COLD &
DEADLY

COLD & **DEADLY**

Toni Anderson

Cold & Deadly

Print Edition

Cover design by Regina Wamba of ReginaWamba.com

Contact email: info@toniandersonauthor.com.

For more information on Toni Anderson's books, sign up for her newsletter or check out her website: www.toniandersonauthor.com.

ALSO BY TONI ANDERSON

COLD JUSTICE® SERIES
A Cold Dark Place (Book #1)
Cold Pursuit (Book #2)
Cold Light of Day (Book #3)
Cold Fear (Book #4)
Cold in the Shadows (Book #5)
Cold Hearted (Book #6)
Cold Secrets (Book #7)
Cold Malice (Book #8)
A Cold Dark Promise (Book #9 ~ A Wedding Novella)
Cold Blooded (Book #10)

COLD JUSTICE® – THE NEGOTIATORS
Cold & Deadly (Book #1)
Colder Than Sin (Book #2)
Cold Wicked Lies (Book #3)
Cold Cruel Kiss (Book #4)
Cold as Ice (Book #5)

COLD JUSTICE® – MOST WANTED
Cold Silence (Book #1)
Cold Deceit (Book #2)
Cold Snap (Book #3) – Coming 2023
Cold Fury (Book #4) – Coming 2023

"HER" ROMANTIC SUSPENSE SERIES
Her Sanctuary (Book #1)
Her Last Chance (Book #2)
Her Risk to Take (Novella ~ Book #3)

THE BARKLEY SOUND SERIES
Dangerous Waters (Book #1)
Dark Waters (Book #2)

STAND-ALONE TITLES
The Killing Game
Edge of Survival
Storm Warning
Sea of Suspicion

For Karen Bell,

For years of love and friendship.

PROLOGUE

THE SHOOTER NESTLED behind the low brick wall on top of the four-story building. The wet asphalt was rough on the knees, but the wall was the perfect height to support the barrel of the Browning X-Bolt Micro rifle with its Ledsniper hunting scope.

A quarter of a mile away, across a busy highway, a group of men and women in somber suits crowded around a hole in the dirt. Diamonds of moisture clung to the tips of fragile blades of lush green grass. A slight breeze ruffled the dense leaves on the sturdy oaks.

Details of the grief-stricken mourners' faces were razor-sharp. The crispness of pressed, white, cotton shirts. Grizzled whiskers poking through wind-reddened cheeks. The soft, plump curve of an earlobe pierced by an expensive, gold earring.

Crosshairs found the handsome face of Dominic Sheridan. His dark blue eyes were reddened at the rim, skin pinched as if consciously holding back emotion. A cleft marked his chin, underscoring a wide mouth set to grim.

Funerals did that to a person.

People milled about, supporting one another, united in grief, blind to danger—sad, devastated, hurting.

Would this tear them apart?

Would it *destroy* them?

Would it make them wake, screaming in the darkness, night after night, year after year, victims of relentless, perpetual anguish?

Would they understand? Or would they remain oblivious to the last man?

The trigger was smooth and silky to the touch. Index finger perched, delicately balanced on the precipice of life and death.

Vengeful.

Powerful.

Godlike.

A long, slow indrawn breath. A breath that marked the moment everything changed. The moment the darkness became visible. Death became a reality.

A steady exhale found the body's natural pause. Then, that seemingly endless moment of inertia as the trigger was gently squeezed, forcing the firing pin to strike the explosive charge in the bullet and retribution to obliterate flesh at 1700 miles per hour.

Now the endgame began. Now everything changed.

CHAPTER ONE

VAN STAMOS—FBI RETIRED—HAD eaten his gun. According to the powers-that-be it had been an accident. Van had gotten hammered one night last week and mistakenly shot himself with the service weapon the Bureau had so generously let him keep after thirty years of dedicated service.

Dominic Sheridan wasn't fooled.

Van had been walking around occasionally drunk and in charge of a loaded firearm for four decades, first as a beat-cop and then as an agent. It seemed like a hell of a coincidence the guy suddenly got careless enough to make a hole in the roof of his mouth right after he retired.

Dominic pressed his lips together as he and his fellow pallbearers eased the casket onto a pedestal beside the grave. He silently fought the frustration and anger that filled him every time he thought about this kind, decent, hard-working man taking his own life. Dominic should have been there for him. He should have known this might happen. He blinked away searing tears that burned for release. He wanted to walk away and find a dark corner and howl out his grief, but he knew how to hide his emotions better than most.

Van had done more to keep him alive and employed in those early days as a new agent than the rest of the FBI combined. Dominic had loved the guy but was still too pissed or repressed or goddamn screwed up to cry at his funeral. What was worse, Van would have totally understood and forgiven him. He was that *good* a person.

Sweat beaded Dominic's temple. The fine wool of his black jacket was too heavy for the hot, sticky humidity of a late Virginia summer. His shirt clung to his back, making his skin prickle uncomfortably, the same way his mind itched for answers. The monotonous rumble of the priest's voice competed with the incessant buzz of a deer fly who wanted a piece of him. He ignored them both, the same way he tried to ignore his friend's body laid out in that wooden casket.

Right now, it was hard to think about anything else.

Dominic had known the transition was gonna be hard on a guy who'd been a mover and shaker in his time, who'd helped put away notorious mobsters and violent serial killers. Playing golf and joining the local bridge club was hardly in the same league as keeping America safe, although Van had assured Dominic he was looking forward to peace and quiet after a long, satisfying career.

He'd put in his time, Van had told him with one of those ironic little smiles. And then he'd eaten his own fucking gun.

A bead of sweat ran down Dominic's temple and into his starched collar. This was the third funeral in the last year for agents he'd worked with at the New York Field Office (NYFO). Dominic was fast thinking the most dangerous thing a G-man could do was retire.

The fact Van's death had been officially deemed an accident rather than suicide meant Van could be buried with his beloved wife, Jessica. If the diocese had denied Van that right, Dominic would have come down here in the dead of night with some fellow agents, a few good shovels, and moved the damned casket himself.

A woman's voice cut through the service. Angry and sharp. It punctured the somber atmosphere the way a shard of glass pierced flesh. Dominic recognized Special Agent Ava Kanas arguing with Supervisory Special Agent (SSA) Raymond Aldrich, the man who'd become her boss upon Van's retirement.

Realizing she'd caught people's attention, the agent lowered her voice. Judging from her body language, though, she was doubling down on her argument with her boss. Her jaw was iron hard, body tense, pale fingers gripping the material of her black blazer so hard that her knuckles gleamed.

Dominic narrowed his eyes. He'd been introduced to Kanas at Van's farewell party a couple of months ago. She was a rookie agent in her first office assignment (FOA) and looked young even for that. She'd worked with Van at the Fredericksburg Resident Agency in Virginia—Van's final posting—and they appeared to have been close. His old friend and mentor had had only good things to say about the woman but then, even before his wife's death, Van had always been a sucker for a pretty face. Dominic liked to form his own opinions and hadn't had the chance nor reason to assess Kanas's capabilities. He'd been busy catching up with Van and other old friends. Many were also here today. Nobody felt much like partying.

The younger agent hadn't stuck around for glory days or good-old-boy stories. Dominic didn't blame her.

She grabbed Aldrich's arm. Her boss tried to pull away, but she wasn't letting go. *Dammit.* They were about to cause a scene. Dominic excused himself from Van's two grownup daughters and went to head off the brewing confrontation. It only took a few seconds to reach the fuming agents who were standing beside a gnarly, old oak at the edge of the crowd.

Kanas eyed him warily. Her brown hair was pulled into a pony so tight it tugged at the skin beside her eyes. Maybe that explained the furrows of pain etched on her brow, but he didn't think so.

"Whatever the two of you are arguing about," Dominic said quietly but firmly, "how about you rein it in until you're back in the office." He masked his ire but not his impatience.

Kanas's chin lifted, and he was pinned by fierce, hazel eyes.

Dominic stared right back. He didn't want Van's funeral to be anything other than the respectful memorial the man deserved. More importantly, there were a lot of powerful people here today. Dominic didn't want Kanas creating a spectacle of herself and possibly ruining her fledgling career. Van would have wanted Dominic to look out for her—the way Van had looked out for Dominic all those years ago.

He called upon all his experience as one of the FBI's top negotiators to dampen his own grief and anger and contain the situation. "I can see you're angry, which sucks. But whatever the issue is, this isn't the place." He used a soothing voice without any inflection that could be misinterpreted as antagonistic. It was mellow and understanding and had helped talk down prisoners and desperados in hostage situations around the world.

Kanas opened her parted lips to speak, but her boss beat her to it.

"She doesn't think it was an accident," Aldrich murmured softly and nodded toward the coffin.

Dominic's gaze slid sideways to Kanas. The anger in her pretty eyes was replaced by a pain so raw it almost hurt to look at. She bit her lip and steadfastly examined her sensible black leather shoes.

"None of us believe it was an accident." Dominic's gaze shifted back to the polished wood of the casket, and a fresh wave of guilt crashed over him. "But the last thing the family needs is anyone questioning Van's right to be buried beside his late wife."

He shifted his feet, and the scent of wet grass and damp earth rose around him, thick and cloying. Combined with the setting, the scent spawned a sudden surge of memories that bombarded his brain. He shook them off.

Suicide pissed him off.

"You don't understand." Aldrich's lips barely moved. "Ava thinks someone *murdered* Van. She wants the funeral stopped so the ME can conduct more tests."

Dominic's eyes widened in surprise.

"It doesn't make any *sense*," Kanas hissed, her voice low and urgent. "He called me last Tuesday afternoon." *The day he died.* "He was fine. We had plans to meet for coffee after work on Wednesday."

Dominic urged her and Aldrich farther away from the rest of the mourners, out of earshot. Some people were starting to glare.

"I'm assuming there was an investigation into Van's death?" Dominic stared the rookie in the eye. He stood only a few inches taller, which made her close to six feet.

"Evidence Response Team treated it like a crime scene, and there was an autopsy. No indication of foul play," said Aldrich.

Kanas looked mutinous. Dominic touched her arm to try and calm her and felt her jolt through the thin material of her blazer.

"What makes you doubt the findings, Agent Kanas?" Because as sick as it might be, the thought of Van being murdered was a whole lot more appealing than the idea that his old friend had committed suicide. Guilt was a terrible thing. Catholic guilt was a bitch on wheels.

And maybe that was Kanas's problem too. Guilt that she hadn't saved the man. That she hadn't realized he was depressed or suicidal.

"It doesn't feel right." She pressed her lips together and couldn't hold his gaze.

He'd never tell anyone to discount their gut feelings, Van had taught him that, but now wasn't the time to cast doubt based on nothing more substantial than wishful thinking.

He took in the devastation in her eyes and the slight trembling of her hands, and something else occurred to him. She was a beautiful woman and Van had technically been single…

Dominic cleared his throat. "Do you know something the rest of us don't? Were the two of you…involved?"

Her chin snapped up. "I loved him, the same way you loved him and countless other people loved him. How many of them have you asked if they were sleeping with the guy?" She kept the volume down, but every word felt like a whiplash against his skin.

"No one else is causing a scene at the man's funeral." He searched those angry hazel eyes for truth. "Except you."

She swallowed and looked away. "We were friends, nothing more." Then she whispered urgently back at him, "I don't believe it was an accident, and I don't believe he took his own life."

Dominic took a deep breath. As tempting as it was to buy

into her theory, there was no proof. Stopping the funeral would cause hurt and uncertainty for Van's daughters, and the man would not have wanted that.

"Look. He'd just retired from one of the most exciting jobs on the planet. His wife of thirty-five years lost a long battle with cancer less than two years ago. Van was hurting. I don't want to believe it either—"

"Except you're not exactly fighting to figure out the truth," she said bitterly.

Ouch. That stung.

He leaned in close so not even God almighty could overhear them. "Because the *truth* is he shot himself." Grief and anger merged. "And that *truth* will hurt the people who have more right to mourn him than we do." Dominic looked pointedly towards Van's daughters who were leaning on one another in their sorrow. "Just because we don't want to believe it, doesn't mean it isn't true."

Wasn't that the goddamned truth.

Kanas's face crumpled, and tears swam in her eyes, and Dominic felt like an asshole. He put his hand on her shoulder, to give some comfort, but she jerked away.

He let his hand drop, and the impulse died. "How about we get back to the service and discuss this later—"

A loud crack rang out through the blustery morning. It took Dominic a fraction of a second to identify the sound.

"Gunshot!" he yelled, turning and grabbing the nearest civilian and pushing her behind the tree. But rather than running for cover, people were milling around in confusion. Some were bending down near the graveside. Had someone been hit? *Damn.* Another gunshot echoed through the morning air so loud and lethal it gave him chills. "Active shooter! Everyone find cover. Active shooter!"

The crowd finally understood what was happening and spilled in different directions. He ran towards Van's daughters who were so wrapped up in grief they hadn't heard the shot and were bewildered by the sudden surge of movement. He wasn't gentle or easy. He wrapped an arm around each woman's shoulders and forced them into a position where they were protected by Van's coffin and a large marble mausoleum.

"Stay here and stay down." He would never forgive himself if anything happened to Van's kids.

Dominic crouched as low as he could, pulling his Glock-22, scanning the surrounding area to assess the situation even as he called it in. The priest was cowering behind another tree, and people were crying as they huddled in terror behind any cover they could find.

Goddamn son of a bitch.

"Gun shot fired at St. Michaels's Catholic Church." He peeked his head over the marble and saw a crumpled form lying in the wet grass. Calvin Mortimer. *Shit.* They'd worked together in New York.

The emergency operator was still on the line.

"Federal agent down—we need immediate medical help. Might be an active shooter situation," he added, even though it would delay the ambulance. He couldn't in good conscience let first responders walk unsuspectingly into gunfire.

Another bullet pinged off the tombstone above his head, making Van's daughters shriek in fear.

"You're okay as long as you keep your head down. Do *not* break cover." *Assuming the shooter didn't move firing position.* He didn't tell them that. He doubted that would happen. It seemed more like a sniper attack than a terrorist assault and law enforcement should be able to isolate and capture this UNSUB *in situ.*

His gaze went back to Calvin lying motionless on the wet grass. The perfect target. *Dammit.* Dominic couldn't leave the guy exposed like that. The distant scream of sirens sliced the air.

He looked around and locked gazes with Ava Kanas who had drawn her weapon. She tipped her head toward Calvin. Dominic nodded, tucking his weapon back in its holster before sprinting from behind the headstone, expecting a bullet for his trouble.

Out of the corner of his eye, he saw Kanas dodge from one tree to another, hopefully drawing the shooter's attention away from him for a few precious moments. His ragged breath and the loud beat of his heart reverberated in his ears. He hauled Calvin up and over his shoulder, never hesitating even as a bullet bounced off a grave marker nearby.

Dammit.

Dominic ran for cover, holding tight to the man, hoping like hell he wasn't doing more harm than good. He laid Calvin carefully on the ground behind the engine block of the nearest vehicle.

Another shot rang out, splintering wood inches from where Ava Kanas sheltered. She raised her Glock and took aim, but whoever was firing the long gun was well out of range, and Kanas resisted returning fire and potentially injuring innocent civilians.

Cool under pressure. He admired that.

He turned his attention back to the wounded man. Calvin didn't seem to be breathing, and there was a bullet hole on the right side of his chest close to his heart. It looked bad, and the basic first aid Dominic knew wasn't nearly sufficient enough to deal with this situation.

"Let me through." One of the mourners crawled toward him. "I'm a trained RN. Let me in."

Dominic tapped the man crouched beside him on the shoulder. "What's your name?"

"Richard."

"Help the nurse, Richard. Try to keep this man alive until the ambulance arrives."

The man nodded, and the nurse started working to stem the blood flowing from the wound, before moving on to chest compressions.

Calvin had lost a lot of blood.

Dominic scanned the area. Most people were keeping safely out of the line of fire. There had been a short lull in the shooting. Dominic didn't know whether the gunman was waiting to pick off anyone foolish enough to give them a clean target or if he was making his escape. It all depended on the shooter's endgame.

A few agents closer to Van's casket were working their way gingerly toward where the shots had come from, but they were going to be hampered by a wide-open piece of ground they'd have to cross to get there. Dominic glanced at Calvin's blanched features. Blood covered the man's shirt, and Dominic's. The clock was ticking for his survival, and the bastard who shot him might be getting away.

"Stay down until local police tell you to move. I need to make sure the shooter is no longer a threat before the ambulance will be allowed in."

As he spoke, Agent Kanas took off sprinting down the road behind him, using the line of parked vehicles as some measure of cover.

Shit.

Dominic ran after her, half expecting a barrage of gunfire. Neither of them had body armor, but there was no way he'd sit around while another agent attempted to tackle the gunman alone.

She was fast, but he was faster. He caught her as she reached the road, and they raced across four lanes of traffic together, dodging oblivious drivers who honked their horns at the two handgun-wielding lunatics. He heard the screech of brakes and hoped the shooter wasn't poised in a position to take out innocent civilians who stumbled onto the scene.

The idea of being in the crosshairs pissed him off, but not as much as having one of his colleagues shot in front of him.

"Did you see where the gunshots came from?" Dominic shouted at Kanas as they sprinted full out.

He glanced at her face. Blood dribbled down her cheek. His mouth went dry. She'd been only inches from death.

"I saw muzzle-flash on the roof of a low, yellow-brick apartment block two streets over."

"You okay?" he asked quickly.

"Yeah."

Dominic concentrated on doing his job. Ava Kanas was a trained professional same as he was. Still running, he hooked his creds on his belt not wanting to get nailed by a local cop mistaking him for the gunman. Kanas did the same.

They hit the main street, dodging pedestrians.

"Active shooter," Dominic shouted. "Find somewhere to shelter and don't come out until the cops tell you it's safe."

"This is it." Kanas's lungs were bellowing by the time they reached a century-old building.

"Get behind me." He held his pistol high and waited for Kanas to fall into position with her gun barrel pointed at the ground. They went through the apartment building's unlocked front door, falling back on basic training to start clearing the area—training Dominic hadn't used since transferring to the Crisis Negotiation Unit five years ago.

"You take the stairs, I'll take the elevator." Kanas's voice was hoarse. At least he wasn't the only one out of breath.

"No. We stick together and take the stairs." The idea of being trapped in a tin can while someone opened up on them with unknown firepower… Nightmare scenario.

Her eyes narrowed in disapproval, but he was the senior agent on the scene and she had to follow orders. Another reason he loved the FBI. They cautiously opened the door to the stairwell and went quickly up, clearing each flight, fluidly covering one another against potential threats.

At the top of the stairs, they paused at the door that led onto the roof. His heart hammered, sweat slick on his body, as he deliberately slowed things down to prepare for whatever lay beyond. It could be anything, from an innocent bystander to a terrorist, to a person experiencing a mental breakdown to a gangbanger with a grudge. This whole scenario might be a trap to lure law enforcement officials to their death. He glanced at Kanas. He did not want to lose another agent today.

He wiped his brow on the shoulder of his jacket, forcing himself to ignore the stark reality of Calvin Mortimer's blood vivid on his white shirt.

They used hand signals to communicate which direction to go. Dominic eased open the heavy fire door, but stood clear. The most important thing was to get through the portal quickly as it made them easy targets. It wasn't called a fatal funnel for nothing.

He and Kanas exchanged a look as they waited. No shots were fired. He couldn't hear anything beyond the sounds of traffic and distant police sirens.

Dominic counted down with his fingers and stepped through the doorway, hooking right as he swept his gaze and weapon over his section of the rooftop. Kanas simultaneously went left and did the same. They moved swiftly, circling the heating vents and maintenance hut, working in formation as if they'd practiced together for years. They made a good team, seamlessly following each other's lead.

The roof was clear.

Neither of them dropped their guard. They scanned nearby rooftops in case they were mistaken about where the bullets had originated or the sniper had moved.

There was no one to be seen, but then snipers weren't always obvious.

"You sure this was the place?" Dominic asked finally, catching his breath.

Kanas bristled. Clearly the woman did not like her word being questioned.

"I'm sure."

That was good enough for Dominic. "We need to call in uniforms to help canvass this whole area."

They walked to the southwest corner of the roof—the area with the best view of the graveyard.

Both kept their eyes peeled for footprints or other evidence but the gritty surface of the flat roof revealed no obvious evidence.

Sunlight gleamed off something brassy on the ground beside some litter.

Dominic photographed the bullet casing with his phone before popping it into a plastic evidence bag. The sooner they got that to the lab the better.

He dialed an agent on the ground. "Shooter's in the wind. We need this building cleared and secured. The other rooftops in the area also need to be checked, roadblocks set up. Send an evidence response team to this roof." He waved his arm in case they didn't know his exact position. "How's Calvin?"

The answer made him close his eyes and draw in an unsteady breath. He hung up without saying another word.

"He didn't make it?" Kanas asked.

Dominic ran his hand over his face and shook his head. Calvin had a wife and two kids in high school.

"You were friends?" she asked.

He nodded again, the lump in his throat expanding until it was too big to talk around.

"I'm sorry."

She was beautiful close up, her expression warm with concern, skin smooth and fine—except for the cut on her cheek with its ugly smear of blood. He raised his hand to check the wound, and she flinched away, arms coming up in instinctive defense.

They both froze.

His gaze narrowed and lifted to the scar that rode the delicate arch of her right eyebrow. She held herself with poised readiness. Not just the wariness of a law enforcement professional, but the hyperawareness of someone who'd been a victim.

"You're bleeding." He was careful to keep his tone neutral as something hot and virulent surged through his blood. He wanted to ask what had happened, but it wasn't his business and this wasn't the time.

She raised her hand to her cheek. "It's just a scratch."

He nodded, and they both pretended she hadn't given away something important. They holstered their weapons, and he watched her out of the corner of his eye as she rested both hands on her hips, staring intently at the tiny figures in the graveyard a quarter of a mile away.

"I told you there was something hinky with Van's death," she said as they watched as ambulances arrived on scene.

He frowned. "This might not be connected."

Her expression raked him with so much scorn he almost laughed. Almost. Because a few minutes ago someone had opened fire at his best friend's funeral and shot dead a good man, endangering countless others.

Someone had murdered a fellow member of the FBI, and there was nothing even remotely funny about that.

CHAPTER TWO

PEROXIDE SEARED THE small cut on Ava's cheek. The fumes made her eyes sting and her brain hurt. She'd come close to dying today but hadn't had time to process that yet. She'd been too pumped up on adrenaline. Too focused on doing her job. The aftermath left her shaken, but she didn't have time to fall apart—that could come later when she was alone in her apartment.

The paramedic paused before applying a butterfly bandage to her cheek.

"You okay?"

She nodded.

He smoothed the bandage over the ragged edges of the cut and placed a reassuring hand on her shoulder. "Looks clean. I doubt it'll scar. You'll be fine."

Ava forced out a shaky laugh. "I hope so. Death by splinter. The FBI would kick me out for sure."

"Where'd you get this one?" He indicated the small puckered scar on her right eyebrow. It was the second time today someone had noted that childhood injury.

"Kickboxing." She touched it. The image of flying across her father's office flashed through her mind. "Didn't move fast enough." At least that part was true.

"You were fast enough to dodge that bullet today."

"Ha. Got lucky I guess." Training was one thing, but not enough to outrun a bullet. Being shot at definitely wasn't her favorite feeling in the world, but she hadn't had time to be scared on a conscious level. She'd just wanted to make it stop. "Thanks for the patch job. Be sure to tell your colleagues how much we appreciate their hard work."

The EMT smiled slightly as he finished cleaning her up.

It was a miracle Calvin Mortimer had been the only fatality here today. Others had been hurt in the chaos and rush to safety. Twisted ankles. Nasty gashes. One woman had suffered a suspected cardiac arrest.

Ava sympathized. Her own heart had pounded so hard she'd thought it was going to explode.

"It's what we do." The paramedic's eyes held an amused sort of interest. He was good-looking in a dark, smoldering kind of way and reminded her of a boyfriend from her beat-cop days. Another time and she might have asked him out on a date, but she had other priorities.

"Thanks again." She ditched the gauze she was holding and searched the crowd for Supervisory Special Agent Dominic Sheridan.

There. Standing beyond Van's casket. She hopped off the step on the back of the ambulance and headed toward him. Sheridan was speaking to her boss, Ray Aldrich, and a bunch of suits while Evidence Recovery Technicians combed the area for slugs embedded in the ground or in tree trunks.

She eyed Sheridan as she skirted around the crime scene tape to the high-powered huddle. He was an attractive guy in his mid-thirties. Tall with brutally short, dark hair, and a strong jawline. It was his eyes that grabbed her. The irises were a rich indigo that saw way too much. She cringed at what she'd given away on that rooftop that morning—things she never revealed to anyone. Things she'd spent most of her life trying to hide. He'd caught her at a weak moment. She'd be better prepared in the future.

Van had always sung Sheridan's praises, but she doubted he'd been talking about the broad shoulders, slim hips or brooding persona.

Van...

Her lungs squeezed, and the pain in her heart was a reminder he was never coming back. Van Stamos had been her idol and mentor, the person who'd inspired her to join the Bureau. More importantly, he'd been her friend. He'd had faith in her abilities and in her strength of character. He hadn't cosseted her. He'd pushed and let her push back. Challenged her to be her very best.

Thanks to Van's support, she had more experience and arrests to her credit than any of her graduating class in their first office assignments. He'd given her that. Given her an advantage within the Bureau because he'd believed in her. He'd *always* believed in her.

And today he was being buried in a furtive rush as if the world was ashamed of him. The man deserved a heroic sendoff befitting a veteran agent who'd dedicated his whole life to the FBI with unfailing loyalty. Instead he got this dismal dirge.

Kill himself?

Van would *never* kill himself, and she intended to prove it. He'd been there for her when she'd needed him, now she'd be there for him. She wouldn't let him down.

Ava strode toward the higher ups, determined someone was going to listen to what she had to say even if it made her unpopular.

She was used to being unpopular.

A headache was starting to grow, gnawing at her energy reserves but if she didn't do this now, she'd lose momentum, not to mention her nerve. She approached the group, doing her best to be inconspicuous, but these people were all high-level FBI personnel. They stopped talking as soon as she came within earshot and waited as SSA Sheridan introduced her.

"This is Agent Kanas." His voice was soft and dark and caressed her skin like a velvet fingertip.

Get a grip, Ava.

"She spotted the shooter's firing position and created a distraction at great risk to herself while I tried to…hmm." Sheridan's voice cracked. "…tried to move Calvin to safety."

He'd braved the line of fire while others had hidden in fear.

"Good work," said the man standing closest to her right.

"Thank you." She looked up and her eyes widened. "Sir." She was standing a few inches from the Director of the FBI. "I-I was just doing what I'd been trained to do, sir. I wish we'd caught the guy." She glanced at Sheridan. If he'd let her take the elevator, they might have cornered the shooter on the roof.

Sheridan calmly held her gaze as if he could read her mind. It wasn't a feeling she appreciated.

"He won't get far," the director assured her. "We have the full weight of the FBI behind this. Teams of agents are scouring the area for evidence and canvassing the neighborhood. Hopefully traffic cams can help us identify all the vehicles in the vicinity and we can get a name."

Ava braced her hands on her waist. "Could the shooter have anything to do with Van Stamos's death, sir?" She eyed the coffin sitting in the sunshine. Van would have been amused by his front row seat at the proceedings. One final case in his illustrious career.

The director frowned and Ray Aldrich jumped in. "Stamos's death was deemed accidental."

The headache pressed against Ava's forehead, but she ignored the pain. No one believed it was "accidental."

A third man Ava didn't recognize mused. "Maybe the shooter saw Stamos's obituary and figured it was a prime opportunity to take aim at the FBI, knowing other agents would be in attendance?"

"Or maybe Calvin Mortimer was targeted specifically," said another man.

Ava clenched her hands into fists, holding back emotions that wanted to leak.

One of the men standing there, a classically handsome, chisel-jawed superior, watched her with a keen, icy blue gaze. He looked familiar, but she couldn't place him. From the academy maybe? A heavily pregnant brunette stood beside him, resting a palm on her swollen abdomen. She was armed.

Ava wished she knew who these people were but could hardly demand they identify themselves. Technically, for the next few weeks, she was still a rookie, while these guys probably had over a hundred years' service between them.

The director nodded. "We can't afford to rule anything out at this stage."

To Ava, that sounded like a brush off. She opened her mouth to share her theory about Van's death when a sharp tug on her jacket sleeve stopped her.

It was Sheridan. She glanced at his face, but he wasn't looking at her. The guy was subtly trying to tell her to stay quiet. Dammit, this might be her only opportunity. She didn't have a direct line to the director and doubted she'd ever again be this close to him in the flesh. She wasn't going to waste this chance because someone she barely knew thought she should shut up.

"Does that include a scenario in which this shooter deliberately staged Van Stamos's murder as a suicide so they could target mourners at his funeral? And the Bureau missed it?"

Sheridan coughed, dropping his hand away, cutting himself loose from any association.

"Kanas," Aldrich warned.

She sent him a mutinous glare. Aldrich was an okay guy, but Van had been worth ten of him as an investigator.

"You think someone is actively targeting federal agents?" the man she thought she recognized from the academy asked.

"Any evidence of this?" This from the director.

She shook her head. All the evidence suggested Van had blown his own brains out, but she knew that wasn't true. "No, but as you said, sir, we *can't afford to rule anything out.*" She parroted the director's own words back at him, hoping for a positive reaction. "We should definitely investigate every avenue."

The expressions were all skeptical, except for the pregnant woman and the icy blond. Sheridan wore a slight smile. He could afford to, his career wasn't on the line. The others looked annoyed. She'd broken protocol and upset the patriarchy.

The director gave her a look that told her how close to the line she was getting, but his words also gave her hope.

"It is a possibility we can't afford to ignore," he agreed. "Aldrich, go back over the files regarding Van Stamos's death and look for anything suspicious. Submit your report directly to me. I will coordinate with the task force being set up to investigate this shooting."

Ava doubted Aldrich would do more than a cursory investigation whereas she'd turn the world inside out and upside down looking for answers.

"I'd like to be the one reviewing the case, sir." Ava winced, knowing it was a mistake as soon as the words left her mouth.

"That will be up to your supervisor, Agent Kanas," the director said sharply, taking a step away from her. The FBI was all about procedure. He checked his watch. "I need to brief the president." He stared hard at her then. "I do not want to hear your theory on any media channel or Twitter account. Am I clear, Agent Kanas?"

"Of course, sir." She stood stiffly. Pissed. She was no more likely to leak the suggestion than anyone else here. Less, considering even the thought of Twitter made her gag. She was too antisocial for social media, not to mention too busy actively working cases.

The director nodded brusquely and stalked away, most of the suits following him in a swarm as he headed to his big black car.

Sheridan, the blond-haired man, and the pregnant woman remained behind. The woman held out her hand in greeting. "Agent Rooney. Nice to meet you, even though the circumstances suck."

Ava pressed the other woman's fingers in a firm grip. She'd heard of Mallory Rooney. Almost everyone in the Bureau had. Rooney was married to some shit-hot, ex-CIA dude, and worked for Lincoln Frazer, the legendary profiler from the Behavioral Analysis Unit—and Ava finally identified the blond man at Mallory's side. Assistant Special Agent in

Charge (ASAC) Lincoln Frazer had taught Ava all about the grisly aspects of serial murder during the blur of New Agent Training.

"What makes you think Van Stamos was murdered, Agent Kanas?" Frazer wasted no time on pleasantries.

"The fact he was a devoted Catholic who wanted to go to Heaven?"

Frazer looked unimpressed.

How did she articulate what she couldn't explain herself? "Van believed he'd see his wife again in the hereafter. No way would he kill himself and deny himself that eternal happy ending."

It sounded sappy, but it was true.

"So, no actual evidence?" Frazer's gaze was assessing.

She straightened her spine. "Except the fact he was enjoying retirement and talked about visiting Italy and writing a book. Also, we were supposed to meet for coffee the next day."

"People who commit suicide often make plans." Frazer wasn't known for his tolerance of foolish ideas, but she was disappointed he wasn't more open.

"Van wasn't depressed," she said stubbornly.

"That we know of," Sheridan put in.

She swung toward him. "He wasn't, and you'd have known that if you'd bothered to pick up the phone occasionally."

Sheridan's lips tightened in irritation, but screw him.

"Van wouldn't have done this to his daughters." *He wouldn't have done it to me.*

Sheridan's stare grew too intense for her to hold his gaze. She looked away, but Frazer was watching her with the same hawk-like focus, silently dissecting her argument and abilities.

It reminded her of the way Sheridan had stared at her on

that rooftop that morning. Like he could read her life experience from the lines on her face and memories scrawled behind her eyes. She'd given herself away to Sheridan, but she didn't intend to make the same mistake again.

She forced herself to hold still under the scrutiny.

"Contact me at the BAU if your boss finds any discrepancies in the circumstances surrounding Stamos's death, Agent Kanas. He was a good man. He didn't deserve this and neither did Cal Mortimer." Frazer squeezed Sheridan's shoulder like they were buds. Mallory Rooney shot her a wry smile, then she and Frazer headed off to their car.

Ava was suddenly alone with Sheridan. They both stared at Van's casket, the hot sun making her cheeks heat. The funeral was on hold until the crime scene was processed.

"You realize you could have handled that with more tact if you'd been driving a bulldozer?" Sheridan said softly.

She shoved her hands in her jacket pockets. "Because I said what I was thinking rather than sucking up to the big bosses?"

That slight smile touched his lips again, suggesting she amused him. Well fuck him.

"Because you made your boss look like a jackass who can't control you and he's gonna be pissed."

She raised a brow as they eyed one another. It was beyond obvious Aldrich was a jackass and couldn't "control" her.

"I only want the truth." Ava crossed her arms over her chest, and he took in her body language with a sweeping gaze that saw everything she wasn't saying. That she was pissed and frustrated and hurting. And maybe she was being too hard on her boss. Aldrich was harmless. He might be angry, but he wouldn't screw with her career even though she'd just screwed with his.

Dammit.

Sheridan shifted even closer until his breath stroked her ear. "You need to be careful, Ava." Her name on his lips sent a shiver of awareness down her spine. "Pulling a stunt like that in front of the director is going to get you a reputation as a blue flamer and that will lose you a lot of friends."

Was he testing her for a reaction after what had happened on the roof? She lifted her chin, and they stared at one another. So close she could smell the scent of his skin and count the dark lashes around his eyes.

"The FBI is a team, and in this business, we need all the friends we can get—Van taught me that." His gaze never wavered from hers.

"Kanas!" Aldrich shouted as he strode up behind them, making her startle. "What the hell was that? Are you trying to make me look like an imbecile?"

She winced.

Dominic Sheridan murmured again next to her ear. "Told you." And then he turned and walked away. She watched him cross the road and climb into a black Prius, driving down the road and taking a right turn out of sight. Aldrich's words bounced off her like hard rain. She looked over at Van's coffin baking in the sun. What would her mentor have done if he'd been here? A small smile touched her mouth. He'd have done exactly what she'd done.

"Are we finished, sir?" She touched her injured cheek. "I'm feeling a little woozy."

The man threw his hands in the air. She'd played her trump card, and he knew it.

"I want you in my office at eight o'clock tomorrow morning to talk about this, Ava. I'm serious. Do not be late."

She almost snorted as she walked away. Late? He was the one who kept bankers' hours.

Circling the enormous crime scene took time and only increased the feeling of sweaty isolation she felt from her colleagues. Why was no one else buying the idea Van had been murdered? Was she deluding herself? Had they known him so much better than she had? Were her instincts nothing but heartbreak and wishful thinking?

She hadn't been lying to Aldrich about feeling woozy though. She climbed into her Bucar and drank out of the water bottle she kept in the cupholder, placing a hand on her stomach which gurgled and groaned. The headache had grown and stabbed her brain like a knife in her skull. She popped a couple of pills from her purse with another mouthful of water and squeezed her eyes closed for a few seconds' respite.

Another glance at the Evidence Recovery Technicians searching on their hands and knees through the wet grass made her more determined than ever to figure out the truth. Van hadn't believed in coincidence. She saluted the coffin with a sad smile. "Don't worry, Van. I've got your back."

He'd tell her to keep digging until everything began to make sense—and right now nothing made sense. Not Van's supposed suicide, not the shooter at his funeral, not the seeming indifference of his fellow agents, especially the one with intriguing dark blue eyes.

THE CHIEF NEGOTIATOR of the FBI and his immediate boss, Unit Chief Quentin Savage, looked up from the report he was reading when Dominic walked into his office late that afternoon.

"Heard about the shooting." Savage's gaze was thorough and assessing. "Did you know the victim?"

Dominic sat heavily and rested his elbows on his knees. He'd showered and changed into a spare shirt and suit he kept in his go-bag. He'd thrown the bloodstained clothes in the garbage. "We were friends at the New York Field Office. The guy was married with kids."

"I'm sorry." Savage leaned back in his chair. "Do they have any idea as to the shooter's identity or motive?"

Dominic shook his head. So far, they had a big fat zero. "I'd like permission to work the case."

"Denied."

Dominic looked up. "But—"

"I need you here, Dominic. We're already overstretched, and you're one of our best negotiators. Let the street agents deal with the murder investigation and if they need our services, they'll call."

Dominic opened his mouth to argue but then closed it again. Savage was right. The Crisis Negotiation Unit was highly specialized and perpetually overstretched. There were never enough agents. Never enough time.

"I understand if you need to take some personal days..." Savage let the statement hang even though he'd just made it impossible to ask for time off.

"I'm fine." Dominic would have been more fine if some asshole hadn't just shot dead one of his friends at his mentor's funeral.

"Hey." Charlotte Blood poked her head around Savage's door, her expression a mass of sympathy. "I heard you've had a terrible day. You need anything?"

Dominic shook his head, knowing questions and concern were inevitable, but not ready to talk about what had happened or how he felt about it. He'd go see the Bureau shrink and do the mandatory hot wash and talk about his *feelings*. He'd tell the doc what she wanted to hear and get the all-clear. God knew, he'd visited a lot of shrinks growing up. He knew the drill.

"A bunch of us are going to grab a beer and dinner after work. You guys wanna join us? It might help to be around friends." Charlotte was the bleeding heart of the unit, one who could bring stone-cold killers to their knees with a bit of active listening and emotional labeling. She'd honed empathy to the sharpness of a 14th Century Samurai blade and wielded it ruthlessly.

Quentin smiled at Charlotte, and she smiled back. She was somehow impossible to resist. If Dominic was ever in a tight corner that required a negotiator, he'd want Charlotte doing the talking. He pitied the guy she fell for because he wouldn't stand a chance. For some inexplicable reason, his mind flashed to the image of Ava Kanas on that rooftop looking so isolated and aloof—the opposite of Charlotte's all-encompassing warmth. He pushed the image aside. The inexperienced rookie was her own worst enemy.

"Unfortunately, I have to write my keynote for that conference in Indonesia next week," Quentin grimaced. For all he was considered one of the best in the field of negotiation tactics, he did not enjoy the spotlight.

"What about you, Dominic?" Charlotte asked again.

"Not tonight, Char," he told her. "I have some case files to catch up on."

Quentin frowned at him. Charlotte's smile dimmed.

"We'll be there for a while. It's Eban's birthday. Join us if you get hungry or want company." She sent him a worried look before she left which made him feel warm and guilty all at the same time.

Yup, the woman knew how to twist the heartstrings. And the fact she genuinely cared was why she got away with it, even with the most hardened criminals and hard-assed FBI personnel.

Dominic stood to leave.

"Where are we on the Alexander case?" Savage asked quickly.

The Alexanders were a retired couple whose dreams of sailing round the world had been shattered when they'd been kidnapped in the South China Sea five months ago.

It reminded Dominic he wasn't the only person in the world having a bad day. "No new updates as of last night. The negotiator we have in the embassy in Jakarta has another week before his rotation ends."

"See if he can hold off on his return for another week and meet me in Jakarta. I'll get an onsite brief then. Then call State and see if there has been any update in the security situation in the region."

"Gotcha." Dominic was aware what his boss was doing. Keeping him busy. Not letting him dwell on the awful events of today.

He headed to his office two doors down, which he shared with another negotiator who'd just returned from secondment at SIOC at HQ.

Time was always the friend of the negotiator, wearing down kidnappers, stretching their resources, lowering their expectations. But for the hostages and their friends and family, every second of every hour had to be torturous, not knowing if their loved ones were alive and suffering, or already dead.

Dominic got on the phone to the State Department before everyone went home for the day. As he waited to be connected, he thought again about Ava Kanas, the way she'd flinched away from him when he'd gone to touch the injury on her cheek.

At some point someone had hit her hard enough to scar her. Was it an old injury from her childhood or something more recent? It made him furious, but she didn't seem like the sort of woman who would want his sympathy or his pity.

He clasped the back of his neck as State put him on hold. There was definitely something about her that intrigued him. Maybe it was seeing that vulnerability combined with her bravery...not only when going after the shooter but in voicing her opinion in front of the director. That took balls.

Did she have a Charlotte in her life to make her feel better? Would her boss make sure she didn't suffer any ill-effects from the shooting? Make her visit the Bureau shrink?

Van would've.

Would Aldrich?

Dominic tossed down his pen and rubbed his eyes as he was passed from person to person in Washington. There was probably a boyfriend on the scene to hold Kanas's hand if she needed comfort. The idea sat sourly. Which was stupid. It wasn't like he'd see her again and even if he did, he never dated agents and that went double for younger agents.

He laughed at his own ego. Who the hell said she'd look at him twice? She was a beautiful woman and might not even be into guys.

He pushed her out of his mind as he finished with State and then called Savage with an update. Then his cell rang and Dominic looked at the caller ID.

The Governor of Vermont was on the line.

He stared at the screen until eventually the call went to voicemail. Then he stood and grabbed his jacket. Maybe he needed that drink after all.

CHAPTER THREE

THE PIECE OF paper on the table contained a list of ten names. Two had died of natural causes. One man's cancer traced to his work at Ground Zero. Sad, yes, but only because he'd gotten off easy. Three names had already been crossed out this year. Each death had been deemed natural or accidental, including Van Stamos, whose suicide had been perfectly staged and made gratifyingly ugly.

A thick green marker was dragged over the name "Calvin Mortimer" with a sense of grim satisfaction. It had been a tossup, who to shoot. Only three names remained on the list, the most important being Dominic Sheridan. It had been tempting to put a bullet in him today, but like the man who'd succumbed to cancer, that would be letting him off easy. Sheridan deserved to suffer the most. The prospect of the slowly dawning horror he'd feel once he realized he was being hunted was extremely satisfying.

Carefully, the green marker was capped, the piece of paper folded and slipped into a desk drawer. Then the drawer was locked.

A phone rang in the distance. Revenge needed to be total, complete. A veritable masterclass in murder. Peter would be so proud.

CHAPTER FOUR

"MAKE JENNIFER MCCREDIE out of the San Francisco Field Office your lead negotiator, but don't put her in first." Dominic was talking to a police chief of a small town outside Sacramento where a man had holed himself up with his ex-wife, young son, and a smorgasbord of semi-automatic weapons. "Get one of the other negotiators to do some of the preliminary leg work. Get the man talking. Make him feel like you're listening to his problems and that you care about what's happening to him and no one is going to get hurt. After a few hours let Jennifer talk to him." It would take her that long to arrive on scene anyway.

There was a pause on the other end of the line. "The guy shot a waitress at a fast food joint and seems to have a raging hatred of women. What makes you think he'll want to talk to this Jennifer person?"

Because Jennifer is the top negotiator on the west coast?

Dominic rubbed his face, glad he wasn't on video. He didn't indulge very often but after yesterday's debacle he'd allowed himself a few beers with the others and had woken up with a hangover. Charlotte had poured him into a taxi at midnight.

The woman was a saint.

Dominic drank from a bottle of water he kept on his desk.

"My experience is that getting a woman to really listen to him is exactly what this guy craves." The waitress had insisted the hostage-taker leave the restaurant when he made a scene with the ex-wife. The waitress had threatened to call the police when he'd refused to go quietly. So, he'd shot her. "Jennifer can get him talking, provide an empathetic ear."

Over the years, Dominic had noted that many of the people who took hostages were men who felt like they were losing control of what they saw as their property. Their wives left them or simply wanted some independence, and the men couldn't handle it.

The police chief grunted. "I asked his old boss and brother to come down here to talk to him. Was that a mistake?"

Dominic squeezed the bridge of his nose. "It's great that you interview them, but don't let them talk to the hostage-taker."

"Why not?"

"Because you've no idea the type of relationship they have or what resentments the husband might harbor. If the hostage-taker is the suspicious type he might think one of them is involved with the ex-wife. Trust me, it's happened." With deadly consequences.

The chief made a frustrated noise.

"Have SWAT secure the perimeter and see if you can get a visual on the guy in the event you need a tactical solution. Then let the negotiation team do their work. It will take time, but that's a good thing." Giving time *time* was an idea an experienced negotiator at the NYPD had taught him. "The longer we draw this out the more chance we have of everyone walking away from this thing alive."

A lot of people considered negotiators and behavioral

scientists to be the social workers of law enforcement. The hand holders. The "let's talk this out" or "this UNSUB was probably abused as a child" types. As if that meant they were somehow less dedicated to putting the bad guys behind bars or getting hostages released without harm.

Stats were pretty convincing that when crisis negotiators got involved tempers had time to cool and things resolved with less violence and harm to those involved.

The police chief swallowed audibly. "There's a little kid in there…"

Dominic's grip on the phone tightened. "I realize that, but as tempting as it is to rush in with guns blazing, that's the most dangerous thing you can do for the child at this point. If the situation deteriorates, you'll have that tactical team in place ready to respond."

Dominic never failed to see the futility of the hostage-takers' actions. What did they think would happen? That the cops would leave them alone while they held their family at gunpoint? That rape and enslavement would be fine as long as they didn't bother anyone else?

A good negotiator had to put all judgment aside, to convince a hostage-taker—usually a person in crisis—that life was still worth living, and that although things seemed hopeless right then, there was still hope. It got considerably harder when someone committed a capital crime in a death penalty state.

If law enforcement were forced to go tactical then mother and child could easily wind up dead in the crossfire. But if crisis negotiators did their job effectively there was no need for the flash bang or storming the barricades. Getting someone to release their captives and lay down their arms was the most empowering thing imaginable.

The chief seemed hesitant. "I'll do it your way, but the mayor isn't going to like it."

"Tell him to butt out. This is a law enforcement matter, not a political one."

"Her." The cop corrected. "I'll tell her, but she probably isn't going to like it."

Getting local politicians and the brass to cooperate in a cohesive manner was often challenging, and lack of communication between various agencies could dangerously undermine the negotiator's position.

Dominic rolled his shoulder. "Tell the mayor to call me if she wants any clarification on negotiation tactics." He rang off, knowing the police chief had his hands full with a set of circumstances he wasn't used to dealing with. Unlike Dominic, who dealt with some variant of this situation on an almost daily basis. It didn't mean all siege or hostage situations could be run the same way with the same results. Emotions drove events and so did the unpredictable actions of everyone involved. Humans were notoriously fickle. Hence the need for trained negotiators who didn't react or lash out in frustration and who knew how to de-escalate tension even when lives were on the line.

He grabbed his water bottle again and took another large gulp, wishing he hadn't finished off the night with a few whiskey chasers. Beer was one thing. Fifteen-year-old Glenfiddich was something else.

He checked the wire, but there was no update on the UNSUB in Calvin's murder. The image of Ava Kanas challenging the Director of the FBI to delve deeper into Van's death flashed through his brain. The woman had *cajones* even if she lacked subtlety. He picked up the phone and called Fredericksburg and was put through to Ray Aldrich almost immediately.

"Any updates on the shooter?" Dominic asked.

Aldrich sighed. "Nothing that points us to an identity. There's a basement parking garage, and we believe they drove away before you even got there on foot. No surveillance cameras anywhere in that building or in the vicinity."

"What about Van's death?" Ava Kanas's conviction had been compelling, but maybe neither of them wanted to admit they'd failed a man who'd mentored them both.

"I've been over the notes again but can't find anything that looks suspicious."

"Could I look at the files?" Dominic closed his eyes as he made the request.

"You sure you want to do that?"

Did he want to view the death scene and autopsy photographs of one of his best friends? No, he didn't. "I might be able to help."

"Okay, I'll send you the access information but don't say I didn't warn you," said Aldrich.

"What about Agent Kanas? How's she holding up after the shooting?"

Aldrich sighed. "She's a good agent, but she's like a dog with a bone and doesn't know when to let go. I put her on a lead we were sent from the New Mexico Field Office, which should keep her busy for a few days or weeks."

So, she'd probably be even more frustrated. "Do you believe her?" asked Dom.

"Honestly? No. I think she's overwrought and upset."

Ava Kanas did not seem like the overwrought type. She

seemed determined and passionate.

"She and Van were close?" Dominic asked.

"Not intimate like you suggested yesterday, at least, not as far as I'm aware."

Dominic winced. Not his finest moment and probably reflected more his thoughts regarding Agent Kanas than anything else. She was *very* attractive.

"But they were close. This is her FOA, and Van took her under his wing. I guess she imprinted on him in a big way."

Van had done the same thing with Dominic over a decade ago. Dominic had never figured out why. Had he looked like such a newbie that Van had known he needed help? Probably.

Something about Ava Kanas's conviction seemed deeper than that of a mentee's reaction to a mentor's death, but as Dominic sucked at relationships in general, what the hell did he know?

"I'm getting another call," Aldrich said. "Thanks for taking a look at the files. I do not want to look like an idiot in front of the director."

Dominic grunted as he hung up. He didn't give a crap about appearances, but some might suggest he didn't need to, which was probably true and pissed him off.

Dominic's email dinged and there was the case file number of Van's death investigation and a permission key to access it sitting in his inbox. His mouth went dry, and his heart started to pound as his finger hovered over the button. He wasn't looking forward to this. Not even a little bit.

AVA SAT IN her Bucar down the road from the home of the

girlfriend of a prisoner who'd escaped from the Penitentiary of New Mexico. The converted older home had three apartments, one on each floor, and backed onto the city and historic Confederate Cemetery. It was mid-morning in a quiet neighborhood, not exactly conducive to surveillance when strangers sitting in parked cars stood out like flashing neon signs. She kept an eye on the front door by watching her rear-view mirror.

She'd dressed down in a The National t-shirt and her oldest, rattiest jeans ripped at the knees, and a pair of red Vans meaning she could run if necessary. She wore shades and a blue, evil eye bracelet her mother had sent her when she'd graduated the academy. Her gun was on her hip, with the shirt tugged over it. A backup strapped to her ankle.

Everyone else from the Resident Agency had been assigned to the investigation into yesterday's shooting. It looked like she'd hamstrung herself by opening her big, fat mouth in front of the director. Rather than being involved she'd been sidelined. The knot in her throat threatened to choke her.

Van would be so mad at her for screwing that up. She didn't care. She wouldn't let it drop. He'd warned her to always make sure she followed the rules and to do her job properly.

The public relied on the FBI to get the bad guys off the street and agents had to be willing to get the job done no matter the sacrifice. Agents were allowed a personal agenda, but the Bureau's work came first. He'd drummed that into her from the moment they'd met.

So here she sat outside Maria Santana's apartment, drinking coffee and watching the door when she'd rather be tracing Van's last movements or going door-to-door searching for clues as to the identity of yesterday's shooter.

A fly buzzed, and she swatted it away. Despite it being early and her being parked beneath a large, leafy tree, it was hot as Hades inside the Impala. She had the engine and AC off and windows rolled down as an idling car would draw too much attention. This promised to be a long and tedious assignment.

Maria Santana's boyfriend, Jimmy Taylor, had been held on charges of drug smuggling and two counts of first-degree murder, one of which involved a cop sent to arrest him. Ava had no idea how Jimmy had escaped custody but the idea he'd travel back to Virginia when he was right next to the Mexican border seemed ludicrous. So what if Maria was sex on legs? There was no way he'd come back here. This was a waste of her time.

Ava forced herself to not react when Maria emerged from the building looking pretty and feminine, wearing dark shades, a long floral skirt with a peasant blouse. Ava weighed her options. Follow Maria on foot or hang out here and wait for her to return home? Alternatively, she could drive around the block and park at the Sugar Shack and watch the apartment from there while refueling on donuts until Maria returned.

Follow on foot. She could do with the exercise.

Ava was reaching for the door handle when a big, black Suburban pulled up behind her down the street.

She froze.

The driver was a white male wearing dark shades and a red ball cap pulled low. Was it Jimmy? Nah. He couldn't be that stupid, could he? Ava forced herself to remain still and not draw attention. At the same time, she peered in the mirror, attempting to make a positive ID.

Maria climbed in the truck and locked lips with the guy like she was gonna nail him then and there in the front seat. What the hell?

Holy shit.

It *was* Jimmy Taylor. Obviously, Maria was *sex on legs* and worth the risk of a lengthy prison sentence. Was that true love or the ultimate in stupidity? Considering Maria could have flown out to meet the guy anywhere in the world, Ava was hedging toward them both being morons.

She let them pull away and watched them turn down Sylvania Avenue before she started the engine and cut quickly down Mortimer, parallel, one street over. She floored it, catching sight of the Suburban crossing Littlepage, and floored it again. By the time she got to the next intersection, she'd caught up and watched them veer left before she indicated and did the same. She called dispatch.

"I have a sighting of the suspect, Jimmy Taylor, traveling west on William with his girlfriend, Maria Santana, in a black Suburban." She gave them the license plate. "I'm in pursuit and need immediate backup. Get a chopper in the air if possible."

Maybe she could patch into some local police cruisers, and they might be able to box Taylor in before he got away.

She squinted at the vehicle now traveling in front of her. Ideally, she'd be part of a team—unlike what Sheridan had suggested yesterday, she *did* know how to work as part of a team—and they'd operate in tandem changing positions and taking different routes, but today she was on her own. It was unusually quiet on the road, which was both good and bad. They took a right onto Highway 3, and she stuck closer than she wanted because she didn't want to get caught at a light. She held her breath as they passed the exits to Route 1, grateful he didn't take either. Unfortunately, they were only a mile from the intersection that took him onto Interstate 95, which ran the entire length of the east coast. The cops couldn't afford a high-speed chase on such a busy road and if they lost him, Jimmy could escape to anywhere along the eastern seaboard.

She eyed the conditions. They were on a four-lane portion of Route 3 with a lot of shops and restaurants—too much of a risk to pedestrians to try what she had in mind.

"I'm going to attempt to pull him over as soon as I find some green space," she said to dispatch.

"Roger that, Agent Kanas. Backup is on the way."

Ava got close to Taylor's vehicle and turned on the flashing lights in the dash. She laid on the siren, and Taylor's car jumped ahead.

Shit.

Dispatch was still on the line.

"He took off." The on-ramp for the interstate came into view a half mile away. Taylor was going to make a run for it.

Ava weighed her options. The Impala was fully fitted out with reinforced bumpers as it was one of the few surveillance vehicles they had at the Fredericksburg Resident Agency. "I'm going to attempt a PIT maneuver to prevent him getting onto the interstate."

She'd practiced the Pursuit Intervention Technique a hundred times in training as a patrol cop, but never for real and never on her own while trying to arrest an alleged murderer.

He ignored the northbound ramp, which suited her purposes. Southbound had more waste ground and less trees on the side of the road.

She put her foot on the gas, and her car shot forward. It took a few nerve-wracking seconds to position the nose of her hood just behind his rear, driver's side wheel arch. He swerved away as if he knew what she was planning. Maybe he did. She couldn't afford to hesitate in case he had a weapon and started shooting.

She checked her surroundings again and saw the flash of lights in her rear-view. Backup was close.

"Going to try to force him off the road." She matched her speed to his, hoping the Impala had enough power in reserve to accomplish what she intended. Holding tight to the steering wheel, she nosed the Impala inches from Taylor's Suburban as he hit the ramp. She punched the gas, jerking the wheel toward the other car. The fleeing vehicle abruptly spun sideways across the tarmac and careened onto the shoulder, coming to an abrupt halt, a complete one-eighty to where it had started.

Ava managed to keep control of her car and pulled up onto the shoulder a little distance away. Jumping out, she drew her Glock even as she pulled the lever for her trunk. She grabbed her ballistics vest and pulled it over her head, strapping it on one-handed and never taking her eyes off the Suburban.

The other car still rocked slightly in the dirt at the side of the road.

Knowing backup was close, but not knowing the state of the people inside the rig, Ava carefully approached the vehicle from the driver's side. Her heart pounded from the exhilaration of the chase and the uncertainty of what lay ahead. Did Jimmy have a weapon? Did Maria?

"FBI. Open the door and show me your hands," she yelled.

Slowly the door creaked open. Jimmy Taylor held his

hands out to show they were empty and turned his body so both feet were visible. She moved around so she could see past him into the passenger seat. Maria was slumped, apparently unconscious, against the passenger door. Blood matted her hair. More blood coated Taylor's chin.

"You ran us off the road?" His voice was high-pitched with shock. "What the fuck? My girlfriend is hurt. I need to help her."

Ava balanced her weight on the balls of her feet. "She should have worn her seatbelt."

"You *fucking* bitch." His words were clipped. Eyes hot with rage.

"Ambulance is on the way." Not quite true, but it wouldn't be long. "Get out of the car, Mr. Taylor. Nice and slow."

"Who? You've got the wrong guy, darlin', and I'm going to sue you and your department for everything you have."

"Get out of the car, Jimmy."

"You made a mistake, and I'm gonna sue your fucking ass so bad…" He slid out of the car slowly, then lunged so fast he caught her off guard. She dodged, cursed and then moved in closer, keeping her gun out of his grasp while she kneed him in the groin. As he curled over in agony, she caught one of his wrists and used it to force him to the ground. Patrol cops were pulling up as she drew her cuffs out of her back pocket. She identified herself. One officer handled traffic. Another approached with his weapon drawn, pointed at Jimmy. Ava read the guy his rights and slowly registered the sound of a chopper overhead.

"There's an injured passenger." Ava told the police officer. "We need them both checked out at the hospital before they get processed." She helped Jimmy to his feet and passed him over to a third cop who turned up. "Call the Marshals. Tell them we found something they lost."

Ava and another cop saw to Maria until the paramedics arrived. The woman had banged her head on the side window and claimed she didn't remember a damn thing, not even her name. Not the first person in the world to claim amnesia, but as a defense tactic it generally didn't go down great with the judge.

The cops put Jimmy and Maria in separate squad cars, and Ava was happy for the cops to take credit for the apprehensions. It built rapport between departments and was considerably less paperwork for her. Then she checked her own car for damage. There was a slight dent in the side, but nothing major. She might get her knuckles slapped by the mechanics, but her boss should be happy enough.

Van would have gotten a kick out of the whole thing. She looked up at the sky and grinned, missing him so acutely it felt as if someone had carved out a piece of her heart.

Her work cell rang. She checked caller ID and pulled a surprised face. "What can I do for you, SSA Sheridan?"

She hadn't expected to hear from him again after their exchange at the funeral yesterday.

"Can you meet me at Van's house in the next hour?"

Her heart gave a hard *whump*. Had he found something?

"Agent Kanas? Are you still there?"

"Yeah. Yes. Sorry." She looked at the strewn motor vehicles and the mile-long line of traffic with drivers all craning their necks to see what had gone down. She had some paperwork to write up and a report to make, but… "I'll be there in thirty minutes."

She hung up because she didn't like the way she responded

to SSA Sheridan's voice. A lot of men had sexy voices. Didn't mean anything, even though it was packaged well. She climbed into her car, knowing she'd ache tomorrow but for now, she was still riding the adrenaline high. She'd helped get another bad guy off the street, and that was why she'd joined the FBI in the first place. And why she stayed.

CHAPTER FIVE

As Ava drove up to Van's house, a feeling of immense sorrow sank into her bones. It didn't look like Sheridan was here yet and she was glad. It gave her a moment to grieve in peace. It was an older neighborhood, a lot of small family homes built in the fifties and sixties with some newer, larger homes here and there.

She stepped out of the Impala and headed slowly across the street to the neat little bungalow Van had shared with the wife he'd worshipped. The air was still warm from the heat of the day and the scent of roses from Jessica's garden scented the air. Jessica had passed away by the time Ava had worked with him, but every room reflected the woman who'd made this house a home. As far as Ava knew, Van hadn't altered a thing.

When her father had been murdered, Ava and her younger brother and sister had been packed up with barely the clothes on their backs and whisked clear across the country. The only reminder of her father had been a framed photograph kept in her mother's bedroom. That, and Ava's recurring nightmares.

Ava missed her dad even though she could barely remember him now.

The smell of fresh cut grass snapped her out of her memories. The sound of someone approaching from around the side of the house made her tense.

Supervisory Special Agent Dominic Sheridan appeared wearing dark slacks, a bright white shirt—complete with his service weapon in a shoulder holster—and expensive-looking, black leather shoes, now covered in grass shavings. His tie was gone, sleeves rolled, revealing tanned, strong-looking forearms and nicely shaped hands.

He stopped short and looked momentarily nonplussed. Cleared his throat. "Van didn't like the grass getting too long."

They looked away from one another. Their individual grief too raw to share.

"My jacket's around back." He tilted his head toward the rear of the house in a walk-with-me motion.

Ava said nothing as she followed him. Van lived in a corner plot with a big wedge-shaped yard. Sheridan's Prius Bucar was pulled up outside Van's garage. Sheridan's jacket hung off a fence post, a red tie sticking out of the pocket. Ava watched as he rolled down his sleeves and buttoned the cuffs, the muscles in his arms flexing. Her cheeks heated. Hopefully he hadn't noticed her ogling him and he'd blame the blush on the sun. He shrugged into his jacket but left his tie in the pocket.

"What can I do for you, SSA Sheridan?"

Those deep blue eyes probed her face. "Call me Dominic."

"Okay." She made it sound like a question, feigning a nonchalance she wasn't feeling. His face was attractive. His voice was attractive. So was his stupid name. He oozed power and confidence, wealth and charm. If she had any smarts at all she'd stick to calling him SSA Sheridan.

When she didn't say anything further, he pulled a key from his pocket. Ava crossed her arms. "You want to go inside?"

He nodded.

A shiver of trepidation hit her. "Did you look at the reports?"

His lips thinned. "I decided to take a look at the house first."

"Do yourself a favor. Don't look at the autopsy photos."

"Did you?" Those denim eyes were intent on hers. She didn't want to show weakness in front of a superior but this was about the loss of a friend. A good friend. For both of them.

"I wish I hadn't." She admitted as she turned toward the house.

"I'll keep that in mind."

Ava met his gaze then. "Aldrich won't be happy that I'm here."

"My boss won't either, but I hadn't planned on telling him."

"Good plan." They shared a quick smile.

In silent agreement they approached via the back door, the one Van insisted friends and family use when they came by.

"When was the last time you were here?" he asked.

"Monday last week." She hadn't wanted Van to get lonely—at least that's what she'd told herself. In truth she was the one who was lonely but she wasn't about to welcome SSA Sheridan to her pity party. "What about you?"

He grimaced. "May. I had a busy few months."

Ava could tell he regretted that now. She stood aside and allowed him to turn the key and swing the door wide.

She went to take a step forward, but he touched her arm. "Put these on."

He held out a pair of latex gloves and then pulled paper booties out of his pocket. She eyed them with surprise. "You think this is a crime scene?"

"Isn't that what you've been trying to convince people?"

"But no one is buying it." She took the gloves and tugged them on. "You said you didn't read the reports, so—"

"I started to," he admitted. He stretched the latex over his fingers with a snap. "It felt like I was reading about a stranger. I figured I'd get a better sense if I first looked at the scene myself."

They both slipped the paper covers over their shoes. A ball of dread congealed in her stomach. "Has anyone else been in here since…?"

Sheridan shook his head. "Van's daughters were waiting until after the funeral to deal with the house."

She squared her shoulders and stepped inside. A wave of memories pummeled her. Van standing next to the coffeepot. Van making scrambled eggs for dinner because it was one of the few things he knew how to cook and he was always happy to share.

Sheridan's mouth was downturned as if cataloguing his own memories of happier times. "Why did you come over last Monday?"

It felt like a lifetime ago now. "I'd made an arrest on a child pornography investigation that started when he was in the office. He liked to know the status of things. When I was able to tell him anything, I mean." Once retired, former agents were no longer privy to information on active cases but she'd sometimes bent the rules a little if she'd thought Van might be able to offer insight.

"Child porn cases are the worst."

They exchanged a look. That kind of case was so common that almost every law enforcement officer dealt with one at some point. Many agents working them long-term required therapy afterward. One of the most effective therapies Ava had found was taking those monsters off the street.

An odor stirred in the stale air. Unidentifiable to most people, but not to law enforcement. It became ingrained on the palate like salt or pepper. Sheridan led the way down a short corridor that opened out onto a large, open-plan, living room off to the left and a half bath and then an office off to the right.

A black feeling pressed down between her shoulder blades. What if she was wrong about her theory? What if she was making Dominic Sheridan suffer this ordeal simply because she was reluctant to accept Van had decided to end it all? People killed themselves all the damn time, though she could never understand why. Hopefully she never would.

What if she was right? Sheridan was the only person who'd even pretended to believe her.

He paused with his fingers on the doorknob. "Ready?"

"Nope." She braced herself. "Let's do this anyway."

He opened the office door and flicked on the light switch. They both stood for moment, feet made of matching lumps of clay. The fetor of death hit the back of her throat, and she wanted to gag. Somehow, she forced the impulse away. Blood and brain matter were sprayed against the wall behind the desk, blackened with age.

As ghastly as this was, it was still Van, a man who'd been like a father to her. When it came to father figures, apparently, she was bad luck. She touched the beads on her wrist.

"This sucks." Sheridan took a step into the room and skirted the edge, careful not to touch anything. She liked that he didn't pretend to be unaffected. Anyone unaffected by a scene like this when the victim had been a dear friend couldn't be anything other than a sociopath or an asshole, and she generally avoided both.

Ava followed without a word. Someone had turned off the air conditioning. The fusty air combined with the biological decomposition made the stench unbearable. Iciness rushed over her, and her stomach started to churn. She strode over to open first the blinds and then the window, the outside air blowing over her face, immediately helping her breathe. The scent of freshly cut grass wafted inside and made her smile even as tears pricked the back of her eyes. Van would have appreciated Sheridan cutting his lawn even if, right now, the smell made her want to retch.

"The window was open the night he died," she recalled, swallowing repeatedly, desperate to moisten her throat.

A screen of shrubs covered most of the view.

She didn't know why she was suddenly shivering when the house was so stuffy and hot.

Dominic came over and stood beside her, the heat of his body warming the air between them. There was a key in the other window which was locked. He touched it with his index finger.

"No screen?"

Ava shook her head. "I don't know if there was ever one here."

"I'll check with Sarah. She'll know."

Van's daughters lived in Baltimore where they'd both gone to college. Ava had met them briefly a few times when they'd visited, although she'd tried not to intrude on family time.

Sheridan walked around to the far side of the desk. Blood and gore coated the back of the hard, wooden swivel chair Van had insisted on using. Drips of something stained the carpet beneath.

Ava averted her eyes. This was harder than she'd expected. "They took whatever he was drinking that night, the glass, his weapon to the lab."

Sheridan nodded. "Makes sense."

Nothing else did. No note. No hints of depression. No warning.

"Who found him?" he asked.

"A neighbor called it in Wednesday morning."

"You talk to him?"

She shook her head. Everything had been such a whirlwind of grief and denial, followed by anger and frustration leading up to the funeral she hadn't even thought of it.

"Wanna do it now?" he asked.

She'd rather get her stomach pumped. "Sure."

AS MUCH AS he wanted to sprint out of Van's study, a death scene now ingrained on his brain more effectively than any photograph, Dominic carefully closed and locked the window before leaving. It wasn't like Van to be lax on security, but maybe that had changed after Jessica's death and his subsequent retirement. Maybe he'd stopped caring. Dominic hadn't come around often enough to know for sure, and the gnawing feeling of guilt kept running its sharp teeth over his flesh. As far as friends went, Dominic was bottom of the heap. Unlike the agent he followed down the hallway.

It made him feel ashamed. It also meant he wanted to help Ava Kanas find answers to any loose ends, to gain closure.

They strode through the kitchen where Van had spent so much time drinking coffee and reading the newspapers. Van had claimed he got more in-depth information scouring newsprint headlines than reading online articles. Dominic rarely had time to read the papers anymore, which was another reminder that he shouldn't even be here. He should be finalizing the timetable for the negotiator courses CNU ran four times a year and checking in with various sieges throughout the country and overseas. But someone had taken a shot at them yesterday and, like Agent Kanas, he couldn't ignore the possibility it was somehow related to Van's death. The task force was working all angles, but he'd known this man intimately and so had Kanas. If there was truly something "hinky" about Van's demise, they'd figure it out faster than anyone else.

They stood for a moment on the back porch inhaling lungfuls of clean air trying to eliminate the pervasive odor of death that clung stubbornly to anything it came into contact with. This was so much worse than being at some random crime scene. This was someone he'd loved. Someone they'd both loved and respected.

No way should Van's family have to deal with that. He'd talk to the company that cleaned his home and see if they could recommend a professional cleaning service. He wouldn't ask permission to get this place sanitized. It's what Van would want.

Van's house stood at the end of a row, but there were properties to the front and the rear. "Which neighbor?" he asked gruffly.

Ava met his gaze, and he caught a glimpse of the devastation he'd been feeling all week reflected in her hazel eyes. She jerked her chin to their right. "Couple with the poodle next door."

Dominic had first met them when Jessica had become sick. More than neighbors. Friends. Reluctantly he led the way.

He checked his watch. His boss had gone up to HQ today to discuss budget needs, and he'd be there again tomorrow. Savage was staying in Dominic's DC apartment. It was nicer than a hotel and Dominic liked it to be occupied whenever possible by people he trusted.

It was the same thing every year, negotiators desperately begging for more funding while HRT and SWAT seemed to just breathe a request, and it was miraculously filled.

It was true that sometimes talk couldn't beat bullets. Sometimes the hostage-taker was determined to kill their captives. Sometimes they were narcissistic assholes who couldn't be reasoned with. But often negotiators could work magic simply by slowing things down and listening.

Waco was arguably the Bureau's biggest failure and had sullied the organization's reputation for more than a decade. If the negotiators had been left to do things their way, the slow trickle of people leaving the compound might have become a rush and eventually David Koresh could conceivably have been left with no one to lead but his own inflated ego. More than eighty people might not have died in the conflagration. Kids might have survived into adulthood.

And maybe that was wishful thinking on the negotiators' part.

Dominic knew some of the agents involved were still haunted by what had happened on that day in April so long ago, by the mistakes the FBI had made. None of them wanted a repeat of that fiasco.

He held the gate for Agent Kanas. She looked like a leggy teen today, dressed down in tight jeans and a soft t-shirt that outlined her breasts in a way that warned him to keep his gaze north. She walked ahead and his attention drifted to her ass. He mentally kicked himself and pinned his eyes back to her long hair that was once again tied up in a messy bun.

What was he thinking? He did not get involved with other agents. Not even for steamy one-nighters. The potential for complications was too great, and he was careful to keep his job and his sex life in strictly different lanes.

Not that Kanas was offering.

At the neighbor's back gate, she stopped and put her hands on her hips. "You want me to take the lead?"

The neighbors' house was a large, new bungalow with small windows. "It might be better for your career if I do it."

She shrugged one shoulder. He noticed a bruise on her forearm and wondered how she got it—sparring? Arresting a suspect? Rough sex?

She flashed him a quick grin, and it transformed her face. It was the first time he'd really noticed her smile, and it softened her features and made her eyes glow with mischief. "If anyone asks, I'll say you ordered me to do it."

He huffed out a laugh. He'd seen how well she took orders when she'd been interacting with her boss. "Let's hope no one asks."

He didn't mind taking responsibility for today's "investigation," but he hoped it wouldn't come to that. He'd survive the flak better than she would if they were discovered. As long as they kept their questioning discreet, they should be fine.

She knocked firmly on the door, and they both stood to one side of the doorframe, even though he wasn't expecting trouble.

A dog barked and scratched at the other side of the door.

"Who is it?" The voice was muffled behind the thick wood.

Dominic nodded to Ava.

"This is FBI Agent Ava Kanas. I'm here with Supervisory Special Agent Sheridan, Mr. Gabany. We were hoping to talk to you about Van."

Dominic wasn't surprised Ava remembered the neighbor's name. Van didn't waste his time with new agents unless he thought they had potential and that was regardless of whether or not they had pretty faces. Something about the way Kanas had conducted herself since the shooting hinted at a keen intelligence and innate competence. Sure, she was pushy and lacked tact, but there was an honesty and integrity about her that would have appealed to his old friend.

It appealed to him.

The lock turned, and the door cracked open an inch. After a moment of cautious assessment, the man's eyes grew large, and he opened the door wide. A poodle Dominic had met on several occasions scrambled out to inspect them.

"Sorry, Dominic, I didn't recognize the name. After the shooting yesterday, the wife and I are both a bit jumpy. Did you catch the shooter?"

Dominic reached down to pet the soft curls on the dog's head. "We're still working on it. How's your wife holding up?"

"She's still pretty shaken."

"We have some questions." Kanas flashed Dominic a look and got straight to the point. Patience was another thing she needed to learn. "We believe you found the body?"

The man paled, flesh going dull gray. "Yes. Yes, I did. Worst thing I've ever seen in my entire life."

"Would you mind if we came inside?" Dominic asked quietly. The last thing he wanted was to further traumatize one of Van's friends.

Gabany checked his shoulder and shook his head, instead motioned them out onto the back porch. "Reza is asleep. I don't think she'll ever leave the house again after what happened."

"I know how she feels." Kanas took a step back and waited for Sam Gabany to be seated.

Dominic couldn't imagine Kanas running from anything. More like standing on a hilltop, shaking her fist at the world. But everyone dealt with grief differently. He buried his under a stoic front. That was how he'd learned to survive. He saw no reason to change now.

"Can you tell us if there was anything unusual about the night Van died, or any of the nights leading up to it?" Dominic asked.

Sam Gabany shook his head, clasping his hands between his knees. His dog took turns sniffing first Dominic and then Agent Kanas.

"I spoke to Van on the Sunday when we were both doing yard work. I borrowed his lawnmower because mine wouldn't start." Gabany's watery eyes glimmered with fresh tears. "I thought I heard what sounded like a gunshot around 10 PM on the Tuesday night. The TV was on, and I didn't get up immediately as I thought it was part of the show I was watching. Reza was in the tub and called through to me. Said she thought she'd heard something too." He scratched his nearly bald head. "I checked the window, but it was dark outside, and I didn't see anyone in the street. I called Van's cell." He cupped his face with his hand over his mouth. "I liked to get his advice on security issues." His indrawn breath sounded like a sob.

"Go on," Dominic said softly after a few moments of pained silence.

"I checked the back yard and saw Van's car in the driveway—he didn't generally put it in the garage except in the winter."

A kid on a bike rode along a footpath that ran along the back of the property. They all watched him turn the corner out of sight.

"I figured if he was home and there had been a gunshot, he'd have been outside, investigating, you know? I forgot about it. Convinced myself it must have been on the TV and went to bed. I never imagined…" He sniffed. "Next morning, I noticed the newspaper on Van's lawn so I picked it up and let myself in—I still keep a spare key on my fob. Reza and I used to spend a lot of time over there when Jessica was ill and Van was working." The man closed his eyes as grief washed over him. "I should have spent more time with him when he retired—"

"We all should have," Dominic told the man, razors carving out his heart.

"I thought he was doing okay. I never thought…" Gabany gulped loudly.

Dominic let the silence linger. Silence was a much-underutilized tool for getting answers. Kanas watched him, clearly trying to gauge where they were going in the interview.

"He was sad about Jessica, but she'd been so sick there that at the end I think he was secretly relieved her suffering was over."

"Cancer sucks," Agent Kanas said, her jaw working.

Dominic wondered if she'd lost someone close. He knew nothing about her family or her background. The poodle headed into the yard. For a moment it felt as if they were all waiting for Van to appear on his back porch and wave before joining them.

"No one should ever have to doubt how much they meant to one another," Gabany said cryptically.

Dominic glanced sharply at Gabany. "Do you know if Van had started seeing anyone since Jessica died?"

Gabany turned his head away and stared at the big maple that dissected his and Van's yard. "No."

Kanas caught Dominic's eye. They'd both noticed the defensiveness. The clipped response compared to his previous answers.

"No, you don't know or no, he didn't start seeing anyone?" Dominic probed. There was something here worth digging at. Something meaty and meaningful.

Gabany shrugged but wouldn't meet his gaze. The man had put his shields up. The question was why?

"Aside from Sarah and Amy, she's the only woman I saw visiting." Gabany nodded toward Kanas, resentment gleaming in his eyes. Sarah and Amy were Van's daughters.

"We were colleagues and friends," Kanas reassured the man, which seemed to make Gabany relax a fraction. "Van was like a father to me."

"It sounds as if you're upset by the idea of Van being involved with someone new," Dominic said carefully.

"It's not that, I…"

"What is it then?" Kanas pushed.

Dominic sighed. Patience was a virtue. Thankfully it could be learned.

Gabany pressed his lips together. "We all met at church, okay? Reza and Jessica were best friends. I know Jessica is gone and all, but the idea of having...relations outside of marriage...bothers me."

"Relations?" Dominic held Kanas's gaze, willing her not to say anything. To let the other man fill the silence.

There was something Gabany wasn't telling them. Maybe it was nothing. Maybe it was gossip or narrow-mindedness. Whatever it was, Dominic wanted to know.

Gabany scratched his head and lowered his voice to a whisper presumably so his wife didn't overhear. "Sexual relations."

Again, Dominic let the pause ride and could practically feel Kanas grinding her teeth. She remained silent this time, fingers clenched in her lap as if physically holding back the need to force answers from the man. He felt like he'd won a major victory.

Finally, Gabany spoke again. "I know a man has needs, but it felt wrong."

"Felt wrong?" Dominic mirrored the words, pulling out information one word at a time. Mirroring built rapport and forced the speaker to expand on their thoughts. It was a common technique negotiators used to build trust.

"Yes, wrong. When I went into the house, I could tell from the smell something terrible had happened." Gabany shuddered. "I went into the office and found Van..." His knee started to bounce.

The dog whined, ran back to the deck and went over to comfort his master.

Two shiny stripes appeared on Gabany's pale cheeks. "I didn't want everyone to see him like that."

"Like what?" Kanas asked.

"His pants were undone and..." Gabany swallowed. "He was exposed."

"His genitals were exposed?" Dominic clarified.

Gabany nodded, red deepening in his cheeks.

"So, you, what? Zippered him back up?" Agent Kanas's eyes were huge. She needed to work on her poker face.

"I didn't want him found that way," Gabany said defensively.

He'd messed with the body which could mean nothing or could mean everything.

"What do you think happened?" Dominic asked softly, shooting a quelling look at Kanas.

Gabany shifted his feet. He was obviously uncomfortable talking about sex in front of a woman. "I don't know."

"Well, there are two choices. Either he masturbated alone or there was someone with him." Kanas had no such qualms. "Was there any evidence of semen?"

Gabany's mouth dropped open in shock as if a woman wasn't supposed to know about basic human biology. Yeah, tact was definitely not high on her list of attributes. Kanas had switched to full-on investigator and Gabany was still thinking about the death of his friend.

Dominic was trying not to think about Van at all. "Can I clarify a point?"

The man looked aghast but nodded.

"You adjusted his boxer shorts to cover his penis?"

A quick nod.

"What about his pants?"

Another nod. "I zipped them up and fastened the button."

"He never mentioned another woman? Not even in passing?" asked Kanas. "Because he definitely didn't mention anyone to me."

Gabany shook his head, looking defeated. "No."

Dominic paused. He wasn't sure quite how this changed things. Perhaps Van had been knocking one out before ending it all. But would he really have wanted to be found that way?

Or was Agent Kanas right and someone else had been in the study, someone who'd helped that bullet find his brain?

Or had Van had a sexual encounter that evening and been so overcome by guilt and remorse and self-hate for cheating on his dead wife that he killed himself and left his humiliation right out in the open for everyone to see as some sort of twisted self-punishment?

The trouble with that scenario was that no way Van would have wanted anyone in the FBI finding him that way. Van understood the black humor and notorious urban legends that abounded within the Bureau. He simply wouldn't have wanted that humiliating detail to be his legacy.

But if there was another woman involved who was she and when had she left? Before or after Van ended up with a bullet in his brain?

"Would you be willing to make an official statement?" asked Dominic.

"Will it get me in trouble?" Gabany sounded defensive now.

Dominic let out a breath through his nose. "It might get you a caution. But as long as you tell the truth I can't see the District Attorney being keen to prosecute."

Gabany went white around the mouth. "Does my wife have to know? Or the general public? I did it to protect Van's reputation..."

"I can't guarantee someone won't find out," Dominic told him honestly. "But no one inside the FBI wants to see Van's memory sullied in any way. He was a highly respected agent whom we loved and esteemed. No one is going to release the information unless we have to."

Gabany nodded slowly. "Give me your card, and I will send you a signed statement."

It didn't quite work that way, but Dominic would figure out how to handle it when he had the document in hand. No way would the DA go after a conviction for this. Dominic handed over his card, and Kanas did the same.

The poodle whimpered as they walked away and made Dominic think about his own dog who was probably curled up on his bed even though he wasn't supposed to be there.

"What are you smiling at?" Kanas asked between gritted teeth.

He raised his brow at her. "You have a problem with me smiling?"

"Considering what we just learned about Van, yes."

"Lighten up, Kanas. Van's dead no matter the state of my face."

Her eyes did a shocked flick around his features and darted away. She muttered something he didn't catch.

He checked his watch. "I need to get back to Quantico."

"What?" Kanas stopped and faced him, incredulous. "We need to go talk to the medical examiner. See if they took swabs for DNA. We need to trace Van's movements the day he died. We might be able to place him with someone—"

"We're not actively assigned to this investigation, remember?" Although he had an excuse as Aldrich had asked him to look at the files. Kanas didn't. "*You* need to get back to the office before your boss notices you're AWOL. I'll contact the ME and the lab and—"

"No. No way." She put her hands on her hips, her t-shirt stretching tight across her full breasts. He had to force himself not to let his gaze get distracted. Ava Kanas had the sort of body that could make a man break every rule in the book, and Dominic was not a rule breaker.

"You are not sidelining me on this," she insisted.

And the sort of mouth that could drive a man insane. Not in a good way.

"Sidelining you?" Was she serious? "Taking the lead on something is not sidelining. Ever heard of teamwork? Cooperation? Or plain old saving your ass?"

"Saving my ass?" Gold flecks sparked in the depths of her eyes. "You wouldn't even be here if it wasn't for me."

Dominic strove for his natural calm, the one that usually came so easily to him. "I'm *trying* to protect your FBI career from the kamikaze spin you seem determined to put it into."

Her lips parted and her chest rose and fell rapidly as she clearly tried to hold on to her temper.

"There are rules and procedures for this. We have no solid evidence. We have no witnesses. All we have is a man who claims he adjusted the clothing of what is most likely a suicide victim." He reined in the temper that was starting to fray. Ironic that he found it easier to deal with bank robbers and terrorists than Ava Kanas. "I'll check the files and see what evidence was collected at the scene and ask the ME what samples they took during the postmortem." The funeral had been postponed but, given the embalming process, Dominic couldn't be sure what evidence might still be present. At least he was in a position where he could get them to check without losing his job.

She swallowed tightly. "What am I supposed to do?"

"Just do your job until we have more answers." He pulled his tie from his pocket and slid it along his collar.

Her eyes followed every movement of his fingers. "I'm not letting this drop just because my 'superiors' are telling me to. That's not what Van taught me about conducting investigations. Question everything. Don't let anyone tell you to ignore your gut. Trust your instincts."

God, she was infuriating. "You're deliberately missing the point. I'm not letting you fuck up your career because you're torn up with grief."

"You're not *letting* me?" A muscle flexed in her jaw.

"That's right, Ava." He got in her face. It would have been a hundred times easier to stare her down if he hadn't wanted to crush her against him and kiss her until she couldn't breathe. *Fuck.* "I'm not letting you. That's what Van taught me—how not to fuck up a career."

She stilled at his vehemence. After a long beat of silence, she finally said, "Fine." But it sounded more like "fuck you."

She brushed past him, her stride long and confident and pissed. "Let me know if I can do anything else to assist you, *sir.*"

He shook his head. God she was stubborn, but pissing off her superiors was not a great way of keeping her position. No way in hell would Ava Kanas let this go. The question was, how far would he be willing to go to protect her?

CHAPTER SIX

AN HOUR LATER, the sun was slanting through the blinds at an oblique angle that seemed determined to burn out her retinas, although that wasn't what was bothering Ava.

She was still so mad with Dominic Sheridan that even writing her FD 302 for the incident with Jimmy Taylor that morning hadn't cooled her off. Jimmy was safely back in custody and Maria, the girlfriend, was at the hospital suffering from a concussion after hitting her head on the dashboard. They were saving her a place in jail.

Ava spied Ray Aldrich coming into the office where she had a cubicle along with the other agents in their little Resident Agency. She eyed him warily.

He was all smiles and charm today. Even at their meeting first thing that morning he'd calmed down. He was like a dog with no teeth, but he might grow some if he figured out she'd been investigating Van's death against his explicit instructions.

"Nice job on the arrest this morning, Ava."

"Thank you." She gifted him a belated, "Sir."

Van had always said you caught more flies with honey than vinegar, and Sheridan wasn't the only one who was good at manipulating people.

"The damage to the Impala was minimal. Did you know it had reinforced bumpers before you rammed Taylor's SUV?"

Did he think she was an idiot?

"I wouldn't have attempted the PIT maneuver in an unmodified vehicle, nor would I have done it if I hadn't seen the patrol cars in close pursuit. I had only a few seconds before Taylor reached I95 and the potential harm to civilians would have increased dramatically."

"I'm not doubting your choices, Ava." *Liar.* He laughed. "I'm shocked he turned up at all."

Yeah, she'd gathered. Aldrich had been trying to keep her occupied and away from the office and the investigation into Calvin Mortimer's shooting. Jimmy Taylor had messed up his plans.

"No one ever said cons were rocket scientists." She turned slightly in her chair, feigning nonchalance. "Any news into Mortimer's murder?"

Even though the shooting had occurred in Virginia, higher ups had moved the investigation to the Washington Field Office (WFO) as they had more available personnel and space than the Richmond office. Plus, WFO was geographically closer to the crime scene and the national laboratory and the director who had apparently requested hourly briefs on the task force's progress.

Aldrich stuffed his hands in his pockets. "Lead investigator is an agent called Mark Gross who was recently promoted to squad leader at WFO. I know they're pursuing leads into vehicles seen on the traffic cams in Fredericksburg yesterday, although if the attack was planned it's likely they used false plates, and they're still waiting on the ballistics report."

"No forensic evidence recovered from the roof of the apartment complex?"

"Unfortunately not. Just the brass casing you and SSA

Sheridan discovered." Aldrich leaned on the edge of her cubicle. "How are you doing today?"

How was she doing? Lost. Adrift. Angry. "Fine."

"You talked to the psychologist yet?"

Her mouth pinched. "I was busy with the Taylor surveillance and arrest. I'll call to book an appointment now..." She reached for the phone. It was after five and the shrinks would all have left for the day. As she'd expected, no one answered. She made a show of checking her watch. "I hadn't realized it was so late."

"Do it tomorrow. Losing Van was bad enough and then Calvin Mortimer shot dead in front of us. It's important to get the help you need."

The help she needed involved everyone else getting out of her way so she could figure out exactly how Van died.

"Well, you were there too," said Ava. "I know it's not my place but don't forget to book your own appointment."

Aldrich was one of those people who was generally harmless but did everything to protect his own standing within the Bureau. She needed to play this situation carefully, to lay the groundwork for when he eventually found out she'd gone behind his back.

"I'm putting you forward for a commendation for yesterday's heroics in the face of grave danger."

What? She didn't want a commendation for doing what she was paid to do.

"I appreciate that." She smiled at him and tried to make it reach her eyes. Would she also get a letter of censure for pursuing the facts behind Van's death? Probably.

She thought about Dominic Sheridan again. She didn't need him to *protect* her. She was an FBI agent, not some frightened civilian. They had a solid indication that Van's death wasn't as cut and dried as everyone assumed and it made her crazy not to be taken seriously. Not to be respected as an equal.

"Did you find anything when you went over Van's files?" she asked.

Aldrich straightened as if knowing what she was angling for. "Nothing to indicate foul play."

She thought about what the neighbor had told her regarding pulling up Van's pants.

She opened her mouth to say something and then closed it again. If she copped to continuing the investigation by questioning the neighbor, she'd face disciplinary action and lose any hope of continuing her search for the truth. As a rookie agent she might also lose her job. As much as she hated to admit it, Sheridan was right.

"I know it hurts, but perhaps when he left the Bureau, he decided he didn't have anything else left to live for..."

Except the trip to Italy he'd planned and the book he'd started to write about his life as a G-man. His friends. His family.

Aldrich reached out as if he was about to pat her arm. She bared her teeth in the parody of a smile, and his hand paused mid-air.

Yeah. Do not touch.

"I better finish my report, sir." Hopefully Maria Santana would be convicted for conspiring with an escaped felon. People were stupid. People in love were particularly witless.

For a split second, a vision of her holding hands with Dominic Sheridan flashed through her brain. Her heart started pounding, and a flush of heat filled her face. Where the hell had that come from?

"Are you okay?"

It must be bad if Aldrich noticed.

"Still a little shaken up after yesterday," she lied, touching the scab that had formed on her cheek.

He nodded firmly. "Tomorrow morning. Call the psychologist."

She watched him walk away then dropped her forehead to the cool surface of her desk. She definitely needed her head examined if her subconscious was envisaging some sort of fairytale romance with the other agent. Sure, he was ruggedly good-looking and charming when he wanted to be, but he was also the sort of guy who was difficult to read and didn't let anyone close. She'd worked with that type plenty of times before and was sick of constantly striving to prove herself worthy. He was a Supervisory Special Agent ten years her senior, and someone who played by the book. She was a rookie who followed her gut. And, so what if he had a nice face and nice forearms, possibly six-pack abs under that shirt, but it didn't mean he knew what to do in the bedroom.

She huffed at her own thoughts. How had her imagination escalated to the *bedroom*? He could be married with kids for all she knew.

Please, please, let him be married. Then she wouldn't have to worry about making a damn fool of herself over a man who thought of her as nothing more than an annoyance, an irritation, a responsibility he'd inherited from Van.

She didn't need romantic humiliation to compound all the other issues going on in her life. Better to keep everything professional and concentrate on figuring out what exactly had happened to Van. She could get her heart broken in her own time.

DOMINIC PULLED UP outside Van's house later again that same evening in his personal vehicle, a black Lexus. It was nearly 9 PM now and dusk. The quiet settled around him, and he realized with a thick sense of despondency it was almost exactly one week since Van had died.

Dominic got out and closed the driver's door quietly and walked around the hood. He'd always liked this part of Virginia. It was quiet and relatively peaceful, but close enough to both DC and Quantico to have been in the running when he was looking for his own place when he'd transferred to the Crisis Negotiation Unit from LA. He'd chosen a home more in the country, and closer to work so he'd be able to spend more time with his dog and a little less time driving—theoretically at least.

He opened the passenger door and unclipped his black lab who jumped out and milled in a circle, head down, tail wagging like a truce flag. Ranger was eight now. A present from his father, presumably chosen to demonstrate how incredibly awkward and time-consuming Dominic's chosen career was—as if being a lawyer had better hours. But, with the help of a doggy daycare near Quantico, fellow agents who loved dogs, and a neighbor who owned horses and took Ranger whenever Dominic needed to go away overnight, they managed. Ranger was beyond the crazed exuberance of pupdom and supposedly more sensible nowadays. At least he'd stopped eating drywall.

Dominic clipped on the dog's leash and strode across the

street. Ranger nosed the scents along the white picket fence as Dominic opened the front gate. The motion sensing security light flashed on, almost blinding him. He walked around the side of the house staying on the grass he'd cut earlier that day. A large shrub hid the window of the study from the street. Crickets chirped loudly and a drop of sweat ran down Dominic's spine. Ranger whined.

He glanced around. The street was empty. No one sat in nearby parked cars. Still, the sense of being watched lingered.

The unanswered questions from earlier kept circling his brain. Why had Van's pants been undone? Why had the window been open?

Dominic had checked the evidence logs, but no one had mentioned checking the outside of the property.

Using his cell phone as a flashlight, he pushed back the rhododendron branches, dislodging leaves in a gentle shower. He ran the beam of light over the ground beneath the window, careful to keep Ranger well away from the loose soil. It had rained last week on Wednesday around five PM. A quick shower that had soaked the parched ground. But this space was protected by the bushes and overhanging eaves.

The beam of light picked up a bunch of impressions in the dirt. Footprints. A frisson of alarm traveled over his shoulders and down his spine. Someone had been here. It could be kids daring one another to check out a death scene. It could be reporters looking for a grisly scoop. He was glad the blinds had been firmly closed against prying eyes.

But there was another possibility. Ava Kanas's theory. Where Van had been murdered...and these could be the footprints of his killer.

Shadows thickened and deepened as the motion sensors

timed out, cloaking him in a dense darkness. Dominic backed up and started walking toward the fence on the west side of the property, keeping Ranger close to heel. It was heavy dusk now. No moon. No streetlights illuminating the immediate area. He faced the house and paced about fifteen feet before tripping the motion sensors. He tried the same thing for the security lights at the back of the house. They had even less of a range due to the covered porch.

Ranger sniffed his way along the ground like a dog on a mission. Dominic wished he had the lab's nose. How much more convenient it would be to be able to identify someone from the scent they left behind.

He walked back to the original spot and stared at the window to Van's study. He pulled out his cell and made a call, wondering if he was making a massive mistake. "Agent Kanas?"

"Dominic?" The use of his first name caught him off guard. Warm. Intimate. *Massive mistake.* "What is it?"

She sounded confused. Hell, she was probably home or in bed.

"Meet me at Van's place. I've got something to show you."

"When?"

"Right now." He hung up on her, knowing she'd come and not sure how he felt about the bond that was forming between them. As much as he wanted to, he couldn't exclude her from this search for answers. He sure as hell couldn't ignore her.

These footprints could have nothing to do with Van's death and everything to do with people's obsession with the macabre. But the question kept tugging at him. What if Kanas was right? What if someone had murdered Van and then used his death to target another FBI agent? And what if they'd done it before?

CHAPTER SEVEN

AVA SNAGGED A booth for her and Sheridan at the back of a bar called the Mule & Pitcher on the outskirts of Fredericksburg not far from where she'd taken down Jimmy Taylor. A friend of hers in the RA had let her sneak a look at Van's case file earlier. Bank records showed he'd had dinner in this bar. Then he'd gone home and, according to most people in her organization, had *accidentally* blown his brains out.

She peeled the foil from her bottle of beer with her thumb and tapped the fingers of her other hand on her thigh as she waited for Sheridan to join her. She was surprised he'd called her, but grateful.

She glanced around. She'd never been here before. She preferred Netflix to nightclubs. Except for the occasional night out with the guys after work she tended to spend her spare time in the gym or at the firing range. The last time she'd gone on a date, months ago—to the movies, she remembered now—she'd spotted some loser ripping someone off at an ATM and had chased the sonofabitch four blocks until she'd caught and cuffed him. Her date had been long gone by the time she'd gone back. He'd never called her again.

Van had told her she could be a little intimidating, but she wasn't going to pretend to be something she wasn't. She wasn't about to let somebody get attacked and not do anything about it because her date couldn't handle it.

She ignored the glances she was getting from a few of the guys in the place. There were still plenty of men who thought a woman alone in a bar meant she was hoping to hook up. She took another swallow of beer and let her expression dispel the notion.

The joint was hopping. Didn't people know it was a Tuesday night? Surely some of them had to work the next day? Ava winced as one woman fell off her chair and started laughing where she lay on the floor. So, did all her girlfriends. Ava was about to get up and assist when the lady rolled onto her side and heaved herself up.

Good times.

The bar itself was off to the right against the back wall with a small dance floor tucked in near the window. Thankfully no one was dancing and so the music wasn't too loud. Most people sat in small groups, drinking and laughing. Clientele looked to be early twenties to mid-thirties. Some people had obviously come straight from work while others were dressed more casually, shorts and t-shirts, jeans. Ava touched the evil eye bracelet on her wrist. It was a silly Greek superstition, but the amulet never failed to make her feel better.

Sheridan walked in still wearing that expensive-looking, dark suit and the same blood-red tie he'd stuffed in his pocket earlier that day before cutting Van's lawn. He looked like a smoking-hot politician or a scorching CEO. Common denominator seemed to involve sex and heat and things she should not be associating with a senior agent at the FBI. She let herself enjoy the view for as long as it took for them to make eye contact and then she lifted her hand in acknowledgment.

She scanned the bar. Several pairs of female eyes were

following his progress across the room. Apparently, she wasn't the only one who'd noticed his good looks.

It was ten thirty and many customers were on the other side of tipsy. According to the signs, Happy Hour lasted from five until midnight, which suggested the manager needed a basic math lesson but certainly explained the raucous crowd.

Sheridan reached her booth and slid into the seat, moving close so they could talk without being overheard. His thigh brushed hers before he shifted away, and she jumped at the brief contact.

Way to play it cool, Ava.

She cleared her throat, searching for a nonchalance she wasn't feeling. They weren't on a date. This was business. This was about Van. "Where'd you leave your dog?"

He shrugged, and she tried not to notice the broadness of his shoulders. He was just a colleague. Hell, she didn't think he even liked her very much, and she wasn't a masochist.

"In the back of the car. I cracked the windows." The night had cooled off.

The fact he cared more about his dog than the security of his Lexus ramped up his attractiveness by another factor of a thousand.

"You aren't worried about those fancy leather seats getting chewed up?" She took a sip of beer. She wasn't surprised his personal vehicle was a luxury model. He was a luxury model kind of guy.

An amused gleam lit his eyes. Her heart wanted to give a little flip, but she forced it to remain frozen in place.

"There was a time there would have been nothing left of the interior, but nowadays..." He shrugged. "He's getting old. Slowing down, thank god. Like me."

"Sure."

The guy was in his prime and knew it. He sure as heck hadn't looked like he was slowing down when they'd chased after the shooter yesterday morning.

"It's true." He laughed quietly, more relaxed than she'd seen him before. But the creases at the edge of his eyes were more pronounced today. She wondered if he'd gotten any sleep last night after the shooting. She certainly hadn't.

Her server came over with the bucket of wings Ava had ordered. Ordering food had been the only way she'd been able to secure a table.

"What can I get you?" the server—"Caroline" according to her name tag—asked Sheridan with a big smile before running through the specials.

"Water, please." He tapped his coaster on the table. "You have a big crowd in here like this every Tuesday night?"

The waitress wore a bright smile and a tight top that showcased a killer cleavage. Sheridan got top marks for not dropping his gaze below the woman's chin, although those cherry lips were probably already accumulating a large tip.

Ava had once been those lips and that smile. She'd put herself through college waiting tables in a high-end joint in Portland. She'd had her ass pinched so many times it was a wonder she hadn't stabbed somebody with a cocktail stick. Swapping high heels for steel-toe boots when she'd joined the Portland Police had been one of the happiest moments of her life, eclipsed only by graduating from the FBI Academy.

"Help yourself." Ava indicated the wings when the server left. The chicken smelled good and she was drooling, but she wasn't going to be the only one to eat and get messy. Sheridan already held too many aces. Good-looking, powerful, strong.

Independently wealthy if his car was anything to go by—otherwise he owed the bank a lot of money.

He took a drumstick, chowing down as if he'd forgotten to eat lunch and dinner. Maybe he had. They were both using what precious little spare time they had to dig deeper into Van's death. Food seemed irrelevant.

"You managed to get an evidence team out there?" She was surprised he'd contacted her to look at the footprints he'd found before calling Aldrich. Surprised and pleased. It didn't mean he'd include her in anything else. But he'd wanted a second opinion before he'd reported it. The fact he'd called at all...maybe he wasn't so bad.

Were those footprints proof of anything besides morbid curiosity? Were they from Van cleaning windows or doing some weeding? Or had someone gotten into Van's house through that window? Shot him and staged a suicide? The main thing was to make sure the evidence was properly documented before it disappeared in case this thing ever went to court.

"ERT arrived before I left. After all, the director did leave orders he wanted 'no stone unturned.'" He wiped his lips and fingers on a napkin and took a long drink of water.

Was that a dig at her? For what she'd done at the funeral?

"You called the director?"

She got the vibe Sheridan was connected to the higher ups, but she didn't know for sure. Maybe he'd worked with them before. Maybe he knew them socially.

He shook his head, but something about the way he did it suggested he could have, if he'd wanted. He was connected all right.

"Aldrich. You going to eat anything?"

She picked up a drumstick and bit into the warm meat and the flavor dissolved onto her tongue. "Oh, my god, this is good." She groaned. Fried chicken was the reason she could never be a vegetarian.

He glanced at her quickly and she slowed down, chewing her food self-consciously. He had a way of unsettling her, which irritated her. Her family were all about food. She'd grown up above a Greek restaurant in a small town in Oregon. Was it the fact he was senior to her? He was only a few years older, but being a Supervisory Special Agent was a world apart from someone who hadn't yet officially graduated from New Agent status. Van had also been senior to her and she'd never felt self-conscious with him…

The structure of the FBI had appealed to her when she'd signed up. It gave her a target to aim for. She just hadn't considered how it would feel to be on the bottom rung of that ladder after she left the academy with so many years to go.

Forcing herself to eat because she was hungry and her body needed fuel, she nibbled the meat down to the bone, then wiped her fingers. "Did you tell Aldrich I was there?"

"I told him that I was at Van's house taking care of the place when I noticed footprints outside the office window. I let him suggest we get an evidence team back out there." He picked up another wing as the server refilled his water. When she left, he continued. "I also persuaded him that it was his idea to dust the window for prints and check for any contact DNA. Just to be thorough." He grinned and her heart gave a panicked little jolt.

"You're good at manipulating people," she blurted—anything that didn't sound like she found him attractive. She could not afford to get a crush on this guy. It would be too humiliating.

A dimple cut into his cheek, but the smile dimmed. "Most people call it charm. You should try it some time."

Ouch. The dig hurt more than it should.

The fingers of his hand tightened around his glass. "It's an important part of my job, getting people to do what I want but making them think it's their idea."

"You like being a negotiator."

"I like kidnap victims going home. I like people not dying."

She liked that too. She took a sip of beer. "You sound defensive."

He gave her a long, hard look and ignored the observation. Maybe she was imagining it anyway.

"This is where Van spent last Tuesday night?" Sheridan changed the subject back to what they should be talking about.

"Yup." She looked at a table full of laughing women who were clearly celebrating something. "Not where I'd expect him to hang out."

"Maybe he met someone here." Sheridan's dark blue eyes connected with hers. The conversation with the neighbor flashed unspoken between them.

She looked away and scanned the crowd. "Most men I know would not blow their brains out after a blow job."

Remembering the scene and the photographs of Van's body she felt sick. She thrust her plate away. She shouldn't have read the autopsy report, but she'd been so sure the investigators had missed something obvious, something she'd spot immediately. She closed her eyes at the image that flashed through her mind. Some things you could never unsee.

"It's okay to be upset," he said softly.

"Thanks for the permission," she snapped and then immediately regretted it. "I'm sorry. It's just so…" She swallowed hard.

"I know. I get it." The depth of his understanding made her feel small and petty for lashing out. "Van was a good man. He deserved better than what happened to him. However he died, he deserved better."

She nodded, unable to speak now. Maybe this was why Sheridan was a top negotiator. Apparently, he could talk to people about anything. Even the prickly and temporarily insane.

A sense of loneliness and isolation overwhelmed her. She missed Van, she missed her mom and her siblings who lived clear across the country. Most of her friends were there too. Van had filled a million gaps in her life. He'd helped shape her decisions for so long, and now he was gone. It didn't seem fair to lose him.

Losing her father had been a graphic and terrifying experience. Losing Van felt worse. Maybe because she'd known Van longer, or because it had just happened. She took a drink of her beer, and Sheridan let the silence ride. Slowly the tightness in her throat eased.

Being lonely sucked, but it was still better to be alone than involved with someone who wasn't completely right for you. She hadn't met anyone even vaguely right yet, and at twenty-six, she was starting to wonder if she ever would.

Sheridan let her wallow as he devoured more wings. "Even if there was someone with him before he died, I'm still leaning towards him taking his own life," he admitted. "He was too good an agent to be taken unaware."

"I could pull my gun and shoot you dead right now."

His mouth twitched in amusement. “Is that a threat, Agent Kanas?”

She pinched her lips over the reluctant grin that wanted to escape. “You know what I mean. If you aren’t expecting it and the other party is planning something, they can get the drop on you easily.”

He frowned at her.

She sounded like a nut job. “Why would he shoot himself?”

“Who knows why people kill themselves,” he said bitterly. “Maybe because of the guilt?”

“Guilt?”

“That he’d betrayed Jessica.”

His dead wife.

“I know he loved his wife. He spoke about her all the time.” Ava still didn’t buy it. She tapped her fingernail against the thick, green glass of the bottle. “If the guilt was strong enough that he’d kill himself over screwing around on her, why screw around in the first place?”

“Men can be pretty weak in the face of temptation.” His gaze dropped to her lips but then he glanced away, so quickly she was sure she’d imagined it. “He was pretty religious.”

She shook her head. “The church doesn’t care—it’s until death do us part, not for all eternity. Why commit the ultimate sin when he’d knew he’d end up in purgatory? Why not confess and do penance like all the other Catholics?”

Sheridan frowned. “You’re right. It doesn’t fit with the man I knew, but if he’d been drinking…”

The server came up to them again with a big jug of water. She refilled Dominic’s glass.

“Another beer?” The server pointed a finger at Ava.

"No, thanks." One was her limit when driving.

Sheridan picked through his wallet and showed a photograph to the woman. "You ever see this guy in here?"

Ava leaned over Sheridan's arm. He didn't move away. It was a photo of him and Van at a ball game. The grip around her throat tightened. Some of the things she'd said to him had been unfair. He'd clearly loved the guy.

The server's eyes widened for a moment in a flash of recognition. "Maybe. He looks familiar."

"Were you working last week?" Ava strove to sound casual.

"I worked three shifts. Tuesday, Friday, Saturday. I'm in grad school and need the extra cash."

"Do you remember seeing this guy in here last Tuesday night?" Sheridan asked quietly.

The waitress eyed the photograph of Van and frowned. "I've definitely seen him around, but I'm not sure when." She glanced back up. "The shifts all start to blur together after a while." She shrugged. "Sorry."

"Who else was working last Tuesday?" Ava aimed for casual but failed if Sheridan's frown was anything to go by.

Caroline divided a look between them. "Is he missing or something?"

"He's a friend." Sheridan gave her a nod that was technically the truth.

The woman hadn't recognized Van despite the news coverage, and Ava blanked her expression. She wasn't about to give away the fact that Van was dead.

"We're trying to track his movements. We won't cause you any trouble." Sheridan slid a fifty-dollar bill across the smooth wood. "He's a friend of ours and we need to know if he met anyone here. It's important. You have any security footage we might be able to access?"

The server sidled closer with her water jug to block the view of the cash from any observers as she slipped the money into her apron, refilling their glasses with more water as she did. She probably thought they were private investigators looking for evidence of one spouse cheating on another. "I wouldn't go asking the owner for security footage if I were you." Her mouth tightened. "He's not a nice guy."

Ava exchanged a look with Sheridan.

The waitress looked nervously over her shoulder. "I need to check in with my other tables."

Sheridan slid a business card across the table. "Call me if you remember anything else."

Caroline read the card and her skin blanched. "Of course." She pasted on another big smile, one that failed to reach her eyes this time, and quickly stuffed the card into her apron pocket and walked away.

Obviously, she didn't like the fact they were Feds, but there were a million reasons why that could be.

"What do you think?" Ava asked Sheridan.

"I think the FBI needs to talk to the manager and take a look at that surveillance footage."

Which meant him taking the information to Aldrich and the task force and her pretending to not exist. Again. They carried on eating their chicken wings until all that was left was a pile of small bones. Ava licked the salt off her fingers.

They were no further forward than they had been yesterday except for a few more loose ends—like why had Van's pants been down and why had he come to this bar? Did he even have a specific reason? The slowness of their fact-finding mission frustrated the hell out of her.

Over Sheridan's shoulder, Ava watched a massive guy wearing a plaid shirt walk up to another guy seated at the bar and tap him on the shoulder. When the man sitting down turned around, the big guy plowed a sledgehammer fist into his face.

"Bar fight." Ava scanned the area for any other threats.

The injured man wiped a hand over his face, clearly shocked as his fingers came away bloody.

Sheridan slid out of the booth. She followed.

"How'd you like it when someone bigger 'un you picks a fight, asshole?" the big guy shouted, obviously very drunk and very angry.

Awesome combo.

The injured guy swore and scrambled to his feet, using the momentum to land a left hook that made the big guy stagger back into a table full of drinks. People scattered. Beer and wine went everywhere, glasses flying across tabletops and smashing onto the floor.

Bar patrons cleared a space around the brawling men. Some people were getting the hell out of the bar. Others were settling in for the show.

"I don't start fights, motherfucker," the man who'd been hit yelled, "but I sure as hell know how to finish them."

The two men started pounding one another, and Ava rolled her shoulders. Not how she'd planned to end her day.

Sheridan held his badge high and shouted over the din. "FBI. Let's break this up, fellas."

The man with the bloody nose took a quick breath. "You see what he did to me?"

The big guy leaned forward. "That's what happens to

assholes who hit women."

Ava narrowed her eyes on the injured guy who she'd been mentally rooting for until that moment.

"I don't know squat about what you're talking about." He ducked a punch that might well have put him down for good.

"That's enough!" Sheridan shouted, pushing through the crowd. "Party's over."

Sheridan had the larger man in handcuffs before the guy registered his presence, controlling him easily despite his size. Ava watched Sheridan's back. Sheridan murmured to the man who'd been attacked. "You want to press charges, sir?"

The guy touched his broken nose. "How long would it take?"

"A couple of hours." Sheridan spoke over the large man's whining.

"Hell no."

A man who had to be the manager pushed through.

"Do you want to press charges?" Sheridan asked him.

The manager shook his head. "Just throw him out. You're banned, buddy," he shouted after the guy.

Sheridan walked the troublemaker to the door and paused, talking to him in a low, fierce tone.

Ava went back to the table to ask for the check.

When Sheridan reappeared, she asked, "You didn't arrest him?"

A rueful gleam lit his eyes. "More trouble than he's worth. The man—Karl Feldman—says he found a woman crying near the restroom. She claimed the guy at the bar smacked her around."

"Should we try and find her? Get a statement?"

Sheridan downed the last of his water and pointed at the

crowd who'd resumed their night out with barely a blink now the excitement was over. "How exactly?"

"By looking for someone who's been crying?" Ava huffed out a long breath as she looked around. He was right. It was virtually impossible, and the woman might not want to talk to law enforcement even if they identified her.

Caroline came over wearing a big smile. "Manager says it's on the house."

Sheridan shook his head, and Ava thrust out some bills.

"I'll get it," Sheridan tried to push her money away.

"I ordered. I'll pay," she insisted.

"Fine," he muttered. "Thanks for dinner."

Did Sheridan roll his eyes? It was hard to say.

"I'm just going to go talk to the guy at the bar for a moment," Ava murmured. "Make sure he thinks twice before taking another punch at his girlfriend. Don't bother waiting for me—"

"I'll wait."

"It's okay—"

He planted his feet. "Unless you're planning to stay here to party or maybe take one of these guys home, I'll wait."

Ava reared back in shock. Was that what he thought of her? She put her hands on her waist and raised her brows. "Fine. Knock yourself out. I'll be five minutes."

DOMINIC SAT IN the booth and watched Ava at the bar. Why the hell had he said that? People literally lived and died depending on his ability to keep a cool head under pressure, but an evening with Ava Kanas and he was reduced to some dictatorial bone head who couldn't keep his fat mouth shut.

The fact she wouldn't accept his support, refused to acknowledge that the FBI worked best as a team, drove him insane. She always had to go it alone. Ava Kanas against the world. No wonder Van had taken her under his wing. Kanas was her own worst enemy and, unless she learned to trust the agents she worked with, she wouldn't survive in the Bureau.

It was his duty to stay here and back her up in case something went sideways at the bar. But would she accept his help graciously? Hell no. It pissed him off, and he'd lashed out and said something inappropriate that had hurt her feelings, which meant they both had something to learn.

True to her word, less than five minutes later, she turned away from the guy with the bloody nose whom she'd been lecturing at the bar. Dominic almost felt sorry for the man—except for the whole potential domestic abuse thing.

Together they headed through the heavy front doors into the fresh air and he walked her to her vehicle—a Nissan Vecra he wasn't sure he could physically fit into.

She heaved a sigh. "I can take care of myself you know."

"You're welcome." He gave her his sunniest smile, determined to make things right.

"Yeah. Thanks." The words left her mouth reluctantly.

"I shouldn't have said that back there. That was out of line." He'd sounded like a jealous fool. He'd sounded like his goddamn father.

She gave him a smile with serrated edges. "For future reference I generally only hook up with strangers in bars on the weekends and holidays."

He wasn't rising to her bait. "That's great. Drive safe, Ava. I'll talk to Aldrich about tracking down the surveillance footage of the bar first thing in the morning. See if we can get an image of Van here with someone."

She glanced around the street. "There's an ATM machine over there. Ask him to pull that video too."

"Good idea." He hesitated.

"I know what you're going to say." She held up her hand to stop him from speaking.

Why that amused him so much he had no idea. "What?"

"Not to get my hopes up, that Van might have gone home alone, and even if he didn't, it didn't mean he was murdered."

He pressed his lips together and held the car door for her.

"I'm not stupid." She climbed into her tin can of a car and started the engine.

"I don't think you're stupid, Ava."

She held his gaze for a long time, eyes shadowed, uncertainty worrying her mouth. After a few long moments he closed the door and watched her drive away. He wandered back to his car, feeling so tired he could barely drag one foot after the other.

Ranger licked his ear when he climbed into the Lexus. He patted the front seat and the dog jumped over from the back. He attached the specially designed dog seatbelt and gave the mutt a quick scratch on his ribcage, thinking about Ava Kanas and the effect she had on him. Despite her lack of teamwork skills, she was a good agent. Sure, she had trouble with authority, was overzealous, blunt, and a little conspiracy prone, but she had integrity, and grit, and a work ethic to rival his own. He could see why Van had liked her so much.

And that wasn't even considering the pretty face and incredible body.

"Not thinking about those," he muttered to himself.

His eyes felt heavy, and his sinus felt clogged as if he was suddenly coming down with a cold. Home was twenty minutes away, and his bed was a siren call for the weary.

Out on the highway the road was clear. He put his foot down, wanting to hurry before he fell asleep at the wheel. He hadn't slept much over this past week and even before that, work was always full on. Savage was gonna be pissed if he got sick. All he needed was a good night's sleep and…

Lights flashed at him and a horn blared. He jammed his eyes open and jerked the wheel back into his own lane as a truck whizzed by.

Holy shit! He'd almost nodded off while driving. Things were worse than he thought.

He rolled down the window. Sucked in the cool night air and stretched his eyes as wide as possible. Ranger whined.

"S'okay, boy." He was slurring words like a drunk. Shit. He squinted at the signpost. Almost home. Just a couple more miles.

The flashing, blue strobe lights in his rear-view told him he was in deep shit.

He concentrated intensely and pulled over onto the shoulder. Except he was going way too fast and couldn't find the brakes as his feet had quit working. He tried to jerk the wheel, but a telephone pole came out of nowhere. He swore and grabbed onto Ranger's scruff and closed his eyes.

The detonation of the airbags snapped his head back like a punch. The impact jarred every bone in his body. His shoulder felt as if it was being ripped out of the socket. The terrible scream of steel crashing against wood penetrated his brain. Pain stabbed at his torso, across his face and down his legs. Blackness numbed the edges of the agony, then consumed him whole.

CHAPTER EIGHT

DRIVING HOME FROM the bar, Ava had initially turned the police scanner on for company, but the need to hear her mother's voice overwhelmed her. Ava lived in an apartment above an antique store close to the Rappahannock River. The biggest noise pollution was the clopping of shod hooves on a Saturday morning when the horse-drawn carriages full of tourists drove by.

It was wonderfully quiet.

On nights like this, however, quiet turned to lonesome and combined with the quiet desperation she was feeling over Van's death, lonesome became unbearable. To remind herself she had people she loved, who loved her in return, she picked up the phone.

"Hey, Momma."

"Ava. Sweetheart. How are you? When are you coming home?"

Her mother wasn't talking about a visit.

Ava ignored that. "Christmas. I told you already."

"It's late. Are you just leaving work?" Her mother thought she worked too hard. This from a woman who'd run a restaurant six nights a week while single-handedly raising three kids. "Did you eat?"

Greek parents liked to feed their kids like guppies, until

they burst.

"I was out."

"On a date?" Her mother was always trying to pair her off. Her younger sister had married her high school sweetheart a few years ago now and had already popped out two kids, taking the pressure off a little. Ava loved her niece and nephew but wasn't ready for kids. Not to mention the whole lack of a partner thing.

"Someone from work." It wasn't a lie but it was misleading as hell. That's how pathetic she was.

"Is he Greek?"

"No, Momma, he isn't Greek." Were all parents like this?

"Is he good-looking?"

"He's a colleague, Momma."

"So, he *is* good-looking. Is he married?"

"Let's pretend he is."

"So, he's good-looking, and single. Is he rich?"

Ava didn't know whether to laugh or cry. She hadn't called to talk about Dominic Sheridan with her mom—more to stop thinking about the man. "Is rich more important than kind?"

Her mother stopped laughing. "No, Ava, but I know you wouldn't be with anyone who was cruel."

Suddenly Ava's eyes stung. They'd both learned to avoid evil men, unless she was slapping handcuffs on them. "I'm not *with* him. We were working."

"You work too hard…" The nagging resumed.

Ava tuned her out. Something on the police scanner caught her attention and she turned it up. A black Lexus had crashed into a telephone pole on Route 17.

A fluttery feeling stole through her stomach. "I gotta go, Momma. I'll call you again on the weekend. Love you."

It couldn't be Dominic Sheridan. That didn't prevent her from swinging the car around and heading back to check it out for herself.

It took twenty minutes to reach the scene of the accident. She slowed to a crawl. Two police cruisers, a firetruck and an ambulance were already pulled up on the side of the road. Amber, blue and red lights swept the area, lighting it up like a war zone. A patrolman directing traffic waved her through. She rolled down the window as she drove by, telling herself that although it was the same make of car Sheridan owned, it couldn't be him.

Then she saw the dog being held on a leash by another officer, and she swerved onto the side of the road.

"Get back in the car and move along, ma'am," the patrolman yelled at her.

"FBI." She flashed her creds at the cop. "What happened?"

He blinked in surprise. She was still in her stakeout clothes from that morning. Ripped jeans and graphic tee hardly screamed "federal agent."

He stared at her badge, clearly dubious. "Looks like a DUI. Guy crashed into a pole."

"Is he alive?" She held her breath for the answer, her lungs hurting.

"Banged up pretty bad, but he's alive."

She exhaled. Thank god. How badly was he hurt? "Can I see him?"

The sound of a saw sent dread racing through her. The firemen had the jaws of life on the side of the car and were opening that sucker up like a tin can.

"Why? Who is he?" The cop eyed her suspiciously.

"He's a fed. Supervisory Special Agent with the Crisis

Negotiation Unit."

"Might not be a Fed much longer. Guy crashes into a pole on a nice day on a clear highway he's probably drunk."

She shook her head. "He wasn't drinking. I was with him all night. He drank nothing except water."

The patrolman shrugged and looked at her with a knowing glint in his eyes. He'd assumed the same thing her mother had, that they'd been out on a date. "Drugs then."

No way did Sheridan take drugs.

"Can I see him?" She lifted her chin in challenge as she waited. She didn't need his permission, but she believed in working with the cops. Sheridan had been fine at the bar. "I'll take his dog to get checked out at the vet," she added.

The patrolman's lips thinned. "Fine." It was obvious the cops here had already reached their own conclusions as to the cause of the crash. Either that or this guy didn't like Feds.

She walked past him, reminding herself what it was like to work this sort of scene day in and day out. She headed over to the officer holding Sheridan's dog, flashing her badge. She craned her neck, but it was impossible to see past the emergency personnel. She squashed the desire to push through and see for herself. She'd only get in the way.

"Hey, buddy." She sank to her haunches to hug the poor disoriented dog, ignoring the wet grass soaking her jeans, absorbing the soft fur against her cheek. She looked up. "How is he?"

"Seems fine. He was secured so he's mainly just shaken and scared with no obvious injuries. Hey." The man holding the leash narrowed his eyes. "Aren't you the agent who pulled the PIT maneuver on the escaped prisoner this morning?" He passed her the dog's lead as she rose to her feet.

It felt like a million years ago since she'd arrested Jimmy Taylor. She held out her free hand to shake his. "Yes, sir. Name's Kanas out of the Fredericksburg office."

"That was the perfect execution. One of the choppers in the air caught it on camera."

"Yeah? I'd like to see that sometime." She ran her hands over Ranger's silky head.

"We're going to use it in training—proof not all Feds are dummies."

She laughed even though apprehension was crawling through her chest. "Sergeant out of Portland PD drummed that maneuver into me a hundred times. I better send him a copy of that tape to prove I was paying attention."

"Portland PD, huh?" He looked her up and down, assessing her physical attributes like a coach checking out an athlete. "You enjoy being an agent?" The question in his eyes suggested he'd thought about the transition himself.

"Yeah, I do, but less so when my colleagues are involved in car wrecks." She swallowed the nausea that swirled as the fire service did their thing. "That's a friend of mine in there. Negotiator out of Quantico." Most cops liked negotiators—they weren't glory seekers. Her hands went to her throat. "Can you tell me how he's doing?"

The officer rested his hands on his equipment belt. "Let's go see."

Less than three years ago, she'd been walking around with one of those heavy, cumbersome belts strapped around her waist. The worst thing had been figuring out what to do with it whenever she needed the restroom. She didn't miss it. And thinking about her former life as a police officer was much better than worrying about Dominic Sheridan.

A flurry of activity around the Lexus had Ava and the police officer pushing forward to see if Sheridan—it *had* to be Sheridan—was alive or not.

She spotted his bleached features covered in blood. "Oh hell." For a moment her knees went weak, and the uniform supported her with an arm around the waist.

"Don't faint on me now. He was unconscious when I got here, but he was breathing."

"Jesus." She covered her mouth with her hand. "Did someone run him off the road?"

"Nah. I was following him as he swerved all over the place. Probably got tanked—"

"Did you smell any alcohol on his breath?" she demanded, pulling away.

The cop slowly shook his head. "Now you mention it, no, ma'am. It could have been a brain aneurysm."

Oh, God. The idea punched her in the throat. She didn't want Sheridan to be hurt or to die and didn't want to examine why it upset her so much.

"Or drugs…maybe it would be best for him if the doctors don't take a blood sample straight away—"

"No way." Ava shook her head. "There is no way Dominic Sheridan did drugs." Suddenly the bar fight occurring out of nowhere and the guy with a girlfriend whom he said didn't exist took on a different meaning… "Get the medics to take a blood sample right now."

The trooper reared back on his heels. Tilted his head. "If he did take—"

"He didn't." She didn't know why she was so sure. Because Van had believed in the guy? Because of what she'd seen in the short time she'd known him? "Either it's a medical emergency," the idea was also terrifying, "or it's possible someone spiked his water when we were at a bar earlier. I want him tested straight away for roofies." If Sheridan had done drugs or secretly drunk alcohol then he'd have to pay the consequences like everyone else. But she didn't believe it. The guy was a straight arrow. Serious and dedicated.

Ava excused herself and called the FBI switchboard. She asked to be put through to the CNU in Quantico, hoping against hope someone was still there. The agent who answered the phone sounded pissed she'd interrupted his evening.

"You need to get down here ASAP." She gave him directions. "One of your people, Dominic Sheridan, has been in a car wreck." Ava watched the fire service ease Sheridan into a neck brace and then onto a hard stretcher. The only good news was he was still breathing. "He's alive, but it looks bad."

EXCITEMENT WAS LIKE a drug through her blood. The flashing yellow and red lights made the scene of the accident look like a dance party. The car was jagged, twisted metal, ripped open and glittering like a tin can. Blood covered one of the airbags.

Well, that didn't look good.

Suppressing a grin so as not to rouse the attention of the patrol cop wasn't easy. But nothing worthwhile ever was. Bernie was going to be very, very happy.

CHAPTER NINE

IT WAS NEARLY two AM when Ava knocked on the door of the neat little craftsman tucked into a quiet bay about a quarter of a mile from the Mule & Pitcher. She'd barely stopped shaking since watching Sheridan carted away in the back of an ambulance. One of the firefighters had assured her that although he was unconscious, all his vitals were good, and he hadn't suffered any obvious injuries aside from a possible broken shoulder. Didn't mean he hadn't suffered some sort of head injury or brain damage or internal injury—

She shut down that train of thought. Dominic Sheridan was in good hands, and her time was better spent trying to figure out what had happened this evening. Something about the bar fight no longer rang true, and her cop instincts had been aroused.

She eyed the big black truck in the driveway. Even though it was walking distance from the bar, Ava had a feeling Karl Feldman hadn't used his feet.

She knocked on the door again, and a light went on inside. She held up her badge to the peephole. She also wore her raid jacket because she didn't want anyone in any doubt that she was here in her official capacity.

"Mr. Feldman? This is FBI Special Agent Kanas. We met earlier tonight. I need to talk to you about what happened in the bar."

There was a shuffling sound, and Ava eased her hand onto the grip of her Glock. Maybe she should have told someone where she was going.

The door opened wide, and there stood the giant who'd started the bar fight, wearing pajama bottoms, an off-white t-shirt, and a loose cotton robe that didn't meet in the middle. Ava was five-ten and this guy made her feel like a gnat. He was balding with glasses and a bristly mustache. His eyes looked like those of every photograph of every serial killer she'd ever seen. Maybe this wasn't the smartest idea she'd ever had. He squinted at her and sighed gustily. She got a face full of stale booze and bad breath.

"I didn't realize a bar brawl was a federal offense."

Disturbing the peace, assault, battery—there were a lot of potential charges to arise from something as seemingly innocuous as a bar fight. And if Ava and Sheridan had arrested this man, maybe Sheridan wouldn't have driven into a telephone pole.

"I'd like to ask you a few questions."

"Come on in." He let go of the knob and walked away, leaving her little choice but to follow.

But before she stepped inside, she texted Feldman's address to Sheridan with a time stamp and "Going in." It might not prevent anything happening to her if this guy was a psycho, but at least her colleagues would know where to start looking for the body.

She walked inside the house and was pleasantly surprised by the simple decor and classy color scheme. The floors were hardwood and the rugs looked Persian but could be Ikea for all she knew. She followed him through to the kitchen which looked freshly renovated with pale shaker cupboards and a large farmer's sink. Feldman sat on a sturdy kitchen chair at a big wooden table.

"You have a beautiful home, Mr. Feldman."

He looked at her with small beady eyes. "It's what I do."

She raised her brow in question. The strong smell of metabolized alcohol pervaded the room and stole some of its charm.

"I renovate old homes and restore them to their former glory. Actually, I make them even better." He went over to the freezer, grabbed a bag of frozen peas, wrapped them in a dishtowel and pressed them to the knuckles of his right hand as he sat back down again. "The guy I hit changed his mind? You came to press charges?"

"No, sir. Although Mr. Gardner"—the man he'd punched—"might still file charges."

Feldman grimaced. "It's probably a good thing I'm self-employed."

"You get in fights often?"

He grimaced. "It's been known."

Ava ran her hand over the smooth surface of the island, hoping to put the guy at ease. "This is a nice piece. Marble?"

"Actually, it's a rare piece of pale granite I found. Easier to look after than marble. Stains less."

"Nice."

Feldman nodded and picked up a tall glass of water. He drank deeply.

"You said that a woman told you Mr. Gardner beat her. Did she approach you directly and ask you to intervene on her behalf?"

A frown pushed bushy eyebrows together. "I came out of

the washroom, and this woman stumbled away from me and started sobbing. I asked her if she was okay. At first, she wouldn't tell me what the matter was, but finally she admitted she was scared of the guy in the red shirt sitting at the bar."

"What did you do then?"

He gave a slightly embarrassed shrug and placed the frozen peas against his jaw. "Charged off like an idiot to deal with the guy."

"What did the woman do?"

He shrugged, and Ava avoided looking at the strip of stomach that movement revealed. "I don't know. I was thrown out. I didn't see her again."

Ava had no proof that someone spiked Sheridan's drink, or even knew what it meant if someone had. Was it opportunistic? Some clown sticking it to the Feds? Or had someone followed them from Van's?

If she was wrong, if Sheridan had snorted some bad coke or had an aneurysm behind the wheel, she was going to look like a goddamn fruitcake with her conspiracy theories.

Hence coming here alone…but she often worked alone. She was in a small office and there weren't always the resources to work in pairs—especially as everyone else was working overtime on the Mortimer shooting.

Worry for Sheridan kept tugging at her nerves. She wanted to see him and make sure he was okay, but she had no right. He wouldn't want her there—she barely knew the guy.

"You ever seen the woman in the bar before tonight?" she asked.

"No, it was my first time in the place. Plus, I was so drunk I could barely see."

And yet he'd driven home…

"Would you consider talking to a police sketch artist and trying to recreate a likeness of the woman?" Ava didn't know if it would be useful or not.

"Why are you so concerned with her? Why not go after the boyfriend?"

Ava rolled her lips. "The thing is, Mr. Feldman, Mr. Gardner says he doesn't have a girlfriend and denies hitting anyone—except you."

A cold smile tugged at Feldman's lips. "Do they ever confess to being wife beaters?"

She recognized it immediately, that soul deep knowledge of abuse reflected deep in his eyes.

"No, they don't admit it, but…I'd really like your help trying to track her down."

If the woman had been telling the truth then maybe Ava could help her. If she'd been lying to create a diversion, then Ava wanted to know that too.

After a few moments Feldman nodded and climbed to his feet, looming over her with a pained expression. It crossed her mind that this guy could have made up the woman, or be working in conjunction with her. Coming here alone was unwise to say the least.

He grimaced and pressed a finger to his temple. "I'll work with a sketch artist, but I don't know that I'm going to remember much in the morning."

There was no way she'd be able to persuade anyone to come out in the middle of the night based on nothing more than one of her crazy hunches. But Karl Feldman had been more accommodating than she'd expected. "I appreciate your willingness to help. I'll show myself out."

Ava hurried out of the house, irrationally unnerved by the

guy, especially considering she was both armed and dangerous. She shivered as she escaped into the warm night air. She wasn't proud of herself for being nervous, but she put it on the long list of flaws she was working on.

Her phone beeped as she walked to the car. The veterinarian left a message to say Sheridan's dog was fine and that they'd keep him until morning when she could pick him up.

She sent Sheridan a quick text to tell him his dog was okay.

Had the results come in from tox screens yet? She didn't know who to call to ask. Sheridan? It seemed like an imposition when she didn't know if he was in a coma or worse. Texts were one thing, a phone call something else entirely. And if the tests confirmed narcotics in his bloodstream what was she gonna say? Sorry I helped destroy your career?

Should she call his boss? Hers?

Her cheeks burned at the thought. What right did she have to ask about his medical condition? What would they think?

Dammit. She smacked the steering wheel in frustration. She'd have been this concerned about anyone who'd been in a serious accident. She looked at her phone. The fact he was attractive had nothing to do with her worry, and she didn't want anyone misinterpreting her concern. She closed her eyes, frustrated by her own indecision.

She put the Nissan in drive and headed back to the bar to see if anyone there remembered anything. After that, she'd head to the hospital and check on Sheridan's condition. Because that's what colleagues did.

THE BUSINESS CARD was handed over along with a fierce kiss.

"Two Feds were asking questions about that guy from last week. So, I slipped a cap of Liquid E into their drinks and passed the wreck of their car on the side of the road."

Bernie's fingers ran over the embossed circular shield on the business card. United States Department of Justice, Federal Bureau of Investigation, Critical Incident Response Group, Dominic S. Sheridan. The name "Dominic S. Sheridan" was printed in bold letters.

What did the "S" stand for?

A strange mixture of rage and grief hit. Questions raced. Heart pounded. "They'll know it was you."

"I created a distraction." Caroline started undoing the buttons of her fitted black shirt and smiled as Bernie watched. Caroline was hot enough to melt glass and fucked like a rabbit even without GHB. "And I'm a very good liar."

Caroline was a good liar. She was also horny. She was often horny when she came over at two in the morning. Bernie didn't mind. Caroline thought she was the smart, streetwise one in the relationship, and Bernie didn't mind that either.

The fact the FBI had started asking questions about Van Stamos's last movements was concerning when there were three people still on the list left to kill. Perhaps they weren't as dumb as they seemed.

"Are you sure he's dead?"

"No." Caroline undid her pants to reveal a matching lace thong. Hot as fuck. "But even if he's not, he's not going to be asking questions anytime soon."

"You said two agents. Who was he with?"

Caroline shrugged. "Some woman. Didn't get her card or her name."

Stupid bitch.

Caroline had proved very useful, first as a fuck-buddy, and then with information that mobsters were running drugs out of the back of the bar where she worked. Bernie had let her stick around, spending more and more time here. Getting comfortable. Too comfortable.

"Ricky got pretty spooked when he found out they were Feds." Caroline laughed.

Ricky was the manager of the bar. If the guy had a brain it was so small and so far up his ass it would probably be mistaken for his tonsils.

"He and the boys were going to move the coke tonight. Idiots. They should have cleared it all out last week after the other Fed blew his brains out."

At Bernie's request, Caroline had called Van down to the bar with the lure of information about the drugs. Then she'd slipped something into his beer.

Caroline's glance turned sly. "Did I mention I came over last Tuesday night but you weren't around?"

So Bernie's CCTV camera had shown.

"I had a business meeting out of town."

Caroline snorted. "Sure. You asked me to drug the guy but you never told me why. And then he turns up dead the next day..."

This was how shakedowns began.

Caroline held her hands high. "But I didn't ask any questions."

"I like women who don't ask any questions." Bernie ran a finger down the center of Caroline's chest, hooked the black lacy pushup bra, and pulled her closer. A long, deep kiss had Caroline rubbing her whole body against Bernie's.

Bernie pulled back. "How about I run you a nice hot bath

so you can soak your poor aching feet. You did good tonight. I want to show you how grateful I am."

Caroline's smile was wide and sultry. "Only as long as you promise to join me." She pouted prettily.

"I was planning to."

Bernie arranged olives and a plate of cheese and crackers on a tray. Poured two glasses of *Bollinger,* adding a little something extra to Caroline's glass.

Inside the en-suite of the master bathroom the mirrors had steamed up. Bernie turned the lights low.

Bubbles frothed everywhere as Caroline lay back against one side of the enormous tub. Bernie put the tray on the side. Within arm's reach.

"Oh, my god, I could get used to this." Caroline took the drink Bernie handed her. Then Bernie stripped, slowly, making it good and hot how women like Caroline liked it. Caroline watched with lust dancing in her eyes.

Bernie climbed in and straddled the naked woman. Their skin was slippery against one another.

Bernie picked up the other glass, and they chinked glasses and drank the lot in one go, laughing. Bernie poured more Champagne and dribbled liquid over Caroline's shoulders and breasts. Licking it off was exactly the sort of attention Caroline craved. Bernie's fingers dove lower, between shaved lips that were as hungry as Caroline's mouth.

It didn't take long to get her off. They both knew how the other liked it. Rough, fast, unrelenting.

"This is so good. I think I could do this all night." Caroline sounded drunk now.

Bernie started over, giving her another orgasm before pulling her to lie stretched out on top. She jerked suddenly.

"Relax. I've got you."

It took a few minutes for Caroline to go completely slack, her thighs floating in the water.

"So good," she murmured as her mouth slid beneath the surface.

She struggled when she inhaled, but Bernie wrapped strong arms around her chest and pinned her legs. It wasn't too hard to hold her securely beneath the bubbles.

After five minutes, Bernie got out of the tub and dried off.

Killing was the easy part. Getting rid of the body was always the challenge.

A STEADY "BEEP, beep" brought him slowly back to life. Dominic groaned and tried to raise his hand to his aching head, but someone gripped his wrist. He cracked open an eyelid and saw his boss standing there.

"Why don't I get the good-looking nurse?" His voice bounced around in his throat.

"Some people think I'm good-looking." Savage's piercing gaze was intent on his face. "Rip out the IV and I'll beat you with it."

"Didn't know you cared." He huffed out a soft laugh and winced as pain radiated from his nose along his cheekbones. "I thought you were in DC? What happened?"

Savage pressed a button, presumably calling for the nurse. "You were in a car accident so I came straight back."

"Car accident?" He had a vague recollection of loud noises and lots of pain.

"Tell me what you remember."

Every time Dominic inhaled, he tasted blood. Nausea swirled in his stomach but the last thing he wanted to do was vomit in front of his boss. "Can't this wait?"

"No."

Damn. Dominic mentally ran through his day. He remembered going to Van's house. Finding the footprints. Going for a drink with Ava Kanas at the bar Van had visited a week ago. He remembered arguing with Kanas, but couldn't remember about what. Getting in his car… His eyes shot open. "Ranger. Is he okay?"

He tried to sit up, and pain exploded in pulsing waves along every nerve fiber. He fell back against the pillows in agony.

"Ranger is fine," Savage assured him. "Agent Kanas took him to an emergency veterinary clinic to get him thoroughly checked. He's still there I believe."

"Kanas?" Dominic frowned in confusion. "She was at the crash scene? What was she doing there? Is she okay?"

"She said the two of you had met for a drink in a bar to talk about Van Stamos as you were both close to him." Savage's tone suggested he knew there was more to it than that. "On her way home, she heard on the scanner that a black Lexus had hit a telephone pole on 17. She swung around to make sure it wasn't you. Unfortunately, it was. What do you remember?"

Dominic wasn't sure. "Driving home and suddenly feeling really sleepy. Being barely able to keep my eyes open. I think I tried to pull over. Then nothing." Maybe that was a blessing. Panic shot through him. "Did I hit anyone?"

"What did you have to drink?"

Drink? "Nothing."

"Not even one beer?"

"Water." He wanted water now as his throat was sore. The fact he'd woken up with a hangover that morning was why he hadn't consumed any alcohol at the bar. He wasn't a saint, but he did not drive while over the limit. He shook his head and tried to quench the resulting queasiness that swirled in his stomach.

"Drugs?"

What the fuck? "No, Quentin. You *know* me. I am not a drug user. Tell me no one else was hurt tonight. Tell me I didn't hit anyone." He didn't think he could live with himself if he'd crashed into someone and injured them—killed them.

Savage pressed his lips together before replying. "You know I have to ask. No one else was involved in the accident, but the fire department had to cut you out of your vehicle. Your Lexus looks like someone took a giant can opener to it."

Dominic didn't care about the car. He could feel cuts on his legs and remembered the sound of a saw. Panic raced through him as he looked down and wiggled his toes. Relief surged inside when he saw them respond under the blankets.

His heart pounded.

A nurse entered the room. Flirted with Savage, took a few readings, adjusted his IV, and left again. She didn't give them any answers.

"So, how bad am I?" Dominic asked.

"You were lucky."

Dominic did not feel lucky.

"No broken bones, no internal injuries. A dislocated shoulder which they already re-set. Mild lacerations. Bruising—you are going to hurt like a sorry sonofabitch tomorrow."

He hurt like a sorry sonofabitch today.

Savage frowned. "Like the nurse told you, doctors are running tests to rule out a brain aneurysm, but you seem okay to me and it strikes me there would be a lasting impact on your motor skills and cognitive abilities if you'd suffered that kind of trauma."

Savage sat heavily in the single chair in the room. "Agent Kanas had another theory—one that she insisted the doctors run blood panels for immediately, so I hope to god you're telling the truth about the alcohol and drugs."

Dominic gritted his teeth. It seemed Ava Kanas had more faith in him than people he'd worked with for years. He was thirty-five years old and a respected federal employee. He wasn't an asshole although those things weren't necessarily mutually exclusive.

"Kanas thinks someone roofied your water at the bar."

What?

"She said there was a fight?"

Dominic tried to clear the fog from the memory. "I maybe remember breaking up a bar fight."

"Kanas thinks it might have been used as a distraction."

Could she be right? Had he been drugged? It would explain the sudden onset and severity of the fatigue as well as the fact he was now awake with relatively minor injuries. He was thirsty. His voice was scratchy. He hurt like a bitch, but he was talking and his limbs more or less worked.

"Why would someone roofie my water?" Dominic asked.

"Why *would* someone roofie your water?"

"Don't use that shit on me, Quentin. I'm too fucking tired and sore to deal with it right now."

"Why were you really at that bar?"

Dominic closed his eyes and drew in a deep breath. "I

asked Agent Kanas to find out Van's last movements." Not technically true, but his career could weather a lot more storms than Ava's could. "The bar was the last place he visited, that we know of, before he died, so we checked it out."

"You're investigating his death." Savage's tone was clipped.

"Double-checking some aspects. I also found footprints outside the window to his office and *suggested* to Ray Aldrich at the Fredericksburg RA that he get the Evidence Response Team out there again."

"Why'd they miss it in the first place?" Savage asked.

They shouldn't have. "Probably because it was such an obvious suicide, and no one wanted to list it as such. I don't know," Dominic said tiredly.

"Why would someone target you?"

"I don't know if they did." The pounding in his head wasn't making it easy to think. "I identified myself as a Federal Agent to the waitress hoping she had information about Van. And again, to break up the bar fight. That's the only time my drink was out of my sight. Perhaps someone in the bar didn't like Feds."

"It seems a lot of people lately don't like Feds," Savage observed. He was talking about Calvin Mortimer's murder.

Dominic grunted. Was it possible the FBI was really that unpopular? With criminals and politicians maybe. Most law-abiding citizens were glad to have the Bureau's assistance fighting bad guys. Did seem like a hell of a string of coincidences, or incredibly bad luck, or something else entirely…

"What about Agent Kanas? Do you trust her?" asked Savage.

"Why wouldn't I?"

"She's ambitious. She could have been the one to drug your drink and then follow you home, waiting to act as savior—assuming you survived..."

"Ava Kanas couldn't care less about being anyone's savior." She was driven by the love of a good man and a determination to get to the truth. "I trust her." Dominic tried to open his mouth to defend her further, but his tongue refused to cooperate. The nurse must have given him another dose of sedative. That pissed him off. He drifted off wondering how Ranger was and whether or not Kanas was okay. He hoped so. He really hoped so.

CHAPTER TEN

LIGHTS WERE ON inside the Mule & Pitcher. Despite the "closed" sign in the window, Ava tried the front door and was surprised to find it unlocked. All the stools were up on the tabletops, and the floor was wet after a recent mopping.

Three guys sat drinking at the bar. The manager was at the till, the machine spitting out totals. He looked up at her with an "*oh, shit*" expression.

"I thought that door was locked." He raised his voice over the din the register was making and gave one of the men sitting at the bar a glare. "What can I do for you, Agent…?"

The atmosphere grew increasingly tense as Ava slid onto a bar stool. Finally, the cash register finished churning out data and silence reverberated around the room in the aftermath. "This a private party?"

"A couple of friends are keeping me company while I cash out," the manager answered.

"Huh." This might be the leverage she needed to get him to hand over the surveillance tapes for tonight and a week ago when Van had come here.

"What's your name?" She turned to one of the men peering into his beer. She watched him debate whether or not to tell her the truth.

"Bo." He had a deep voice. Nice enough face.

"You know Lanny Gardner, Bo?" she asked.

He shrugged one lean shoulder. "Lanny? Sure. He's a regular."

"He beat up all his girlfriends?"

Bo huffed out a laugh and shook his head, but she didn't trust his pretty blue eyes. "I don't know anyone who beats up women."

"Is that a fact?" She raised one thoroughly disbelieving eyebrow. One of her mother's boyfriends had once casually punched her in the face before holding her against a wall and sticking his hand down her pants. Fingering her as if he had the right to do whatever the hell he wanted to her body. As if he'd owned her.

She'd been thirteen.

He'd been too drunk to do anything worse. She'd waited for him to fall asleep on the couch and then held the sharpest knife they owned against his throat. Every time he'd exhaled it had bit into his flesh. It had taken him a long time to notice, to wake up. By that time blood was running down his neck in rivulets and had soaked the collar of his shirt.

She'd told him which part of his body she'd cut off in his sleep if he ever touched her again. He'd run out of the apartment, screaming that she was insane.

Afterwards she'd told her mother, and her mother had called Van. He'd arranged to have an FBI agent pay the guy a visit. Van had been watching out for Ava for a very long time.

The bar manager put an open bottle of beer on the counter in front of her with a heavy clunk. Ava eyed it warily. Everything about this felt wrong. At Feldman's she'd been reacting to preconceived notions and pop culture fear. Here her instincts were crawling all over her nerves and screaming that she'd screwed up. She hadn't told anyone where her next stop was going to be after she'd questioned Feldman. She hadn't expected anyone to still be working in the bar much less for the front door to be open.

It crossed her mind that the waitress could have spiked her and Sheridan's drinks, and that the bar fight could have simply been a distraction so Caroline wasn't the only suspect.

Ava hadn't finished the beer she'd left on the table. Sheridan had finished his water when she'd been over talking to Lanny Gardner.

Had the manager seen them questioning the waitress? Did he have something to hide? Had Van suspected the bar was the site of something illegal? Was that why he'd been here in the first place? Had these people been involved in his death?

Lots of questions and no answers except for the beads of sweat starting to form between her shoulder blades.

Ava wrapped her hand around the neck of the bottle wishing she weren't so impulsive. Van had tried to curb the habit, but she'd never quite got the hang of caution. Apparently, she only learned lessons the hard way.

"You have CCTV cameras in here?" Ava shot a look at the lens above the bar.

The manager gave a shrug as he continued doing something with the cash register. "Some."

"I want to see tonight's footage." It wasn't a question.

His expression turned sullen.

"Or I could bust you for operating after-hours."

His eyes hardened, but he didn't look intimidated or contrite. He looked irritated. This was not going how she'd anticipated.

"I want to identify the woman who claimed Lanny Gardner hit her. I can get a subpoena and a full team down here to go over the footage in the morning if you'd prefer. Your choice."

The men exchanged glances. She knew immediately it had been the wrong play. Their stances shifted.

Bo stood, wooden stool creaking ominously, and moved behind her. He ran the tip of his finger across the nape of her neck, and she repressed a shudder. "Anyone know where you're at, sweet cheeks?"

"I'm an FBI agent, *Bo.*" She derided him. "What do you think?"

"I'm thinking you're bluffing. I think you came down here on your own on a mission to save some whiny little bitch. That's why your sidekick isn't with you."

"He's sitting in the car outside." She forced herself to breathe normally. To show no fear.

Bo shook his head. "He isn't."

What the fuck? What did he know?

"Anyone gonna miss you if you disappear, sweet cheeks?"

She used one hand to grab his wrist and ducked under his shoulder, bringing his arm behind his back and one-handedly driving him to his knees. She planted her foot on his back, exacerbating the bite of the angle, then smoothly pulled her Glock left-handed and pointed it straight at the manager who'd started to bring up a shotgun.

"Raise that one more inch, and you'll be wearing a 9mm slug between your eyes."

He hesitated.

"Put it *down*! Get around here and on the floor. All of you. Get on the floor." A light sheen of sweat formed on her brow. Holy crap. How had things gone south so fast?

The three other men eased onto the floor, watching her for an opening. If they found one, they'd kill her, she knew it the same way she knew her own face.

Did they kill Van?

"Hands on your head," she shouted. "Spread your legs. Wider."

"I thought that was my line." Bo gave a dark chuckle that crawled over her nerves, and she gripped his wrist tighter.

"No talking." Obviously, these guys were involved in something illegal.

Duh, Ava, ya think?

Had they drugged Sheridan? Was that why they knew he wasn't outside waiting for her in the car? She cuffed Bo behind his back, making sure the metal bracelets were snug. For the others she pulled out the cable ties she kept coiled up in her jeans pockets in case of emergencies. She jerked the plastic teeth firmly into place, forcing the manager's wrists close together so he couldn't twist free.

She had the third guy contained before calling dispatch.

"This is Agent Kanas out of the Fredericksburg Resident Agency. I need immediate law enforcement assistance at—"

The fourth guy slid his hand under his plaid shirt at the back of his waist band.

"Keep your hands where I can see them," Ava yelled.

Too late. He pulled a gun and rolled onto his back, bringing the weapon up and aiming it at her, pulling the trigger, but not fast enough. Ava swerved to the side and fired three times at his center mass, the noise enormous in the vast space.

The men on the floor were swearing and shouting, but she stepped away from them, keeping her back to the one wall in case the gun shots brought someone else in from the back.

She realized the dispatcher was still talking to her.

"Yeah, yeah, I'm all right. Yeah. Send a bus." She gave them the address with a shaky voice. "One of them pulled a gun on me. I'm all right, but he's wounded. Maybe the EMTs can save him."

IT WAS EASY to be invisible in a hospital. Just sit around and look tired and worried with a coffee cup near anxious fingers, or pace the corridors with clasped hands and tight lips. It was, however, more difficult to get answers to questions like whether or not Dominic Sheridan was alive.

Caroline had fucked up.

It didn't matter.

As soon as the next agent died—hopefully sooner rather than later—even the FBI would figure out the connection and realize they had a serial killer on their hands, hunting them like the animals they really were.

How surprised they would be.

Was Sheridan dead? Bernie hoped not.

Extreme pain and suffering would be acceptable, but not dead, not yet, and not by someone else's hand. Bernie wanted him to eventually figure out why this had happened and who was responsible before dying an excruciating death.

What about the female agent who'd accompanied Sheridan? Who was she? What had happened to her?

A flurry of activity stirred around the door to a private room. A group of FBI agents marched past, huddled around Sheridan's tall, lean figure like secret service bodyguards.

Sheridan was alive. Good.

The Fed looked pale and gaunt. Bruises darkened his eye sockets and there was a cut across the bridge of his nose, probably from the airbags in his fancy Lexus. He wore sweats and a plaid shirt, and his right arm was in a sling.

Hopefully it fucking hurt.

No sign of the woman he'd been with last night. Maybe she hadn't been in the car. Or perhaps she hadn't made it.

Hopefully he cared for her and the pain of her death would eat him alive until it drove him insane with grief.

Was his daddy involved, yet? Must be nice to have a politician for a father, but not nice enough to stop what was coming. Nothing would stop what was coming.

Oh, yes. It was good he wasn't dead yet.

This was far too much fun for it to be over so quickly.

"WHAT THE HELL do you mean 'she's been put on administrative leave'?" Dominic closed his eyes against the throbbing pain in his head and the news he'd just received about Kanas.

His boss had wisely waited until they were alone in the car before updating him on the latest developments.

"She was investigating Van's death explicitly against her boss's orders. She went into a dangerous situation without backup, not once but twice, and the second time she ended up killing a man."

"She was following up on what happened earlier at the bar. Trying to figure out if someone drugged me." And someone had. The results had come back positive for GH-fucking-B.

"She should have told her boss. She should have followed procedure and not gone in alone—"

"At two AM? On a hunch? Agents often work alone in small Resident Agencies, you know it. If it had been me following up on a crash involving Agent Kanas would you think I'd been foolish to go alone to get what she thought were witness statements? Isn't that what we're trained to do?"

"We're trained to follow procedure." Savage shot him a glare. He was driving Dominic home, with orders from the doctors to make him rest. *Sure.* Dominic didn't have any serious injuries except for the shoulder they'd reset. The sling he'd been told to wear was already a royal pain in his ass. Thankfully he was left-handed and it was his right shoulder which had been injured. The biggest problem was he wasn't allowed to drive for at least a week and his house was rural with just a couple of close neighbors.

Dominic couldn't see himself getting much rest, especially knowing Ava was in trouble. None of this would have happened if he hadn't involved her in the case again.

No wonder she had a giant chip on her shoulder if this was how she was treated. "You said she facilitated a massive drug bust."

"Which would have been great had the DEA not already had the place under surveillance."

Shit.

He sat up straight. "Do they have any video tapes? From last night or last week?"

Savage grunted.

"Do the DEA at least have evidence of these assholes spiking my water?"

Savage overtook a tractor trailer hauling hay. Dominic held his breath and tried not to envision a horrific death. He'd come damn close last night. Only the fact his car was packed with safety features had enabled him to walk away from the accident without major injury.

"Not that they've given us yet. They're still pissed we crashed their party. It makes sense though. You're in the bar asking questions, and they have a half ton of coke in the back room. Maybe they thought you were onto them."

"Seems like a weird way to throw Feds off the scent—drugging us. Why not split with the coke?"

"No one said these guys were geniuses."

Dominic drummed his fingers on his thigh. "You know, without Ava Kanas we might never have figured out what happened to me. I'd be in the hospital, and you'd all be checking my blood panels for narcotics and alcohol and giving me censorious looks until they came back negative. The docs might have missed the GHB altogether."

Savage's fingers tightened on the wheel. "She's also the one who came up with the theory Van was murdered and dragged you into something that almost got you killed."

Dominic's lip curled. "Because I'm so easily led."

"Doesn't mean her actions weren't indirectly responsible for you ending up in the hospital." Savage shot him another look and swerved around a dead skunk on the road.

"I'm the one who called her." Dominic's fingers dug into the dashboard. "And slow the hell down. I've had enough excitement for one day."

Savage took his foot off the accelerator. "Sorry."

"You have to admit something weird is going on. Van commits suicide after going to that bar. A shooter kills an FBI agent at his funeral. I get roofied and almost die in a car wreck…"

"They might be completely unrelated."

Dominic's laugh was unamused and even more so when pain sliced through his ribs. He grabbed his side with his good arm. He hated to think what he'd feel like without a seatbelt or airbags. Dead, no doubt. "What happens now?"

"You go home, rest, and keep away from Agent Kanas."

"To the investigation." Dominic ignored the jab about Ava.

"You know you can't be involved in any way—"

"Some fucker tried to kill me. I am already involved." Dominic rarely raised his voice. It wasn't a great negotiation tactic, but they all had their off days.

Savage made a visible effort to control his own temper. Too many strong-willed males in an enclosed space, but Dominic was not in any mood to back down.

"Maybe you should take some time off. Go on vacation. Take a break."

"You need me in the office."

Savage's mouth thinned. "I'm not compromising your health—"

"Stow it. I'll be in tomorrow."

"Thanks." Savage cleared his throat. "We need you, but you look like shit. I asked headquarters for enough money to fund another five full-time negotiators at CNU, which would take some of the pressure off us. They said they'd think about it."

Dominic grimaced. "Don't hold your breath."

Savage pulled up in Dominic's driveway in front of his three-car garage. The place was way too big for one person but had a pool, good security and a large fenced back yard for Ranger to patrol. Talking of his dog, there was Charlotte opening the door and holding Ranger on a leash. The dog practically dragged her down the steps when he saw Dominic.

He pushed open the door, holding onto the plastic bag of belongings, swearing as his damaged shoulder screamed. Nothing was broken, he'd heal, but in the meantime, he'd need to lay off the chin-ups.

Ranger ran towards him, tail wagging, tongue out. The dog shoved his nose into his junk—*ugh*—and they both whimpered pathetically.

"He's definitely okay?" Dominic asked Charlotte, not liking the fact he kept looking over her shoulder waiting for Ava Kanas to appear. How pissed was she gonna be with him?

What could he do to fix it?

"Ranger's fine. Vet checked him over, and Agent Kanas dropped him off at CNU this morning."

Dominic bit down on asking how Kanas had looked. Was she okay? What the hell had happened last night? Had she discovered anything about Van's final moments? Had she been hurt? But his boss was watching and would not approve of his interest.

Interest?

Yeah, that's what the cool kids were calling it nowadays.

"I bought you some groceries and brought over some home-made soup from my freezer. Put it in your fridge for when you get hungry." Charlotte often house-sat when he was away so she had a key. She winced at the state of his face. "You should, you know, hire someone to buy food for you. You already have a cleaner and a gardener. It's just one more step." She laughed and rubbed her hand down his good arm in a maternal way.

He blinked. He wasn't used to anyone taking care of him. The Sheridans weren't that kind of family.

"I think you should go the whole hog and hire a live-in housekeeper," Charlotte joked.

"Or a nanny," Savage muttered scathingly under his breath.

"You're just jealous," Charlotte told their boss with a grin.

"He has a freaking cinema in his basement. Of course, I'm jealous." Savage grinned.

Dominic gave Charlotte a one-handed hug. "Thanks, Char. I appreciate your help." Already overcome by fatigue, he petted his dog, and they shuffled tiredly toward the house.

"You sure you'll be okay?" Savage asked. The guy didn't miss much. It was that innate perception and attention to detail that made him so good at his job.

"I can stay if you like." Charlotte looked anxiously at his battered face. "I don't like the idea of you being out here alone. I could work in the basement. You wouldn't even know I was here."

He kissed the top of her head affectionately. "I'll be fine, but thank you."

He liked his own company. Having lots of rooms meant it was easier to avoid his family when they occasionally descended on him. And that thought reminded him he needed to respond to his father's phone messages, even though Savage had given the governor a medical update earlier. *Great.*

"I'll take another pain pill and sleep like the doctor ordered. Thanks for everything. See you at the office tomorrow." He shut the door on Charlotte's exclamation of distress. Let her lecture Savage on time off and recovery. Dominic had a hunch he needed to check out. A thought that kept niggling at his brain and wouldn't go away. He picked his personal cell phone out of the plastic bag, dialed a number and listened to it ring.

Eventually she picked up.

"Kanas? Get your ass over here."

CHAPTER ELEVEN

AVA SAT IN her little Nissan in Sheridan's huge driveway. It was nearly two o'clock in the afternoon, and the sky was full of dark clouds that threatened to rupture at any moment.

What was she doing here?

After the shooting at the bar last night, she'd called Ray Aldrich to give him an update. Aldrich had been more worried the incident made him look soft than the fact she'd almost died. She'd told the guy she'd been following up on what had happened to Sheridan while memories were still fresh, but as soon as he'd discovered she and Sheridan had chosen that particular bar because it was the last place Van had been seen alive, he'd freaked and put her on indefinite leave.

The fact he hadn't supported her after she'd been forced to kill a man in self-defense made the anger inside her froth and boil and scratch at the back of her eyelids with watery claws. While she was glad Sheridan hadn't been disciplined considering he'd almost died in a car wreck, the differing standards were staggering.

So, she'd been shocked to hear from Sheridan. Shocked he'd been released from the hospital with only minor injuries. Shocked he wanted her to come over to his house to discuss what had happened.

She'd come, but she wasn't sure why.

He was a Supervisory Special Agent and at this rate she'd be lucky to graduate probation.

It was an impressive-looking house. Huge and gorgeous with classic stonework on the lower level and an upper story clad with siding painted a warm gold. Pinky-red shutters flanked the multi-paned windows. It was a color combo that shouldn't have worked but did, making it appear even more sophisticated to her design-challenged eye. The building was L-shaped with three separate garage doors on the left-hand side and white painted Doric columns supporting a covered entrance straight ahead. Cozy chairs were tucked onto the veranda. Elegant and original, fitting the man completely.

Her fingers gripped the wheel. She couldn't get out of the car.

The DEA were pissed she'd steamrollered their case, but the criminals hadn't given her much choice. Turned out they'd been distributing coke out of the back of the premises for months. Was that why Van had been there? Had he received some sort of tip off? Had somebody in that bar killed him because he'd found them out?

She didn't know and was off the case even though it had been her arrest.

FBI had given the case back to the DEA. DEA had apparently held off raiding the place, wanting to nail the top dog. They suspected the Russian mob, but the kingpin was a slippery bastard who'd so far evaded capture. The guy she'd killed had been traveling on a Ukrainian passport, but he was probably just the link man. She shuddered as she remembered the moment she'd pulled the trigger. No amount of training could prepare you for killing another human being, but she wasn't sorry. She had too much of a strong desire to live to be sorry.

She understood why the DEA was angry. She would have been furious if it were the other way around. If she'd known they had the bar under observation, she would never have gone near the joint. But she hadn't. DEA might have surveillance footage, but the chances of them sharing it with her now she'd busted open their op? Better chance of smashing the glass ceiling and becoming the first female FBI Director.

A tap on the window had her jumping in her seat. She jerked around, and Dominic Sheridan stood beside her car, dressed down in a pair of gray sweats and a blue plaid shirt with the two top buttons left undone. He was barefoot.

He looked awful. Both eyes were black, and an ugly gash split the bridge of his nose. Right arm rested in a sling. Her heart gave an unsteady thump at the sight of him, probably because he'd startled her. He still looked too handsome for her peace of mind, but she'd always been attracted to bad boy types, so the battered features actually worked for her more than his clean-cut side did.

There was obviously something wrong with her. Not exactly breaking news.

He stared at her, waiting for her to get out of the car. She lifted her chin. What was she even doing here? Talking about the case, pursuing this investigation, was going to get her fired.

Large splats of rain started pinging off the windshield. He just stood there. The guy was gonna get soaked.

She cracked the door, and he opened it the rest of the way. Then he held out his good hand to assist her out of the car, but she didn't take it. She sat there looking at him.

He didn't seem mad at her reticence to touch him. He

appeared patient and understanding.

Goddamn it.

She didn't want his pity, and she wasn't used to chivalry. Men were a mystery to her. She had a younger brother and nephew she adored, a father who'd died when she was only seven years old, and a series of boyfriends who'd never quite fit. Van had been the best man she'd ever known. And Van had told her over and over again that Dominic Sheridan was a great guy.

Still, trust wasn't something she easily bestowed.

"I don't blame you for being angry, Ava. It isn't fair that you've been suspended and I haven't. I will do everything in my power to make sure you are fully reinstated."

With those words he broke the spell she was under.

She turned to grab her laptop case and purse from the passenger seat. Sheridan insisted on taking the items from her. She told herself not to be charmed. This was work, and she was more than capable of carrying her own belongings. She'd fought hard to be treated as an equal. He carried them anyway.

"Thanks for insisting on the blood work last night. They found GHB in my system. You saved my ass." He held her gaze unwaveringly as she got out of the car. "And for taking care of Ranger. If anything had happened to him…I don't know what I'd do."

Rain dampened his short hair.

"You'd have done the same for me." How she knew that she wasn't sure, but she did.

"Were you hurt last night?" His low voice resonated through her bones.

Rain dotted her skin with pinpricks of sensation. She waited for the lecture on being reckless, but it didn't come. She shook her head. "Feldman wasn't hostile, and I handled the four guys in the bar."

His eyes widened despite their bruised state. Obviously, he hadn't known there were *four* men at the bar.

She should shut her mouth before she got herself into more trouble, but she'd never been good at backing down or backing off. She probably needed to figure that out before she got herself fired or killed.

"I made a mistake going back there alone," she admitted.

"You did what any good agent would do when following a lead—but in the future if you do something like that, send the status update to someone who isn't in the ICU." His quick flash of eyebrows told her he'd received her text message about visiting Feldman.

She nodded wearily. She felt more chastened by his calm understanding than by Ray Aldrich chewing out her ass. "You're okay? Aside from the obvious." She indicated his face and arm.

He nodded.

"I'm sorry you were hurt. Sorry they destroyed your ride."

He shrugged. "I got off lucky. I'm glad you weren't targeted."

If she'd finished her beer it could easily have been her looking like a bit actor from a Rocky movie.

Sheridan's expression remained impassive, but his gaze slipped briefly to her lips, and a shiver of arousal ran over her flesh.

He took a step back, and the moment passed. "You're getting wet. Let's go inside."

The rain intensified, and they started jogging toward the house. From his pained expression moving fast hurt, but he kept up the pace before pushing open the extra-wide front door. Ranger greeted them with a tennis ball in his mouth and a tail that never stopped sawing the air.

"Nice place," she muttered, after greeting the dog.

Sheridan placed her belongings on a long, thin table in the hallway and ducked into a small room down the corridor. He came out with two fluffy towels, one of which he tossed to her. She wiped it over her hair, face and neck, grateful she hadn't bothered with makeup after the lousy couple of hours' sleep she'd managed to steal.

She wasn't trying to impress this man with anything except her abilities as an agent.

Sure.

She looked around. The structure hinted at possibly being an old converted barn that had been added to. She shrugged out of her wet blazer and slipped off her shoes and left them beside the door. The air conditioning caused gooseflesh to rise up on her arms.

Before she could ask exactly why she was here, he said, "Come on through to the back. It's where I'm set up."

He moved inside, and she grabbed her stuff and followed along with Ranger, admiring the dark hardwood floors and artwork on the walls—abstract and vivid, and probably original. She passed an office, a living room with two big, oatmeal-colored couches, and beyond that a dining room, which had an enormous, dark wood dining table with eight fancy wooden chairs set around it.

Even though the timber was dark, the overall effect with the large, pale floor rug and light blue-green walls was bright and welcoming. There was a wine rack in one corner along with what was probably a fridge, although it looked like a custom piece of furniture.

"Do you live here alone?" She didn't know much about the guy, which meant those little tendrils of attraction she was feeling might be completely inappropriate if she was suddenly introduced to Mrs. Dominic Sheridan.

"Yeah." He looked self-conscious and stuffed his good hand in his pocket. "I know it's a little big but I wanted somewhere in the countryside but close to work. This place came on the market…" He shrugged as if that explained everything.

She saw a pool through the window, complete with a pool house and pagoda.

Holy crap, he must be loaded.

She'd be lying if she said she wasn't intimidated. She'd grown up over a restaurant and had waited tables through college. The concept of having money, of not scraping by from paycheck to paycheck and wondering if she'd ever have enough in her bank account for the deposit on a house of her own was mind boggling.

She followed Sheridan through to a spacious kitchen with a tall granite island that had four stools lined up alongside it. It wasn't the pretty, off-white cabinets or the top of the range appliances that caught her attention. Instead it was the laptop sitting next to a half-eaten sandwich. Sheridan moved the cursor, and an image of a man smiling at the camera filled the screen.

"Who is that?" Her teeth chattered.

Sheridan didn't answer immediately. He went over and boosted the thermostat and then took her towel and tossed it with his into a room off the kitchen.

He walked back to where she stood beside the laptop, the

tightness around his eyes indicating every step hurt.

"That," he said slowly, "is a guy named Brian Andrews. He was my supervisor when I worked the violent crimes squad in New York. Great guy." Sheridan's tone was grim. "He died in a car wreck in Ohio last September."

Ava held his stare, afraid she knew where this was going.

"While lying in my hospital bed, I started thinking about how many funerals I'd attended in the last year and decided to check out who else might have died that I didn't know about."

He flicked the cursor, and another image appeared. "This is Preston Daniels. He and his wife died the previous Christmas in Utah. Carbon monoxide poisoning from a faulty heater."

"Let me guess, he also worked with you in the New York Field Office."

Sheridan nodded.

Crap.

Another click. Another face.

"Arnold Biro died of cancer early last year—linked to his work at Ground Zero. He was living in California at the time of his death." Another photograph. "Ira Mallic suffered a fatal heart attack on Long Island. Jamal Fidan drowned following a boating accident. They all died in the last couple of years."

Ava's knees started to buckle, and she sat on the nearest stool. She and Sheridan stared numbly at one another.

"You think someone is targeting FBI agents who worked at the New York Field Office same time you did?"

He rubbed the hint of stubble on his jaw. "Some of these deaths might be natural, but the rate of attrition is way above the national average, especially when we add Van and Calvin Mortimer to the list."

"Not to mention you…"

"I'm not dead yet."

The grin he sent her made her mouth go dry. "I suspected Van had been murdered and Calvin Mortimer obviously, but if you're right…"

"If *we're* right, the FBI is looking at a serial killer targeting agents."

Ava's fingers clasped one another. "You need to talk to Aldrich again."

Sheridan looked away. "I thought we could take this information to someone higher than Aldrich."

"Who?" Ava crossed her arms over her chest. She was so cold she felt like there was a winter storm brewing inside her. A soft, woolen blanket settled over her shoulders. Sheridan moved on as if the act of kindness meant nothing.

"I've made a couple of inquiries to people I know," he said grimly.

"Aldrich isn't all bad." She wasn't sure why she was defending the man. Probably because no one could have replaced Van. Aldrich had never stood a chance as her boss.

"He was an accountant," Sheridan said like that explained everything.

"I shouldn't have ignored his orders."

"He suspended you after someone shot at you—"

"I know what he did!" she snapped and immediately regretted it. Sheridan's expression turned blank.

"Sorry…" Ava began.

"Forget it." His tone was brusque and had lost that low urgent intimacy. "What you might not know is Aldrich not only suspended you but also reported you to OPR, and if he finds out you're still pursuing this case you will lose your job. I guess I should have spelled that out when I called you."

Ava's mouth opened in surprise. *OPR*? The Office of Professional Responsibility. Internal affairs for FBI agents. They could take her job from her in an instant, all because she was trying to get to the truth. She slumped her head onto her arms as they rested on the kitchen island.

She couldn't lose her job. This was all she'd wanted to do since she was seven years old. "We can't ignore the evidence—"

"We don't have any evidence." Sheridan's fist clenched as he sat heavily beside her on a stool. He rested his injured arm on the granite counter. "We have a lot of dead agents and a really bad feeling and nothing but curious circumstances suggesting the cases might be related."

A doorbell chimed throughout the house. Sheridan's brows rose. Ranger started barking.

"Want me to get that?" Ava asked, climbing to her feet. She dropped the blanket onto the stool.

"No, it's fine. I asked someone to meet us here, but they're earlier than I expected. Someone who can help us figure this out and possibly help you keep your job. Assuming you *want* to keep it?" Those battered indigo eyes assessed her searchingly.

"More than anything in the world, SSA Sheridan."

The grin that tugged his mouth took her by surprise. "Then you may as well start calling me Dominic. Looks like we're going to be stuck with each other for a while."

Ava followed him into the hallway, unsettled by the appeal of that statement. Could Dominic Sheridan really help her get her job back or was she gonna crash and burn just like he had last night?

DOMINIC STRODE TO the front door and threw it open, expecting ASAC Lincoln Frazer from the Behavioral Analysis Unit. He blinked at the sight that greeted him.

A neighbor from the opposite side of the road stood on his doorstep carrying a large casserole dish. Her black Mercedes was parked in the driveway. Rain sluiced off her designer raincoat, hair and makeup perfect despite the weather.

"Suzanna. What can I do for you?"

"Oh, Dominic. Hi. I heard what happened yesterday…about the accident. And, oh my gosh—your poor face. Does it hurt?"

He wanted to laugh. Of course it hurt, especially as he was avoiding taking anything stronger than acetaminophen. "Looks worse than it is."

She raised the dish in case he'd missed its significance. "I know you don't keep much food in the house so I brought over that beef casserole you like…" She trailed off as Ava strolled into view. "*Oh*, you have company. Sorry, I assumed you were here alone. I worried you'd be hungry and in need of someone to look after you, but obviously not."

He looked at Ava who raised both brows as she stuck her hands in her back pockets. Amusement danced in her eyes. "Hey."

"Suzanna, this is a, er…*colleague* of mine." He deliberately paused over the word colleague, giving it an emphasis that suggested much more than a working relationship. Ava smiled politely, not missing a beat.

"Would you like to come in?" Dominic offered.

"Oh, I-I," Suzanna stammered. "Well, now, no. I can see

you are working. I'm *so* sorry to interrupt." The pot that had been raised high slumped slightly. "Please take the casserole. I wanted to make sure you had something healthy to eat."

"This is really kind of you, Suzanna. Thank you." He took the heavy dish from his neighbor. His injured shoulder screamed in protest, but he didn't complain.

Ava tilted her head to one side. "Man, I wish I had a neighbor like you. Mine are more likely to hold me at gunpoint than bring me food."

Suzanna's brown eyes went wide in shock. "Oh, okay then. Well then, I hope you *both* enjoy it."

Dominic started closing the door with his foot.

"I'll come back tomorrow for the pot."

"Don't worry. I'll drop it back onto your doorstep as soon as we're done. I don't want to cause you any inconvenience," Dominic insisted.

"Okay—" Suzanna's reply was cut off by the heavy door slamming shut.

Ava stared at him knowingly in the damp cold of the quiet hallway. "That was mighty neighborly indeed." Her expression was an invitation to share.

He grunted. "Hold you at gunpoint? You live in Fredericksburg."

She laughed. "A little color doesn't hurt from a *colleague*."

He ignored her smug expression and headed into the kitchen, putting the pot in the oven and leaving it on warm. Suzanna did make great stew.

"Funny how she knew about the state of your fridge." Ava's eyebrows did the rest of the talking.

He rubbed his face and gave up. "She stayed over after a party at another neighbor's house last Christmas." He had little recollection of what happened between them except for the fact they'd both woken up naked in his bed. He'd been mortified. "I should never have..." He pursed his lips. "Anyway. She, hmm, wanted more."

"You didn't. I get it. Trust me, I get it." She smoothed her hands down the front of her jeans, and he felt like an asshole.

"She deserves a lot more than I have to offer. She has a kid, although I've never met him. Lives with his dad apparently." He cleared his throat feeling sheepish. The guilt he'd felt for the last eight months swirled inside him, amorphous and unpleasant.

Ava breathed out heavily. "Did you ever think that if maybe you talked to her like an adult, she might stop trying so hard?"

Why was he immediately the bad guy? "I did talk to her. I sat her down the morning after we had sex. I sat her down again a week later after she came to my door hoping for a repeat." And again, a month later. Talking hadn't worked, and every time he saw the woman, he felt more and more of a reprobate.

Ava's mouth thinned in disapproval.

"It didn't make me feel good, Ava. I felt like a jerk, but I'd have been more of a jerk not to have that conversation. I don't ghost people, I'm upfront and honest."

She looked at him dubiously.

"And I like sex, okay? Is that a crime between consenting adults?" Christ, why was he even talking about this?

"Of course not." Her voice squeaked. Her cheeks flamed beet-red. The idea he could make Ava Kanas blush did something to his insides. He didn't like that either.

She hadn't seemed bashful yesterday when they'd been

discussing blow jobs. But they'd gotten personal rather than talking about work. Ironic, as he was not the sort of person to over share. Something about Ava Kanas made him do things he didn't normally do. He wanted to know her. Wanted to know what made her tick.

Not physically. Nothing physical could happen between them. He was too old for her and did not date other agents, especially junior agents. He wasn't about to take advantage of someone younger or more vulnerable. He cleared his throat. "Anyway, I thought we were working this case?"

She chewed her lip, which didn't help his resolve to keep things strictly professional.

"How can we if we don't have access to the case files?" she asked.

The doorbell rang again.

"We have something else. Something better."

"More beef stew?" she asked dryly, trailing behind him to the front door.

He turned so abruptly she bumped into him. Electricity shot through him. It had nothing to do with the pain from his injuries.

He steadied her with his good hand. "There's no line up of ex-lovers. I don't usually get involved with women who don't realize upfront what I'm interested in, and I'm only ever interested in short-term."

Their gazes locked, and he could feel his heart beating just a fraction too hard. He wasn't proud of his commitment issues, but his mother's death, combined with a rotating door of temporary step-mothers had left him leery of even the pretense of emotional attachment. Why get invested when chances were it wouldn't work out anyway?

He reached out and couldn't stop himself from hooking a lock of hair that had escaped out of her tight bun behind her ear. "I'm sorry I used you to try to drive Suzanna away, even if it was only implied. I won't do that again."

She trembled in his hold.

Was she cold or did she feel this inconvenient attraction too? He hoped to hell it was all one-sided, because that would make it much easier to keep his hands to himself.

Her hazel eyes were huge and full of shadows. She swallowed noisily. "Sorry. I was projecting. I've been on the receiving end of enough brushoffs to feel sorry for Suzanna. It sucks."

"I've been there too, Ava. Most people have." His gaze flicked to the blemish on her brow and the fresh graze on her cheek. "Is that how you got the scar?"

"No."

"Not gonna tell me that story?"

"I doubt it."

He laughed. At least she was honest.

The doorbell rang again.

Ava blinked, and he stepped back. He wasn't doing a good job of keeping her at arm's length but here came the cavalry. Dominic checked the peephole this time.

Lincoln Frazer, head of BAU-4, peered back at him, looking pissed at being kept waiting.

Dominic swung the door open. Lincoln stepped inside to be greeted by the dog who went ballistic sniffing the guy's pant legs. Lincoln was followed by the heavily pregnant agent who'd accompanied him to the scene of the shooting at Van's funeral. Agent Mallory Rooney. The senator's daughter.

He winced because he hated when people did that—

labeled him by his father's achievements rather than his own.

Another man stood behind them, assessing Dominic with quiet gray eyes.

Lincoln eyed his bruised face. "Hurt much?"

Dominic shrugged.

"Thought so." The man grinned. "So, I guess the big question is, who wants you dead and why?"

CHAPTER TWELVE

"YOU GUYS REMEMBER Special Agent Ava Kanas?" Dominic asked as he closed the door behind the newcomers.

"How could we forget the Special Agent who is single-handedly saving America," Lincoln Frazer commented dryly, but his tone was amused rather than critical.

The third man stepped forward and held out his hand. "Alex Parker. Agent Rooney's husband. I consult for the FBI on cybersecurity matters."

Ava shook his hand. This was the guy rumored to have worked for the CIA before he was incarcerated in a Moroccan jail. Ava noted they wore matching scars on their brows. She wondered if he'd got his from being pistol whipped after watching his father's murder. Something in the depths of his eyes suggested worse. Much worse.

He smiled, and she found herself smiling back.

Sheridan led the way to the dining room. Ava followed, walking beside the heavily pregnant agent. Parker played with the dog as he brought up the rear.

"When's your baby due?" Ava asked.

Rooney shot her a rueful glance. "Three more weeks. I feel like I've been pregnant forever."

"You're working right up until the birth?"

"To the bitter end, which is why Alex is hovering even more than he usually does," Rooney said with a smile that suggested she didn't mind. "I'm actually surprised he hasn't signed up for a midwifery course just in case something goes wrong."

"Where do you think I go every Thursday afternoon?" he asked with a straight face.

Rooney gave her husband a quelling look, then nodded toward Frazer. "The boss banned me from traveling for work, but this is within easy driving distance of Quantico. I'd rather do something useful than sit around wondering where my toes went."

Ava laughed. "Enjoy the freedom while you can."

"You have kids?"

Dominic glanced sharply over his shoulder.

Ava shook her head. She had no idea how she'd be able to meld a family with a successful FBI career, or unsuccessful one for that matter. Rooney obviously had a supportive husband, but not everyone was a millionaire who could consult for the FBI.

Ava was only twenty-six and, despite her mother's incessant nagging, wasn't in any rush to get hitched. She didn't want to be tied down any more than Sheridan did. "My sister has two kids under two. We talk."

Rooney blew out a breath that made her bangs dance. "Now that's bravery."

Dominic led them to his fancy dining table and invited them all to sit. He went and grabbed his laptop, then sat at the head of the table. He moved stiffly, obviously in pain, but too stoic to admit it. He probably shouldn't even be out of bed, never mind working a case.

Ava didn't know what was going on between the two of them. Work, for sure. A vested interest in Van's death and figuring out what the hell was happening. But something else too. Some undercurrent of attraction they were both pretending didn't exist.

Seeing Suzanna, the poor besotted neighbor salivating on the doorstep had made Ava take a giant mental step back. But who hadn't made a mistake when it came to relationships? She was pretty sure every man she'd ever slept with had been a major error in judgment. She pushed the thoughts out of her mind. She needed to concentrate on getting her job back.

"What have you got for us?" Frazer asked intently.

"Agent Kanas and I have determined that a total of seven agents who I worked with in the New York Field Office are now deceased, including Van Stamos and Calvin Mortimer."

If Sheridan was right about his theory it would be the first time in the history of the FBI where agents had been ruthlessly and systematically targeted. Ava held her breath.

Frazer swore. "Which squad?"

"Violent Crimes."

"You think someone purposely murdered Mortimer, Stamos, and the other men in that squad because of something that occurred in New York?" Rooney asked.

Sheridan nodded.

"Any cases spring to mind that might have incited this level of vengeance?" asked Frazer.

"It was New York so could have been anything. Mob stuff,"—Ava forced herself not to react—"serial killers, serial rapists, kidnapping, murder, intimidation, witness tampering, bribery, corruption. We had a piece of anything that turned nasty and a lot of people went to prison." Dominic shrugged and continued. "Some of the deaths might be natural causes—cancer, heart attacks, but I have trouble believing seven men below the age of sixty just happened to die unexpectedly within the last twelve months."

"Seems like a hell of a coincidence," Parker commented.

Sheridan went into the kitchen and brought back a coffee pot and five mugs. Parker fetched a jug of milk. The smell of beef stew floated through the air, making Ava slightly nauseous.

Frazer got up and stared at the view of the pool, huge lawn and nearby woods. "We're going to need to re-examine the details of those agents' deaths."

Rooney broke in. "Do you think your accident last night was related?"

"The GHB in my system suggests it wasn't an accident," Sheridan said easily.

"But was it related to these other deaths or was it related to the drug smuggling operation being run out of that bar?" Ava asked in frustration. Too many questions and possibilities.

"I can see the guys in the bar trying to get rid of a couple of Feds who got too close," Parker put in.

"Organized crime knows that messing with Feds is the surest way to bring a whole load of attention to your illegal activities," Frazer objected.

"Sometimes the Mob gets bold," Parker stated quietly. He looked at Ava as he said it. Did he know about her past? It was secret, but maybe if you were a really good cybersecurity expert nothing was secret. She feigned nonchalance.

"Why was Van Stamos in that bar last week? Was it a place he regularly visited? Could he have been investigating the drug runners?" Rooney turned her head to one side as she asked the same questions that had been swirling in Ava's mind for hours.

"He never mentioned going there to me." Ava shrugged. "Maybe someone contacted him with information…I don't know."

"Where's Van's cell phone?" Parker asked.

Sheridan looked at him. "I can get it for you."

"Alex is a wizard with cell phone data." Rooney's eyes sparkled as she took a sip of coffee her husband poured for her.

"I don't need the phone but I need to know his carrier," said Parker.

"I'll find out," Sheridan wrote a note for himself on his cell.

"Anything back on the shoe prints?" Ava asked Sheridan.

"Shoe prints?" Frazer queried.

"When Van's body was found the window in his office was open," Dominic explained. "When I checked outside the window last night, there were distinct impressions in the soil. I asked Ray Aldrich to get the evidence response team back in to make plaster-casts and to check the surface of the window for contact DNA or fingerprints."

"Why use the window? If someone was there why not use the door?" queried Rooney.

"You can avoid tripping the security lights by going out that side window and heading straight to the fence," Dominic answered.

Ava's eyes widened. He hadn't mentioned that snippet of information last night, but it explained why he'd been snooping around in the dark.

"How would the dealers from the bar know that?" Parker

handed her a coffee and offered her milk which she accepted gratefully.

"They wouldn't," said Ava. "Only someone who'd staked out the house would know that."

"Then someone might have been stalking him beforehand," said Frazer contemplatively. "Watching him and waiting for the perfect opportunity, which doesn't scream drug dealers to me."

"But the coincidence with what was going on at the bar..." Ava hated coincidences. "And there is still no proof Van was murdered."

"Except your conviction and Dominic's," said Frazer.

"There's something else weird." Dominic glanced at Ava, and she pressed her lips together. If they were wrong and this got out, Van's legacy would be blighted. No one would remember the arrests or his work with victims. It would be all about the fact he'd died with his johnson hanging out.

Dominic knew it too. "We spoke to the neighbor who found Van's body. He said when he arrived Van's pants were undone. The neighbor adjusted the clothing before calling the cops, because he didn't want his friend to be found that way."

Frazer stared at Dominic and then at Ava. The iciness in his gaze was like frost on a windshield. Ava suspected it was something he cultivated to keep people at a distance.

"Neighbor's theory was Van had a sexual encounter and was so overcome with guilt for cheating on his dead wife that he shot himself," Dominic continued.

Frazer's lip curled. "I find it hard to believe a retired agent would leave himself exposed in that fashion even if he'd felt guilty enough to kill himself. He knew how law enforcement talked." He narrowed his eyes. "It *is* the sort of thing an

UNSUB might do if they wanted to humiliate a victim."

"We need the surveillance footage from the bar the night Van was there. See who he spoke to." Dominic adjusted his sling, lips twisting into a grimace.

Frazer eyed Ava. "That's not going to be easy."

"Once the higher ups see the list of dead agents surely the DEA will cooperate?" she said defensively. "And the DEA saw us enter and leave that bar. We weren't exactly low profile. I'm assuming they had someone inside the place. Why the hell hasn't one of them contacted us about Van being there the night he died? Don't they read the damn news?"

Frazer spread his hands on the table. "It's all circumstantial."

"It seems to me like we have several different things we're trying to establish here that are muddying the waters." Parker leaned forward. "Whether Van Stamos or any of the other agents were murdered and who spiked Sheridan's drink last night. And are the events linked?"

"How do we find answers if the DEA won't cooperate with their surveillance footage?" Ava asked.

Parker shrugged. "I might be able to see what the DEA has if they keep the digital evidence stored in their system, but it could take time."

"There's also an ATM machine opposite the Mule & Pitcher." Ava had forgotten about that with everything else that had happened.

"What about the guy who started the bar fight last night?" Dominic asked her.

Ava shifted on the hard, wooden chair. "He said he'd be willing to work with a police sketch artist but wasn't sure what he'd remember when he sobered up. I was suspended before I could follow up."

Frazer made a note on his phone. "I'll check in on the status of that and get a background check run on the guy. Then, while Alex is conducting pen-tests on the DEA's system—"

Alex grinned at Ava's startled look. "They pay me to find faults in their network."

Frazer grunted. "Too damn much. Anyway, I'll talk to a friend there and explain this thing might be bigger than a drug bust or even the attempted murder of two agents. If nothing else they might be able to get us some information on whether or not the men in custody admit to roofying Dominic. Dominic—you check into the status of the task force investigating Calvin Mortimer's murder. If we get any definitive evidence that these other deaths are connected then the investigation will most likely be taken over by that task force. Mark Gross is in charge. He's a good agent."

"I'd go question the waitress—if I wasn't suspended." The reality of Ava's situation hit her all over again.

Dominic cleared his throat. "I was hoping you might put in a good word for Agent Kanas with the director…"

So that's why he'd invited her over here with these guys. Ava rolled her eyes. She wasn't going to beg for favors from people she didn't know.

Frazer laughed. "I don't have that kind of pull with the director."

"Bullshit." Dominic started to fold his arms and then winced in pain.

"Not bullshit." Frazer sent Rooney a rueful look. "I used up all my favors over the last nine months. And if Agent Kanas isn't reinstated, she can't work this case, not even on the periphery. It could throw any evidence we collect into jeopardy once it gets to court."

Ava felt the blood drain from her head. The idea of sitting around in her apartment waiting to be fired was soul destroying.

"You do it," Frazer said to Sheridan. "With your personal connections you could probably get her reinstated at Fredericksburg while OPR conducts its investigation." Frazer played with his mug as he spoke.

"What 'connections'?" Ava bit out.

Dominic stayed stubbornly silent.

"His father is the Governor of Vermont." Frazer's expression was cloaked, but a slight smile played around his lips.

Ava blinked slowly. She'd guessed Dominic came from power and influence.

"And his godfather is Joshua Hague."

Ava's eyes stretched wide. "Joshua Hague?"

"Yes, Joshua Hague, the President of the United States of America." Frazer seemed to enjoy outing Sheridan's connections, but Ava felt as if she'd been punched in the stomach.

Dominic refused to meet her gaze. "My father and godfather have no influence on anything within the Bureau."

"They shouldn't have." Frazer's smile was cynical. "If you ask Ray Aldrich to reinstate her, he'll do it. You know he'll do it for you."

Dominic grunted. "And what does that say about my integrity? I've spent years making sure I never crossed that line. Never asked for favors based on who I might be related to."

So much for Dominic using all his influence to help her get her job back.

"That's very convenient when it's my career on the line, not yours." Ava should admire the man for not using his connections for personal gain. Except this wasn't about him. She was the one with everything to lose.

"I won't compromise my integrity."

"You don't think I'm even worth the trouble of picking up the phone." The realization stung.

"Of course, I think you're worth it. But these are politically powerful men—they are not FBI. They do not influence the day to day running of the Bureau. And I can't approach the director because I don't want him feeling like if he doesn't do something for me then he gets in trouble with POTUS."

So, she got to rot after almost dying trying to figure out what happened to him. Angry tears pricked the back of her eyes, but she blinked them away. She'd rather die than cry in front of these people.

"I won't put the president in a difficult position." Anger flashed in Dominic's usually calm eyes.

The fist in her throat expanded. She thought about her life. The difficult life-altering and life-threatening choices she had made over the years. And this man who'd offered to help wouldn't even put in a good word for her. Ava climbed slowly to her feet. "I don't care about your political connections, but you don't even have the balls to stand up for me as a fellow agent."

He stood too, and they were staring each other down over the dining table. "My integrity is important to me."

His integrity wouldn't pay her rent. "We were both doing things our bosses told us not to do, but I'm the only one who got canned. Is that the FBI bureaucracy treating us equally or is the fact you have political connections already in play?"

Dominic's mouth tightened. "Maybe they didn't want to suspend a man while he was unconscious."

He'd almost died, but so had she. She'd killed a man last night.

Ava began to gather her things together before she lost it in front of these people.

"Fine," he bit out. "I'll talk to Aldrich. Sit down, Ava. We have work to do." His narrowed eyes met hers, expression resentful. She was sure hers looked exactly the same.

She fought with herself and her pride and the desire to storm out. That would only prove to these agents that she was rash and impetuous, something Van had tried to coach her against. She needed her damn job. She got a tight grip on her temper and paced the length of the dining room waiting for the anger in her blood to cool.

"There's something else no one has mentioned yet." Rooney placed a hand on her stomach. "Determining who else might be in danger."

Ava hadn't even thought that far ahead which showed how much she was off her game.

"Write a list of everyone on that squad." Frazer agreed. "I'll talk to HR for their official list too."

"It's possible other people may have been targeted. If this was a case that went to trial there could be witnesses. Prosecutors. Judges." Dominic dragged a hand over his face. He looked haggard. She felt guilty for yelling at him. Maybe she hadn't been fair. She'd known she was crossing a line when she'd investigated Van's death in spite of Aldrich's orders.

"You know you're a target, right? Regardless of who roofied your drink last night. If we're right about this then someone wants you dead," said Ava.

"I can look after myself."

"Like you did last night?" Frazer said sarcastically. "If you are right about this then the UNSUB has used various methods to successfully murder several experienced Federal Agents without raising suspicion. Until now."

"You want me to go into protective custody, or into hiding? CNU is severely shorthanded and can't afford to lose a full-time negotiator."

"They'll be more shorthanded if you wind up dead," Frazer stated. "Anyway, you might not get a choice."

"Yeah," Dominic's lip curled. "I don't think so."

Frazer raised a patronizing brow. Ava crossed her arms over her chest and huffed. So, Dominic would use his unspoken influence to keep himself in the game without even batting an eye, but she'd had to beg for him to support her.

"Why don't we get Ava reassigned as your bodyguard until this is over?" Rooney suggested brightly. "You need someone to drive you around anyway, right?"

"What? No." Dominic looked horrified.

Ava flinched.

"It's the perfect solution. She can work the case while you're doing your negotiator thing and watch your back the rest of the time."

Frazer was staring at Ava in an assessing manner. "It's not a bad idea," he mused. "You could pose undercover as Sheridan's girlfriend and that way the killer won't necessarily know we're onto them the way they would if he was suddenly surrounded by HRT agents."

Dominic said, "You think they're watching me?"

Fraser nodded. "Unless they just happened to be at the bar last night, they're probably stalking you. Same way they must have stalked the other victims."

The saliva in Ava's mouth dried up.

Dominic's usually smooth voice rumbled through his chest. "I don't want a bodyguard."

"I don't want to be suspended," Ava shot back.

"Then you should learn to work with the FBI rather than in spite of it," Dominic bit out.

Ava sucked in a furious breath.

"Here we go again." Frazer rolled his eyes. "How about we take this one step at a time. Alex can look for any surveillance footage he might be able to find from the bar. I'll talk to the DEA, but don't hold your breath. Mallory can follow up on getting the police artist out to the guy who started the bar fight and talk to the waitress who served you. I'll approach the director with our suspicions. You," he looked at Dominic, "put in an appeal to Aldrich to get Kanas's suspension lifted and her assigned to work with you. OPR are investigating anyway, no reason for her not to be useful in the meantime."

Ava blinked at his callous matter-of-factness.

"You'll need to take basic security precautions which includes having someone with you at all times. If not Kanas then we'll arrange someone else—until the higher ups decide to make that decision." Frazer pinched his lips together. "I suspect they'll want an HRT unit on you whether you like it or not."

"No way am I wasting the time or resources of HRT," Dominic said forcefully. He shot her a look. He didn't want her either, that was for damn sure.

Rooney's stomach rumbled audibly, breaking the tension. "Sorry." She rubbed her distended abdomen. "Junior is hungry and whatever is cooking smells good."

"Beef stew courtesy of a neighbor. You want some?" Dominic asked.

"Only if you don't mind." Rooney smacked her lips. She looked at her boss.

He shrugged. "Far be it from me to come between a pregnant woman and food."

"Linc?" Dominic asked. The use of Frazer's shortened first name suggested they were good friends as Ava had suspected.

The blond man shook his head. "Not for me. I'm taking Izzy out for dinner."

"I'm in." Parker accepted the offer without being asked.

"Ava?" asked Dom.

No way she was eating the neighbor's infamous beef stew. "No thanks. I'm thinking of turning vegetarian."

Dominic's lips quirked. "And give up chicken wings?"

She gave a reluctant laugh, and some of the lingering tension eased away. "Maybe not. But I'm not hungry. Go ahead and eat."

Dominic went into the kitchen, and they all strung along behind him. Ranger was dancing excitedly under his feet. Ava saw what happened like some slow-motion Rom-Com disaster. Dominic put on an oven glove and retrieved the casserole dish awkwardly with his one good arm. Then he turned, tripped over the dog, and knew he was going down. He lobbed the casserole dish so that it wouldn't hit Ranger who yelped in confusion and shot out of the way as Dominic crashed hard to the floor. The casserole dish shattered. Stew went everywhere.

Ava rushed to where Dominic lay writhing on the floor.

"Are you okay?" She clutched his good shoulder, and his hand grabbed hers as he rolled onto his back, gasping for breath, gripping his ribs with his elbows, clearly in pain. He squeezed her fingers so hard she winced.

Under the blackened bruises, his skin was milky pale, eyes scrunched up and watering.

"Jesus, Dominic, say something. Do I need to call an ambulance? Did you break a rib?"

Then his shoulders started shaking, and he started to wheeze.

"Are you okay? Speak to me dammit before I smack you."

Finally, a shout of laughter erupted, and he let go of her hand to wipe the tears from his eyes. "You'd make a terrible nurse."

"Did you break anything?" she asked urgently.

"Suzanna's fucking casserole dish. Now I'll have to buy her another one. Help me up, Agent Kanas, and then I'll show you to a spare room you can use in the short-term until we figure out what the hell is going on."

The dog started to lick up the stew.

"There's broken glass in there," Ava warned sharply.

Frazer caught Ranger by the collar and dragged him away. "Come on, boy."

Dominic looked up at Rooney from his prone position on the floor. "Stew's off the menu. How about some homemade soup?"

CHAPTER THIRTEEN

EVERY MUSCLE IN Dominic's body hurt. Every nerve, every bone, every sinew. It was getting worse rather than better, and no way was he taking anything stronger to numb the pain. The epidemic of opioid addiction scared him far more than any temporary discomfort.

He and Ava Kanas had spent most of the early evening going over the reports on the other agents' deaths looking for commonalities. The only thing they found in common was the fact they were now all dead. In terms of cases worked by the New York squad there were hundreds of instances where they'd all worked together to some degree. The FBI tended to do takedowns in overwhelming numbers as a deterrent against criminals thinking they stood a chance of escaping and to crush the will to fight back. It was a tactic that worked.

He and Ava had kept everything strictly polite and professional and had both been as uncomfortable as hell. She was set up at the opposite end of a long work table the previous owners had left in the basement.

His gaze kept drifting to her. Intelligent eyes narrowed in concentration. Shiny brown hair loose around her shoulders rather than tied up in its ubiquitous bun. She wore a baggy cable sweater with tight jeans. Her Glock-22 sat on the table beside her computer. A reminder she wasn't here for a social visit.

Dominic did not want to be shadowed by anyone. He was a loner by nature—he had a feeling Ava was too. He didn't want to waste Bureau resources protecting him when there were other people in greater danger. Chances were his would-be attacker had left the area and if they hadn't, they sure as hell would bail if Dominic were surrounded by a bunch of HRT meatheads in Kevlar.

He wanted to catch this bastard not have him run away. But he couldn't do it alone right now. Hell, he couldn't even drive. So, he was stuck in close proximity to a woman he found increasingly attractive, a woman who seemed to like him a hell of a lot less than he liked her—which was a good thing, he told himself.

He was supposed to be making a list of everyone he remembered working with at NYFO, but he couldn't concentrate with the other agent in the room. Maybe he was tired. He touched the bridge of his nose which was now as black as his eye sockets. He looked like a goddamn raccoon—made worse by the lack of sleep.

"Want a drink?" He nodded toward the fully stocked bar. The previous owners had also left a pool table and darts board down here. Not to mention the fully functional cinema with seating for eight.

Ava looked up from her computer where she was casting an eye over the lists of cases he'd helped work on at NYFO to see if anything jumped out. Perhaps Van had mentioned a particular defendant and the list might jog her memory. Basically, they were clutching at straws.

"No. Thanks. Better keep a clear head. Just in case."

Just in case some UNSUB decided to take another crack at

him—and she what? Threw herself in front of a bullet to save him? Hell, no. Not happening, but he figured it would be better if she didn't realize that.

She'd gone back to her apartment and grabbed some belongings. Who knew how long it would take to catch this bastard. At least his home had good security. He'd drawn all the blinds to prevent them becoming easy targets for a sniper upstairs, but here in the basement they didn't need to worry.

"You can have one beer—"

"I know you don't think much of me, SSA Sheridan." Those eyes of hers narrowed to laser points of disapproval.

Dominic opened his mouth to argue, but she spoke over him again.

"I know you think the idea of me acting as your bodyguard is ridiculous and the last thing you want, but I take my job seriously. So, no alcohol, thank you."

He held onto his silence when all he wanted to do was dive in to protest with both feet. After a few moments he said carefully, "It isn't 'you' I object to, Ava. It is the idea of anyone—including yourself—putting themselves in danger for me."

She looked up, and something flickered in her eyes. "I don't believe you."

Dominic realized he needed to treat his interactions with Ava like any other high stakes negotiation so he started with some emotional labeling. "It seems like this is upsetting for you."

She rolled her eyes dramatically.

"It seems like you think I don't value you as an agent."

Her eyes went wide in feigned surprise. "What gave it away?"

"The daggers in your eyes."

Her eyes narrowed again.

He winced. "That was a joke." Apparently a bad one. She brought out the worst in him and he decided to use that by listing all his worst characteristics in an accusation audit. "Look, I'm an asshole. I take myself and my job way too seriously. I am hypersensitive about my political connections. I don't want anyone thinking I got my position for any reason other than the fact I'm good at what I do."

She was watching him now with a little less hostility.

"I don't like the idea of some scumbag hurting people, especially my friends and colleagues. If we discover Van was murdered, I'll never forgive myself for not being there to protect him. If he committed suicide, I'll feel the same way." And the idea of anyone harming this woman because she was with him drove a stake through his already aching body. He cleared his throat. "I'm a private person. I like my own space, and I don't like having to hide from this bastard. I don't want them to think they are winning. I don't want them to think I'm scared." He paused briefly. "I guess that's pride. A deadly sin where I come from."

She let out a long breath that sounded like she might be letting go of her resentment. "I get that. I overreacted earlier. Van always said I had a hair trigger. I apologize. I just feel like no one is taking my opinions seriously—"

"I take you seriously. You're a good agent."

She raised a brow in question.

"You held fire when we were being shot at during Van's funeral. A hot head would have returned fire."

"We were out of range."

"Which proves you were thinking and not just reacting.

And this thing with the circumstances surrounding Van's death. You kept hammering away at the case even though no one believed you."

Her lips pulled tight, and she looked away. "I might still be wrong."

"You're not wrong." He knew it with certainty now. There were too many unexplained deaths. Too many coincidences. "I'm sorry I wasn't keen to go out on a limb for you with the higher ups. I figured if I persuaded Frazer to do it, I'd have been able to help you while maintaining my puritanical stance." The ease with which Ray Aldrich had agreed to reinstate her while OPR did their work had made his stomach crawl.

"I had no idea about your political relations. Van never mentioned your family to me." She picked at a piece of fluff on her sweater. She was curious but didn't want to admit it.

"Because he knew I hated it when people brought them up—especially at work." Dominic got up and poured himself a small whiskey. Enough to feel the kick, not enough to blunt his faculties. "My father and I don't have the easiest relationship, but he's a politician so I try to not talk about it."

"Why don't you get along?"

He looked at her, the whiskey warming his tongue. "We get along fine, he just tends to put his career before the rest of us, and that can be hard."

"I googled your family earlier," she admitted. Her voice dropped low with sympathy, and he knew what she was going to say before she said it. He braced himself. "The article said your mom killed herself when you were a kid."

"And that's just one of the many things I don't like to talk about." He poured himself another shot. Crap. "What about your family?"

Her eyes went wide. "What about them?"

"The name Kanas is Greek, right?"

She nodded but shifted uncomfortably.

"Something you had in common with Van?"

She threw her pen down and stretched her arms above her head. A blue, beaded bracelet caught the light. Dominic looked away. Did not need to be reminded she had breasts.

"Van converted to Catholicism to marry Jessica. He pretty much left the tight-knit Greek community behind at the same time," she said.

"You seem to know a lot about him." How close had they been?

"We talked about it a lot." She laughed. "Ask any Greek kid about Greek school, and you'll understand why growing up 'Greek' is such a big thing."

"You think the fact you both come from a Greek background is why you two got on so well?" If he hadn't been watching her so closely, he wouldn't have noticed.

Her hand went to the bottom of her neck in a move that screamed self-protection. "Probably."

He frowned. He didn't believe her. Why would she lie about something as simple as that? "You come from a big family?"

She climbed to her feet and started to pace. "Not really."

He raised one brow. She seemed even more reluctant to talk about her family than he did. She yawned. The dark circles under her eyes told him all he needed to know about how exhausted she was. He also knew that until he turned in, she wasn't going to budge.

His cell phone started to vibrate. It was his father. Damn.

"I'm gonna take this in my room and then get some sleep."

"I'll sleep on the couch upstairs."

"There are five other double beds in the house," he said in exasperation.

"They're all on other floors to where you're sleeping. I'll be fine on the couch," she insisted.

He ground his teeth, picked up his service weapon from the table, and headed upstairs. Ranger was already in his dog bed by the back door and half-heartedly wagged his tail when Dominic walked by.

He went through to his bedroom on the ground floor, placed the Glock on the bedside table. If Ava wanted to sleep on the couch that was her problem.

She'd be fine.

He'd slept there plenty of times, but it still felt weird to have anyone, let alone a woman he found attractive, sleeping so close by. On the couch. "Protecting" him.

He pressed redial on his cell.

"Dominic, how are you, son?" It probably wasn't his father's fault that he perpetually sounded like he was on the campaign trail.

"Pretty good, considering." Dominic forced himself to smile because people could hear smiles even on the phone. "Been a hell of a week."

"I called you after the shooting on Tuesday."

"Sorry, Pop, I meant to call back but I got tied up at work."

"Joshua was asking after you…"

Dominic had been ecstatic when his godfather had won the election, it was only afterward it had become awkward. "Please give him my regards."

"You could pick up the phone yourself you know. Better

yet, pay the man a visit."

Tension pulled at the muscles across Dominic's chest. "I'll try to do that the next time I'm in DC." And he probably did owe the man a visit. It just felt so incredibly freaking awkward visiting his godfather at the White House.

"I was calling for another reason." His dad cleared his throat. "I asked Tracy to marry me, and she said yes."

Dominic blew out an audible breath and dragged off his sling, tossing it on the bed. "That's great, Dad." Maybe fifth time was the charm.

"We're having an engagement party next week. Would love for you to come up and meet her and her family. Your brother and sister will both be there. Bring a date."

A date? Was he serious? Last time Dominic had taken a date home his brother had seduced her. Dominic unbuttoned his shirt and eased out of the sleeves. The bruises on his ribs were darkening beneath the surface of his skin. Dominic shucked his pants and tossed them on a chair. He had pajamas around here somewhere. He went to the walk-in closet and fished out some loose plaid pants. Ava Kanas probably wouldn't appreciate what he usually slept in.

"Tracy wants a big, white wedding as this is her first time..."

Dear Jesus.

"I was hoping you'd be my best man."

"You told Franklin about that?" His older brother would be pissed.

His dad laughed. "Not yet but he did the last three. Figured I might have better luck if I asked you this time."

His brother wouldn't like being usurped. For some unknown reason, Franklin had been in competition with

Dominic for as long as he could remember. Sports. Grades. Women. His father's attention. Franklin hadn't liked it when Dominic had rejected the idea of joining the family law firm where he'd already made partner. He didn't like the fact Dominic had signed up for the FBI. He didn't even like the fact it was Dominic's godfather and not his who occupied the Oval Office.

Their father was always trying to force them to get along, but Dominic was the only one making concessions, and he was done with the pretense and the bullshit.

"I'm hoping this is the last time. I think you'll like Tracy."

His father might have better luck if he didn't marry women half his age who wanted his money and position more than they wanted the man himself. Not that Dominic was an expert in relationships. His dad definitely had him beat there.

His father cleared his throat. Their interactions always seemed to stumble on the unresolved damage from Dominic's childhood. "Anyway, hopefully you'll come." His dad rattled off a date and time. "Your sister misses you."

He knew that was the only way his father could even come close to admitting he missed him too. At least the governor was no longer living in the mansion where Dominic had found his mother overdosed in bed when he'd been a kid.

He remembered every detail from that day. From the quietness of the house, to the stuffiness of his mother's bedroom. He'd known he wasn't supposed to bother her when she was sick—he had a new baby sister and waking his mom up when she was sleeping was punishable by a sharp smack across the back of the legs. But he'd skinned his knee falling off his bike and had wanted his mother's comfort.

Yeah, well that hadn't happened. He pushed the memories

away.

"I'm not sure I can get away to Vermont right now, Dad. There's some stuff going on at work."

"Well, that's okay because we're holding the party in DC so that everyone can attend."

By everyone, he meant the president. Dominic couldn't help being cynical. "Well, that's great. I can't guarantee I'll be in Virginia though. If a situation arises—"

"Surely the FBI can spare you for one lousy night especially after you were in a car accident?"

Guilt twisted his insides. Last time he'd visited had been at Christmas, and his father sounded genuinely keen to see him. "I'll see what I can do, but no promises."

"At least I know what to get you for Christmas this year."

"What's that?"

"A new Lexus."

Dominic closed his eyes as images from the crash bombarded him. "I don't need you to get me a car, Dad."

He thought he heard a catch in his father's voice. "But I'd like to, son."

It was always like this. Clawing through years of guilt to try and have a normal relationship and then throwing money at it in the hopes of a quick fix. He cleared his throat and returned the favor. "So, what do you want for an engagement present?"

"You. I want to see you."

Shit.

"And bring a date. Otherwise I'll have Tracy invite all of her single friends to try to set you up."

"Fine. I'll bring someone." He closed his eyes and hung up, praying for a hostage situation to arise. How the holy hell had he been trapped into this? Maybe Charlotte would come with him. But even as he thought it, he knew who he'd be taking to the goddamn party.

Maybe they'd get sent to Alaska, or an oilrig. He could hope.

He headed out of his bedroom to grab a glass of water and some pain meds but stopped on the threshold of his darkened living room.

Ava was stretched out asleep on the couch wearing sweats and a green camisole. Ranger was curled up beside her.

"Traitor," he muttered to the dog who gave him the side eye.

He grabbed an afghan from the back of the other couch and draped it over the two of them.

Then he went back to his oversized and empty bed and lay there awake not knowing what the hell he wanted anymore.

WATCHING SHERIDAN'S HOUSE from the woods wasn't as satisfying as it usually was. The blinds were closed, and drapes drawn flush against one another. No gaps. No easy spying on Dominic Sheridan. No fantasizing about putting a bullet in his unsuspecting forehead.

There were no cars in the driveway, but he was definitely home. Not dead. Hiding.

Was he alone?

Reports hadn't indicated any fatalities last night so the woman he'd been with was presumably alive too. Pity. Caroline's death wouldn't be quite so pointless if at least one of them had died. But Caroline had interfered and had known too much. Plus, she'd served her purpose.

Would they blame Caroline for the murders? It was distinctly possible. An idea took shape. It would require another night of no sleep, but sleep was elusive these days anyway. Too many ghosts begging for retribution.

A light snapped off inside Sheridan's bedroom, leaving only the dim lights on inside the pool. The G-man had an excellent alarm system, video cameras and motion sensors on every corner.

It was too risky to attempt a break-in, and it was preferable to pounce when the prey wasn't expecting it. Like poor pathetic Van Stamos. So earnest in his desire to fight crime.

Fucker.

Impatience started to bite. To finish this. To destroy this asshole. The desire to smash all the windows with a baseball bat and piss in the pool was appealing, but it wouldn't win the prize of complete and utter revenge. Only three more dead bodies would do that.

The challenge was harder now.

The wind rustled the leaves on the trees, and darkness encompassed the world. A grim reaper walked through the shadows, patient and ready. Now for the real test. Now to kill the last three murderers and have complete and utter revenge. Soon. Very soon.

CHAPTER FOURTEEN

DOMINIC WALKED INTO his boss's office the next morning, sat down and waited for the opening salvo.

Quentin Savage looked up from the report he was reading. "I just got off the phone with the director."

"Yeah?" Minimal positive encouragers worked to keep the other person talking, which was more effective when the other person wasn't a trained negotiator.

"Yeah," Savage repeated and eyed him narrowly. "Lincoln Frazer managed to persuade him we need to look into the possible scenario that FBI agents from the NYFO have been deliberately targeted and their deaths staged to look like accidents. Now the director wants WFO to expand the task force into Tuesday's shooting into a task force that investigates all these deaths to see if there's a link. They are assigning bodyguards to anyone who worked on that squad during that time period, including you. Did you have anything to do with this?"

"I discussed a few things with Lincoln Frazer yesterday afternoon."

"When you were supposed to be resting?" Savage had a reputation for no bullshit, brutal honesty. When negotiating, he was absolutely unflappable, but the rest of the time he was fiery and unpredictable. It kept everyone on their toes.

"I started to think back on how many agents who I'd worked with had died recently. I couldn't rest until I spoke to someone who might recognize a pattern."

"And who better than the head of BAU-4?" Savage said snidely.

BAU-4 was the behavioral analysis unit that dealt with crimes against adults.

"Can you think of anyone from the cases you worked on back then who might hate the FBI this much?" Savage asked.

The idea someone wanted him dead was unsettling. Sure, plenty of bad guys he'd put away had threatened him with violence when he'd arrested them, but they generally didn't take it personally. They were the ones breaking the law and—as long as they weren't narcissists—they understood they got what they deserved. "Anyone who hates the FBI that much is either still serving time or dead."

He'd checked the most obvious, high-profile villains last night. Lincoln's team were checking the rest while the task force got organized.

"They could have hired someone or possibly have a family member who felt wronged," Savaged mused.

Dominic grunted. If he knew who it might be, he'd have said already.

"And here's me thinking you were the charmer of the group," Savage grumbled after a few moments.

"Apparently someone missed the memo." And the killer wasn't the only one. Dominic thought of Ava Kanas. She'd barely spoken to him since breakfast when he'd informed her they might have to attend his father's engagement party in DC next week if this situation wasn't resolved.

She'd asked what to wear, and he'd told her a dress, and

she'd been pissed ever since. Showing up in body armor was bad form.

He didn't think anyone would make an attempt on his life at this thing because security would be tight if POTUS was expected to attend. He and Kanas could use the trip to glean more information out of the case agents. Visit the WFO and the task force before the party. They didn't have to stay long. A quick in and out was always the best way to attend these things, especially if his family were involved.

He snapped back to whatever Savage was saying. "They've had at least two opportunities to kill you, and yet they haven't. Why?"

"Maybe I'm just lucky?" said Dominic evenly.

"Maybe they want to torture you before they kill you," Savage suggested.

Dominic laughed. "There's a cheery thought."

Savage was right though. He'd been a potential target at the funeral, and GHB wasn't the only thing someone could slip into a drink—assuming that was the same UNSUB and not the drug dealers. Whoever wanted to kill him had had several opportunities.

Dominic scrubbed his good hand over his face, trying to erase the image of Calvin's bright red blood on his white cotton shirt. The image flashed into his mind, and he was horrified all over again. Furious. Devastated. He was so tired, the sling he was forced to wear was cumbersome and restrictive, and his whole body throbbed with low grade pain, but he wasn't going to whine. Unlike Van and Calvin and the others, he was alive.

"Ballistics confirmed that the bullet casing found on the rooftop was the same caliber and composition and probable make as the one that killed Calvin Mortimer," Savage said.

"That's hardly helpful," Dominic said derisively.

The Unit Chief shrugged. "It's as much as we have to go on right now. Slug that came out of Mortimer was virtually destroyed, and they can't get ballistic markings off it, nor any of the others."

But if they found the shooter and the gun, they could match the brass casing, which might make it possible to get a conviction. The shooter had cleared up most of the brass which suggested the one left behind had been a mistake.

"Any update on eye witnesses or surveillance footage in the area of the apartment complex?" Dominic asked.

Savage shook his head. "I spoke to Mark Gross from WFO who said that they'd canvassed every residence in a square mile block, reviewed all the images taken in the area but there are no cameras that cover the front of that building. They are running plates from any vehicles caught on camera or registered in the local parking meters but no red flags so far."

"Someone did their research beforehand."

"We're lucky he was a lousy shot."

That was true, Dominic realized. The shooter had only hit Calvin, who'd presented a non-moving target. It suggested the shooter wasn't military or particularly skilled. As soon as people had started to scatter the shooter hadn't hit anyone. Closest they'd come was to nailing Ava with that shard of shattered wood.

Dominic pressed his lips together. She'd come close to death that day and had still gone head-to-head with the top man in the FBI an hour later. If he could teach her how to talk to her superiors with tact then there'd be no stopping her in the Bureau. In ten years, she'd be running her own field office.

"So, we've basically got no progress on finding Calvin's killer?" Dominic said.

"Basically."

"The shoe prints I found outside Van's window were a size seven." Pretty small. Could have been a kid being nosey. "They are running DNA."

"Which will take a few days," said Savage leaning back in his chair. "I hear we have a new member of the team." He smiled without it touching his eyes and stared out into the bullpen where Ava had set herself up to work. She was still trawling through cases from the NYFO, looking for something that screamed blood-thirsty vengeance.

"Lincoln Frazer suggested using Kanas to watch my back."

"I'd prefer a team from HRT." Savage's black gaze was unwavering.

"She's a good agent." Dominic held his stare. "I am not wasting the time of an entire detail of folks from the Hostage Rescue Team."

"That is part of HRT's remit. Guarding FBI members and their families." Savage's expression was stern. "And you know it."

"I'm not having a security detail," Dominic spoke loudly. He liked and respected his Unit Chief but he wasn't backing down on this.

"And here's me thinking I was the boss." Savage was testing him.

"We want to draw the UNSUB out. We won't do that if I'm surrounded by men with MP-5s. They'll just go to ground until we drop our guard."

"You think Ava Kanas is up to the job of keeping you safe?"

"I've seen her in action. She's a good agent." Dominic shrugged. No one was taking a bullet for him anyway.

Savage exhaled loudly. "Just don't go anywhere alone, not even a public restroom."

"I don't usually hang out in public toilets so it shouldn't be a problem." Dominic checked his watch, eager to escape his boss's office and return to some semblance of normality. "I need to head back to work, unless there's anything else…"

Savage glanced at his computer monitor and swore.

"What is it?" asked Dominic, getting that tingle between his shoulder blades that said something big was about to happen.

"Prison siege in New York State."

"Send me—"

"No."

"But—"

"No," Savage said, exasperated. "You're grounded until we catch this killer."

"What the hell? You think this shooter is stupid enough to follow me into a siege area that probably has more SWAT and security than anywhere outside a war zone? That's the safest spot I could be. Come on…" Dominic raised his good hand in the air.

"They were stupid enough to murder an FBI agent at an FBI agent's funeral." Savage mirrored his pose. "I'm sending Charlotte and Eban. HRT have been assigned too. I'm sure they can handle it."

"You're gonna need more negotiators there than that," Dominic stated softly.

"You're a liability."

Dominic climbed to his feet. "Someone attacks me and I'm forced out of my job? I'm supposed to sit here arranging teaching timetables for training classes?"

"Someone has to do it. Why not you?" Savage gave him a look.

Dominic's lips curved into a confident smile. "Because I'm one of your most experienced negotiators?"

"And?"

"And…my skills are better off being used in the field than being squandered in the office."

"I'm not seeing it." Savage deadpanned.

"If you were captured by terrorists who'd you want on the other end of the line?" Dominic was not going to sit here twiddling his thumbs because of some asshole.

"I'd prefer a team of negotiators over any one individual negotiator."

"Well, obviously." They always worked in teams. "But if some bad guy started chopping off your extremities, it's me you'd want talking the guy down, right?" Dominic grinned when Savage crossed his legs.

"You had to go there." Savage's lips twitched.

"That's right," Dominic said.

"With my luck you'd dare my kidnapper to kill me just to get my job," Savage grumbled.

"I didn't think of that." Dominic placed his palm on Savage's desk. He knew he had him.

"I guess you're probably safer up there than here. It wouldn't surprise me if the UNSUB pays your house a visit trying to get to you."

"I have great security. I'll know if someone tries to break in."

Savage followed him out of his office. "Don't forget your bodyguard." His voice dripped with sarcasm.

"Grab your flak jacket, Agent Kanas," Dominic shouted.

She sat at a desk apparently trying to vanish into the office carpet. Chances of Ava becoming invisible were next to zero.

"What's going on?" She climbed to her feet looking uncertain.

A ribbon of excitement shot through him as it did every time something big started to go down. "We're going on a field trip."

MALLORY PUT A hand to support the bottom of her baby bump as she made her ungainly and inelegant way down the west bank of the Rappahannock River. It didn't help that she couldn't see where to place her feet.

Sweat trickled down her back and soaked into the waistband of her maternity, black dress pants. She looked like the side of a mountain.

The ground was dried, cracked mud, and the river was low thanks to a long, hot summer and the distinct lack of rain. Birds sang in the trees and squirrels chattered angrily at the police invasion.

An hour ago, she'd got a call from a local police chief about the missing Mule & Pitcher waitress she'd been trying to track down. Because of the nature of the investigation—both the drug angle and the murders—Mallory had put out a BOLO when it turned out no one had seen the woman since the FBI had busted the guys at the bar for drug smuggling. Mallory had figured she was involved in the drug operation, but it was also possible the DEA had whisked her away into protective custody as a witness for their case.

"You okay there?" A police officer in a dark blue uniform

held his hand out to assist as she clambered over a decaying tree trunk.

She gripped his hand and awkwardly followed him to the water's edge.

"A couple of anglers found her. They were hoping for smallmouth bass, got a whole lot more than they bargained for." The glint of dark humor in the officer's eyes made her release a small laugh. This she was used to. This was her world.

The baby kicked under her ribs, trampling her lungs as he-or-she squirmed, reminding her that her world was about to change. For a long time, the baby hadn't seemed real, but now it was a fully formed human being, and she was already fiercely overprotective of the little bean.

The idea of being a mother was also terrifying. She knew better than most the dangers that existed in this vast and beautiful country. She knew her faults. She hoped she did a good job and didn't screw the kid up too badly.

She followed the officer along a narrow pathway probably made by deer or anglers. It was the sort of place she liked to bring her rescued Golden Retriever, Rex, for a long, tranquil walk—minus the dead body, of course.

Up ahead she saw a small group of people gathered around something milky pale. She signed a logbook and leaned against a tree as an officer helped her slip paper booties over her shoes.

The fact she couldn't bend in the middle was proving to be more of a hardship than she'd anticipated.

"Less than three weeks," she muttered. She wasn't ready for motherhood, but had realized over the last few months that she'd never be fully prepared, and that was okay. She had Alex and between the two of them they would figure it out. She was concentrating on preparing for the birth, which at least she could plan and have some control over.

Mallory walked on, feeling all eyes on her. She recognized the ME from other cases and nodded to him.

"You were looking for this woman?" the man asked.

Mallory drew closer and stared down at the naked and battered form of a young, adult female. Mallory had been shown a driver's license photograph of the waitress, but the face was so puffy it was hard to tell if this was the same person.

"You ran prints?"

The cop next to the ME nodded. "Came back as Caroline Perry. Grad student at Mary Washington." The waitress at the Mule & Pitcher.

Mallory nodded. "Any idea as to the cause of death?"

The ME raised experienced eyes up to meet hers. "It's a little early for a determination."

"Did she die before or after she was in the water?" Mallory asked. Getting a scientist to make a definitive statement required pliers and fingernails.

"Again, it's hard to say."

Mallory eyed the cuts and lacerations all over the body. "Looks like she was beaten…"

The ME frowned. "Again—"

"It's hard to say." Mallory finished for him.

"It's pretty rocky upstream of here and with the low water it's a rough ride along the river. There's no bruising so there's a chance the skin damage is postmortem rather than antemortem."

Mallory pinched her lips. "Any idea how long she was in there?"

"Not long," the ME surprised her by saying. "Given the relatively warm water, decomposition and animal predation would have been much more advanced and extreme if she'd been in the river for a full day even. I suspect she's only been in the river since sometime last night."

No one had seen the woman since she'd driven away from work on Tuesday night, but it was apparent she hadn't gone home, and her car hadn't been found. Where'd she been? When had she died?

"Any evidence of sexual assault?" The woman was naked. Had she been assaulted or gone skinny dipping and drowned?

The ME pulled a non-committal face.

"Anything else you can tell me?"

He frowned as he examined the body. "No obvious evidence of manual strangulation, gunshots, or deep stab wounds. No loss of limbs or decapitation."

"That's why they pay you the big bucks," one of the cops joked.

Mallory felt the baby give a big push against her diaphragm with both feet. She rested her hand just beneath her rib and sucked in a breath. He-or-she better not twist around again. She didn't want to deal with a breech birth. That was not in her plan.

"How come the BAU are involved?" the ME asked.

The interest in the gazes of the other men sharpened.

"We have a serial killer around here?" the ME asked.

As tempting as it was to tell him it was too early to tell, she didn't want to bait the man.

"I don't believe we have a sexual sadist on the loose, but we're looking into some other incidents in other states that might be linked."

"How is she involved?" A cop nodded at the body on the banks of the river.

Empathy for the dead woman washed over Mallory. She'd

said goodbye to her sister when she'd finally buried her, but every corpse, every victim made the old feelings well up like blood in a fresh wound.

She met the ME's gaze. "We're not sure how she connects except she worked at the Mule & Pitcher. We wanted to question her about the events of Tuesday night."

From the looks on the men's faces they were all putting that together with the widely reported drug bust and the drugging of a Federal Agent that had led to a nasty car wreck. If Sheridan and Kanas were right about someone targeting FBI agents this whole thing would explode into a media sensation. Mal hoped they'd solve the puzzle before it became public knowledge. She didn't want the killer feeding off that kind of buzz. They might never stop.

She handed over her card to the ME and to each of the local cops. "Please call me if you find out anything else."

She turned and trudged back the way she'd come, reversing the process of logging out of the scene and removing her paper booties. The officer who'd escorted her helped her climb up the steeper sections of the bank. If she got stuck, she'd need a mechanical winch to get her out.

She left him at the top of the bank, thanked him and got into her Bucar which was currently a RAV4. Called Frazer. "Waitress is dead. I'm meeting the police sketch artist at Karl Feldman's in forty minutes."

"Either she killed herself because she drugged Dominic and knew she was going to go to prison, or someone killed her so she couldn't reveal anything," said Frazer.

"Dead women tell no tales," Mallory agreed.

"And revenge is a dish best served cold." Frazer was grimly amused. "We need to figure this out before the UNSUB kills again."

CHAPTER FIFTEEN

Ava boarded a C-17 military transport with a bunch of pumped up macho-types from HRT and enough equipment to start a war or, hopefully, end a siege. She hated flying but had decided not to mention the fact to Sheridan in case he decided to leave her behind.

According to the short briefing they'd been given, two rival gangs had started a fight in a cafeteria in a medium security Federal Correctional Institute. Another group of three inmates had taken advantage of the guards' distraction to barricade themselves inside the prison kitchen with four hostages, one of whom happened to be the warden.

A pulse of excitement ran through the assembled agents shimmering like a heat haze. She could only imagine the sort of training these men undertook and how good it must feel to put that training into action.

Her equipment was her creds, her Glock-22, her backup, a large go-bag and a laptop. She followed Dominic and strapped into an uncomfortable-looking seat beside him. He hadn't said much to her on the drive up.

Everyone was tense, except the female negotiator who Ava had handed Dominic's dog off to yesterday morning. That seemed like a million years ago. Ranger was now staying with a neighbor of Dominic's who kept horses. The third negotiator accompanying them, Eban Winters, was quiet and laid back. In general, the negotiators seemed a lot more chilled than their tactical counterparts, except for the head of the unit. Quentin Savage was pretty intense, like an angry John Wick looking for revenge over his dead puppy.

A massive guy with shoulders so broad they took up more than the space provided sat next to her. He looked past her and gave Dominic a nod, his gaze traveling over her speculatively on their way back to front and center.

"I recognize you from somewhere." The guy spoke out of the side of his mouth.

Ava shrugged. "I have one of those faces."

The guy shook his head slowly. "That's *not* it."

Ava was aware of Dominic stiffening on her other side.

"You a negotiator?" he asked.

She felt like she was in a spaghetti western. CNU had decided to call her a trainee negotiator to mask the threat to Dominic's life and keep a lid on news of this possible serial killer hunting Feds. They did not want to give anyone ideas. "That's right."

The man grunted and turned his attention to Charlotte Blood who was doing a meet and greet with most of the HRT team.

Ava turned to face Dominic and found him looking at her from just inches away. The pilot started the engines and even though Ava opened her mouth to say something, the noise from the engines meant it was impossible to be heard. She closed her mouth and couldn't help notice the way Dominic's gaze settled on her lips briefly before moving away. Maybe she wasn't imagining the attraction that made her aware of every time he moved, every time he spoke. She remembered the feeling from high school along with the accompanying acute embarrassment when someone figured it out.

No way was she letting Sheridan or his pals figure it out.

Charlotte walked past on the way to her seat and gave her a reserved smile and squeezed Dominic's arm which made the HRT guy on her right tense.

Interesting. Did the HRT guy know the female negotiator or did he *want* to? She had a feeling it was the latter and couldn't help a smirk.

After an hour on the transport, the smirk was gone. A storm front had made the ride rocky, her butt was sore, and her head ached from the roar of the engine. She white-knuckled the webbing on the seat as they came in for landing and exhaled a happy sigh when they taxied to a military hangar where they could unpack the Hostage Rescue Team in relative secrecy.

"Scared of flying?" Dominic asked her when they were finally able to talk again.

"Scared of crashing," she corrected.

They exited the aircraft and left HRT to sort out their equipment. An agent from the Buffalo Field Office picked them up and took them straight to the prison, a low gray affair with more razor wire than no-man's land.

Half a mile from the main building, an outer perimeter had been established to prevent the press or public getting too close and to prevent any enterprising inmate from taking advantage of the situation to stage an escape.

The negotiators arrived at the main door and hurried inside the building to be greeted by another agent from Buffalo.

"Who is talking to the hostage-takers right now?" Dominic

asked. He'd been furiously writing notes on the journey up.

"We have a Bureau of Prisons trained negotiator on the line."

"Good. Are they talking? Making a list of demands?" asked Dominic.

Ava had to walk fast to keep up with them all. Dominic seemed to have forgotten his injuries and had ditched his sling despite doctor's orders. Charlotte Blood and Eban Winters followed close behind. Ava felt like a bit of a fraud pretending to be one of them, but she knew how to stay out of the way.

"They have a *long* list of demands but..."

"But what?"

Ava recognized the blistering authority in Dominic's voice.

"Each of the hostage-takers has a different list of demands."

"*Great.* Who's the leader?"

"Two of them are vying for top spot. A former drug dealer out of Albany, Frank Jacobs, who swears he's born again, and an old mobster hitman called Gino Gerbachi, AKA Gino-the-snake."

Ava stumbled, and Dominic caught her by the arm before she fell flat on her face. Gino Gerbachi couldn't be here. He was in Otisville, Orange County...

"You okay?" Dominic asked.

"Yeah. Sorry. Thanks. Tripped." Her heart pounded as if someone had plugged her into an electrical socket. She forced herself to step away from Dominic's support.

Did she tell him she had a connection to this guy or not?

"The third guy is a convicted serial killer."

"Who?" Dominic asked.

"Milo Andris."

Dominic scowled. Ava wondered what the man had done. "We have any visuals on them inside the kitchen?"

"We have cameras and audio in there that they seem unaware of at this time."

"Any women in there?" Dominic asked.

"The warden is female."

A shiver ran over Ava's shoulders at Dominic's closed expression.

"What weapons do they have?" Dominic fired questions at the man.

"Kitchen knives and other implements. I expect they all have at least one homemade shiv on their person."

Ava didn't want to interrupt this exchange. Lives were at risk. If Ava told Dominic about her connection to "Gino-the-snake" he'd remove her from the prison, and if he removed her she couldn't act as his bodyguard. And if she wasn't his bodyguard then she was pretty sure she'd be back on suspension until Aldrich figured out a way to get rid of her.

She rubbed the Mati bracelet on her wrist. It was supposed to protect from the evil eye. It might only be an old superstition but she wasn't above a quick prayer.

It wasn't like she'd have to deal with the inmates. She'd stay in the background. Strictly anonymous. Gerbachi wouldn't even recognize her if he saw her. Her name was different now, and Kanas was common enough in Greek communities as to make tracking her mother and siblings difficult. She could work on leads from the murders while Sheridan did his thing, sleep when he slept. These separate worlds did not need to collide.

She set her teeth against one another. All the times Dominic had accused her of not being able to work as part of a team came back to her. But it wasn't just her secret she was protecting. It was her mother and siblings and niece and nephew. This wasn't the sort of secret you shared, it was the kind you buried.

But she would tell him.

Eventually.

Just not in front of all these people.

"Where's the Incident Commander?" Dominic asked as they strode along past multiple locked doors and crowds of uniformed cops and correctional officers.

The local agent opened a side door. "Right in here."

She followed behind Dominic. Eban and Charlotte were right behind her. The idea of anyone getting to Dominic in here seemed crazy but until they figured out who the baddy was, Ava wasn't going to relax her guard. Maybe it was a fellow agent with a hidden agenda? She eyed the other two negotiators and Eban met her gaze quizzically.

She looked away.

The room they'd entered was attached to another room which they could see inside of courtesy of a glass wall. A group of four men sat at a table all wearing headsets but only one guy wearing a mike. The others were scribbling notes.

There was a large notice board on the wall with lists of instructions.

Dominic shook hands with a large man wearing a brown suit just inside the door who introduced himself as Special Agent in Charge of the Buffalo office, Derek Hamner. The Incident Commander.

Dominic looked around after the introductions were made. "Is there a room farther away from the action we can use?"

The Incident Commander appeared to bristle.

"It's generally a good idea to keep the negotiators isolated and separate so we aren't distracted by everything else going on and don't inadvertently communicate anything to the hostage-takers about what the tactical team is doing. I mean we need to know what is going on, but it's better if we aren't part of that energy—we don't want to communicate it to the hostage-takers."

The IC relaxed. "There's a couple of trailers in the parking lot just around the corner from the front door."

"We'll need comms set up there, along with any video feeds."

The Incident Commander nodded. "It'll be ready in an hour."

"And if we can have accommodation in the same area? That way we will always be close to the action if needed?"

"There are two cabins there. One has a kitchenette, shower and bathroom facilities. We can throw in some mattresses, and you can rotate your people on shifts."

"Just make sure the mattresses are unused. No offense," Charlotte piped up with a smile that made the IC smile back in return.

Ava was surprised by the request and grateful. The woman seemed to charm everyone she met, but her attitude toward Ava had cooled considerably. Ava had no idea why.

"I'll arrange it." The IC puffed out his chest. "HRT will be billeted in an old aircraft hangar nearer the airport."

The negotiators exchanged cell numbers with the Incident Commander.

Sheridan said, "If we could meet up with the Tactical

Team Commander at eighteen hundred hours, we can discuss best options to proceed. In the meantime, I want to listen to the negotiator in there and see what the risk assessment is."

The IC nodded. "I'll send someone to fetch you at six."

When he left, Dominic knocked on the glass and waited until someone let them inside. He held her gaze and pressed his finger to his lips before they entered. She understood. No talking.

She braced herself as she entered, knowing she was going to see and hear the voice of the man who'd murdered her father in cold blood and who'd smashed her across the face with a pistol before leaving her for dead.

She squeezed behind Dominic and found a chair in the corner of the room with a small desk. She sat down and drew in a long breath and settled herself. She'd faced the bastard in court, she could do this. But probably best if Gino Gerbachi didn't know she was here—considering she was the reason he was serving consecutive life sentences and would die in prison.

DOMINIC CHECKED HIS email as he listened to Joe Booker and saw that Mallory Rooney had written to him. He didn't read it, just forwarded it to Kanas. He couldn't afford to get distracted.

Joe—the Bureau of Prisons' negotiator—was doing a great job, slowing everything down, telling the hostage-takers that "nobody wanted to hurt them" and asking "how can I help you?" over and over again.

Time was a negotiator's friend.

Dominic watched on the TV screen as the hostage-takers paced the large kitchen area. Frank Jacobs and Gino Gerbachi took it in turns to rant their demands into the speaker phone but so far, Milo Andris hadn't talked to them at all.

The four hostages had their hands bound behind their backs and sat on the floor beside the double-locked, heavy duty door that formed the rear exit of the kitchen. The rear exit led through a corridor to an exercise yard. There was the warden, a prison guard, a cook from a private company, and another inmate who clearly wanted nothing to do with this situation.

The trouble with prisons from a siege perspective was they were so secure it was hard to do a full-on tactical assault without a lot of people dying in the time it took for the security forces to gain access. No one wanted that to happen, but should the hostage-takers start hurting people then the authorities would have no choice except to act.

Dominic wondered what the Black Swans of this situation were—the unknown unknowns. Information so far outside expectations that no one even imagined they existed. Black Swans could give the negotiators the leverage they needed to end this thing, or it might cause the situation to blow up in their faces. The whole point was they couldn't know what these Black Swans were until they were revealed and that was why the FBI had people digging into every aspect of the hostage-takers' and hostages' lives.

Dominic wrote a note to Joe. "Ask Gino to put Milo on the phone. We want to know what his demands are."

"Hey, Milo, get your freak-ass over here," Gino yelled after Joe relayed the message.

Joe held the headphones from his ear for a moment. Gino was an old-style, bullish mobster who used bullying and intimidation techniques to try to get his own way.

Milo ignored the guy and continued sharpening a kitchen blade on a wet stone. Every dull scrape of that blade was like a chalk drawn down a dry board and made Dominic's teeth fuse.

Why Milo was sharpening that knife was anyone's guess, but Dominic didn't like it. Each of the hostage-takers carried a weapon and he noticed neither Frank nor Gino ever turned their backs on Milo.

"He doesn't want to talk," Gino said finally, moving closer to the speaker phone and talking loudly. "When do we get our helicopter?"

"Gino, I can't even begin arranging for a chopper until I have assurances from all three of you that the hostages aren't going to be hurt."

Dominic watched Gino face Milo again.

The man pulled an ugly face that bunched up his mustache. "Milo promises not to hurt anyone as long as you get us what we want."

A helicopter with enough fuel to get them to Canada.

Apparently Canadian authorities welcomed escaped felons much more readily than the US. Someone better inform the RCMP.

Joe looked at him, and Dominic circled his finger.

"Can you get Milo on the phone to confirm that for me, Gino? I need to hear it from him," Joe persisted.

"He doesn't want to talk to you motherfuckers!" Gino screamed into the phone.

Joe didn't react. "Gino, we just want to make sure everyone gets out safely and unharmed. Tell me what I can do for you right now to make you more comfortable."

Dominic nodded his approval. Joe was good.

The problem was a lot of the usual tactics didn't work with

inmates in these sorts of desperate situations. These types of prisoners had very little to lose.

Negotiators were stalling for time, waiting for the tactical team to come up with a viable assault strategy and to practice it enough to be able to pull it off blindfolded. Alternatively, they'd settle in for the long haul. Talk them down for weeks until the prisoners gave up all hope of freedom and surrendered.

Obviously, the helicopter was never going to happen unless they used it as bait to get these fellas out into the open.

Milo's constant knife sharpening made Dominic anxious for the safety of everyone in that kitchen. The man had raped, murdered, and dismembered six people in rapid succession ten years ago showing little or no remorse when he'd been caught. Since being incarcerated he'd been a model prisoner, but who knew what cravings lurked in the mind of this sort of sadistic killer? Dominic was waiting on psych reports.

Video of how the situation had unfolded suggested the three men hadn't planned the event beforehand. Gino and Frank had exchanged a look when the rival gangs started fighting and headed into the kitchen. Milo seemed to simply tag along.

The talk continued, but that was good news. As long as hostage-takers were talking, they weren't hurting hostages.

Dominic rolled his sore shoulder. Although his body still hurt, and his face looked like he'd taken a beating, he was getting better.

A tap on the glass had him looking up. Charlotte. Dominic checked his watch. Midnight already. It was time to rotate shifts. He muted the mic and told Joe to tell the hostage-takers he was going off shift in a few minutes but that other people were going to be here if they had anything at all they needed to make them more comfortable.

Dominic glanced at Ava who was staring at the TV screen with a look of intense concentration. She'd spent the last few hours poring over documents in the corner of the room. He wondered if she'd come up with any suspects for the serial killer stalking FBI agents, or if Rooney had got anything out of the waitress.

Ava caught him looking at her. Dark shadows painted the hollows beneath her eyes. He wondered if she was hungry. Neither of them had eaten since breakfast.

"Time to go," he mouthed.

She nodded and began quietly gathering her stuff together. Technically she didn't have to be here but at least this way he could keep an eye on her the way Van would have wanted him to, and she could work the case without getting into any more trouble. Plus, if she helped figure out who the killer was, she could get back into the Bureau's good books.

They stepped into the adjoining room to update Charlotte and Eban on the situation before they started their shift. Despite the initial promises from the Incident Commander they were still in the main prison building. The guy said maybe tomorrow, but Dominic knew better than to hold his breath or get hung up on stuff he couldn't control. That way lay lunacy.

"We've set up two beds with a makeshift curtain between them for some privacy." Charlotte told him. "Took the plastic off the mattresses ourselves. I persuaded one of the local agents to drive me to Walmart and picked up some cheap bedding. Who knows how long we'll be here. Eban and I also ordered Chinese food and left some for you guys in the fridge there."

"Appreciate it, Char." Dominic edged her and Eban over to one side of the room to talk privately. "It's quiet in there right now. Joe is doing a great job calming them down and beginning to win their trust. I'm trying to get Milo on the phone, but he doesn't want to talk and doesn't seem to have any demands. I think the other two had considered this breakout plan in the past and they are as surprised as anyone to have ended up with Milo for company."

Which made for a volatile situation. Milo was a serial murderer and there was no telling what he might do. "Have someone in the room assigned to watching Milo at all times. I'll talk to the IC before I grab some food and sleep."

"Think they'd want to talk to a woman?" Charlotte asked.

Dominic pressed his lips together, considering. "I think at this stage Eban should try to keep the continuity Joe had going. Keep reassuring them we want to help them, want a peaceful resolution and don't want anyone to get hurt. They keep asking for a chopper. See if you can get Milo to agree not to hurt anyone and then we can start to talk about a chopper."

"Might be the best way of getting them out of there," Charlotte agreed.

"But not until we have Milo saying he won't hurt the hostages," Dominic emphasized.

"Got it, Dom," Eban assured him. "You two go get some rest."

Dominic let out a long breath. He was so keyed up but knew that he needed rest to stay sharp. "I'll see you at eight."

He stopped briefly to talk to the tactical commander in the hallway. HRT had a team in place should they need to move fast, another team resting and a third team practicing an assault.

The hostage-takers had stored water in containers and had enough food to last for weeks in those big refrigerators. Dominic had a horrible feeling that these prisoners had so little to lose—especially Milo—that the tactical response might be the only way to end this thing.

He hoped not. The chances of hostages dying in those circumstances increased greatly.

Finally, he headed outside the prison building to the trailer. Tension buzzed through the air from the huge numbers of heavily armed personnel milling around, having low, murmured conversations.

He ignored the curious looks and walked around the corner to where the trailer was situated. He opened the door, relieved it appeared clean, had a working air conditioner, and small kitchenette. Compared to some places he'd stayed in over the years this was a palace.

"Rooney identified a body pulled out of the Rappahannock this morning as that of the waitress from the Mule & Pitcher." Ava pulled the door shut behind her and dumped her bags on the bench seat.

He stopped and turned, immediately too close to the woman in this enclosed space. He hadn't thought about the fact they'd be stuck in here together. Alone. Hadn't had to time to think about anything except getting those hostages to safety.

He was sweaty and dirty, and his body ached from the car accident, but mostly he was starving and determined not to be attracted to Kanas. He grabbed the cartons of Chinese food out of the fridge and threw them all in the microwave. "What else?"

He found two beers in the fridge and popped the lids off

both and handed her one. For once she didn't argue with him about drinking it.

"Caroline Perry's shoe size is comparable to those we found outside Van's window. A man's seven or woman's size nine."

"They run Perry's DNA next to any found at any of the other scenes?"

"It's being done but the lab is backed up."

He scratched his forehead and caught sight of his black eyes in the microwave door. "The lab is always backed up. How'd the waitress die?"

"ME hasn't said yet."

"Any sign of a gun at her place?"

Ava shook her head. "Mallory was going to visit Karl Feldman with the sketch artist this afternoon. I assume we'll get a sketch in the morning." She sounded dubious.

"Except…" he encouraged.

"Except if he was in cahoots with the waitress, he's hardly likely to admit it so we'll have no idea if the image is real or an attempt to throw us off the scent."

"I assume someone is retracing Caroline Perry's steps to see where she was during Van's funeral, and at other key times when agents died?"

Ava nodded. "Rooney said they were also tracing her background to see if there were any connections to any of the NYFO cases you guys worked."

"All the other agents who worked in the squad have protection?"

Ava undid the band that kept her hair tied up and ran her fingers through the long tresses as they fell around her shoulders. He tried not to watch.

"Bunting and his wife went to a safe house. Gil Reiz in San Antonio has an agent assigned with him at all times to act as backup. Fernando Chavez has a team assigned to him and his family."

Dominic wondered if Reiz's bodyguard was half as attractive as Ava Kanas. He tried to push the thought away. The fact that he was even thinking it made him feel like a lecherous, old goat. And even though the age difference was less than a decade, his superior rank made the situation ethically wrong. He didn't want to take advantage of anyone and could only imagine how bad a relationship between the two of them would look on paper.

Relationship?

Shit!

Desire was not a basis for anything except sex. He did not do relationships in general, and he definitely didn't do them with fellow agents. He had to stop thinking of Ava as anything except a colleague.

He grabbed disposable chopsticks and divided the food equally onto plates. Then he started shoveling food into his mouth like a starving man.

Ava ate more delicately. He just needed enough fuel to get him into the shower and then collapse into bed for a few hours' sleep and hope no one interrupted him in the meantime.

"Alex Parker get anything from the DEA?" he said between bites of Kung Pao chicken.

"He said the DEA isn't storing the surveillance online. Lincoln Frazer put in a formal request to see the footage. Parker had better luck with the camera on the ATM across the street but he said the footage was grainy as hell."

She paused, and he could tell she was thinking something through.

"It seems likely our waitress roofied your water after she found out we were agents—otherwise why is she dead?"

"Maybe the drug dealers saw her talking to us and thought she was snitching on them," Dominic suggested.

"I guess." Compliant and agreeable, Ava was obviously tired.

He polished off his food and restrained himself from licking the plate. Ava put her food down, half eaten. He eyed it. "Are you finished? Can I have that?"

She gave him a smile. "You gave me cave man portions so sure. I'm going to grab a shower and pass out."

"Don't use all the hot water. I'm next."

She nodded and hit the minuscule bathroom while he finished his beer and her food, and forced his mind away from the knowledge a wet, naked Ava was standing just a few feet away.

He thought about the siege. Milo was the unknown factor in this dynamic. The guy could start killing the others as soon as his knives were sharpened to his satisfaction. Dominic had requested all the files from Milo's prosecution. The prison psychiatrist had prescribed medication to help control his paranoid fantasies and they claimed the results had been extremely effective, but Milo wasn't getting his meds while they were barricaded inside that kitchen. Who the hell knew what that would do to his mental state.

The door to the bathroom opened a crack. Ava poked her head out, fingers curled tight around the door.

"Sorry. Could you pass me a towel, please?"

Dominic started. So much for getting his overactive imagination under control. Her wet hair was dripping water onto the floor and her naked shoulder taunted him like a fourteen-year-old boy.

"Of course." He went over to Ava's bag and pulled out a towel. He grabbed his while he was at it, and fresh boxers and a t-shirt to sleep in.

He held the towel out so she could take it. "Here you go."

She let go of the door to grab the towel, but the damn thing started to swing open. Dominic stuck his foot to stop it.

God. Even the idea of seeing her naked was stirring his blood. Dammit. "If you're finished in there, how about you get dried and dressed out here while I grab a shower?"

"Good idea. Just give me a second." She came out wrapped in a towel that hit mid-thigh. Her shoulders were bare. Perfect collarbones emphasized a long, slender neck and pointed chin. She was brushing her wet hair completely unaware that she looked absolutely stunning. "It's all yours."

If only.

Dominic hated himself for being turned on by this woman, this rookie agent. But there was nothing he could do about it right now except *not* get involved. They were stuck with each other.

He went inside the tiny bathroom, stripped off and turned on the cold water before stepping under the freezing spray. Anything to get his body under control and his blood cooled.

CHAPTER SIXTEEN

AVA WOKE IN the middle of the night disorientated and confused as to where she was and why she was sleeping on the floor. Slowly her night vision made out the slivers of light coming through cheap venetian blinds. Muted sounds of police radios crackled in the distance.

She was in the trailer near the prison just outside Buffalo. She rolled over and tried to get comfortable, but no matter what, she was wide awake.

Yesterday had been traumatic, but she'd got through it without Sheridan suspecting anything was amiss. Hearing Gino-the-snake's voice had whipped her back to the night her father died. The long, tedious months of living in safe houses with a team of US Deputy Marshals protecting them from threats of intimidation and death before she'd been called to testify against the man.

Gino had shot her father and then smashed the same gun into her face and kicked her as she lay unconscious on the floor, left for dead. They were to be examples in the tough Greek community as to what happened if you didn't pay "protection" money. Her mother had found her alive and called the FBI rather than the cops because she had a cousin who had a cousin who worked for the FBI in New York. That cousin of a cousin had turned out to be a man named Vangelis

Stamos—who'd had a profound effect on Ava's life from the day they met.

Van was the man who'd persuaded her terrified mother that the only way they'd get justice for her husband was by pretending little Emmeleia Stophodopolis was dead—until she turned up and testified in court. Emmeleia had her own white coffin and her name was engraved on her father's tombstone. Van had talked her mom into changing their identities and entering the witness protection program. Considering it meant leaving behind her entire life, this was not a minor undertaking.

Ava's mother was her hero. She'd sacrificed so much to keep her kids safe while still standing up to the bad guys.

Van had helped them when they'd moved. He'd suggested a small town just outside Portland, Oregon, where many of his relatives lived. The tight Greek community had helped hide them and also supported them by giving her mother a job and a place to live.

Then the court case had happened. DNA and ballistics evidence, combined with photographs of Emmeleia's injuries, of her father's brutally slain body, and her unshakable eyewitness testimony had been enough to convict Gino and one of his associates. That associate, a man who'd only recently been initiated into the crime family, had rolled on the others and enabled the Feds to dismantle the entire corrupt empire as well as landing most of the players in prison for life without parole. To say Ava's real identity was unpopular with *Cosa Nostra* was an understatement. But no one knew who that girl was anymore. No one. Not even Dominic Sheridan.

Ava had joined the police force with the aim of never being powerless again. Being an FBI agent reinforced that need. She wasn't sure what she'd do if her job was taken away from her.

And now Dominic was trying to negotiate with a man who'd decided a seven-year-old girl wasn't even worth a bullet.

Did she tell Dominic the truth and risk him sending her away? The thought of losing her job made her feel physically ill. But she wanted to be braver. She wanted to trust…

Was he awake? She listened attentively for the sound of his breathing, but she couldn't hear a thing. Slightly panicked that he'd left her here alone, she caught the bottom of the makeshift curtain and raised it high enough to see the man lying on his back, features softened in sleep.

She stared, taking in the straight nose, thick brows and stubborn jaw. The bruises from the accident looked like darker shadows in this dusky twilight. His lips were parted, and she found herself wondering what it might be like to kiss him.

He rolled onto the side facing her and suddenly opened his eyes.

Ava froze, then whispered slowly, "I thought you might have left me behind…" She tried to swallow her mortification at being caught staring at him. The words revealed more than she wanted.

He reached out and touched her cheek, which was more or less healed now. "Still here, Kanas. Go back to sleep. It's four AM."

Her heart pounded crazily as she held his gaze. She should tell him about Gino. Confide the truth. He'd understand and wouldn't send her away. His palm was so hot against her skin it burned. She wanted to get closer to that heat. The craving was so overwhelming it terrified her, paralyzed her.

He removed his hand with a slight smile that she could get

used to and sleepily closed his eyes. Murmured, "Go to sleep, Ava."

She lay there staring up at the ceiling, until dawn flooded the room with light. She didn't sleep another wink.

WHEN DOMINIC WOKE at six, he discovered Ava had left a breakfast sandwich in the kitchenette along with a cup of coffee, which he assumed were for him. He got dressed and took his breakfast outside.

Where was she?

He found her talking to one of the HRT guys. She was dressed in another black pantsuit with the sleeves rolled up, blue, beaded bracelet adorning her wrist. Combined with the shoulder holster and long hair pinned up in a messy bun, the woman looked hot as hell.

Dominic was friendly with most of the team even if there was some residual institutionalized rivalry between these two sections of the Critical Incident Response Group (CIRG). HRT and SWAT guys were the tip of the spear when it came to the Federal Government's toolbox, but at the end of the day everyone wanted to go home. Negotiators helped end standoffs nonviolently when at all possible and after the debacles of Ruby Ridge and Waco—*thank you, ATF, for those fuck ups*—the FBI had been authorized by Congress to use peaceful means to end sieges when at all possible.

Dominic walked over and nodded to the guy and recognized the male glint of interest in the agent's eyes. The guy was hot for Kanas and probably trying to get her number.

Who wouldn't?

Dominic remembered reaching out and touching Ava's cheek in the small hours and mentally winced. The touch had settled something deep inside him. And she hadn't flinched away like she had on the roof the day of Van's funeral—he still didn't know where she'd gotten that damn scar, but he'd find out eventually. Dominic had had to clamp down on the desire to draw her close and tuck her in beside him. Who knew what would have happened then. In his imagination some scorching hot sex where they both got off multiple times. She'd probably lain on the mattress terrified all night.

"Morning." He greeted them both. "Thanks for breakfast," he said to Ava, finishing off the sandwich and crumpling the wrapper with one hand.

"Any progress with the prisoners?" the HRT agent asked him.

"I got out of bed five minutes ago so you probably know more than me." His voice came out a little sharp, which he did not need. "Ava, can I have a word?"

Her hazel eyes went wide. She thought she was in trouble. "Of course."

A small smile twisted the HRT agent's mouth, and he backed away out of earshot. He knew why Dominic was snarky. Fucker.

"So about last night—"

Her eyes went massive. "I am so sorry—"

"Why the hell are you sorry?"

"Because you must think I'm a freak to have been staring at you like that."

Dominic blinked. He hadn't even thought about it which was odd considering how rarely he slept so close to another person. "That's not it. I was going to apologize for touching your face."

"My face?" Ava touched her cheek in the same place he had last night. The graze had healed well with just a small, brown scab marking the spot.

"I realize I overstepped what is probably considered appropriate boundaries." His face heated. He hadn't been this humiliated since he'd woken up in bed with Suzanna after a drunken hookup he couldn't even remember.

Lines appeared between her brows as her forehead crinkled. "I didn't think you touching my face was inappropriate." She sounded confused by the idea. "Maybe it depends on whether or not the other person wants to be touched?" Her cheeks filled with the same amount of color as his, and she went to take a step back, but there was a wall behind her.

Compelled by the need to know, he stepped closer and lowered his voice. "And did you? Want to be touched?"

She met his gaze then, hazel eyes warm, vulnerable, tentative. "Yes."

He swallowed his shock at her honest admission and the hint she might have welcomed more. Yet it shouldn't have surprised him. Ava Kanas was unflinchingly honest.

"Look, Dominic, there's something I need to tell—"

"Sheridan!" Another member of HRT yelled at him from the corner of the prison building. "You're needed in the command center ASAP."

Dominic squeezed her arm briefly, keeping everything strictly professional to the casual observer even though his blood was pumping erratically through his veins. "Tell me later. I need to get back to the negotiation room."

Ava pushed off the wall to follow.

He gave her a quizzical glance. "You don't need to be

trapped in there all day. Work in the trailer."

"Charlotte and Eban need to rest." Her mouth turned down. "Plus, it's my job to watch your back, remember?"

Dominic's mood plummeted. She was right and had reminded him of another reason why even thinking of getting tangled up with Ava Kanas on a personal level was a terrible idea. It didn't stop him imagining the taste of her mouth the entire way into the building. Or from seeing the smooth curve of her naked shoulders. As soon as he entered the prison doors, however, he shoved distraction to one side.

Charlotte and Eban were headed towards him down the corridor. Both looked strained with exhaustion.

"Any progress?"

Eban shook his head. "We kept them talking for most of the night, but the HTs are getting more and more strained. They're tired. Milo still won't talk to us. We suggested sending his medication in via the ductwork and they went for it. No idea if Milo actually took the drugs or faked it. He might fear they're sedatives."

"Were they?" Dominic asked.

"Not this time," Eban smiled ruefully. "Figured we'd try and win a little trust first time around."

"Go get some food and sleep." Dominic checked his watch. "I'll radio you if I need you." Cell service was blocked, so they used small radios instead.

The two walked sleepily off into the sunshine, and Dominic headed down to the Command Center to find the Incident Commander.

"You better wait outside," he told Ava when they reached the door. He didn't want to draw attention to her or explain his own situation of being in danger. None of this was about him.

Inside he found the Incident Commander, SAC Hamner, talking to Kurt Montana, the tactical commander from HRT.

"Any progress?" the IC asked.

"I'm just heading back in there now. The overnight negotiators say the hostage-takers are getting tired. Hopefully we can wear them out further today."

The Incident Commander rolled his shoulders. "How long is it going to take to talk them out?"

Dominic cocked his head. "How long?" he echoed.

"Yeah. This entire facility has been on lockdown and there are hundreds of prisoners who need to be taken care of."

The prisoners were all fed and watered. The authorities had started transferring some of the lesser offenders to a minimum-security prison nearby. Ironically, this situation might hasten the release of some of the other prisoners while extending that of Gino, Frank and Milo—not that Milo was ever getting out into the general population again. He was lucky not to have been put on death row down in Florida where he'd committed some of his atrocious crimes.

Dominic knew the Incident Commander was stressed and worried about the fate of the hostages. Dominic was worried too, but rushing the process didn't help. "I realize this must seem frustrating to you, but progress is being made. So far they haven't harmed the hostages and they are talking to us—except Milo." Dominic hoped to talk to the prison psychiatrist today. The guy had been on a European vacation. Now he wasn't. "I think we need—"

"What about pumping gas into the kitchen area via the air ducts?" the IC shot out.

Dominic crossed his arms and shot Kurt Montana a cool

look. "That hasn't been used very successfully in the past. I'm thinking specifically of the 129 hostages who died during the Moscow theater siege, 126 of whom were believed to be killed by the anesthetic the authorities pumped into the theater prior to the rescue attempt."

The Incident Commander pursed his lips worriedly. "I don't want any hostages to die, but this is costing a fortune. Surely they don't think they can get away with it and actually escape?"

"Waiting these guys out is the best way to achieve a peaceful outcome." Dominic mirrored Hamner's body language. Talking to the bosses was often a negotiation in itself.

"I suppose you're right." He sounded doubtful.

"Not to mention the millions of dollars in wrongful death suits that the families will bring if we don't at least try to talk these guys out."

The Incident Commander frowned at Kurt Montana who adjusted his thigh holster with a tight smile. Kurt was a man of action—a great guy, but not one who enjoyed the waiting part of the game.

"How long will it take you to get inside the kitchen if we need to stage an assault?" Dominic asked the tactical guy.

Kurt threw back his shoulders and pushed away from the wall. "With the hostages being kept next to the outside exit door we can only assault through the cafeteria. I have a team figuring out exactly how much C4 we need to unequivocally blow the hinges without killing everyone inside. Hopefully once we perfect that part of the assault the siege will be over in under a minute."

It only took a few seconds to slice someone's throat.

From the look Kurt threw him, he knew it too.

"Let's continue to tire them out. If things deteriorate, we'll do it your way," Dominic agreed. "But we need to be very sure we have exhausted all peaceful avenues first."

Kurt looked surprised by that. Surprised Dominic would consider an assault at all.

"I'm worried about Milo," Dominic admitted. "He's not communicating with the negotiators, and he's incarcerated for horrific crimes. He has nothing to lose by killing everyone in that room."

"Maybe he'll do us a favor and off the other two hostage-takers first," Kurt quipped.

"It's my job to try and get *everyone* out without them coming to any harm." Dominic stared the man down.

Kurt's lip curled.

"Obviously we prioritize the hostages."

"That's good of you." Kurt sneered.

Dominic didn't drop the other man's gaze. "I'm sorry if this job is coming between you and your playtime back at Quantico but saving lives has always been CNU's main goal."

Kurt bristled.

"Even if we do stage an assault, I'd suggest waiting a few more days to prove we really did give negotiation time to be effective. Otherwise the senate oversight committee in DC will eat you alive."

"Well, I'm sure daddy's connections will allow you to sail right through that process." Kurt got in Dominic's face.

Dominic didn't know what had crawled into Kurt's craw, but they didn't need it here. He kept his expression bland, but he didn't back down. In fact, he took a step closer. "Following the code of conduct and doing everything we can to talk these hostage-takers out peacefully until such a time as the hostages are deemed to be in immediate danger is what will get me through any review. But you be sure to blame all your mistakes and fuck ups on me and not your inability to see past your dick. And remember, if any of your guys die when we decide to go in guns blazing if we haven't exhausted all peaceful options, that will be on you. Now get the hell out of my way and let me get back to work."

CHAPTER SEVENTEEN

FERNANDO CHAVEZ HAD done very well for himself over the years and was now a supervisor in the FBI's Reno Field Office. One of his favorite pastimes was waterskiing on Lake Tahoe with his wife and their three young children.

Such a pity they all had to die.

Chavez's ego had placed his family in danger. That and the desire to prove he wasn't scared, or changing his routine just because of "some asshole."

They were all so boringly predictable.

When Jamal Fidan had drowned, Bernie had spiked the man's drink and when he was incapacitated, shoved him over the side of the boat, leaving him to flounder and flail until he finally sunk beneath the surface.

This was going to be a little different.

The "friend" accompanying the family on this beautiful Saturday morning was obviously some sort of undercover bodyguard.

The bodyguard glanced over to the other side of the parking lot and gave a nod.

Shit. A feeling of dread swept through blood and bone when the person in the driver's seat of the white pick-up truck nodded in response. Bernie hadn't noticed the backup.

With a shudder, Bernie put the 4X4 into gear and carefully

reversed up the small gradient. No tire spins. No fast moves.

Watching the show would be a mistake. A foolish indulgence.

The eyes of the bodyguard on the boat followed the rented 4X4 as it traveled along the road beside the lake.

Fuck you, asshole.

Bernie hit dial on a pre-programmed number in the cell phone and sucked in a deep breath of anticipation.

Nothing happened.

Pulling over onto the side of the road Bernie tried again. The amount of plastic explosive in the cabin of that boat should be enough to incinerate everyone on board.

A third try had exactly the same results.

Goddammit!

Had they found the bomb? Was this whole scenario a trap? A setup? A cold sweat broke out over Bernie's skin despite the heat of the day.

If it was a trap someone would be following, or maybe there was a surveillance plane high in the sky—or a drone. It would be virtually invisible. The pounding of blood through suddenly hot ears made it impossible the hear anything except for the erratic rush of panic.

Pulling back onto the highway, Bernie ignored the feeling of fear that wanted to consume. It was a glitch. A bad connection. Shitty cell service. Or they were blocking signals...

Bernie glanced up at the sky. The FBI was not following. The FBI was a bunch of incompetent fools. Bernie kept driving. For hours, going nowhere. In circles. Filling up with gas and taking in the sights. At the end of the day Bernie drove past the marina again but the Chavez family wasn't there. The boat was though and the desire to go check why the bomb hadn't gone off was almost overwhelming. But not being able to ignore stupid urges was why Peter was dead. The man could never resist a potential target and had picked up a female the Feds had planted.

Most people called it entrapment. Dominic Sheridan had shot Peter dead and gotten a fucking commendation.

Bernie's fingers gripped the wheel so tight they felt welded on.

Next to Sheridan, the female cop was the most important target to destroy. Without that slut, Peter would never have been caught. Bernie had already set that plan in motion. Fernando Chavez was going to have to wait for now, be put on hold.

He lived in a log cabin in the woods though. Perhaps some gasoline and matches could be arranged. It was a hot, dry summer. The fire would grow fast and consume everything in its path. The perfect sort of vengeance—painful, terrifying.

Bernie didn't even need to see the man die. It just needed to happen. All those responsible for setting up Peter needed to stop breathing on a permanent basis.

After ten hours of aimless driving the small, private airstrip came into view. It was almost tempting to go to Peter. To be with him again if only for a short time, but there was much to do.

Revenge was time-consuming. Soon it would all be over. Soon it would be done.

CHAPTER EIGHTEEN

AVA HAD TRIED to talk to Dominic again in the hallway before going into the negotiation area for his shift, but she could tell from his countenance he wasn't in the mood to hear anything she said. She chickened out and instead sat in the corner plugged into the ethernet cable so she could download her emails. All wi-fi and cell service had been blocked so the hostage-takers couldn't communicate with anyone except the negotiators in this room.

Ava was beyond mortified she'd admitted that she was okay with Dominic touching her. When she thought about it, her head wanted to explode. He'd been shocked and taken aback. He was probably placing her on his list of female stalkers, the ones who mooned after him and wanted him in their beds and wouldn't leave him alone once they got him there.

Ugh.

She wasn't shy about asking men out on a date, but even that tiny admission to Sheridan had shattered her confidence. She was such an idiot. He was effectively her boss right now, and she was supposed to be watching his back, being that extra pair of eyes so he wasn't caught unawares. He'd basically apologized for a sleepy, innocent touch and she'd told him, hey, that's okay, Boss, touch me again, any way you want.

Ugh. She squeezed her eyes shut the same way she gripped the pen she was making notes with. She had to tell him about her connection to Gino, but unless she wanted to yell the sensitive information across a crowded room it was proving completely impossible.

She opened the file Mallory Rooney had sent. Apparently, Lincoln Frazer had finally persuaded the task force investigating the Mortimer shooting in Fredericksburg that the deaths of the six other FBI and former-FBI agents from the NYFO might be related. Members of the task force were double-checking the details to determine if they were truly accidental or natural. Linked or not. The agents at the BAU-4 had agreed to read Ava in on any relevant information that might be useful when figuring out who this UNSUB was. They were emailing Dominic too, but he wasn't even opening the messages any more. He was focusing on this prison siege situation and not allowing any distractions.

Including her.

Humiliation washed over her once again. How could she have said that to him? She pushed the churning thoughts away and also blocked out Gino-the-snake's bellicose voice making his crazy demands. A helicopter and fifty thousand dollars. Each.

Did he really believe he was getting out of here?

Mallory Rooney forwarded an email about the dead waitress. At the time of Van's funeral, Caroline Perry had not been at the bar nor the university. No one could place her anywhere which meant they couldn't rule her out as the shooter. She had been working at the Mule & Pitcher when Van had eaten there and the Feds found capsules of Liquid E in her bedroom of her shared apartment, suggesting she was probably responsible for drugging and nearly killing Dominic. Had she drugged Van and staged his death? ME's tests were inconclusive, but GHB metabolized out of the body fast.

No long gun. No evidence she'd ever owned or even fired a rifle, but they were still looking for the waitress's car.

Had she finished whatever she'd set out to do? Maybe she thought Dominic was dead in that car wreck? Had she committed suicide rather than go to prison?

ME said she'd probably drowned but hadn't been absolutely certain. They were waiting on lab test results. And DNA results.

DEA were immovable on sharing their video footage. Boy, were they ever pissed with her for ruining their op. Lincoln Frazer's team was doing its thing creating a profile. Alex Parker had examined Van's cell phone data and discovered her friend and mentor had received a call from a burner the morning of his death. The call had lasted fifteen minutes.

Alex was trying to find out when and where that burner had been bought and used. Maybe they could catch the UNSUB on surveillance images somewhere.

If this was an intricate plot designed to kill a specific group of FBI agents then Ava doubted the UNSUB would be sloppy enough to be caught on camera. Planning had been too detailed, too thorough. Even figuring out the names of the agents on the squad would take work for someone outside the Bureau.

Could they have hired an investigator?

Ava looked up as some sort of scuffle broke out on the TV monitor. The sound was on very low so the headset Joe—the guy doing all the talking—was using wouldn't pick it up or produce feedback. The hostage-takers had their phone on speaker.

Gino had grabbed the lone woman in the room—the warden—who cried out as the mobster dragged her by her bound arms across the floor into the center of the room.

"What's happening in there, Gino?" Joe kept his voice calm even though the tension in the room felt like something was about to shatter.

"Nothing's happening, you fucking prick. That's the fucking problem. We want out of here. Do you get it yet?"

Joe closed his eyes and seemed to be mentally bracing himself. "I'm sorry, Gino, that this is taking some time, but how am I supposed to arrange that helicopter when I don't have the assurance from all three of you that you won't hurt the hostages?"

Dominic pressed his lips together. Although he was still in his seat, he looked animated and full of energy. And handsome. Those bruises were faded to pale gray now and did not detract from the outer package.

And did you? Want to be touched?

Ava closed her eyes and looked away before he caught her staring.

"How about this, *Joe*? How about if we don't get a helicopter in the yard in the next thirty minutes then I'm going to slice this bitch from throat to snatch." Gino's voice oozed venom. "But only after I've had a little fun."

Gino tore the warden's shirt open, and everyone in the room froze. The woman had maintained a brave front until that moment, but now her face crumpled as Gino ran the edge of the knife across her flesh, leaving a thin red welt in its wake.

Joe didn't look up at the screen.

"Gino, talk to me. You know that if anything happens to

the hostages it won't look good and the chances of the higher ups delivering that helicopter gets increasingly less likely—"

Suddenly the third hostage-taker, the one who'd sat in the corner sharpening his knife and refusing to communicate for days, stood and walked over to where Gino held the trembling warden.

Milo Andris spoke quietly into the receiver. "You have my assurance that none of us will hurt any of the hostages, as long as you provide us with a helicopter as my colleagues have requested, by noon tomorrow. Now you can move forward." And then Milo took the warden gently by the arm and sat her on the floor in the corner beside him, and he carried on sharpening that damned blade.

Gino grinned like Milo's reaction had been his intention all along and went to rummage in the refrigerator, but Ava didn't buy it. Gino wasn't smart enough to pull off that level of manipulation, but he didn't want to look foolish or take on the other guy.

Serial killers even freaked out mobsters.

A man knocked on the door of the negotiation room and entered. Joe muted his mic.

The newcomer wore old jeans and a t-shirt with a beer logo on the front. "Hi there, I'm Dr. Jones. The prison psychiatrist. Just got off the plane from Lisbon so apologies for looking like this. What can I do to help?"

Dominic hustled the guy over to Ava's side of the room and sat in a chair so close to her his knee brushed her thigh. She tried not to react.

"Tell me everything you can about Milo Andris," Dominic asked the psychiatrist. "Especially his relationship with the warden."

THE AREA WAS remote and densely wooded. A couple of hikers had reported finding the car, seemingly abandoned, ten miles upstream of where they'd pulled Caroline Perry out of the Rappahannock River.

Mallory stopped to take a breath.

"You okay?" Alex asked, taking her elbow.

"Junior is kickboxing my lungs, a favorite pastime, and I'm roughly the size of a hippopotamus, but apart from that..."

"Take it slow. The vehicle isn't going anywhere."

"Unless the local sheriff tows it."

"He won't tow it," said Alex. She hated how reasonable he sounded. "Not when it belongs to a suspect in Tuesday's shooting."

Mallory pulled a face. "I suppose."

She was grumpy and irritable. Her back ached. Alex was nothing but supportive, but she was still hugely pregnant and waddling like a freaking duck. At this point she wanted it all to be over with, but she also wanted a healthy baby.

Alex rubbed her lower back with a prescience that sometimes amazed her.

"I'm still terrified I'm going to be a lousy mom," she muttered quietly as if that would somehow minimize her fears.

"You are going to be the most incredible mother in the world." That's what he always said.

"What if I'm not? What if I yell at the baby?"

"Mom's yell. It's a thing."

"But—"

"You," he stopped and looked down at her, smoothing her bangs to one side. "Are going to be an amazing mother.

And"—he interrupted her again before she could argue—"you will also sometimes make mistakes. It's allowed. You don't need to pretend to be perfect."

"You're perfect," she muttered. He always knew what to say to make her feel better.

Alex laughed. "That is a lie, but I intend to give everything I have to you and our family." The gray of his eyes was warm silver. "Together we will figure this baby thing out."

He grinned as she batted his stomach with the back of her hand. "*Baby thing*?"

He took her hand and kissed her fingers.

Married life had been considerably easier than everything that had come before. Even if Alex was right it didn't mean she worried any less. Worrying was part of her nature, but a part she was usually more able to partition off and deal with. Ever since she'd gotten pregnant her hormones had gotten the better of her and made her weepier and more battle ready. It was a scary, unnerving combination but there wasn't anything she wouldn't do to protect this child, or this man. She squeezed her husband's hand, knowing he felt the same way.

Up ahead she caught sight of a sheriff's deputy in a brown uniform. She and Alex approached the small, silver sedan making sure neither of them walked in the tire tracks along the lane.

Looking at the dirt, Mallory noticed a few faint shoe impressions in the dust.

Alex saw them too. He crouched for a moment at the side of the track. "Looks like a man with small feet or a kid with big feet. Could also be a woman."

That narrowed it down.

"Let's get the evidence techs to put down markers and

follow them out as far as they are able. They might match the ones found at Van Stamos's place."

"Or it could be someone out for a hike," Alex suggested.

"Let's collect the evidence."

Alex looked up from his crouched position, and she could barely see him over her enormous belly. "Yes, Boss."

She grinned as she turned away. As agreeable and amenable as Alex Parker was, every single day, there was never a doubt as to who was the real "boss." His skill with weapons, cybersecurity, and computers was legendary. His life experience made him the consummate reader of potentially dangerous situations. Whenever he was around, she always felt one hundred percent safe. It was when he was gone, she got nervous. About the past. About the future. About the uncertainty of parenthood and the fear of messing up.

They planned to be geographically close for the next few weeks so he'd be with her for the birth. She needed his strength for what lay ahead.

The sheriff's deputy held out his hand to Alex first. "Deputy Ortez. You must be Agent Rooney?"

"Mr. Parker is a consultant for the BAU and is also my husband so I asked him to accompany me." The deputy shook her hand and stared at her midsection.

"How far along are you?"

"Nearly thirty-eight weeks." And counting down the days.

"Your first?" Ortez asked.

Mallory nodded.

"Your life is about to undergo a seismic shift," the officer said with a smile.

"Can't wait," Alex replied.

"I've got three of my own so I have some experience in an

emergency, should it be required."

"I'll bear that in mind." Mallory had no intention of having her baby beside a river in the dirt. She'd be in a hospital with every expert and medical machine available to man.

She eyed the car. She had a bad feeling about this case. Things weren't adding up. Was Caroline Perry a killer or had she roofied Dominic Sheridan for kicks? Karl Feldman's police sketch had turned out to look remarkably like Angelina Jolie. He'd clammed up completely once he'd discovered Caroline Perry was dead—or when he realized that law enforcement had discovered her body. He'd lawyered up and shut up.

Maybe Feldman had been so drunk he couldn't remember what the woman had looked like. But it was also possible he and Perry had been working together, and he'd killed her and dumped the body. Analysts were digging up everything they could on Karl Feldman. Background checks had so far come up without any obvious links to the dead FBI agents. Mallory wondered if such an enormous man could have tiny feet.

She didn't like so many clues pointing nowhere. She didn't like the lack of clearly attributable motive.

"There are some shoe prints leading down the track. Did you record them yet?" she asked the deputy.

The man nodded to a technician in white Tyvek booties who was photographing something on the ground. "There are some beside the vehicle too, but it's been dry so they aren't real clear."

Mallory walked around the car and looked at the prints and what looked very much like drag marks. "Catalogue and collect everything. I'll request a bloodhound team to see if they can track the scent back to the road." Although what that would tell them she wasn't sure. Did they have an accomplice who'd picked them up? Had they hitched a ride? Walked?

She peered into the back seat of the sedan. A pile of clothes were tossed on the floor.

"Find her cell phone?" Alex asked the officer.

The deputy shook his head.

"You looked in the trunk yet?" asked Mallory.

"No, ma'am. As soon as I ran the plate, I got a hit on your flag. Figured I'd wait for you guys to turn up."

Mallory nodded. "Appreciate it."

She went to the trunk, but Alex stopped her.

"Let me check it out first." Alex put on gloves and a very unattractive hairnet. He was hypersensitive about leaving his DNA at any crime scene, for good reason. He opened the rear passenger door and eased the back seat forward an inch and shone a penlight inside the trunk.

For a full minute he studied the interior of the trunk in meticulous detail. Then he crouched and looked under the vehicle, working his way around the base. "I don't see any obvious boobytraps."

Because even though she was already dead, if Caroline Perry had killed multiple Federal Agents, she'd presumably be happy to take out a few more should the opportunity present itself.

"Stand over by the trees," Alex told them, but he was looking at her when he said it.

She pressed her lips together but decided it wasn't worth arguing about. She had a baby to protect.

"Be careful," she told him before moving thirty feet away. Maybe they should call the bomb squad, but Alex wouldn't open the trunk if he seriously thought there was a threat. She spread her fingers over the baby bump, feeling the person inside stretch and wriggle.

"What did you say he consulted about again?" the deputy

asked.

She huffed out a silent laugh as Alex carefully eased open the trunk. "Everything."

When Alex turned to face her, she knew he'd seen something of relevance.

Inside the trunk was a Browning rifle complete with a hunting scope.

"Is that the rifle used to shoot Agent Mortimer on Tuesday?" Mallory asked Alex.

"Could be."

She'd bet on it.

The flash went off as the police photographer recorded the evidence. Mallory turned away and walked down to the water's edge. The opposite bank was reflected in the river. It was wide here, clear and shallow at the margins. Tiny fish darted away as her shadow fell across them.

If Caroline Perry had killed herself, how had she done it? Got undressed and then walked out into the river and let the current take her? The drag marks suggested otherwise. It suggested the woman had been incapacitated, or dead, before going into the river.

Mallory called Frazer even though it was a Saturday and he was home relaxing with Izzy. The FBI did not stop on weekends. "We found a rifle. We need a ballistic analysis on it straight away. I'm going to ask the local sheriff about a dog team to track some footprints. Someone should put a tail on Feldman—just in case." Something about this whole thing wasn't adding up. Mallory stared at the footprints walking away from the scene. "And another thing, find out what size feet the guy has."

Frazer laughed mockingly on the other end of the line. "Yes, Boss."

CHAPTER NINETEEN

DOMINIC LEFT THE negotiation room at eight that night. The last four days had been a monotonous grind comprising of twelve-hour stints in the negotiation room—still situated in the main prison admin building—and sleeping a few, short inches away from a woman whose looks and scent were starting to drive him insane with lust.

He'd had a brief meeting with the Incident Commander and Kurt Montana when he'd finished his shift tonight. He planned to be back on duty by six AM sharp tomorrow. If the hostage-takers didn't surrender beforehand the plan was for three tactical snipers to simultaneously shoot all three hostage-takers as they walked to a helicopter that would be waiting for them in the courtyard. A hugely difficult plan fraught with the potential for death of the hostage-takers and the hostages alike, but the authorities were losing patience with these inmates.

In the meantime, the negotiators needed to keep the hostage-takers calm and talk them through all the stages of what they thought was their exit strategy. Making sure each stage was carefully choreographed even though the prisoners would never leave the compound.

The hostage-takers were to leave the four hostages on the ground, and the FBI pilot would serve as their only remaining captive until he set them down somewhere remote north of the border. That was the deal. The pilot would be armed, and the prisoners needed the guy alive as none of them could fly a helicopter. Still it was a hell of a brave thing to agree to, even in principle.

These men were armed and dangerous and, as Milo had proved, completely unpredictable.

Dominic followed Ava back to their trailer, his steps dragging with weariness.

The prison shrink was shocked Milo was involved. The serial killer was doing a doctorate in philosophy and had a good working relationship with the staff at the prison—nothing like multiple life sentences to focus the mind on education. According to the psychiatrist, Milo had been a model prisoner who regretted his crimes and respected the warden and was grateful to her for allowing him to continue his studies. The guy had never been alone with her though, or armed and in control. That changed things.

A lot depended on the sadist's fantasies, and if any of these events fed into them, not to mention whether or not he was swallowing the medications they were sending in via an air vent in the wall.

Dominic did not like the steady deterioration in Gino Gerbachi's behavior. The man only dozed if Frank took a watch. He was sweating, nervous, exhausted, pissed. He was close to breaking. Dominic found his tired eyes instinctively going to Agent Kanas's round ass as he walked behind her to the trailer. Maybe Gino wasn't the only one close to breaking.

He shook his head at himself. She was off-limits and the last thing he should be even thinking about was sex. Except now he was thinking about sex. *Goddammit.*

"I have some news on the investigation," Ava began, turning eagerly to fill him in on any updates.

He touched his hand to her arm and felt a familiar jolt of electric energy pulse through him the same way it did every time they came into physical contact.

"Sorry, Ava, I don't want to think about that tonight. I want to concentrate on this situation until it's over." And hopefully at the end everyone would still be alive.

He'd taken over negotiations that afternoon. He hadn't apologized or explained. He'd just calmly introduced himself. "My name's Dominic. You're dealing with me now."

No drama, no theatrics. Just a done deal.

Joe had been amazing over the last few days, but he was clearly exhausted and Dominic was worried he'd inadvertently let something slip about the takedown operation. He still didn't think he'd uncovered the unknown unknowns in this situation—the Black Swans—but FBI analysts were still digging.

Gino didn't warm to him much but Frank did. They'd begun talking about everything from favorite ski hills in Vermont to scuba diving in the Bahamas. Gino sat with a sneer twisting his puffy features. Milo remained silent sitting calmly beside the warden like he was guarding her, but that might be a crazily off-center assumption.

"Dominic, I—"

He squeezed Ava's shoulder. "I promise I'll be back on the case as soon as this is over, but right now I need a shower, a cold beer and a few hours' sleep." Must be the car accident and the pressure of this incident but he was whacked.

She searched his eyes and must have seen the imminent exhaustion threatening to suck him under. She nodded uncertainly. "Okay. Let me go pick up some food. Anything in particular you like?"

"Not pizza." Pizza was the staple of most late-night, armed standoffs and crisis negotiations.

"I'll see what else is available around here." She dropped her laptop inside the trailer and headed straight out the door. He stumbled inside and had the world's fastest shower and collapsed unconscious onto the mattress he was using on the floor. Ava wasn't back and the image of her talking to the HRT guy the other morning punched through his consciousness. No doubt about it, any number of those guys would love to get into her pants.

Her choice.

He clenched his teeth at the thought.

Five hours later he surfaced to the soft sound of Ava's breathing. The moon was full and everything was lit up inside the trailer with a bright silver glow. He carefully lifted the flimsy sheet that separated them to look at her. She lay on her back on top of the thin coverlet, wearing another one of her camisole tops and a pair of boxer shorts.

God she was pretty, those elegant, winged brows and that lush, wide mouth that gave as good as it got. He shouldn't be looking at her like this, staring like a lover when the sheet was there to give them both privacy in cramped quarters. He was about to drop the sheet back into place when she rolled over and her hand flopped toward him, her palm connecting with his bare chest. He jolted. Her fingers spread wide, and the sear of her touch branded him. Then her eyes slowly opened.

Instead of withdrawing her hand she blinked a few times and then rubbed her palm over his pecs and down his rib cage.

"I imagined you'd look like this…" Her voice was low and

soft as velvet. Her hand stroked up and brushed his nipple.

He gritted his teeth against the pleasure her touch wrought. "You've been imagining what I looked like without my shirt on?"

Did that mean she'd been thinking about sex the way he had whenever he lost control of his thought processes?

Her eyes rose up to meet his, voice husky with sleep. "I wondered what you'd look like naked."

"I'm not naked." His voice dropped two octaves and then he watched as her hand drifted lower and curled around his cock which was standing to attention in an impossible to miss salute.

"Is this where I apologize for touching you?" she asked, eyes dark as they fastened on his.

God, this woman.

He swallowed as lust infused every cell of his body. She was so erotically over the line and yet he didn't give a damn. Between her sultry voice and deft touch, he could barely speak.

"I'm good," he said.

"Are you?" she murmured, discovering the changing shape of him with appreciation that threatened his control to a breaking point.

He closed his eyes briefly, her touch stoking his desire until his blood caught fire. They shouldn't be doing this, but if he didn't have her soon his head was going to explode. He opened his eyes again.

"Do you really want to find out, Ava? You want to have sex with a guy a lot older than you are? One who's theoretically in a position of superiority?" He held her gaze in the darkness.

She ignored the age difference like it was non-existent.

Maybe at this stage it was, they were both consenting adults. But it didn't change their respective positions within the FBI.

"Theoretically?"

"You have my cock in your hand. Trust me, that changes the power dynamic."

"Yes," she bit her bottom lip. "I want to have sex with you, but I don't want it to complicate anything."

Sex always complicated things but right now he didn't care. Let them get as complicated as all fuck, as long as he could get inside her right now.

He hooked his arm around her waist and dragged her onto his mattress, dropping the sheet behind her and rolling her beneath him.

Her hands came up to grip his upper arms and she held on tight.

"You're sure about this?" he asked.

She nodded, eyes on his lips.

He lowered his mouth to taste her and felt her body melt against him as her arms came around him.

He kissed her slowly, nibbling the edges of her mouth, hands cradling her head, holding her exactly where he wanted her. She tasted like the mint of toothpaste and something sweet and sexy and sinful.

Her skin was soft as satin, but hot, feverishly hot. He licked the seam of her lips and waited for her to open up to him. He needed to know they were both in this together. It only took a moment for her tongue to be tangling with his as he unhurriedly discovered her flavor.

Her nails dug into his back, and her thighs parted as her legs went around him. He settled his hard length against her core and kissed her faster, deeper. Those hands of hers slipped into his boxers and squeezed his ass, moving against him in a way that had him careening toward the edge way too fast. He was trying to make this last but Ava was in a hurry.

He grabbed both her hands and pinned them above her head with a firm grip. "Patience, Kanas."

Her eyes flashed and then narrowed.

Oh, was this ever gonna be fun. He dragged the camisole top high enough to uncover her breasts and then leaned down to run his tongue over her plump flesh, edging ever closer to those dark, perfect areoles. Finally, he gave in to her silent demands and sucked one hard tip into his mouth. His tongue tormented her breast until she begged him for more, and then he moved on to the other nipple.

He shifted down her body, and she stiffened and grabbed his short hair when she realized where he was headed.

"You don't have to do that."

"I don't *have* to?" he asked incredulously. "What if I want to?"

"I don't know…guys always say that but…" She seemed to become impatient with herself. "I've never actually come when a guy did it, so…"

Dominic did not want to be reminded of anyone else going down on this woman, but he never could resist a challenge. "How about we give it a try, and if you don't like it you tell me to stop?"

She nodded, appearing a little embarrassed by their frank discussion as she looked down at him settled between her thighs.

She was so ballsy most of the time that whenever she appeared uncertain or worried, he wanted to reassure her and calm her fears. She brought out some sort of savior complex in him he hadn't known he possessed. He didn't like that realization, but it didn't stop him sliding her shorts far enough down her legs that he could see the trimmed triangle of hair at the apex of her thighs. The scent of her made him want to dive deep, but he wasn't usually a greedy lover. With Ava, however, he wanted to do everything.

He slid his tongue down over her clit and felt her rear up off the mattress.

"Should I stop?" he asked with a smile.

"No." Her voice was high and faint. "Give it your best shot."

He laughed against her stomach and felt her muscles twitch in response. He slid his tongue back through her folds and centered his ministrations on the small nub of tissue that held the keys to most women's orgasm. Slowly Ava relaxed and her thighs fell open enough for him to drag her shorts all the way off and for him to taste her more deeply, even as he ached to be inside her.

It took time and concentration to find the rhythm she needed. Thankfully patience was one of his strong points. Her shallows pants told him she was close to losing it, and he sucked on her clit to push her right over the edge. She sobbed quietly, and her whole body shuddered as the first climax hit. He hoped to hell HRT weren't standing outside the door with heat sensitive cameras.

"Okay. You passed that test, Sheridan." She sounded breathless, and she tugged on his hair. "Now get up here and gimme the rest of it," she said it with a laugh, and he could get used to this playful Ava.

He crawled up her body, enjoying every inch of her flesh along the way. She dragged the camisole over her head, and he reared back to get the full impact of her nakedness.

"You are beautiful."

"So are you."

One side of his mouth kicked up. "Guys like me aren't beautiful."

"Whaddaya mean?" She pushed at his shoulder.

"Men descended from knuckle-headed Irishmen." He traced the softness of her stomach and the vulnerability of her navel.

"I think you know exactly how hot you are, but you want more compliments."

He smiled as he cupped her breast and tweaked the nipple with his thumb, pinching it hard enough to make her jolt. "Compliments are good."

Ava huffed out a laugh as her body squirmed. She ran her hand over his jaw. "You have a nice face."

"Nice?" He dipped his mouth to suckle and pulled her nipple into his mouth.

Her body bowed towards him. "I meant stupendous."

"Better," he murmured between tastes.

"I like your nose, and those fierce brows."

He laughed and let his hand trace down her ribs and over her stomach to sink between her legs and tease her opening.

"I love the dark shade of your eyes." She gasped and swallowed rapidly as he slipped a finger inside.

"Blue."

"Indigo."

"Bruised."

She touched his face almost tenderly. "And the scruff on your jaw felt really good between my legs."

"I'll grow a beard."

"Then you can try that again sometime."

"I will." He'd told her he liked sex, and he stored this information away for next time. The idea of pleasing Ava was addictive. He might not usually have sex with other agents, but it would make the next few days or weeks a lot more pleasurable if they could do this as a stress reliever every night.

They didn't *technically* work together.

The FBI was fine with relationships as long as agents were on different squads—and the power balance was firmly in her hands when they were horizontal, not that he'd ever compromise himself or her.

He traced his lips over the protrusion of her collarbone and simultaneously sank his fingers inside her with his palm stroking her clit. Her body was toned and fit, but still soft and womanly. She had the longest legs he'd ever seen, and round hips, and full breasts that could hold his attention for decades.

"I like your chest and your shoulders." She squeezed the muscles at the top of his arms.

He scraped his teeth over her slender neck, careful not to mark her where others could see it.

"And your neck."

He laughed. She was terrible at compliments.

"And I definitely appreciate the rock-hard pecs and those very nice abs, Sheridan." She was teasing him. "Not bad for an old man."

"I'm thirty-five. Nine years older than you are."

She ran her hands down his back and over his ass. Then her hand slipped between his legs and she held him firmly, her eyes on his. "I like this part of you too."

"My ass? Or my cock?"

She huffed out a laugh. "Both."

"Say it, Ava."

"I like your cock, Dominic. I want it inside me."

He could feel himself growing harder at her bold words and touch. She bent her knees and rubbed the end of him against her opening, and he had to force himself not to sink inside.

He grabbed his wallet out of pants he'd tossed aside earlier and rummaged through it for the emergency condom he kept tucked in there. He found it, thank god, but she took it out of his grip before he could open the package.

She tore it open slowly and carefully covered him. He swallowed at the sensation of her stroking him from tip to root and then positioning him at her entrance.

"Did I mention I like your cock?" she asked with a quick grin. "I'm hoping to love it in the very near future."

He grinned, despite the gravity of this episode pressing down on his shoulders. It was just sex. And yet he couldn't remember having this much fun before or having his brains reduced to rubble just from the thought of fucking someone.

He nuzzled her ear as he thrust forward, unable to hold her gaze. Somehow that made it too overwhelming, too real to watch those pretty eyes as he filled her. But he wanted it to be real, he wanted to see everything he was feeling reflected back at him.

He raised himself up onto his good elbow to look at her beautiful face and body, to kiss her long and deep before he began moving inside her.

God, she felt good. Tight. Hot. Aroused. He made sure every thrust hit all the good spots, angling her hips to doubly make sure. His injured shoulder was feeling no pain right now.

He wanted to take it slow, but the desire cruising his blood was stoking his body to a boiling point. He counted to one hundred in French to stop himself losing it. Even when Ava spasmed around him he held on until he could breathe again, slowing it down, wanting it to last forever.

He kissed the sweat from her temple before carefully rolling them over and letting her sit on top of him.

She rode him gently at first, tentative movements, learning him and what he liked until she gained confidence. Then her arms came to rest on his chest, one hand over his heart as she closed her eyes and took what she wanted from his body.

As she started to tighten around him for the second time, he locked his arms around her hips and slammed into her so forcefully he was worried he might hurt her. Then she cried out again and they climaxed together, him gripping her tight and holding back a roar that would have brought backup bursting through the door.

Ava shuddered and sank against him, their hearts beating in unison.

Holy shit.

He swallowed repeatedly, pretty sure his head had exploded. He closed his eyes and wondered what the hell he'd done. Then he wondered how quickly he could get hold of more condoms so they could do it again.

She went to pull away, but he held her still for another moment. Then she rolled over and lay on the mattress naked beside him. He went into the bathroom and when he came back, he looked at her. She didn't seem particularly bashful. Maybe she knew how incredible her body was, or maybe she didn't care.

She cracked open an eyelid. "Is it wrong that I don't want you to stop touching me?"

He swallowed. "I wouldn't call it wrong, but I'm not sure I have the will power to stop fucking you if I do, and I don't have any more protection."

She didn't flinch away from his blunt language. In fact, the way she swallowed and squeezed her thighs together made him think she liked it.

The temptation to see if she did was overpowering. He took a dangerous step forward.

A knock on the trailer door had him swearing and Ava quietly scrambling back to her side of the curtain. He pulled on his boxers.

"What is it?" He stalled to give Ava enough time to drag her top over her head and shimmy into her shorts. He strode over to the door.

"Incident Commander wants you in the command center," came a low, clear voice.

Dominic opened the door an inch. "What's happening?"

The HRT agent's gaze slid behind Dominic into the darkness where Ava was getting dressed.

Dominic shifted his body to block any potential viewing opportunities.

The guy smirked. "I'm just the messenger boy." He nodded and backed away.

Dominic shut the door and climbed back into the clothes he'd taken off earlier. If they'd woken him up it couldn't be good. "Ava, you don't have to come..."

"Remember what I said about sex not changing anything?" She was doing up the buttons of her blouse as he searched for clean socks.

"Probably better if we don't mention the sex part to anyone else." The last thing he wanted was to have Ava put back on suspension because he couldn't keep his dick in his pants.

"It's not the sort of thing I'd broadcast," she said sharply.

Ouch.

"I'm not an idiot," she added in a stern whisper.

He shook his head at himself. He'd handled this badly. As confident as she was in her body, it was a different matter entirely when it came to her job and her position at the Bureau. She knew he didn't do relationships, but she didn't know anything else about how he treated women after sex.

He ducked behind the strung-up sheet and clasped her arms gently, made her look at him. Her eyes were huge in the semi-darkness, bright with emotion he couldn't label. "I have never doubted your intelligence, Ava. I know you're a smart, hard-working and dedicated agent who's honest and has integrity. But if people find out we're sleeping together they'll separate us, and while under normal circumstances I'd agree with that policy for your benefit, right now I want you close to watch my back and help track down this killer." His grip tightened, and he said fiercely, "Also, because having sex with you once was not enough."

She opened her mouth to reply, but someone rapped on the door again.

He gave her a quick kiss on the lips. "Gotta go. We'll talk later."

CHAPTER TWENTY

AVA HAD KNOWN Dominic Sheridan would be good at sex. Passionate. Ardent. Unabashed. Focused. With a keen eye for detail, amazing tactile skills, the stamina to gift her multiple orgasms and still finish with a bang. She felt boneless and energized. Fired up and relaxed. Her whole body trembled with aftershocks of pleasure and that was even as she followed his rapidly moving frame through the sea of muscle-bound HRT personnel.

She hadn't expected to *enjoy* it quite so much. Not only the orgasms, but the entire episode had been something she'd be happy to repeat anytime.

Best. Sex. Ever.

Which was exactly why poor, besotted Suzanna had ended up on the doorstep in the rain holding a freaking casserole dish full of beef stew.

Not gonna happen. Sure, repeat sex like that would be fantastic, but she wasn't going to invest emotionally in this guy. He wasn't going to fall in love with her. He'd told her that. She wasn't stupid. They came from completely different backgrounds and the only thing they had in common was Van. Plus, Dominic was gonna freak if he discovered she hadn't told him the truth about her past.

She waited outside the command center leaning against

the wall as Dominic went inside the room to talk to the IC.

She squeezed her hands into fists, aware that her hair was a mess and she hadn't looked in the mirror recently. God knew what was stamped on her features. Sated lust? She touched her neck where he'd nipped her and prayed she didn't have a hickey. She dropped her hand and straightened her shoulders. It wasn't anyone else's business anyway.

She pursed her lips. She kept trying to tell him about her association with Gino Gerbachi, but whenever she started talking about it, he was busy and didn't have time to talk.

Except she could have told him the truth rather than tell him she was desperate for his cock. She closed her eyes briefly at the realization of all that she'd said to him tonight. She could have mentioned her WitSec background before he'd put his tongue inside her and made her come so hard stars were still imprinted on the back of her eyelids.

Ava inhaled deeply. She'd messed up.

Her connection to Gino might mean nothing, but she had no idea how Sheridan would react to the information or how it might affect his job—or even the perception of how he did his job, which seemed vitally important to him.

She winced.

They'd spent a lot of time together over the last week and had just indulged in mind-blowing carnal adventures, but she didn't really know Dominic very well. Sure, Van had said he was a great guy, but add sex to a "relationship" that wasn't a "relationship" and people started treating you differently. Ava wasn't about to let that happen. She loved her job. She *needed* her job. More than she needed a man.

It took a moment for her to notice that the tension in the prison, usually ratcheted tight, seemed stretched to breaking point right now. What was going on?

She heard raised voices inside the Command Center, Dominic's included. Her eyes widened. She met the gaze of a serious-looking operator type leaning against the opposite wall. He pulled a face indicating he'd also heard the exchange, and it couldn't be good.

Dominic was suddenly striding out of the room, and she launched herself off the doorjamb to catch up with him. Fury radiated off him in palpable waves. So much for that post-coital glow.

She stuck close, clutching her laptop case to her chest, ignoring the curious looks HRT was throwing them.

Dominic headed inside the first door to the negotiation room. Then knocked on the door of the inner sanctum to get the attention of the negotiators working there before he burst inside. Ava followed close enough to be his shadow. She had the feeling he'd completely forgotten she was there.

Her eyes shot to the screen. Frank was holding the warden down on the steel countertop with a knife to her neck, and Gino was between her legs, dragging her pants down.

The moisture in Ava's mouth evaporated.

Eban Winters was talking to the hostage-takers with his gaze averted from the screen, still pretending he couldn't see what they were doing. He muted the mic.

Dominic leaned over the table and asked, "What happened?"

"They somehow found some liquor. Got drunk then decided they wanted a little fun. Gino smashed Milo on the back of the head when Frank distracted him. He's lying on the floor unconscious or dead."

"They rape her already?" Dominic's voice was cold, but

Ava recognized the emotion in it.

Eban's skin was pale, and Charlotte reached out and squeezed his hand.

"Not yet. We need to get their attention off of the warden and back onto us, but they aren't listening to me anymore," Eban stated in frustration.

"The IC is arranging a helicopter to arrive in twenty minutes. We're bringing up the timetable, but if they continue what they're doing, HRT will stage an immediate assault," Dominic said grimly.

Ava didn't need to be a negotiator to know if that happened, they probably all died, including the warden.

Eban relayed the message about the helicopter.

Frank yelled toward the speakerphone. "That's good news." But he continued to hold the knife to the warden's throat as Gino pulled the woman's underwear from her body. Eban kept talking in calm tones reminding them not to harm the hostages, but from the almost feral look of concentration on Frank's face, and the fact Gino was undoing the front of his prison jumpsuit, they'd both stopped listening to Eban. That they both intended to rape the warden before they made their escape was obvious.

Ava looked through the glass window. The tactical commander of the HRT was watching, obviously about to give the order to stage the assault.

"Let me talk to him," Ava burst out.

"You're not trained—" Charlotte snapped.

"I can get Gino's attention for a few minutes, trust me. It might be enough."

"How?" Dominic asked, pinning her with a razor-sharp gaze.

"Gino-the-snake is how I got this scar." Ava touched her brow. "He murdered my father and left me for dead. I testified and helped put the sonofabitch away in here."

Dominic's blue eyes held a glint of anger but also of opportunity.

"I might get his attention long enough to get him away from the warden for a few minutes."

"Stalling for time is the best we can do," Eban agreed. "We have nothing to lose at this point."

Tension stretched around the room.

"Put her on." Dominic nodded. "Make sure there's a note in the file that the warden is seconds from being raped by Gino Gerbachi." He looked at her critically. "This might be crazy enough to buy us some time. Do your worst, Ava. Give it all you're got. We need to shock this guy out of his current mindset. Shake him to his foundations. I'll be right by your side to coach you through it."

Ava sat and took the headset from Eban. Charlotte thrust a list of talking points in front of her. Ava took the list, but it wouldn't help. It was hard to bargain with psychopaths even for experts. She was just a rookie agent with a big mouth.

She looked at the monitor, adjusted the mic so it sat below her lips. "Well, if it isn't old Gino-the-snake. I can see now why they call you snake, big boy." She emphasized her Greek accent to sound more like her mother. "I just wonder how the rest of the *family* knew you were such a big dick?"

Charlotte's mouth fell open, but Dominic was staring at her with intense concentration.

Gino froze in the act of jacking his dick into hardness and both he and Frank were staring around in astonishment.

"What? You thought we couldn't see what was going on in

there? You haven't learned by now that the Feds like drilling holes in walls and light sockets? Isn't that what put you in here in the first place, Gino?" She was taunting the man and knew that wasn't how negotiators worked, but they were past the time for tact.

"Oh, no, wait, it was that kid, right? That little Greek girl you got too sloppy to kill."

Gino was standing stock-still in the middle of the kitchen listening to her with rapt attention. Jaws were clenched. Eyes small and beady. He finally put his dick away which was a relief. No one wanted that thing out in the open.

Frank let go of the warden and climbed off the counter. The woman curled into a ball and lay there naked in the fetal position. Ava wanted her off that countertop onto the floor where she'd be safer from crossfire should HRT burst in.

The sound of a helicopter flying overhead and landing could be clearly heard throughout the facility. That got Frank and Gino's attention.

Suddenly Milo, the convicted serial killer, who until that moment had looked like he was unconscious or dead, rolled onto his side and slowly climbed to his feet. The other hostage-takers didn't appear to notice.

"You remember her name, Gino? The little girl whose father you shot like a dog because he wouldn't let you steal his hard-earned money?"

"Emily." He squinted as he scanned the room, looking for the camera, looking for her.

"Emmeleia, jackass. She cleaned your clock in court. Had the jurors weeping in their seats." He picked up a large knife.

Ava could almost see him vibrate with fury. She'd be lying if she said it didn't feel good to mess with him. "You ever wonder what happened to little Emmeleia, Gino?"

"I'm gonna find you and gut you and fuck you until you bleed."

"Well, if you gut me first, it's definitely gonna get messy."

"And I'm gonna gut your mother and your sister and little brother."

She made a tutting sound even though inside she was numb with horror at the thought. That's how these guys won, by being more violent than anyone else. Brutal. Unfeeling. Psychopaths. Didn't matter how much money they had, they were monsters beneath the nice suits and expensive ties. Mobsters were animals and needed to be kept in cages.

But he wouldn't track them down. No links to them existed in her files. They were safe. She laughed. "You'll have to get out of prison for that, and you're too stupid. You're gonna miss your chance because it took you so long to get it up. Need a little blue pill, Gino? To put some pep in your prick?"

Gino walked over and dragged the cook to his feet by his hair. The cook cried out in what had to be excruciating pain. Gino held the knife to the man's throat.

Ava held her breath. Dominic squeezed her shoulder in warning. They both worried she'd gone too far.

"We're going out into the yard now, and that chopper better be waiting." Gino sneered.

Dominic pointed to a line on the sheet.

"If anyone hurts the hostages the deal is off," Ava said. Cold sweat slid down her back. She had never been in a situation this intense before. Even facing down Jimmy Taylor last week had been less stressful than this—because other people's lives were on the line here, she realized.

It was easier to risk your own life than barter for the lives of others.

She wouldn't want this job for all the money in the world.

Everyone in the negotiation room was wired and on edge. She glanced behind her to see the tactical and incident commanders staring holes in her through the window.

She turned back to the monitor. Gino had chosen the cook to be his shield as he was the biggest person in the room. It showed what a coward the man was.

Snake, indeed.

Frank picked another hostage, and they hovered near the exit into the yard.

Helicopter rotors could be easily heard in the distance.

"Is the chopper there yet?" Gino yelled.

Ava had definitely put the guy on edge and reminded him just how much he wanted to get out of prison.

Milo made the third hostage climb to his feet and held him loosely from behind. The warden slid off the counter and crawled out of sight. Good. Finally. They seemed to have forgotten about her, or cared more about their own skins.

Dominic muted Ava's mic. "HRT agents are set to enter the kitchen as soon as the hostage-takers move down the corridor towards the exercise yard."

Frank was unlocking the first dead bolt when Milo thrust the kitchen knife into his back, sliding the blade up under the man's ribs.

Ava's mouth dropped open in shock.

"Fuck," Dominic said in her ear.

She knew HRT was scrambling to get into that room as soon as physically possible, but would it be fast enough to stop Milo killing everyone?

"That was for knocking me out, asshole." Milo turned

toward Gino who was now scrambling away from the serial killer, holding the knife to the cook's throat.

Blood dripped from the end of Milo's blade, and he laughed as he advanced on the other hostage-taker.

"What makes you think I care about him?" Milo flicked the point of the knife towards the cook.

Gino thrust the hostage aside and screamed up at the ceiling, apparently reconsidering his demands for release. "Get me the hell out of here. This guy is a psycho!"

"Not so brave now, are you, Gino?" Milo laughed and tracked the mobster who kept backing away until he hit a wall.

"Where the hell is HRT?" Dominic asked, resting his arm on the desk so close to Ava's it was like he was hugging her from behind.

Ava swallowed hard and then decided to try something. At this stage they had nothing to lose. "This is not how revenge works, Milo." She spoke in Greek. "This man has done harm to my family. I get to decide the price he pays."

Milo paused in his pursuit of the mobster and stared directly at the camera. The man had known all along they were watching. "What about *my* revenge? What about the warden's?"

Gino seemed to sense an opportunity or a weakness in Milo and dashed toward the woman hiding behind the big metal island. Milo stuck out his foot and Gino crashed to the floor, lucky not to impale himself on his own blade. The older man's face was bright red against the shock of white hair. He no longer looked like a gangster, instead he looked like a fat, bitter, frightened, old man.

"He killed my father. He ruined *my* life." Ava insisted holding onto the mic tightly with one hand.

"Then I'll say this is for you," Milo declared like he was giving Ava a present.

"What the hell is going on?" Dominic asked, muting the mic.

Ava had forgotten the rest of them couldn't understand the conversation. "The ancient Greeks were big on revenge," she explained.

"Shit, isn't that what he's been studying? Use English—we all need to understand the conversation." Dominic turned the mic back on.

"Milo." Ava switched to English. "Everything that has happened so far is not your fault. We saw that you weren't part of this plan, that you involved yourself so you could save the hostages."

"To protect the warden," Dominic whispered against her ear staring intently at the monitor. "There's a connection there."

"To protect the warden," Ava repeated. Sweat ran down Ava's temple although she felt icy cold. "The warden isn't going to want you to murder Gino in cold blood. She'll want him punished in accordance to the law."

The woman stood up behind the counter. Naked, arms crossed over her chest but shoulders back, voice strong. HRT was almost there.

"She's right, Milo. I could never have survived this ordeal if it wasn't for you helping me. Thank you for that. Let Gino rot in prison. Put the knife down before they come in here with guns blazing and shoot you for being armed."

On screen Milo and the warden both glanced toward the cafeteria where sounds of the assault team could be heard.

"Put the weapon down," Dominic urged directly into the

mic. "We don't want to hurt you after you've helped resolve this crisis."

Milo looked sadly at Gino. Then he tossed the knife on the counter and raised his hands high into the air. He took a step back and executed a brutal kick that hit Gino in the face. Ava sucked in a startled breath at the ferocity of the attack. Then Milo stepped away with a smile that sent shivers through Ava just as the HRT guys blew the doors and rushed inside.

Ava met Dominic's stare and flinched at the turbulent emotion in his gaze.

"We need to talk," he said.

Ava grimaced. It was her turn to have her ass kicked.

CHAPTER TWENTY-ONE

"DID YOU KNOW about this?" Charlotte demanded angrily as she pushed to his side.

Dominic turned off the microphone and recording instruments. Anger coiled inside him like razor wire. If he said no, Ava wouldn't be suspended, she'd be gone. Kicked out of the Bureau permanently. And she was a damn good agent—one he'd just had sex with.

Complications were multiplying like rabbits and the fact he felt compromised by what they'd done, both by the need to protect her and the need to protect his own reputation and his job, made him so fucking furious that his skin felt like it might char at the edges if he released even an iota of his rage.

"Of course, I knew." He looked Charlotte in the eyes and lied.

Ava was a Black Swan. An unknown unknown that changed everything completely.

It was so *Ava* he should have known. Milo's protective loyalty to the warden was another. Who knew serial killers felt loyalty?

Charlotte threw up her hands when he refused to say anything more and turned away to organize her stuff. He and Ava stared at one another.

She understood exactly how angry he was. Her expression

turned from contrition to resilience to resentment with each breath she took, her mood conveyed by the increasingly belligerent angle of her chin.

Typical Ava.

A loose cannon. A loner. Unpredictable.

The Incident Commander came into the room and shook his hand, but Dominic had not solved this crisis. He'd just stalled for time which hadn't been good enough in this particular instance. Then the IC turned to Ava and shook her hand.

"I don't know if any of that was true, but that was a god-damned beautiful thing to watch."

"What is Frank Jacobs' condition? And the warden?" Dominic interrupted. This operation had been a team effort and the fact the Incident Commander didn't recognize that pissed him off.

"Jacobs has been rushed to the nearest trauma center—he's alive. The warden is physically unharmed."

"I didn't do much, sir." Ava spoke clearly, interrupting what Dominic had been about to say. Ballsy considering his fuse was so short the slightest thing might set him off and she knew it. "The negotiation team worked tirelessly to prevent the hostage-takers harming the hostages. I was a little shock value at the end."

Dominic shook his head.

Shock value. That summed her up perfectly. And she totally cut the legs from under him with the power of her convictions and ingrained sense of honor. It's what Van had seen in her.

The Incident Commander nodded. Goddamn, the man looked infatuated. Hell, they probably all did, except Charlotte who didn't seem to like Ava, at all. "I'm going to recommend you get a commendation."

Ava shook her head. Hazel eyes wide and unnerved. "No. No, sir. I'd rather my part in this be forgotten. Scrubbed from the record if at all possible." She swallowed repeatedly. "I really do have a mother, brother and sister who might be in danger if my name gets out."

"So, it was true?" the Incident Commander questioned.

Ava grimaced but didn't answer. Dominic went still for a long moment realizing exactly what that meant. At a young age Ava, or Emmeleia, had watched her father murdered. She'd been hit so hard on the face that she still wore the scar today. Instead of crawling off and hiding the way he had when his mother had died, Ava had fought back. Changed her identity and gone up against one of the most powerful mob families in NY history.

He put his hands in his pockets to hide the fact they were suddenly shaking. The others moved away, and he and Ava stood staring at one another, surrounded by chaos and frantic activity.

"That's where you met Van?" He had the epiphany out loud.

She nodded.

No wonder they'd been close and the guy had sung her praises. He'd known her since she was a little kid with a target on her back.

"I'm sorry I didn't tell you everything." She spoke low so only he could hear.

And that was where part of his anger came from, he realized. The fact she hadn't confided in him. She hadn't told him her deep dark secrets. Which was hypocritical because

Dominic did not trust easily and guarded his secrets like a miser's gold. WitSec wasn't your average confidence. Lives depended on not revealing information that didn't need to be revealed.

He and Ava had known one another five minutes. Five minutes that felt longer than a lifetime.

Eban and Charlotte were clearing up, gathering the notes they needed to make their reports.

"Remove Ava's name from any of the documents and case notes," Dominic told them.

Eban nodded. Charlotte kept her lips pressed firmly together in disapproval.

Ava's eyes told him she was grateful.

"Want to do the walk-through with us?" asked Eban.

Usually Dominic would do exactly that. See if they'd missed anything or could have done anything differently or better.

"You guys go on without us." He was still trying to put the pieces of his brain back together.

Before Charlotte and Eban could leave though, the warden arrived in the doorway, wearing an over-sized, black HRT t-shirt and the same pants she'd been wearing for days.

She cleared her throat. "I wanted to say 'thank you' to the people involved in resolving this siege, the tactical unit but especially to the negotiators." Her eyes were red, and her hands trembled. The woman knew they'd all seen her naked and at her most vulnerable but here she was, facing them head-on, meeting their gazes with an indomitable spirit. "You kept me from falling over the edge of hysteria in there and allowed me to retain a shred of dignity."

She shook hands with them all. Joe and Eban both had

their jaws clamped so forcefully shut Dominic knew they were holding back tears.

It was impossible not to be moved. He glanced at Ava and although she held herself stiffly, her eyes were glassy. For all her attitude, Ava Kanas had a big heart and had taken a giant risk with her and her family's safety to help rescue this woman, a stranger to her.

And yet she held back with the group hug while Charlotte dove right in.

He narrowed his gaze because he knew from the way she held herself she wanted to join that embrace but didn't feel welcome.

Suddenly he wanted to scoop Ava up in a big hug but was afraid if he did so everyone in the room would be able to read his thoughts and feelings regarding this woman, and he wasn't even sure what they were himself.

He knew he liked her. *Really* liked her. To the point where he'd compromised himself in a way unimaginable a few hours ago. It appeared he'd taken over from Van in trying to protect her within the Bureau—mainly from herself.

For the first time in days his cell phone started buzzing in his pocket. Comms were back on inside the prison. He'd be lying if he said he'd missed being plugged in.

Mallory Rooney was on the line. "Ballistics from a rifle found in the back of Caroline Perry's car match the bullet casing found on the roof after the Calvin Mortimer shooting."

"So, you found her car?"

"Down by the river." Rooney paused. "Ava didn't tell you?"

He ran his hand through his short hair. "I asked her not to tell me anything until this siege was over, which it now is. She can fill me in on everything I missed. Tell me the new stuff."

"The task force is trying to place Caroline Perry at the scenes of any of the deaths of the FBI agents in question. We are also looking at Karl Feldman. Seeing if they were possibly working together. We have someone trying to trace where she purchased the gun but nothing so far."

Dominic rubbed the bridge of his nose. The scab had healed, and his bruises were starting to fade. His shoulder still ached though. And his ribs. But the injuries were fading, and he was keen to put this nightmare behind him.

"Task force is trying to establish a connection between her and any of the NYFO cases your squad worked. Maybe she assumed another identity and isn't really Caroline Perry."

"Have the BAU worked up a profile of the likely offender yet?" asked Dominic, trying to ignore the whirlwind of activity that swirled around him. Ava crossed her arms and stared at him, patiently waiting for news.

"Given the wide-ranging, potential crimes with differing MOs it hasn't been easy," Rooney admitted. "They found plastic explosives on Fernando Chavez's speedboat on the weekend. The guy was insanely lucky that there was a fault with a detonator or else he and his whole family would probably be dead by now. The fact the UNSUB can move across the country so easily suggests they have means and are above average intelligence but we haven't narrowed it much further than that, yet."

Dominic's world slowed. "Wait. Fernando Chavez? Fernando only crossed over with some of the older agents by a couple of months..."

"Task force is examining the cases."

Dominic's mind was racing. It was his life. He knew the

facts better than any task force. "I need to make a call. I'll call you back."

He strode out of the building barely aware of Ava on his heels. He searched for the contact information of a female vice cop he'd worked with during the hunt for a notorious serial killer named the "Lost Girl Killer" by the press.

Peter Galveston had liked to pick up hitchhikers and keep them for weeks or months at his upscale cabin in remote woods where he raped and tortured them. Eventually they died from their injuries or he'd grow bored and finish them off by hunting them in the woods near his house, or strangling them with his bare hands.

The guy had taped much of it in graphic detail, but they'd always thought he'd had someone helping him. Maybe more than one person.

Finally, Dominic found the number he was looking for. Sandra Warren.

"Sheridan?" She sounded exactly the same as she had a decade ago. "What the heck can I do for you?"

"Hey, Sandy. Where are you at, right now?" His heart was pumping fast.

"That's an odd question?" Classic cop, not giving anything away.

"It's really important that you listen to me carefully. This is not a prank. I want you to head straight for Federal Plaza. Don't talk to anyone. Don't drive your own car, don't drink or eat anything…"

"What the hell? Is this some sort of secret society hazing thing? Do I win a prize at the end of it?" She was laughing.

Dominic's mouth was dry. "Where exactly are you now?"

She lowered her voice. "Talking to a sex crime victim in

lower Manhattan."

"Alone?"

"No. I have a detective with me. Why? Hey, come on. You're scaring me, buddy."

"I can't explain, but I *really* need you to do as I ask. Get a cab to the FBI office and wait there until someone contacts you."

"What about my family, Dominic?" Her voice rose with fear. She was taking him seriously.

"Call Ben, tell him to pick everyone up—not in your own car, get a cab—and meet you at NYFO. Call me when you get there…"

"Okay, but if this is a joke I'm going to roast your ass."

"It's no joke."

She hung up, obviously in a hurry to warn her husband.

"You figured it out?" Ava asked, watching him as they threw their belongings into their go-bags. He ignored the sight of the messed-up sheets on the mattresses on the floor, but Dominic did not forget what they'd done.

It paled into insignificance when compared to the deadly actions of this killer—not the act itself, but the associated shame.

"You know who it is," Ava declared, grabbing the wash bags out of the tiny bathroom and tossing him his.

"I think so." He dialed Lincoln Frazer. Nausea swirled in his stomach.

"Who?" she asked.

Frazer answered with a terse, "What is it?"

"Peter Galveston," Dominic said.

"Galveston is dead," said Frazer.

"I know. I shot him." It had been the first time Dominic

had killed a man, but not the last.

"These murders do not share an MO with Galveston," Frazer argued.

"I'm telling you, Linc, it's connected to him. He was our major focus when Fernando Chavez joined our squad. We caught him within a month of Chavez being there and Preston Daniels retired shortly afterwards. Fernando effectively replaced Preston." Dominic's fingers cramped from holding the phone so tightly. "I know it's related to Galveston."

"I'll call the task force and ask them to prioritize reviewing his case files."

Dominic had lived and breathed that case for months. He knew the case files inside out.

"I called a female cop called Sandra Warren who acted as bait for the serial killer. I told her to get to NYFO ASAP and get her family there too. Whoever is doing this will target her."

His phone showed another call coming through. "Wait. She's calling me back. Let me take that."

"Fine," Frazer said. "I'll call the task force."

"Dominic? I can't reach Ben." Sandy was talking quickly, too quickly. "What the hell is going on?"

"Did you check the school?"

"The kids are both in the principal's office. I told her to keep them there until I pick them up."

"Let someone else do that, Sandy. Let an officer—"

"No. Goddammit, if they are in danger, I'll be the one to pick them up. Tell me what the hell is going on."

Dominic took a long breath to slow down his heart. "We believe someone has been hunting down the agents working the Peter Galveston case—"

"Hunting down?"

"Killing."

"Oh, my god."

Dominic could hear tires screeching and a siren go on.

"Oh, no, oh god." Sandy was gulping audibly as if struggling to breathe. "There's an ambulance outside my house, Dominic."

Dammit.

He heard her sobbing her husband's name and then nothing. She hung up on him. Dominic stood there and closed his eyes. If he'd figured this out earlier then he might have prevented this. But that was exactly what the UNSUB wanted. For Dominic to tear himself apart with guilt.

He called Frazer back and told him what had happened and to contact agents at NYFO to get protection on Sandy whether she wanted it or not.

The UNSUB's plan appeared to have misfired and Dominic wouldn't put it past the asshole to have something lined up in reserve.

"What are you going to do?" Frazer asked.

Dominic glanced at Ava. He wished she was safely out of the way back in Fredericksburg—not because he didn't want her around but because he didn't want her to get hurt. And this UNSUB would be more than happy to hurt Ava if she got in his way.

"I'm close by so I'm going to make sure Galveston is in the dirt where I put him. I want an exhumation order signed by the time I get to Chapel Hills on the border of New York State and Pennsylvania. I'll call the RA in Binghamton for assistance. You call the director."

"I'm on it," Frazer replied. "Just one thing…"

"What?" Dominic snapped as he headed out the trailer to

scrounge up a ride.

"Watch your back. Even if Caroline Perry was involved, I don't think she was acting alone."

Frazer was right. The plot was too intricate to be carried out by one lone actor. "I agree."

"Kanas working out okay as protection?" The way Frazer asked made Dominic wonder if he'd guessed something was going on between him and Ava.

"Still saving the world," he told the other man.

Ava's lips pressed together, and he knew she knew they were talking about her. But he didn't have time to worry about her feelings or about what the hell he was going to do with this woman who was complicating his life and his work. Not until they caught this killer. Not until they stopped the madness.

CHAPTER TWENTY-TWO

AVA SAT NEXT to Dominic in the helicopter that had originally been tasked as a decoy for the prisoners' escape. Now Dominic and Ava were using it to head south from Buffalo to somewhere called Chapel Hills.

It was only mid-morning, but considering everything that had happened since midnight she felt like this day had already lasted a thousand years.

They'd got out of there in record time, Dominic barking out questions and updates even when he was on the phone trying to arrange the exhumation of a serial killer named Peter Galveston—the so-called Lost Girl Killer. Now Ava sat in the back of the helicopter, nervously watching the countryside whizz by below. This was her first time in a chopper, and they were traveling so fast her heart was about two feet behind her body. It was deafeningly noisy even with the ear muffs and the mic in her headset wasn't working, so although she could hear Dominic and the pilot talking to one another, she couldn't ask questions or join in the conversation.

After an hour of what seemed like breakneck flying, they touched down in a rural area in Upper Delaware on the border of Pennsylvania.

"Can you wait here? We'll be a few hours," Dominic said to the pilot as the guy turned the engine off. The rotors slowed and Ava heard the pilot agree.

She would be shocked if this didn't last a lot longer than a few hours, but it finally felt as if they were closing in on this UNSUB. Ava grabbed her stuff, opened the door and followed Dominic, both of them avoiding the tail rotor as they quickly strode to a waiting SUV. She'd been so busy filling him in on the details of Caroline Perry's death that he hadn't had time to tell her exactly who Sandy Warren or Fernando Chavez were, but she'd pieced some of it together. Ava had spent a good deal of the flight researching Galveston. He'd been a classic sexual sadist, and Dominic had put a bullet in him during his apprehension. She was guessing Sandy Warren was the woman who'd played the decoy hitchhiker, and Chavez was another FBI agent from NYFO.

"SSA Sheridan and Agent Kanas?" A man in a gray suit and dark sunglasses held out his hand to shake both of theirs. "I'm Agent Pine. The State Governor just signed the order. Everything is ready at the cemetery."

They both got in the vehicle. Dominic had been texting on his phone the whole journey, obviously steamrollering this usually paperwork-heavy event. And he was probably still mad with her about not telling him the truth about Gino and her past.

"Any updates?" she asked, probing for information.

Dominic lowered his sunglasses and looked at her from his seat in the front of the SUV. "NYPD Detective Sandra Warren's husband was found injured in their home. He opened a package that turned out to be a pipe bomb that had been addressed to Sandy and mailed to their house. They got him to the hospital, but he lost a hand and isn't out of danger yet."

Emotion gripped Ava by the throat. "Could Caroline Perry have mailed it before she died?"

The woman had been right in front of them, serving them food and drink and they hadn't suspected a thing.

Dominic nodded. "It's possible. They are putting a rush on all the DNA evidence found during this case and any other lab tests that need to be conducted. This is the Bureau's priority number one. Agents were already tracing every aspect of Perry's background from kindergarten to present day—and trying to ascertain if the waitress actually was 'Caroline Perry' but as far as we can tell she has no living family. So far no one named 'Perry' has turned up with any connection to the Galveston case."

"So, what's the plan?"

"Exhuming Galveston's body shouldn't take long. A couple of hours at most."

"Why exactly are you exhuming the guy's body?" Agent Pine asked.

"Because I need to demonstrate he's actually dead."

"You put him in the ground and now you're digging him up?" Pine laughed. "No wonder people say the federal government is inefficient."

Dominic didn't smile. "As soon as the connection between Galveston and these other incidents become public there will be speculation about whether or not Galveston is really dead. He is. I checked for his pulse after the shooting. I witnessed the autopsy where his brain and black heart were weighed on the counter."

"People will say he somehow faked it. Took some sort of poison to slow his heart. The guy was a multi-millionaire, he could buy off the Medical Examiner, buy off the cops…switch out a body," Ava exclaimed. Conspiracy theorists could get seriously crazy.

"Or that you guys got the wrong person," Agent Pine put in.

"Exactly." Dominic pushed his glasses back up his nose. "And I'm gonna prove that cocksucker can't hurt anyone anymore."

Ava wondered if he needed to prove it to himself too. Van had told her there were cases that shaped your entire career. Her father's murder and taking down the mob had been Van's. Maybe this case was Dominic's.

"How did the shooting go down?" she asked.

"We realized we had a serial killer after the decomposing bodies of three women were found in the woods either side of the Delaware River. The river divides New York and Pennsylvania so the FBI were immediately involved." Dominic pursed his lips. "Who knows how many remains we didn't find. DNA swabs from the cabin turned up forty different profiles, although we were never sure if they were all victims or not. Some might have been friends. According to Galveston's video journals he liked to entertain, often with a girl tied up and incapacitated somewhere else in the house. He got off on that."

Ava shuddered. The mob were vicious and brutal, but it was a different kind of evil to these types of murderers. Still reprehensible. But different.

"We knew the victims generally went missing on a Friday night off highways 178 or 97. We decided to use a female cop to pose as a hitchhiker along a mile stretch of road on a Friday evening. We had a surveillance unit hidden in the woods. We were about to call it a day on our fourth week when this shiny new pickup truck drove past and slammed the brakes for

Sandy.

"She'd been told not to get in the car. We were simply taking names and license plates at that point. Next thing we know she's on her knees on the side of the road, and the driver is getting out and starts manhandling her into the truck."

"Everything happened fast after that. We drive out of the woods right in front of the truck and he almost T-bones us. We caught him by surprise. I jump out and tell him to get out of the truck. He doesn't do it fast enough so I open his door and he's reaching for a .356mm Magnum. Sandy manages to knock it out of his hand despite her being tasered. Once again, I order him out of the vehicle, but he lunges for the gun instead. So, I shot him twice in the chest. It was over in about five seconds but every moment felt like it lasted a century."

Ava blew out a big breath. It sounded like solid ground work and blind luck had caught the serial killer. The razor-fine edge between success and failure was both gratifying and terrifying because sometimes the luck went to the other side. Sometimes the bad guys got away and kept on killing.

Agent Pine pulled into a rural cemetery with a beautiful, old brick church with a white-painted spire, topped with a cross. Old, weathered stones competed with fresh, white marble in the lush, green grounds. Ava got out of the car, trying to conceal the sudden chill that swept over her skin. Maybe it was the fog that had started to crawl in from the surrounding forest. Maybe it was the cool mountain breeze. Maybe it was the ghosts of all Peter Galveston's victims. Whatever it was, her flesh crawled.

In the far corner of the graveyard, a small digger was building a steadily growing pile of soil at the side of a tall marble obelisk.

Ava followed Dominic out of the car and across the damp grass. Right now, Sheridan was very much the remote professional in command of this scene. It was hard to reconcile this man with the person who'd licked her naked body a few hours earlier, but Ava wasn't expecting any PDAs. Didn't want them. Even if they had been in a real relationship, she'd expect SSA Sheridan to behave as a federal law enforcement employee first and foremost. Later when they were alone, who knew what might happen, but she wasn't going to beg like a dog for his affection. She hadn't been needy for attention since her father had been murdered in front of her, and she'd discovered the safety of a strong man was an illusion.

She strode after Dominic, and Pine followed closely behind. She glanced around, checking the area for potential threats. A man and woman were tending a grave a hundred feet away. The woman on her hands and knees pulling weeds. Man filling a watering can. No press. Good.

Dominic walked up to a small group of men watching the excavation, shook hands and introduced himself.

"Where's the tent?" Dominic asked.

Usually with an exhumation there would be a crime scene tent covering the proceedings from prying eyes. Usually they had a little more time to plan…

Pine answered, "ME's office is on the way with a tent and some sampling equipment. ME told me to get the coffin out first as their tent isn't large enough to contain the digger and the dirt too. Said he'd be here by the time we were ready for him."

Ava watched Dominic's jaw clench, but his expression remained neutral. He was skilled at hiding his emotions.

Something she'd never mastered.

A man came towards them from the church and introduced himself as the local pastor, Robin Elgin. He looked to be in his early thirties, a handsome guy, wearing jeans and a green sweater and black trainers.

Hip and trendy for a man of God.

Dominic shook hands with the guy. "Sorry for the inconvenience, Pastor. We won't be in your way for long."

The pastor's lips pulled back in distaste. "I suppose it was inevitable considering whose grave this is."

Ava canted her head to one side. "Do a lot of people visit the grave?"

Dominic perked up at that question.

The man nodded. "Absolutely. We get a lot of traffic because of our famous resident."

"Any regular visitors?" Ava asked.

"Quite a few actually."

"Do you know any of their names?" Dominic asked, his interest sharpening.

The pastor looked surprised. "No, I mean," he shrugged and looked around, "they aren't local residents."

Dominic did that thing he did when he wanted someone to keep talking. "Aren't local residents?"

"Well, I mean they might be, I don't know everyone around here, but I don't think so. They certainly don't come to church on a Sunday, but that seems to be dying off anyway."

"Galveston is buried in a family plot, is that correct?" Dominic asked.

The pastor nodded and cleared his throat. "Yes. I wasn't here at the time, of course, but the Galveston family owned most of the land around here. They donated this acreage to the church on the condition any direct descendants had the right to be buried here."

"Almost like they knew it would come in handy one day," Ava quipped.

The pastor smiled. From the way his eyes drifted over her body he hadn't taken any vows of celibacy.

She blinked in surprise. He made her oddly uncomfortable.

"Do you have some sort of book these visitors might have signed?" Dominic asked.

"Why, yes, although I don't know if they did or not." The pastor's Adam's apple bobbed up and down a few times. "I try not to spy on people when they are here paying their condolences no matter who they happen to be grieving for. If you follow me, I'll show you where the visitor book is so you can look at it."

"Ava," Dominic ordered.

Damn. She didn't want to leave him but could hardly disobey a direct order. Plus, he should be safe enough with Agent Pine.

When the pastor turned around and started to walk away, Dominic stopped her with a hand around her wrist and leaned close to her ear. "Watch your back. I don't trust him."

"Yes, sir. And you watch your back too. This place is freaking me out," she said quietly.

"Scared of ghosts, Agent Kanas?" Dominic's smile was hard.

"No, sir. I'm scared of people." And right now, she didn't trust anyone. Not even the dead guy.

Dominic gave her a grin that made her heart flip like a landed salmon. She heaved a sigh as she followed the pastor to the old church. Despite everything she'd told herself, she was falling for Dominic. If she wasn't careful, she'd be cooking beef casseroles and holding out her heart in her hands for him to trample all over.

Goddammit.

She winced then and went inside the church with a silent apology. It was freezing inside, nothing like the heat of their Virginian summer in this part of the country.

Pastor Elgin led her to the back of the church and picked up a visitor book that sat on a side table alongside a black pen. Part of Ava wanted to bag the lot for evidence, but what would it prove? Nothing conclusive except the need for hand sanitizer was real.

She followed Elgin into a side corridor and through to a room with a small couch and TV, a sink, fridge and coffee making facilities.

"Can I make you a drink?"

The image of Dominic being pried out of his Lexus jumped into her head.

"No thanks. Water would be good though. I'll do it. I don't want to cause you any trouble," she insisted and gave the man a bright smile. He brushed against her to reach up for a glass from a shelf.

Ava rolled her eyes as she took the glass from him. She couldn't decide if he thought he was God's gift—understandable under the circumstances—or was slightly clueless about personal space. Yeah, she'd never been big on the clueless excuse. Different cultures had different personal space limits, but they were all Americans here.

She filled her glass and took a long drink of water without taking her eyes off the guy. She wiped her mouth. "How long have you worked here, Pastor?"

He blinked, and she noticed he had freckles and bright blue, guileless eyes. "About five years now. I can't believe it's been that long, actually. Before that I was in college doing a Ph.D. in theology." He rubbed his hands over his forearms. This place was an icebox.

"Did you pick the parish or did the parish pick you?"

He laughed. She noticed a red patch of skin when he rolled up his sleeve.

"A bit of both, I suppose. I applied for the job when the last pastor moved away and was lucky enough to be chosen. I'd had a position as a deacon in Connecticut before this."

"Good pay?" Ava asked with a smile. You really did get more from people when you were friendly.

He shook his head. "Terrible, but I get decent accommodations included, and it really is a beautiful part of the world."

"Even with a serial killer in the graveyard?"

"Let he who is without sin cast the first stone." The pastor's tone was mocking rather than sanctimonious.

"Very Christian of you." Ava smiled and washed up her glass and put it on the counter to drain. Then she went over and sat at the small table and pulled on gloves to page through the visitor book. You couldn't be too careful.

The first entry in the book was dated four years ago. "Do you have the books for the years before this?" she asked. "Specifically, ten years ago when Galveston was first buried?"

He straightened. "I don't know. They should be around here somewhere. Let me look for them."

"Ever heard of a woman called Caroline Perry? Or a guy named Karl Feldman?"

Elgin frowned. "No. Should I have?"

"Just curious." Ava started leafing through the book, working backwards. The answers were somewhere. It was just a question of figuring out where.

DOMINIC DIDN'T WANT to leave the graveside until the coffin was up and open and he was staring at Peter Galveston's rotting corpse. But as he watched Ava follow the clergyman who could barely keep his tongue in his mouth, Dominic didn't want to leave her alone with the guy either. That was more a personal preference than a professional one so he stayed where he was. Apparently, Mr. Loner had gotten used to his beautiful shadow over the past few days.

Get a grip.

Ava Kanas didn't need his protection. She'd taken down dangerous fugitives and drug dealers and that was just in the last week. Hell, she'd taken on the mob at an age where most kids were playing dress up. What had he been doing at age seven? Probably crying because his mother was dead and then crushing his brother at Mario Kart.

He drew his attention back to where the digger was lifting bucket upon bucket of heavy black soil out of the ground. The noise of the machinery meant it was impossible to carry on a normal conversation. Two more federal agents arrived, probably to check out the proceedings. It wasn't every day they dug up a serial killer.

Dominic used the time to center his thoughts about the case.

This killer had planted C4 in Chavez's speedboat and sent a pipe-bomb to Sandra Warren that had maimed her husband.

He, or she, did not care if other people got hurt. They didn't care if kids got hurt.

If it was Caroline Perry then what was her motive? What was her connection to Galveston?

Dominic raised his gaze to the tombstone and read the inscription. Older sibling. Parents. Nothing for Peter except his name, date of birth, date of death. The man had been an only child after the early demise of his brother. Dominic would bet the farm that Peter had had something to do with that premature death. Psychopaths did not like competition for attention.

The guy had had plenty of friends, but they'd all scattered like roaches after he was shot and claimed they had no idea about the man's murderous pastimes. They were probably telling the truth. *Most* of them. The FBI had never been able to connect any of them specifically with his crimes.

Dominic walked around the obelisk and rocked to a halt. Someone had left the bastard a teddy bear. It was an expensive make, he knew that from the label on the foot. Who the hell left a serial killer a stuffed toy? Someone who loved him, that's who.

He took out his cell phone and snapped a photograph and sent it to Lincoln Frazer. A minute later he got a call from the man.

"Where is that?" Frazer asked.

"Peter Galveston's grave."

"Give me the GPS coordinates."

Dominic texted them and waited silently on the line.

Frazer finally came back to him as the digger hit something solid in the earth with a slight thump. The people around the grave jostled in excitement.

"Alex Parker managed to isolate a cell phone number that had been active around the bar in Fredericksburg, Van's house, and the area where Caroline Perry's body went into the water. It also pinged the tower nearest your house a couple of times. Parker checked, and it pinged the tower nearest your current location on several occasions over the past year."

"Send me those dates." He needed to show the pastor a photo of Perry, see if the guy recognized her. "Where is the phone now?"

"Hasn't been turned on since Tuesday night. Around the Medical Examiner's time of death for Perry."

"What does the teddy bear tell you?" Dominic asked the profiler.

"That someone had strong feelings for Galveston and wanted to prove someone loved him. Probably a female."

Dominic grunted. Men didn't tend to buy teddy bears for loved ones—unless it was for a child. Galveston's parents were both dead.

"This could be the work of more than one person," Dominic stated.

"At this stage, with this many agents targeted, the UNSUB definitely had help," Frazer agreed.

"Gotta go." Dominic hung up.

So, who had left the toy? Could he bag it for evidence? For what end? It wasn't a crime to visit a grave, or to leave an offering.

The gravediggers and laborers had placed chains under the coffin. The earth moving equipment was now doing double duty as a winch. Four men steadied the casket as it came clear of the ground and eased it onto the grass beside the hole in the earth.

Dominic looked around impatiently for the ME. Where the hell was the guy? He was about to open the casket himself when a van rolled into place. Two men, both carrying heavy bags, trudged across the dried grass to meet them.

Dominic held back his irritation but obviously not well enough.

"What's the hurry people? It's not like our fellow is going anywhere."

Dominic forced himself to smile and use his upbeat, friendly voice even though his angry voice wanted to tell them to hurry the fuck up. "It's part of a current investigation that's time sensitive."

"Copycat?" the ME frowned.

Dominic was sure the last thing this man wanted on his table were raped and murdered girls.

"I'm afraid I'm not at liberty to discuss an active investigation at this time."

The man grunted and scowled up at the sky. "Really want the tent up? It'll take thirty minutes to erect."

Dominic thought about it. All they needed was a photograph of the corpse *in situ* and to take a quick DNA sample. "You have any umbrellas in the car?" he asked Agent Pine and the ME's assistant.

Both men nodded and trudged off to fetch them.

The man and woman in the churchyard were watching with interest.

"You guys can leave. We'll call you when we need you again," he told the gravediggers and laborers.

The remaining Feds formed a short wall. Pine handed over a golf umbrella and held a second one himself. Dominic opened the umbrella just as Ava slid up beside him to help form a barrier. The canopy was wide and blocked any viewers from seeing inside the casket from above or the side.

The ME and his assistant both donned masks and then lifted the top half of the coffin lid.

Sonofabitch.

Dominic stared into the box as the world spun around him. Brown stained satin lined the casket but no corpse filled it.

Someone cursed. Agent Pine.

Peter Galveston was dead. Dominic knew he was dead, but someone was trying to mess with his head.

"Can you tell if a body was removed? Or if there was even ever one in there?" Ava asked quietly making sure her voice didn't carry.

"Judging from the stains and bodily fluids there was definitely a body in here," the ME answered.

But it was gone now.

Dominic managed to swallow the huge lump that filled his throat. "Close it up. I want the casket transported to the nearest crime lab for processing. ASAP. Highest priority." He looked at the men who'd assisted getting the coffin out of the ground.

"I need you to question all these people," he told Pine and the other agents. "I don't believe someone stole this body without help. The pastor too. Maybe someone made a donation to look the other way that he couldn't refuse." These people were the main suspects until the FBI figured out different. "Push them hard on accessory to murder of a federal agent. Bag the teddy bear and any visitor books inside the church. Get a warrant if the pastor resists—in fact get a warrant anyway. Courier everything except the coffin to the

National Laboratory." Dominic started striding away, Ava on his heels and Agent Pine catching up behind them to drive.

"Where will you be?" Pine asked.

Dominic checked his watch. "I'm going to check Galveston's cabin. You know where that is?"

Pine shook his head. "But I can find out."

"Don't worry about it. Drive us into the nearest town with a rental office. I can find the way from there." Dominic called the chopper pilot and told him to go home. He had the feeling they were going to be stuck here for some time.

CHAPTER TWENTY-THREE

FROM THE CAR, Dominic had called Frazer who had then called the head of the task force about Peter Galveston's missing body. The press were going to go ape. Now he stood outside the restaurant while waiting for their lunch to be delivered. Neither Dominic nor Ava had eaten anything since last night. Dominic didn't even remember what it had been. He called his boss, who was thankfully distracted by the fact he was about to get on the plane to fly to Southeast Asia.

"I hear you had some unexpected help resolving the hostage crisis," Savage said once Dominic had finished updating him on the Galveston situation.

Dominic scratched his head. He hadn't confronted Ava about that yet. Since the siege ended, his focus had shifted straight back to this case and the fact someone wanted him and his colleagues dead. Everything had been a whirlwind of activity as they struggled to get one step ahead of this UNSUB. He was still trying to figure out whether to be impressed with Ava or furious. Or both.

"How is Frank Jacobs doing?"

"Alive. Doctors think he'll make it. Knife missed his kidneys by an inch. Nicked a lung but didn't do as much damage as first feared."

"Any word about the warden?"

"She's going to take some time off. All the inmates involved will be transferred."

Standard procedure.

"Including Milo Andris?"

"Especially Milo. His attachment to the warden could turn ugly. He could feel she owes him now. *She* might feel she owes him. It's better if everyone starts from scratch. So," Savage was clearly striving for casual, "Ava Kanas was in WitSec?"

"I think officially she still is." Dominic looked up and spotted a pharmacy nearby. Through the window he noted his lunch order hadn't arrived yet. He headed for the pharmacy, still talking on the phone.

"Don't worry," Savage offered, "the information about her full identity has been left out of the official records of the incident. We called her a trainee negotiator and as there is no record of her at CNU, there's no mention of her name."

Dominic blew out a breath of relief.

"Did you know?" Savage pressed.

Dominic might have lied to Charlotte and Eban, but he couldn't lie to Savage.

"No, but looking back I didn't give her much chance to tell me. I was so focused on the siege that every time she tried to talk to me, I assumed it was about the UNSUB killing agents and told her to wait until the siege was finished. She didn't even open her mouth in the negotiation room until Gino was seconds away from raping the warden."

Dominic picked up a packet of condoms and some headache pills. He didn't know whether to be disgusted by his lack of self-control, or impressed by his planning-for-anything mentality.

"I had no idea about her past, but it explains her relationship with Van Stamos. I do know that without Kanas's intervention the siege would not have ended so well for the hostages."

He paid cash and slipped the merchandise into his pocket. Headed back to the restaurant.

"Always expect the unexpected." Savage laughed.

"Don't ever forget it. Keep safe on your travels, Quentin."

The man swore. "Are you sure you don't want to go to Jakarta?"

"Hell, no." Dominic had been there plenty of times and never on vacation. "You'll do great."

"Watch your back, Dom. Someone has a hard-on to put you in the ground."

He thought of Caroline Perry. "That someone might be dead." God, he hoped so.

"And they might not be. The good news is even if they are alive, I doubt they know where you are right now, but that won't last long once the press hears about Galveston's missing corpse. Until we confirm the UNSUB was Perry, and was definitely working alone, do not do anything stupid and keep Kanas close."

Dominic grunted. Keeping Kanas close meant he was definitely going to do something stupid. And that wasn't even what bothered him about the whole thing. Keeping her close didn't seem like a problem, and *that* was in of itself becoming a major issue for him.

"When will you be back at Quantico?" Savage asked.

Dominic crossed his fingers. "Tomorrow. I'll be in touch if anything new turns up."

"Do that. Charlotte and Eban are on their way back here right now. There's some sort of standoff developing in Oregon again."

Fucking Freemen.

"So, everything is normal?" Dominic joked.

Savage grunted. "Some days it feels like no matter how hard or fast we work, there are still a bunch of whackos ready to come out of the woodwork and cause havoc and pain for others."

Dominic thought about Peter Galveston's missing corpse, which hadn't crawled out of that coffin on its own.

"Which is why we're here, I suppose."

Dominic watched a plate of food being delivered to the table where Ava sat talking to Agent Pine.

His mouth watered. He was starving, but even more than his hunger for food was his completely inappropriate hunger for the agent who was smiling across the table at another man.

She was a goddamn rookie. What was he doing? He didn't know. He really didn't know. But he wasn't ready to give her up yet.

He said goodbye to his boss, hung up and pushed back inside the front door.

AFTER LUNCH, JERRY Pine dropped them at the nearest vehicle rental place. Dominic had been insistent about having their own transportation but had forgotten he wasn't medically cleared to drive. Ava hadn't argued with the guy. Whatever their personal relationship, he was still a Supervisory Special Agent and way above her on the pay grade. Instead, she took the keys off the desk and got behind the wheel.

"What?" she asked when he finally slung his bag in the

trunk and climbed in beside her. They both needed to do laundry but neither wanted to waste a few hours on something so mundane when people's lives were in danger.

He shot her a resentful look.

"Where to, Boss?" She smiled determinedly. The fact she was still on the job made her feel grateful enough to ignore his bad mood.

His eyes narrowed further, and he lowered his sunglasses. The bruises were fading fast and the superiority complex was back full force. Rather than replying, he programmed an address into the GPS and then sat back, adjusting the seat so he could stretch out his long legs.

She checked her mirrors and pulled away. This was work, and he was the boss. *Don't screw it up, Ava.*

"Why didn't you tell me about Gino?" he asked after a few minutes of peace.

She blew out a long breath. She'd been anticipating the inquisition now they were on their own, but the question still took her by surprise.

"I didn't know Gino was incarcerated there until we arrived." Her fingers tightened reflexively around the steering wheel. Facing Gino had been like facing one of her demons. Sure, she'd done it before in court, but that had been years ago.

Dominic remained silent. The quiet hum of the engine and weight of accusation filled the void.

Her fingers rubbed the steering wheel. "I never imagined I'd get actively involved with the negotiation." Still he didn't speak. "I know I should have told you, but I didn't think it would make a difference."

"It would have made a difference to me." His words shook her as did the velvet tone of his voice. It wasn't the voice he used during negotiations. It was the one he'd used when they'd had sex.

Her pulse skipped.

She took a right as the GPS indicated and started climbing the hills into a dark forest. "I *never* talk about it, Dominic. I can't risk slipping up and condemning the rest of my family to death. That's the first time I've acknowledged the truth in public since the trial."

He shifted in the seat, the leather creaking. "Most of that crime family is in prison."

"Because of me. And it only takes one. Or for them to pay someone." She shook her head. "I couldn't take that risk."

"You could have trusted me."

"I know I can trust you. I *do* trust you." More than she wanted to admit. "At first, I worried if anyone found out I'd be off bodyguard duty and back on suspension," she told him. "Then I tried to tell you several times but you were either busy or," she cleared her throat, "we got distracted."

He ignored the oblique reference to them getting naked. He folded his fingers in his lap. Her mouth went dry thinking about those fingers on her skin.

"Gino is gonna be searching for information on you again now."

Her attention snapped back onto the threat that had shadowed her for her entire life. "I can look after myself. Should anyone in the FBI or prison service give the crime family information on me then at least my relatives aren't connected to me in any of my official files. Van saw to that... And the Greek community is tight enough that we'll know if someone starts asking questions." A wave of cold hit her. "But I need to warn my family. Tell them to take extra precautions with their safety." Which sucked. It would give her mother even more ammunition about ditching the FBI and coming home.

Those intelligent eyes of his were looking at her differently now. It took her a moment to recognize it was respect she was seeing there.

"No wonder you guys were so close."

Her stomach knotted. "Van saved my life but more importantly, he taught me how to take my power back."

"No wonder you wanted to be an agent."

"Yeah." She laughed. "Ask the mob what they fear most, and it'll be RICO charges and the FBI. So being an agent is all I've ever wanted." She was ripping off layers of armor for this man. She knew he wouldn't return the favor. Maybe that's why she pushed. "What made you join the FBI?"

On cue, he grimaced and looked away. Then he surprised her. "Pretty simple really. My father wanted me to become a partner in a big law firm."

"So, your whole career is you sticking it to your dad?"

The smile caught her off guard. The sparkle in those blue eyes. "That's how it started. Trying to prove he was wrong to push me down a certain path. But it turned out I loved it. Law bored the hell out of me, but being an FBI agent? The adrenaline rush, the danger, making a difference—that was a blast I couldn't resist." He rubbed his hand over his thigh. "Then proving that I got where I was on my own merit turned into a bit of an obsession. Van helped me not mess up too many times as a rookie. When you grow up with a silver spoon in your mouth turns out you have a target on your back."

"I get it."

"You do?" He sounded surprised.

"Sure, I do. Every good-looking woman has to prove she

didn't get where she was by shagging the boss."

She expected him to laugh at her analogy, but he didn't.

"Have people thought that about you?"

"In just about every job I've ever had. Even you thought I'd slept with Van."

He ran his hand around his collar. "I'm an asshole, and I apologize." There was a long pause. "What about us… Does sleeping together put you in an awkward position?"

She checked the GPS and took another turn. "It's best if no one finds out. I mean if it were an actual long-term relationship that might be different. Other agents might still question any promotions I received, assuming I'm not fired"—her heart gave a painful squeeze—"but at least it would be something I'd be willing to deal with. But just for sex…" She shook her head. "I wouldn't want anyone knowing."

She risked a look at him, expecting him to look amused or mocking but instead he was grim-faced.

"I don't want to jeopardize your career, Ava."

"Then no one better find out we're fucking each other."

"They won't hear it from me." He finally gave her the assurance she'd thought she wanted to hear. But it rang hollow inside her.

His eyes lifted to the road ahead. "This is the place where I shot Peter Galveston."

Ava put on her blinker and pulled over to the side of the road.

Dominic got out of the car and walked to the edge of the pavement and stood staring into the thick underbrush.

Ava followed slowly, tucking away her emotions so they didn't get in the way of them doing their job.

"What I don't get," Dominic said quietly, "is why wait this

long to exact revenge? A decade. Who the hell is that patient?"

Ava stood next to him, staring at the opposite side of the woods. "Could they have been serving a prison term?"

Dominic placed his hands on his hips. "I was wondering the same thing." He shook his head impatiently. "DNA results and other evidence should be in by now. Frazer said he'd call me as soon as anything definite came in. Let's head to the cabin."

Ava followed him back to the car. "What do you expect to find?"

He shook his head. "I honestly don't know."

"Who owns it?"

"A corporation based in New York."

"Who owns the corporation?"

His smile was a quick slice of guile. "Alex Parker is looking into that for us."

"Parker? Not the task force?"

Dominic shrugged as he got into the car. "They are presumably also looking into it, but Frazer says Parker is faster, and there are lives on the line."

Ava started the engine, feeling oddly melancholic. She was eager to find out the truth but realized that when they did, she and Sheridan would no longer need one another. They'd part ways. The idea shook her. She wasn't ready to say goodbye to the man.

It took another twenty-five minutes to reach the cabin, up a side road, winding through thick forest with very few houses nearby.

Dominic noticed her glancing around. "Galveston owned most of this mountain."

"Where'd all the money go after his death?" asked Ava.

"A distant cousin I believe. Victims were also compensated."

Ava couldn't imagine it put a dent in the heartbreak of the families.

Dominic leaned forward and peered up the hill on her side of the road. "There's the cabin." He pointed through the trees.

Ava saw a massive construction. A rustic version of a mansion was a more apt description. The fine hair on her nape sprang up.

"Place gives me the creeps," Dominic admitted, tucking his sunglasses into his jacket pocket. It was one of the things she really liked about him. He wasn't afraid to own his mistakes or show weakness. He was comfortable about who he was and confident in his abilities.

She parked in front of the property, and they both climbed out, tense and wary, looking for any signs of trouble. Without talking they retrieved their ballistic vests from the trunk, constantly scanning the trees and the house as they strapped them on.

If she was the person orchestrating these attacks on the FBI in revenge for the death of Peter Galveston, this was where she'd be hanging out. In the place he'd committed his crimes.

Ava tightened the Velcro straps and rested her hand on the handle of her Glock.

"Let's check the garage first. See if anyone is home."

Ava nodded, covering Sheridan's rear, barrel pointed at the ground so no one accidentally got shot.

No birds sang, no squirrels chattered. The only thing that moved were the leaves rustling in the breeze. Ava's pulse gave a few unsteady beats before training enabled her to settle her breathing. This was the sort of situation that made her nerves dance, but she knew what to do, she could handle it. And so could Sheridan.

They checked the garage, looking through the murky glass of the side windows. An ATV and a snow mobile were in there, but no cars or trucks.

Silently they headed to the front door, and Dominic rang the doorbell. The sound echoed inside the cathedral ceilings, but no one answered.

Dominic held her gaze for a moment, the indigo of his eyes as dark as a shadow.

"When Galveston was active, he'd get a victim into his vehicle by first tasering them and bundling them inside, then tying their hands behind their back and gagging them."

Dominic moved along the wraparound deck toward the back door, looking into the house through the large windows. "Once he had them terrified and firmly under control, he'd force them at gunpoint into this house and take them to a make-shift bedroom on the upper floor."

He pointed to a top corner of the property.

Ava's grip tightened on her weapon, but she steadied her breathing, not wanting to look jumpy.

"It was basically an unfinished storage space in the attic at the back of the house with no windows. Galveston turned it into a cell and locked the captives up in chains that were bolted to the floor. They had a toilet and when he was away in the city, he'd leave them some bottled water, a kettle, and Ramen noodles so they didn't starve to death. He had a camera system set up so he could watch them and if they tried to escape, he'd beat them. I think there were other people involved, people who checked on them, but they never appeared in the videos, and we never caught them.

"When he entertained friends here, he'd sedate the captive women by putting GHB into their water." Dominic's mouth tightened as they both acknowledged the connection to what had happened to him. "He filmed himself raping victims and torturing them. He'd bring them downstairs where he had a hook in the ceiling he'd attach them to so they hung there naked. Just out of reach of the telephone." Dominic's footsteps on the wooden boards echoed hollowly. "He kept a couple of them in dog kennels downstairs and made them wear leather outfits and ball gags and crawl around on all fours and eat out of dog bowls. Pretty sure he was going to pretend he was into kink should anyone ever talk to the women. Those were his favorites according to the videos. His pets."

The imagery was caustic.

"Why did he kill them if they were his favorites?"

"They'd displease him in some way, or try to escape, or he'd go too far with his sadism. He kept some of them for months. Often several at once."

Ava shuddered. "How many altogether?"

"Victims?" Dominic knocked harder on the back door.

"Yeah." Ava scanned the forest as Dominic examined the house.

Nothing moved except the ghosts of victims past.

"We identified the DNA of fifteen women on his sex toys—although the youngest was only fourteen years old at the time of her abduction."

Ava felt chilled to the bone. That these monsters existed…

"There's no one here." Dominic glanced upward and frowned.

How many times had those imprisoned women heard someone at the door? How many times had escape and rescue been just out of reach? They'd never know.

"Let's take a scout around as we're here." Dominic seemed reluctant to leave. He wanted answers. They all wanted answers.

Ava nodded and holstered her weapon as they stepped off the porch.

Dominic headed up the hill to the ridge behind the cabin. At the top they both stood for a moment, Ava a little freaked out by Galveston's crimes. The malevolence and narcissistic nature of a psychopath's mindset was one of the things that set them apart from the rest of humanity.

"If you hadn't caught him, he might have carried on killing for years."

"It was luck."

Ava shook her head. "No. It was good police work. You set a trap, and he walked right into it."

Dominic's mouth pulled downward. "I'm going to call Sandy, see how her husband is doing."

The attacks seemed to be weighing heavily on his conscience. She understood it and didn't bother to reassure him. That kind of self-forgiveness took time and perspective.

Dominic looked at his cell and swore. "At least I would if I had service."

Ah, crap. She rested her hand back on her weapon as they went for a short walk around the property. The brush was thick with summer growth, making it possible for someone to easily hide from them. They circled the entire property and came up beneath their rental car. Rather than return to the vehicle, Dominic headed back up to the top of the ridge.

"What is it?" Ava asked, feeling slightly out of breath trying to keep up with Dominic striding up the steep incline.

He pulled a face. "I don't know. Just...something. I feel like there's something here. I want to find it."

"Well, it certainly has an atmosphere," Ava commented dryly.

They walked together back down the hill. Taking another route through a different section of woods.

Ava spotted it first.

She grabbed his arm, and they both stopped, then pulled their weapons.

Slowly they advanced upon a cleared patch of the forest floor. Bushes prevented anyone seeing it from the driveway.

"What is this?" Ava murmured under her breath. She stayed behind Dominic, covering their rear.

"A makeshift graveyard."

"I can see that." There were dozens of white-painted crosses staked into the ground. "You think anyone is actually buried here?"

"I don't know." Dominic walked carefully toward the crosses, some of which bore names. "Molly Jenner. Olivia Lopez. Frauke Holland. These are some of the names of the victims." In the center was a larger cross, one that was more ornate. Peter Galveston was written first in big letters and then in small beneath. No dates of birth or death were listed.

On the right-hand side were crosses bearing the names of the FBI agents who'd caught him. Ava looked closely. Van's name was there. So was Dominic's.

"You have a cross." She felt sick.

"Still not dead."

"I'm glad."

He flashed her a smile.

"So do Fernando Chavez and Sandra Warren. Think this is Caroline Perry's work? Did she set everything in motion and then assume she'd successfully killed you all? She killed herself so she wasn't caught and had to pay for her crimes?"

He sniffed. "I don't know. I do think it's possible. I also think it's possible she's a decoy. Rooney said there were drag marks beside her vehicle next to the river."

"Maybe she was working with someone else, and they decided they didn't need her anymore and didn't want any loose ends?"

"It's a lot of people to kill without someone giving you some kind of assistance. A lot of geography to cover."

Ava took some photos with her cell. Then she squinted at the crosses on the victims' side.

"There are only fourteen victim crosses."

"What?" asked Dominic.

"Fourteen crosses. You said there were fifteen victims…"

"We thought there were from the DNA profiles we found."

"How many bodies did you recover?" asked Ava.

"Eight partial remains on top of the three bodies of the women that led us to believe we had a serial killer operating in the area in the first place."

"So, conceivably, the FBI might have—"

"Accidentally labeled one of the women as a victim when she was actually a willing accomplice," Dominic finished Ava's thoughts.

They looked at one another. "We need to compare any new DNA profiles to those of Peter Galveston's supposed victims."

They stared at one another with the dawning knowledge that they were onto something. This was a new direction for the investigation to follow.

The bullet whizzed so close to the top of her head she felt the air move. It slammed into the garage behind her as the noise of the shot cracked through the air.

Dominic pushed her to the ground, and they rolled through the dirt, scrambling to find cover.

CHAPTER TWENTY-FOUR

"KEEP DOWN," DOMINIC yelled. He ducked toward a slab of rock that stuck out on the left, grabbing Ava and taking her with him, trying to shelter her with his body.

The shot had come from the top of the ridge.

"See anyone?" she asked, glancing over her shoulder.

"No. You?"

She shook her head.

They were pinned down in a gully, another bullet skimming overhead, proving the shooter was still there. "We can't stay here."

"Especially if there is more than one of them," Ava agreed. "You go left, I'll got right. Race you to the top?" Her eyes were alight, and there was a small smile on her lips.

"You look like you're enjoying this, Kanas."

Her grin got wider, but he realized it was forced. The way he smiled during a telephone call in order to influence the tone of his voice.

"No, but damned if I'll show these bastards any fear."

He grinned and kissed her quickly on the mouth. Another shot bounced off the stone above their heads. "Meet you at the top. Don't get cocky."

"I thought that was your department," she teased, beautifully.

God. He hated the fact some asshole was shooting at her, shooting at them. He did not want her to die. But he couldn't afford to think like that. She was a good agent. He didn't intend to let her down by getting her killed.

"It will be, later," he promised. "*If* we get out of this alive. Okay, together." He counted down silently with his fingers. Three, two, one.

They burst in opposite directions, but the shooter must have anticipated the move. A series of shots came straight at Dominic, and they forced him to take cover behind a fat birch. He could hear Ava, deliberately making a lot of noise to try and draw the shooter's attention.

He poked his head forward and back and was rewarded by a bullet in the wood a few inches from his face. They obviously viewed him as the greater threat, but then they hadn't met Ava Kanas. Or—they wanted to finish what they'd started while they still had the chance. He checked his surroundings and grabbed his cell to call it in only to remember the lack of service.

He swore under his breath. Ava was a hundred yards away now. He did not want her facing this bastard alone. He eyed the distance to the next suitable tree trunk. If nothing else, he'd keep the shooter distracted.

He crouched low and bobbed and weaved to the next piece of cover. Bullets shredded the air around him. *Shit.* Cold, clammy sweat coated his temples. Dominic paused, panting, behind another tree. He was never gonna get up this goddamn mountain alive.

Then he remembered what he was good at.

"Hey," he yelled. "We are FBI agents. We had a few questions for the owner of this cabin regarding Peter Galveston.

We mean you no harm."

The only answer was a bullet in the tree trunk, but that was okay. He was going to have to trust Ava to get the drop on this guy while he did whatever the hell was necessary to create a distraction.

"Put the gun down, and we can talk."

Another shot. Maybe the guy was deaf. The issue was, even assuming the person firing the gun wasn't on a psychotic break, it took time to influence someone's behavior. You started with active listening, showed empathy to build rapport, and only then could you bend their will in line with yours. Bullets were hardly conducive to inducing empathy.

Another rule of negotiation was don't lie to people, unless you were about to kill them. "We don't want to hurt you. Tell me what's going on? Why are you shooting at us? Put the gun down, and we can talk."

He couldn't hear Ava anymore. *Shit.* What if there was more than one of them? What if someone had a knife on her?

He closed his eyes and breathed slowly out. Negotiation could only get you so far. Dominic dodged to the next tree, but no shots were fired.

He darted up the hill off the path, using trees for cover, but still no more shots were fired. The bastard was either drawing him out for a clear shot. Or he had Ava and was waiting for him to arrive so he could kill her in front of him. Or he'd run.

The only sound now was that of his own breathing.

Where was she?

He crested the ridge, bracing for a bullet. Scanned the area. Ammunition casings were strewn in the grass. Then he heard the sounds of running and caught sight of a flash of a white shirt through the trees. Ava.

Dominic ran down the hill in the same direction but about two hundred feet parallel still along the top of the ridge. The desire to go to Ava was nearly overwhelming and had nothing to do with tactics or training. It was personal. He wanted to protect her. He wanted her safe. He fought the desire. He needed to trust she could do her job and although she might be a little reckless, she wasn't stupid, and she didn't have a death wish.

A shadow moved ahead of him in the woods. The shooter had cut left rather than right and was headed for the road. He probably had a car there. No fucking way was this guy getting away. Hell no.

Dominic was elevated above Ava and the UNSUB. The guy was wearing black including a ski mask. He'd dropped his rifle at some point and was running in a flat-out sprint toward the car. But Ava was faster, those long legs of hers eating up the ground. She was almost upon him when she tripped and the Glock went flying out of her hand.

The UNSUB realized what happened and stopped, walking back to where Ava lay panting on the ground. The UNSUB looked around but did not see Dominic high above him.

The man pulled out a handgun and aimed it at Ava as she desperately tried to lunge for her weapon.

Dominic put four bullets into the bastard, praying his aim was true and he didn't hit the woman who had somehow snuck under all his defenses. At this distance and elevation, it was a possibility.

Ava covered her ears and curled into a ball, making herself as small as possible. When the UNSUB crashed to the ground, Dominic stopped firing. She rolled to her feet, grabbing her Glock before kicking the bad guy's gun away from his uncurled fingers.

She stood there, holding her weapon on the guy as Dominic found a way down the short cliff.

"You see anyone else?" Dominic asked, glancing around a forest that seemed to echo with the sounds of gun shots and desperation.

Ava shook her head. Her nose was bleeding from where she'd gone down hard on her face. She ignored it and didn't shift her stance over the prone man.

Dominic cuffed the guy and then felt for a pulse. He looked up at Ava's pale features. "He's dead."

He pulled the ski mask up, revealing the man's face.

It was Robin Elgin, the pastor from the church.

AVA SPENT HOURS being debriefed by other FBI agents about what had gone down in the woods. The most aggressive interrogation had been by the head of the task force looking into the FBI deaths, Mark Gross. Gross had gone at her like a bulldozer, less about the fact she'd almost died that afternoon, more about the fact she and Sheridan had been snooping around the house without a warrant.

She'd told him the truth. They'd been so close it had been a natural progression to visit the property where Galveston had committed the crimes and talk to the people who lived there now.

Neither of them had expected to find the crosses, or get involved in a shootout or for her to look down the barrel of a gun and expect to die any second.

"Are we done yet?" she asked after the man was silent for a

good five minutes.

Gross looked up from his notes, but he didn't fool her. The guy was wasting her time to piss her off. Good news. He'd succeeded.

"You can go. Try to remember you're assigned to watch SSA Sheridan's back, not investigate the deaths of the FBI agents."

"Well, I could hardly let him go to the cabin alone, now could I?" she snapped back.

His eyes were hard as the glass beads she wore on her wrist. "I don't expect to see you again, Agent Kanas."

She could only hope.

Her chair scraped against the floor as she pushed back. Rather than stretching out her aching body the way she wanted to, she walked from the room with her chin angled to screw-you.

Men like Gross had a job to do, but it didn't mean they had to be assholes or that she had to like it.

Outside the interview room, the Resident Agency was in total chaos. Half the task force appeared to have relocated here and were working on processing the scenes. Galveston's old home—which, it turned out, was where Robin Elgin lived, and the church. It turned out the same corporation that had donated land to the church also owned the cabin. It was a shell company registered in the Caymans, and someone was going to have to go down there to get more information.

It seemed obvious Robin Elgin had applied for the job of pastor in that church due to either a sick obsession or a previously unknown involvement with Peter Galveston. Now Evidence Response Teams were using ground penetrating radar and cadaver dogs at the site, before digging up the possible graves.

Was Robin Elgin the one who'd orchestrated these murders? Did he know Caroline Perry?

Ava spotted Dominic looking at a report and talking to Jerry Pine. She headed toward him. Some of the local agents were looking a little wild-eyed at the invasion. Makeshift tables and desks had been brought in and set up in every available inch of space. Phones rang constantly. So much for sleepy Binghamton.

Ava squeezed behind a couple of agents who had pictures of Robin Elgin strewn across their desk, including one of him dead. She looked up to find Dominic staring at her.

"I can't believe I tripped over a fricking tree root," she said when she got to him. Without him, she'd have been dead.

He said nothing.

She crossed her arms over her chest, weary beyond belief but not willing to admit defeat. "What's the plan?"

Dominic raised one brow. "I'm *persona non grata* around here. I was waiting for you before starting the drive back."

Ava nodded even though what she really needed was sleep. Since waking in the middle of last night and getting up close and personal with Sheridan, she'd helped end a prison siege, witnessed an exhumation—or an attempted one—and been involved with a shootout. A busy day by anyone's standards.

Getting out of town was a priority. She doubted there was a bedroom to be had in a five-mile vicinity of this town.

They said goodbye to Jerry Pine and the other locals who'd been so much help before the case had blown up in their faces and headed down to the rental she'd parked out front four hours ago.

"Any updates?" she asked, slipping into the driver's seat.

Dominic swore as he opened the door. "Dammit, I forgot I'm still not medically cleared to drive."

Ava shrugged. "Let's start driving and find a motel en route if I start to fall asleep."

"You sure?"

Ava pulled a face. "All in a day's work."

Dominic climbed in and set the GPS so neither of them had to think. She was heading out of town when he finally spoke.

"Autopsy tests on Caroline Perry's body found surfactants in her lungs."

"Surfactants?"

"A constituent of bubble bath."

"Ah. Not something I generally associate with the Rappahannock River. So, she drowns in the tub and is then dumped in the river. Why? Any evidence connecting Perry to Elgin?"

Dominic shook his head. "The burner cell that Alex Parker says was active around Fredericksburg was active around the church and towers nearest Galveston's cabin. He's digging into the corporation that owns the cabin and donated the land to the church. Task force is looking hard into Robin Elgin's background and trying to tie him to Perry."

Ava opened the window to try to keep herself awake, but when she started openly yawning, she knew they needed to find a place to sleep soon.

"Pull over," Dominic told her.

"What?"

"Pull over. I've already been in one car wreck. Don't want to be in another no matter what the doctors say. That's an order, Kanas."

Ava pulled over.

Dominic got out and walked around the car, opening her

door for her to climb out. She swayed when she did so, hyperaware of the closeness of his body. The desire to touch him was almost overwhelming. Just a brief moment of human contact. But she wouldn't be the one to cross the line, not while they were working.

He surprised her by grabbing her arm and pulling her to a stop before she could walk away. Then he sank his hands into the back of her hair and brought her to him for a long, slow kiss. When it was over, he rested his forehead against hers, as her heart pounded madly.

"Glad you didn't die today," he said, swallowing hard.

She reached up and squeezed his wrists. "I'm glad you didn't die today, either. Did I thank you for saving my life?"

"I'm the one who dragged you out there."

"I thought we were in this together?"

"Yeah, but I'm the one he wanted dead."

"Not on my watch," she said seriously.

He laughed, and she felt the sound radiate through his fingers to her skull and down to the marrow of her bones.

"Thanks for having my back," he said softly before releasing her and stepping away.

She climbed into the passenger side, did up her seatbelt, and closed her eyes. Emotions were spiraling out of control beneath the surface of her skin, and she didn't want him to know. She didn't want him to realize she was as weak and stupid as all the other women who fell at his feet.

She cleared her throat and tipped her chair back. "Pull over when you get tired, Sheridan. And don't go breaking the law or else I'll probably get suspended again, and you'll end up getting a commendation." The words emerged prickly and sharp, but they were all the armor she had left, and she needed every scrap of protection she could muster.

CHAPTER TWENTY-FIVE

GRIEF HOT-WIRED BERNIE'S rage. Robin had been a dear friend, an early disciple of Peter's. He hadn't participated in the murders or the torture. He'd just liked to watch. Women liked him and sometimes, Peter had used Robin as a lure for some wholesome little chickadee who didn't stick her thumb out for a ride.

The tire iron dragged through the dirt.

If only Bernie had been with Peter when that slut had been wiggling her ass up and down Route 97.

The pipe bomb had exploded, but the cop hadn't been injured. Her husband had instead.

Maimed.

That's what the news reports were saying. It had a delicious ring to it. Bernie smiled. See how the bitch dealt with getting her loved one fucking "maimed."

The tire iron was heavy. Unyielding. The noise it made as it dragged over the ground made Bernie think of an ancient sword being drawn over rock.

Sandra Warren should be dead. Fernando Chavez should be dead. Dominic Sheridan had murdered Robin and found Peter's grave and should be dead.

Things were not going to plan.

Bernie walked out of the forest and toward Sheridan's

house not stopping, instead increasing the pace and using the momentum to pick up the iron and swing it at Sheridan's bedroom window. The glass shattered, the alarm went off. Bernie moved on to the next one.

Every smash satisfied something dark and resentful inside. Three windows, four. Glass shards rained down, but the ski mask and gloves protected face and hands.

Five, six, seven, eight, nine, ten. The alarm shrieked as the last window shattered.

Bernie stood back and took a long gulp of air, knowing cops were on the way. The tire iron went into the pool, and Bernie backed away from the devastation.

It wasn't Sheridan's blood, but it was a message. They weren't done yet. It wasn't over. He wasn't fucking safe.

The shadows in the woods cloaked the line of retreat. By the time the cops arrived, Bernie would be long gone.

CHAPTER TWENTY-SIX

DOMINIC WAS HEADING east of Hagerstown when his eyes started to drift shut. It was enough to jolt him out of his complacency, and he pulled over in the next town and found a small hotel near the airport.

Ava was fast asleep, her face less sharp angles, her expression unguarded. Her shields were down—something she did with him occasionally now, but less so with other people.

It made him feel smug and like an ass all at the same time. After this was over, they'd have no excuse to be close to one another.

He didn't like the idea of her going back to her "Ava Kanas alone against the world" mentality, and yet there was no room in his life for a real relationship. Losing his mother at an early age had fucked him up.

Van had always told him he was missing out, but he'd never really believed him until now…

Ava said she didn't want any ties either, he reminded himself. He didn't want to be the loser hanging around in the hopes of receiving a few breadcrumbs of affection. He did not want to turn into *that* guy for this woman. He respected and valued her opinion too much.

A valet approached the car, and he touched her arm to gently nudge her awake.

"I need some sleep," he said when she forced one eyelid up.

"I can drive for a couple of hours if I have coffee." Ava stretched out her body in the cramped confines of the car.

Dominic tried to keep his gaze professional even as desire stirred. This might be the last night they got to be together. The idea made him feel sick with loss which was crazy. Maybe it was a side-effect to someone trying to kill them today. Something that would wear off as things returned to normal.

"We both need some rest and some food. A few hours' sleep won't kill anyone." At least, he hoped not. The task force was on the case now, tracking probable suspects.

They grabbed their go-bags and went inside. He sat her on an ottoman near reception while he organized the rooms.

"Come on." He led the way with a hand on the small of her back. A hand that didn't want to let go but did anyway. "Here you go. This is your room."

He opened a door for her and watched her brows hike in surprise and her mouth drop open in what he hoped was disappointment.

She went inside and locked the door with a decisive click.

He headed to the next room along the hallway and dumped his gear on the bed, turning his phone off and plugging it into a charger before knocking on the connecting door.

She threw it open, and he swore he saw tears misting her eyes, but that must have been his imagination.

"I didn't want anyone questioning your reputation should someone check the hotel records," he said quietly.

She dragged him inside by the lapels, and he slid his hands around her waist and pulled her close. He was exhausted, but not so exhausted he wouldn't take advantage of being with Ava while he could.

Her fingers worked on his tie and buttons as he dragged her shirt out of her pants and filled his hands with sleek, warm skin.

She ran her palms over his abs and across his chest, humming as she did so.

She bit her lip, and the action made him as hard as rock, something she didn't miss. Her hands found him and cupped him through his suit pants, and he was literally at her mercy. He dropped to his knees, undoing the buttons on her shirt first, revealing the edge of red lace, then he undid the button of her pants and slowly slid the zipper down.

He looked up, and she was watching him with a look of wonder on her face. The scent of her killed him, but he made himself go slowly, treating her like she was the most precious and delicate thing he would ever touch.

She might just be.

Her pants slid down her thighs, and he tugged off her ankle boots and backup weapon when they stalled there. When she was standing in only her little, red panties and unbuttoned shirt, he urged her back until she hit the mattress. Her knees buckled, and he pressed forward until his mouth was against the warm silk.

"Lie still," he instructed.

She did as she was told. Very un-Ava-like.

He pushed her legs wider apart and ran his nose over the center of her, breathing her in, light touches that teased them both. He ran his tongue down the edge of the lace enjoying the way she moaned. The touch of her thigh against his cheek was so soft he shivered.

He remembered what she'd said last night about liking the feel of his beard between her legs. He hadn't shaved. He tugged the panties down impossibly long legs and put his mouth on her clit, scraping his scruff over the sensitive skin of her vulva, and she damn near shot off the bed.

He reached up to tweak her nipples against the lace that encased them, working her with his mouth and his hands until she was panting and sobbing and grabbing his hair while opening her thighs as wide as they could go and pressing against his mouth.

He was still fully dressed and so hard he hurt. He kept working his tongue over her, unable to satiate himself. Unable to get enough until she cried out and shuddered over him.

He crawled up and laid his head against her stomach, closing his eyes. Her pulse jumped beneath her skin.

"I hope you bought condoms," she said breathlessly.

"I did. Unfortunately, I'm too damn tired to do anything about it."

She laughed. "That's okay. Lie back and let me take care of you."

He crawled onto the bed to collapse beside her. "That's not how I operate."

She took off her weapon holster, shirt and then her bra. She was naked, and he lost the ability to speak.

He slipped his hand into his jacket pocket and tossed the box of condoms to her which she caught one-handed. Then he sat up to shrug out of his jacket and shoulder holster. He placed his weapon on the bedside table.

She moved behind him, and he paused as she kissed his neck, across his shoulders, down his spine.

She touched the side of his ribs, and he jumped. "Hurt?"

she asked.

"Not anymore." Not when she touched him.

She reached around and undid the button of his pants, carefully releasing his straining cock from behind the zipper.

"Breathe," she whispered in his ear. He could hear the smile in her voice.

He closed his eyes as she touched him, but his blood ignited into blind lust, and he shucked his pants and boxers and reached for her, but she backed away.

"Nah uh." She wagged a finger at him. "My turn."

He eyed her narrowly. He wasn't used to not being in control. Especially not in the bedroom. But he looked at her expectant expression and realized it didn't matter. Ava wanted to call the shots for a change and although he couldn't give her that at work, here, in the privacy of their hotel rooms, he could give her anything she wanted.

Maybe it was her damned turn.

He lay back with his head on the pillow and one arm stacked beneath his head. His other rested on her thigh because he wanted to touch her. To be connected in a way he'd never needed to be connected to anyone else before.

She started slow, exploring his body with her hands, followed by her soft lips.

He eased out the band that held up her hair. Her soft tresses fell across his skin like cool silk, tickling his flesh and making his pulse beat stronger. Exhaustion was banished as his cock throbbed and his lungs pumped, every inch of his body hungry and aroused.

She kissed his nipples which felt good but didn't drive him insane the way it did her. *Looking* at her drove him insane. Sliding his palm over the smoothness of her hip drove him insane. Her lips around his cock almost forced him out of his mind.

Holy shit.

She licked him as if he was her favorite flavor of ice cream, and his hand anchored deep in her hair. He had to stop himself from moving. Then she sucked him so deep he touched the back of her throat, and sweat broke from every pore. After a few strokes of her tongue he dragged her away, because this party was about to be over before it had even started.

She laughed, knowing exactly what she was doing to him.

She grabbed the box of rubbers and peeled off the cellophane. She spilled square packages onto the bed and opened one, rolling the slippery latex over his hard, throbbing length. Her touch was light but even so, he had to grit his teeth and remind himself not to go off like a freaking teenage boy.

She straddled his thighs and he watched, glad that the light from the adjoining room spilled through the open doorway brightly enough to reveal every detail.

He slid his hands between her legs. Her pupils widened as he sank two fingers inside, driving her up onto her knees in shocked surprise. Her muscles clamped around him as he found her g-spot and made her cry out.

Her post-orgasmic smile made his toes curl. She inched forward and took hold of him, rubbing the head of his cock against her clit until he was the one squirming.

"Dear God, Ava, if I don't get inside you soon…" he pleaded.

She repositioned her body, and he slid all the way home, mind blanking from the pleasure that flooded his senses.

She held herself still long enough for him to catch his

breath, and then she started moving. Riding him slowly at first, finding a rhythm and a depth that pleased her. And he hung on for the ride, gripping her thighs like a man dangling off a cliff. If she didn't have bruises tomorrow it would be a damned miracle. And still he couldn't let go. Finally, her breath caught, and he drove harder, deeper, pushing for that climax. Wanting and needing nothing except to share that moment with this woman.

It started like an explosion from his balls to his tip, a warm rush that filled him with exquisite joy. Every molecule in his body splitting apart and reconnecting with a click of hedonistic glee. Ava was feeling it too and when she cried out, it sounded as if she were in anguish, but he knew that pleasure-pain battle.

With a sigh she collapsed on top of him, her skin damp with sweat, sticking to his body. He loved it.

He gently rolled them over and ditched the condom. Then he pulled her close and held her tight as they fell asleep.

AVA WOKE TO something hard pressed against her inner thigh and a sweet ache between her legs. It took a moment to remember where she was and who she was with. A moment to relax from a stiffened *oh, fuck*, to a warm *oh, wow* as memories from last night swamped her. At some point she'd stumbled to the bathroom and brushed her teeth. Then she'd crawled back in bed with Dominic as if it was the most natural thing in the world to sleep with another human being. In reality, she had no idea the last time that had happened.

Gray dawn light was starting to creep through the windows, but she stayed where she was, cocooned in warmth and the feeling of finally belonging somewhere.

Nonsense of course, but in this moment, it felt tangible and real. She wasn't stupid enough to pretend it would last beyond this investigation, but she was determined to enjoy it for as long as she could. Before the doubts set in. Before they both started backing away into their solitary shells.

She wondered if he still wanted her to attend his father's engagement party with him tonight or if he'd conveniently forgotten about it—she was fine with that. She certainly didn't fit in with that crowd.

There was a good chance that Robin Elgin and Caroline Perry had collaborated on the murders due to some as yet undiscovered motivation, so the danger was probably over. Plus, she had nothing to wear. She'd thought they'd remain at the prison and miss it, but once again Gino-the-snake was ruining her life.

Neither she nor Dominic were allowed anywhere near the investigation now that both suspects were dead. Justice and FBI investigations needed to be impartial and after several attempts on their lives, she and Dominic Sheridan were anything but.

Dominic was still asleep, but one large hand was clamped over her breast, and his body was like a furnace. She was well aware of his morning arousal. Her nipple hardened against his palm, and she couldn't stop a small wriggle of desire.

Suddenly Dominic's breathing changed, and his fingers tightened and found the hard peak of her nipple and rolled it between his fingers and thumb. She swallowed a groan.

"I guess you're awake." Her voice rose sharply as he pinched the tip her breast.

"I'm awake." His voice was deep and sent a ripple of anticipation through her body.

She heard the rustle of a wrapper, and her mouth went dry with want.

He parted her thighs and didn't even check that she was ready for him. He knew. He knew how turned on she was and how desperate she was for him to fill her up.

She groaned when he did. Panted and clawed the sheets as sensation rocked her. His thrusts made her want this never to end, never to stop. To lie here forever with that delicious friction gliding through her body, ratcheting the tension higher and higher until her nerves felt like guitar strings about to snap.

He shifted them until he was on top of her, the heavy weight of him shifting her thighs wider apart, pressing her hips into the mattress, controlling her range of movement, so that there was no way for her to climax in this position but the arousal still built to almost unbearable levels. Her body was trembling and shaking and still he wouldn't give her what she desperately wanted.

"Dom," she groaned.

He lay flat against her, taking most of his weight on his elbows, but still immobilizing her with his strength, only the tip of him inside her, making her hungry for more, making her want to back into him and take him deeper.

"What?" His breath brushed her ear before his teeth bit gently into her earlobe.

"Please..." It was as close to begging as she'd ever get. As close to telling him how much she wanted him—not just his body—but *him*, all of him.

What was it about this man that hooked into a woman's

blood stream and made her addicted? No wonder women turned up on his doorstep with offerings.

Fuck me and I'll bake for you. Fuck me and I'll do anything...

He held her tight against him and then put his arm around her waist and pulled her body upright, maneuvering them closer to the headboard before bracing her hands against the top of it. She was completely open to him now. He held onto her hips, pumping faster, hitting her g-spot and then spreading his fingers around her clit before clamping down on that sensitive little bud. She pushed back against him, matching his thrusts and his strength. She wanted this madness to reach its peak and to shove her careening off that ledge at a thousand feet without a parachute. She had never felt this out of control, nor this controlled by another person before.

It was heady. It was terrifying.

Dominic's other hand cupped her breast, and she was the one holding them up now as he delivered the trifecta of assaults of her senses. Finally, *finally*, an atomic bomb of pleasure crashed through her, and she shattered into a million sparkling pieces with Dominic crying out as he followed her, holding himself deep inside her as he came.

Slowly they both collapsed onto the sheets, and Dominic wrapped her in his embrace as he nuzzled her neck.

Neither said a word.

CHAPTER TWENTY-SEVEN

MALLORY, ALEX AND Lincoln Frazer stood on the pool deck outside Dominic Sheridan's beautiful home. Except it wasn't so beautiful anymore. The downstairs windows were trashed. Shattered glass everywhere, gleaming edges jagged and dangerous.

The sun was coming up even though it wasn't yet six AM. The security company had been monitoring the place but had been unable to reach Sheridan or Sheridan's boss, Quentin Savage, who was listed as the emergency contact. They'd eventually tracked down someone in the Crisis Negotiation Unit who'd known enough about what was going on to call Frazer. The security company had called the local cops, but by the time they'd got out here nearly forty minutes had passed and the culprit was long gone.

Alex showed her and Frazer the video surveillance footage using his phone. A dark figure approached wearing heavy black clothing, a ski mask, black gloves. There were no identifying features. No tics. No tells. No way of figuring out who the hell had perpetrated the vandalism—or why.

"They obviously knew he was away," Frazer said. "They made no effort to break in. Where's Sheridan's dog?"

"Staying with a neighbor who has a farm," Mallory replied.

"They walk in and out of the woods like they know the

way and aren't in any hurry," Alex said calmly.

"Think they've been spying on Sheridan?"

Alex met her gaze. "They've definitely been watching him."

Mallory glanced at the woods with a shiver. "Should we get tracker dogs in?"

At the place where they'd found Caroline Perry's car the bloodhounds had led them back to the road but they'd become confused about which direction to go in. After an hour the handler had given up.

"Wouldn't do any harm. Might lead us to some sort of hide. Although..." Alex started walking in the direction of the woods.

Even though Mallory didn't want to follow, she did, and so did Frazer. Being summer, the undergrowth was thick and lush, draped in ominous shadows. The scent was of pollen and crushed grass, not the rot and decay of fall.

Mal was grateful that birds were sitting on branches and singing happily. It helped. A little.

Alex followed the path into the trees and led them to a gate in the six-foot tall wooden fence that surrounded the property. Alex stepped aside as Frazer slipped on a glove to carefully open it. Evidence Recovery Techs would dust for prints and DNA later, but it was unlikely the trespasser had left anything behind.

"Why do this?" Mallory asked Frazer, slowing down to catch her breath. No matter how she tried to pretend otherwise, her pregnancy was making it harder to do her job. Maybe she should have stayed in the office like Frazer had suggested. One day she'd listen to someone besides her own stubbornness.

"You okay?" Alex asked, coming back to her side.

Frazer glanced at her sharply and stopped walking.

"I'm fine." She waved them both off, although she could already do with a nap. "Why break his windows? It seems petty and small for someone who has committed murder."

Frazer put his hands on his hips and shrugged. "Maybe it was an associate of Robin Elgin's who knew what was going on and was angry but not murderous about the FBI foiling the plot."

"Or the UNSUB is alive and pissed," Alex said. "The bombs didn't kill Chavez or Warren like they wanted. Sheridan and Kanas found Peter Galveston's corpse, which was obviously important enough to them to dig up and rebury, then Sheridan shot dead Robin Elgin. They can't get to Sheridan so they lost their temper, wanted to punish him and," he shrugged, "this is juvenile but pretty effective in terms of trashing his house."

"Shows a distinct loss of control," Mallory mused.

Frazer nodded. "If this is the UNSUB and not some underling then they're making mistakes, unraveling. They know it's only a matter of time until we catch them."

"Unless they go to ground…" Alex looked up at the trees and then back down at the forest floor.

"We have so much evidence to go through it could take too much time. They might get away." Mallory felt the rising sense of dread she was trying to push down.

"We'll find them wherever they are," Frazer told her gently.

She blinked. Her boss, while not perfect, was a formidable guy. If he said they were gonna catch this UNSUB, then they'd catch them. But the fact remained…*when*?

"Here." Alex had wandered away and crouched on the ground, staring at a shoe print in a small patch of dirt. "This person knows all about covering their face and hands but seems to forget some of the other basics. Get the ERT out here to photograph and cast this sucker."

Mallory went to walk closer, but Frazer caught her arm.

"Careful." He drew her backward, and she realized she'd been about to tread on a piece of evidence she couldn't even see.

She took a step back. "I need to inform Sheridan what happened here. I doubt he even knows yet."

"I'm going to the lab. Put a fire under their asses about the DNA results." Frazer looked pissed.

Mallory was glad she wasn't a lab tech right now. She pressed her fingers into the small of her back and started walking to fetch an evidence tech while Frazer guarded the footprints.

"Did those shoe prints look like the ones from the riverbank?" Mallory asked Alex when he caught her up.

"Yep." He showed her the two images side by side on his phone. Pattern on the sole looked identical. Someone had a favorite pair of sneakers.

"I don't think this is over, Alex."

"Neither do I, baby. Neither do I."

She tried Sheridan again, but the number was showing unavailable so he'd probably turned it off to get some sleep. She didn't blame him.

"Why do people do this? Why hate and destroy when it's so much better to love?"

"Greed, revenge, rage, pain? Maybe they have an appetite for destruction?"

She appreciated the Guns N' Roses reference.

He stuffed his hands in his pockets and shrugged like he didn't care, but they both knew that was a lie.

"We have dinner in DC tonight with my mother. Did you remember?"

"I remembered that I'm probably going to have an emergency come up in the office at the last minute." Her husband wiggled his brows and she grinned.

"It would be nice if we could catch this UNSUB, lock them up and then I can go have our baby in peace." Hopefully too sedated with an epidural to feel pain. She interlaced her fingers around her beachball belly as she glanced at Alex.

His fingers joined hers. "You can stop work any time," he murmured against her brow.

But if Mallory had a flaw, and she had many, not being able to let things go topped the list.

"Can you drop me at work and I'll meet you in DC tonight?" she asked.

"I can drive you to DC."

"I thought you had an appointment there this afternoon?"

"I do but I can—"

She touched his lips with her fingers and they were warm against her skin. "I can drive myself. See you tonight, Mr. Parker."

A grin cut across his face. "Have it your way, Mrs. Parker, but go take a nap on Frazer's couch. He's gonna be busy chasing his tail all day anyway."

Frazer groaned pitifully. "I heard that."

She nodded.

"Promise?" he asked.

"I promise."

"DO WE HAVE to go back to Quantico today?" Ava spoke quietly into the pillow.

Dominic's entire body trembled with aftershocks. This woman had completely destroyed him, last night and again this morning, and he was left wondering what was going on between them. Was it just good sex? Although stupendous was a more accurate word. Had he abstained for so long he'd forgotten what it was really like? He honestly didn't remember having sex with Suzanna which had scared the shit out of him and left him celibate in the months since. Sex with Ava, however, was something he'd never forget.

"Ah, damn." He groaned, remembering something he *would* rather forget.

"What is it?"

"We have to go to DC today."

She turned her head to look at him. "I thought Gross told us to stay away from the task force operation?"

He curved his lips, but it wasn't a smile. Mark Gross had been a pain in the ass. "We have a party to attend."

She swore, echoing his thoughts. "I thought you'd forgotten about it. Or changed your mind about me attending." Ava turned all the way over until she was facing him, and he was treated to the long naked sight of her. He kissed her mouth and kept kissing her until her breath caught.

Finally, when his body was growing hard again from wanting her, he pulled away. To prove to himself that he could. "I don't suppose you packed a ballgown?"

"Ballgown?" she asked, looking startled and aroused and confused.

"It'll be black tie."

"Black tie?" She sounded horrified. He felt her pain.

"My father takes being governor very seriously. Usually he's back home during the summer, but I suspect the president couldn't get away to Vermont. And if the president is invited then it will be formal. I have a tux at my apartment, but I don't have any dresses."

Ava looked down at herself and raised one long leg in the air, pointing her toes. "I could wear a tux."

Dominic laughed, but his mouth was dry as ash. He'd never considered himself a leg man, but everything about Ava defied what he'd considered his norm. "It's tempting just to see what you would look like." He wanted to say something dirty and inappropriate, but they needed to have a conversation about work. They needed to get up, shower, get in the damn rental car and drive back to their real lives. "You don't have to attend." He touched her cheek. "It'll be boring as hell, and my family will take your presence as my date way out of proportion. But as much as they annoy me, I don't want them worrying about me or knowing a killer targeted me—so I will want you to keep that secret even though the threat is probably over."

She held his gaze, and he was struck again by all the faceted colors in her eyes. "We don't know for sure that it's over."

He shrugged. "If the president is attending, security will be tight. I'll be safe enough."

"Would you want me there?" she asked. "If we weren't working together?"

He could tell she regretted the question as soon as she said it because she tried to roll away. He stopped her. She'd made herself vulnerable, and he refused to be any less courageous.

"Yes." Honesty was scary, and his heart revved with fear.

Slowly, she smiled up at him. "Can we stop at Walmart somewhere on the way?"

"Walmart?"

"For a party dress."

He laughed. While he didn't care if she came in jeans and a t-shirt, the society crowd were going to tear her apart. He eyed her carefully, which wasn't a hardship. His sister was too short. He had a sudden thought and went through to the other room, grabbing his cell, turning it back on. He had dozens of missed calls. *Shit.* He dialed one number. "Agent Rooney?"

"I've been trying to get hold of you, SSA Sheridan."

Ava tried to sit up, but he put his thigh over hers. He wasn't done with her yet.

"I turned my phone off to try to get some sleep last night. Before you tell me why you were calling me, would it be weird if I asked if you had a formal gown I could borrow for tonight?" He figured she was a similar height to Ava and when she wasn't pregnant, they'd be a similar size. He could drive to Quantico to pick up the dress and then head back to the lion's den of DC.

Rooney laughed. "I do, but you'll need to talk to Alex about heels."

He chuckled and saw the uncertainty lingering in Ava's eyes. "What dress and shoe size are you?" he mouthed to Ava.

She told him using her fingers.

"Anything in a dress size six and a shoe size seven will work. Agent Kanas is accompanying me to my father's engagement party tonight and is in need of something to wear." He didn't qualify that she'd be his bodyguard. He wanted her there as his date.

"I'll need something where I can access my gun," Ava added.

Dominic repeated that to Rooney, and she promised to deliver something to his apartment that night because she was planning to be in DC anyway. He gave her his address. "So, what's the bad news?" he asked. Because he doubted Rooney would be calling in the middle of the night with anything good.

"Someone trashed the windows at the back of your house."

"Anyone get hurt?"

"No. And by the time the local cops arrived the vandal was gone."

"You think it was the UNSUB."

"Yes."

He dragged his hand down his face. "I thought it was over." He wanted it to be all over. For Sandy and Fernando to be safe, for him to get back to living a normal life. The unsettling thought of Ava not being in it swirled confusingly in his brain. They still had tonight. It wasn't over yet.

"Any update on DNA or lab work or Robin Elgin's cell phone data?"

"Frazer plans to go lean on the lab today until they give him answers."

Dominic winced. He wouldn't want Frazer hounding him, but damn, they needed results.

He realized it was really early and she probably wasn't even at work yet. "I'll call my cleaning company to come do clean up and get a glazier in there ASAP to board up until they can fit new glass. Call me if there's any news and thanks for everything. I owe you."

He hung up and tossed the cell behind him. There were so

many things he should be doing. Returning all those missed calls. Talking to Sandy to check on Ben, talking to Gross about what the FBI had dug up at the cabin. Needling Lincoln Frazer about any other developments and checking in at CNU. Instead he ran his finger over Ava's eyebrows, lingering on the scar on her forehead, then down her nose and across her petal-soft lips.

Down the graceful length of her neck, over her winged collarbones which he found unreasonably attractive. Her breasts were full and pert. Begging for a little attention which he willingly administered. Allowing the hunger to grow, fanning the flames, but carrying on with his exploration all the way down to her toes, which he kissed one at a time.

She watched him, eyes bright as glass. And when he finally started to make his way back up her body, she turned the tables on him before he could sample the tasty bits. She flipped him on his back.

He told himself he could take her if he had to, but from the firm grip she had on him and the fact she knew how to fight dirty, he wasn't sure he was being honest. There were a lot of things Dominic was pretty sure he wasn't being honest with himself about in regards to Ava Kanas and as her lips closed over him and he lost his mind for the third time that night, he was starting to wonder what would be so bad about having a proper relationship with this woman?

As long as his heart wasn't involved, as long as he kept the most vital part of himself separate, so that if and when she left him, he wouldn't be completely destroyed. Maybe, just maybe, they could make this work.

CHAPTER TWENTY-EIGHT

AVA WOULD RATHER go head-to-head with the Russian Bratva than dress up and mingle with the Washington elite.

They drove to the CNU office in Quantico so Dominic could finish the reports and paperwork arising from the prison siege.

She'd checked the documents to reassure herself there was no mention of her name, nor any reference to the Resident Agency where she usually worked. In deference to the Witness Protection Program the FBI had simply labeled her a "trainee negotiator." Aside from the personnel at CNU and the few Hostage Rescue Team agents she'd talked to at the prison no one knew her identity. She'd spoken to her family and they'd supported her decision to save the warden from being raped by Gino Gerbachi. They'd also promised to take extra precautions, but the community was tight-knit, and they didn't exactly list their addresses in the phone book. Anonymity was their friend. It had been from the moment the mob had murdered her father in cold blood.

Once she and Dominic left Quantico, they headed to DC for the party, getting caught in nightmare traffic, and arriving with not a lot of time to spare. Ava scrambled into the shower, washed and conditioned her hair, scrubbed herself clean and shaved with Dominic's razor.

Then she blow-dried her hair and pulled on her panties, but there was no way she could wear a bra with the almost-backless, low-cut, lace and chiffon, lavender gown Mallory Rooney had dropped off.

Rooney also thought to bring shoes, jewelry, a purse that Ava could fit her Glock in and a few items of makeup.

Ava would have to remember to buy the woman flowers because she'd been dreading the idea of this party for many reasons but mostly this one. She didn't know what was appropriate to wear in these situations and certainly couldn't afford clothes like this. It demonstrated exactly how different she and Dominic were in regards to everything outside work—and if they ever had a real relationship, they wouldn't be allowed to work together either.

Which left them with what? Sex?

She could not complain about the sex.

Maybe tonight would be a test for them both. Or simply a reminder that no matter how compatible they were in bed they had nothing else in common.

She shimmied into the dress and managed to pull up the zipper. It had a bit of a Grecian flavor to it, which she liked. She was a little unnerved by the fact her breasts were almost naked, the upper slope concealed only by a scrap of lace. She adjusted it slightly, but it didn't make it any less revealing. At least her nipples were unavailable to the viewing public.

She twisted to look at the back in the mirror. The cut of the cloth draped to only a couple of inches above a ribbon tied at her waist. There was a damn train, which looked amazing but would be a bitch to walk in and not trip over.

Dominic knocked on the door. "Five minutes."

She shot a glare at the door but knew he was no keener to go to the shindig than she was. Maybe less so. Family could be brutal.

She brushed her hair and piled it into the usual bun, making it tidier and tighter than usual, hoping the errant strands behaved for once. It was the best she could do under the circumstances.

She pulled out the makeup and applied eye shadow and some blush and dark eyeliner and mascara. The basics.

Thankfully the lipstick Rooney had supplied was a soft pink rather than a bright scarlet. It felt more like something Ava would actually wear herself.

Ava put on some sparkly earrings and hoped to god they were cubic zirconia rather than diamonds. She ignored the necklace even though it was pretty enough to distract from her boobs. The idea of losing it was too unsettling for Ava's piece of mind. She couldn't afford to replace it. If she flashed someone, she'd just have to live with it. If she lost Rooney's necklace, she'd have to throw herself off the nearest parapet.

Dominic rapped on the door, and she swung it open just as he started to say something.

He blinked twice, and she watched him as he seemed to physically drag his eyes off that titillating edge of the lace.

"Now I really don't want to go to this party." His voice was low and gruff and sent a shiver of lust right through her.

All the oxygen in the room vanished, and she found herself taking fast, shallow breaths that never quite satisfied. She flashed back to being naked and writhing on that bed back in Pennsylvania. She squeezed her legs together and felt a tingle of pleasurable awareness.

Then his eyes met hers. "You look incredible."

Slowly she smiled. "So do you." God, she wanted to advance on him, rip that crisp, white shirt out of that sinfully sexy, black cummerbund and put her hand down his pants and around the erection growing in those expensive-looking trousers.

His eyes darkened, and his nostrils flared. He took her hand and tugged her after him. "Later. Let's get this over with first."

She shivered at the promise in his voice. At the door of the apartment she picked up her silver purse which was large enough to fit her Glock, spare ammo, creds. She carefully slipped into Rooney's heels.

She and Sheridan were now eye-to-eye, and she could see the hunger battling with duty as he watched her.

"Got your gun?" she asked with a suggestive grin.

He took her hand. "Yes, I've got my damn gun." And then he shocked her by pressing her palm against his hardness and pinning her against the door. He wedged his solid thigh between her legs, and she discovered the value of a train as he drew her right knee up to his hip. His other hand rested on her lower back, pulling her toward him. His lips causing chaos in the pulse of her neck.

"I want to kiss every inch of you."

And she totally wanted to be kissed.

The buzzer to his swank apartment rang and broke the spell, reminding them they had somewhere to be.

The guy had two homes. One had a pool and the other had a doorman. Thinking about it, there was probably a pool around here somewhere too.

Ava did not belong here, but she wanted to be with him anyway, and she was beginning to think no matter how much she pretended this thing was about sex and the fact they were stuck together, her feelings went deeper than that. Much deeper.

He swore and pulled away. Pressed the intercom. "We'll be right down." He took her hand. "For tonight, you're not my colleague or bodyguard, you're my girlfriend. Security will be tight so we can relax a little."

A longing so strong shot through Ava that she couldn't hold his gaze. She knew this wasn't for real. Sure, he'd said he wanted her there, but what else could he have said?

Attending the party was to appease his father, and her posing as his girlfriend kept Bureau business private. No one had caught on to the fact there was a serial killer hunting FBI agents yet. Nor did the media know Peter Galveston's body had been removed from his grave probably by the local pastor. When they found out, the public was going to go ape-shit.

But maybe, for one more night, she and Dominic could forget everything and relax—which would be a damn sight easier if she wasn't wearing three-inch heels and her boobs weren't on show to the world.

Courage.

Dominic swept his hand forward so she went first. They headed to the elevator and she stood barely breathing as she watched him in the reflective surface. He looked like a movie star.

He slid on dark glasses as they left the elevator. The glasses hid the last vestiges of his black eyes, and she could imagine he really didn't want to have to explain to everyone exactly how he'd got them.

Outside on the curb was a black Lexus identical to the one he'd crashed in last Wednesday night. He paused mid-stride and almost recoiled.

"What's going on?" she asked, braced for danger.

"Apparently my father sent me a gift."

He didn't seem happy with the notion, and Ava understood. The last time he'd been inside that model of vehicle, he'd been in a terrible accident.

"Let's grab a cab," Ava suggested.

Dominic turned his head sharply, looking at her over the glasses as if surprised by her insight.

She tried not to be insulted. Van had always told her that her biggest asset was her intuition, followed by her gumption. His words. They reminded her of why she was really with Sheridan. Finding the truth behind Van's death. Over the last few days that focus had blurred and shame reared up. After everything Van had done, he deserved better from her.

Dominic took her hand again and squeezed, towing her to the curb where he held up his arm for a passing taxi.

When a yellow cab stopped, he helped her inside and climbed in next to her. She hauled the layers of lace and chiffon into her lap feeling like the heroine in some historical romance. She just needed the cab to morph into a horse and carriage and Sheridan to morph into a Duke. Then they'd make out and possibly have full blown sex, and she'd be ruined and they'd have to get married.

She blinked her way back into the twenty-first century, a little shocked by the fact her imagination was now doling out daydreams where she and Sheridan got hitched.

The problem with grabbing a cab was the fact they couldn't talk about the case in front of the driver. They settled back in silence as Dominic gave the guy an address. Ava wasn't that familiar with DC so turned her attention to seeing the sights as they drove around.

Dominic picked up her hand, and she wondered if he was doing it to get into character or if he needed the comfort for what lay ahead. From the little he'd said he didn't have the best relationship with his family. Hers were loud and boisterous and always interfering in her business, but she loved them.

When they started to pass embassies with the National Cathedral appearing on the hill above them, Ava began to get nervous.

"Anything I need to know about this event?"

"My family is dysfunctional and annoying, the exception being my little sister, Gwen." He spoke quietly so the cabby couldn't overhear. "She's the baby of the family. Blames herself for the fact our mother killed herself even though she was only an infant when it happened."

"Postpartum depression?" asked Ava.

Dominic nodded tersely. "No one ever mentions it, or Mom. It's like we pretend she never existed."

"I'm sorry. I know how much that sucks." Ava was hit by an unexpected bolt of longing. "We don't talk about my dad either. Can't really. I miss him, but it's like I made him up in my imagination."

Dominic nodded and closed his eyes briefly as if letting the emotion touch him for that split second before moving on.

"This will be the fifth time my father has gotten married, and I'm supposed to be the best man for this one." He looked out the window. "Usually he asks my brother Franklin, but I suspect he asked me so I didn't find a way to wheedle out of the proceedings. We've been here so many times. It's hard to pretend it'll last."

"Pessimist." She bumped his arm with hers.

"Realist," Dominic argued. "Between my father's inability to marry the right woman and my brother's need to destroy anything good in the world, my family isn't exactly all hearts and flowers."

"Brothers can be annoying."

He held her gaze. "Franklin isn't annoying. He's an asshole."

Her lips twitched. "Good to know."

His fingers smoothed over her hand as if he were memorizing the length and curve of each bone and knuckle.

"What if people want to know where I'm from?" she asked, trying to distract herself from thinking about his hands on her body.

Dominic's dark blue eyes took her in and seemed to note her raging nerves. "Tell them."

"Which version?" she muttered beneath her breath.

Dominic leaned into her hair. "I forgot to tell you how amazing you are to have done what you did as a kid after watching your father murdered. And how you chased that gunman through the woods yesterday was brave as hell."

His breath on her skin had her nipples hardening against the material of the dress.

"Tell them whichever history you want, but you don't need to try to impress these people. You are hands down the most beautiful and seriously kickass agent I have ever…*known*." His eyes twinkled as he put a certain carnal emphasis on the last word.

She huffed out a soft laugh and rolled her eyes at him. "And how many of those are there?"

He quieted as if carefully considering his answer, then ran a finger over her collarbone. "One. You."

Ava's gaze locked on his, and her mouth went dry.

Then they arrived and she had to laugh as they piled out of a yellow cab while everyone else was being handed out of limos. Then she looked across at the Georgian mansion with enough columns and white marble steps to rival the White House.

Holy shit.

She allowed her skirts to drop, hoping she didn't stick a heel through this beautiful creation, or fall flat on her face.

Dominic took her hand and drew it through the crook of his elbow. "Hopefully we can do a quick in and out, and be home within an hour. Then I plan to lay you on my bed and unwrap you like the best Christmas present I've ever received."

"In August?"

"Birthday present then."

"When is your birthday?"

His grin was sharp. "January."

"I'll have to decide if I'm an early Christmas or late birthday present." She ran her finger down his lapel. "And I'm having a few suit porn fantasies myself."

"Suit porn?"

"And tux sex."

Dominic appeared to choke on his bow tie.

Ava grinned. "I think you get the picture."

CHAPTER TWENTY-NINE

WITH AVA AT his side, some of the dread that usually overwhelmed Dominic at the thought of attending these gatherings dissipated into the ether.

She was funny, didn't take herself or the people at this party too seriously. She was so beautiful she looked like future heartbreak. Which was exactly why he was not falling for her beyond the physical. They could enjoy themselves for a few weeks. Maybe even try this relationship business on for size for a little while. After that they'd go their separate ways.

He ignored the pang that thought caused. Like he'd told her the day after the car crash, he liked sex, and he got lonely sometimes. Didn't mean he wanted anyone permanently in his space, getting in the way of the things he wanted to do, cramping his style.

What things? What style?

He pushed thoughts about his usually solitary existence out of his head. Enjoying the time they had together to the max was a no brainer, even for a knucklehead such as himself.

Galveston's skeletal remains had been found in the make-shift grave behind the garage at the cottage. Well, a body matching the basic anthropological parameters had been found there. DNA and dental records would confirm it by the end of the day. What had surprised everyone was the presence of another skeleton. A child.

No one knew anything about a child. A forensic anthropologist was examining the bones to try to determine how long the kid had been there and possibly how he-or-she had died.

Was it a previously unknown victim? The offspring of a victim? The offspring of Galveston himself? Could the child have been the original owner of the teddy bear that was left on the marker of Galveston's grave?

Where was the mother of this kid and how had the child died? That was the biggest question, right along with who'd buried them in that shallow grave at Galveston's old cabin.

The lab was working 24-7 until they figured this out. Unfortunately, science could only go so fast.

It would be nice to rebury the serial murderer before the press even discovered his body had disappeared. The missing corpse had surely been designed to stir up the man's memory and misdeeds. To instill fear in the population. A way to revictimize the families of the missing and murdered women.

But the presence of the child… Dominic frowned. What did that mean?

FBI agents had been sent to all of Galveston's former residences and any known dump sites to see if this UNSUB had done anything else. They were poised to talk to victims' families as soon as DNA confirmed the skeletal remains really were Galveston's.

So far, no other human remains had been found at the cabin.

Sandy Warren's husband had had two of his fingers reattached, which was hellish but better than having no hand at all. Dominic didn't know how he was going to face Sandy or Ben when he saw them next. Agents from the New York Field Office had set up surveillance on Sandy's property and protection for all her family. Same with Fernando Chavez who had sent his wife and children into protective custody until they caught this UNSUB.

And maybe they already had, but someone out there was still carrying a grudge as they'd smashed his windows. The UNSUB, or an accomplice? That was the question of the day.

The rifle in Caroline Perry's car was the same long gun that had been used to murder Calvin Mortimer. She'd roofied Dominic, possibly Van, too. Probably staged Van's murder as a suicide.

Dominic wanted to know exactly what had happened to his old friend. Guilt washed over him. He wanted to know exactly how badly he had let Van down.

If only they'd figured out the connection beforehand, Van might not be dead, Calvin Mortimer might not be dead. Others might not have died. Sandy and her family might not be going through this gut-wrenching trauma.

Then he realized what he was doing, absorbing guilt about something that was not his doing. The responsibility lay squarely with the UNSUB and their sick needs and motivation.

How were Caroline Perry and Robin Elgin connected to Galveston?

If the task force had figured it out, Gross wasn't saying.

Too impatient to line up with the crowds of people waiting to greet his father and his latest fiancée at the front door, Dominic took Ava's hand and guided her around the side of the house toward the kitchen entrance. They had to show their badges to the security stationed around the house, which was reassuring. Their FBI status and the fact they were on the guest list meant they were both able to enter while carrying concealed. No Secret Service agents visible yet, although they were probably already stationed in and around the house.

The place was enormous, but his father liked to throw these lavish parties so at least he was making the most of the space.

"The house actually belonged to my mother's family." It felt liberating to talk about her for a change. To reject the black stain of her death, so pervasive that they all tried to pretend she'd never existed.

Ava pulled him to a stop. "What did she do? Your mom. When she was alive?"

"Nothing really." He couldn't meet her gaze as the emotions this conversation brought up were too raw. Too fresh even after all these years. "Her family came from old money. Made a fortune in the lumber and mining industries at the turn of the last century. Most of the men in the family perished during the Spanish flu pandemic or during World War II. My grandmother was the only survivor out of six kids. She married late—probably forced to do so by her parents so the money stayed in the family." It was crazy really and yet he reaped the benefits every day. "My mom was the only child from that union and inherited the lot." His fingers tightened on hers. "I think if she had done something with her life, something constructive besides having kids which obviously wasn't enough for her—she might have been able get through that dark time without..." He still couldn't say it. Suicide still pissed him off even though he knew his mother had been mentally ill.

"I'm really sorry you lost her so young, Dominic. Sorry she didn't get the treatment she needed."

Maybe that's where most of the family guilt and resentment came from. The fact that none of them had realized how sick she was and they all secretly blamed one another so they didn't have to blame themselves.

Dominic put his hand on Ava's lower back and pulled her toward him. Her eyes went wide. He lowered his mouth to her lips and kissed her.

"What was that for?" she asked suspiciously when he pulled away. She wiped at his lips that were probably the same shade as hers. He didn't care.

"Come on. Let's find the family and see if we can set a record for the least time spent at one of these things and then go home and have some fun."

When he opened the door to the kitchen the cook threw up her hands and shrieked, at first in surprise and then with joy.

"Dominic! Your father said you were coming but I didn't believe it."

Martha had been with them for years.

"It hasn't been that long..." he tried to defend himself.

Martha wagged her finger at him. "Christmas, and you only live a couple of hours away." She put her fists on her waist. She was wearing a chef's uniform today because it was a formal occasion, but she didn't usually. Most of the food for this size of event would have been catered by an outside firm. He'd always hoped his dad would marry Martha and find some normalcy in his life, but the governor seemed determined to chase the dream of the perfect woman. Pretty. Peppy. Permanently happy. As if that would somehow glue them all back together again. Or maybe his dad liked sex too—with pretty, peppy, permanently happy blondes.

"Who's this?" Martha raised her chin at Ava.

Ava held out her hand. "Ava Kanas. I wor—"

"My girlfriend," Dominic interrupted with a determined smile.

Martha's brows formed a vee in her forehead, and she seemed to look down her nose at Ava for a long, drawn out moment. Ava kept smiling and finally Martha let out a gusty laugh. "She's pretty, but you always did like arm candy."

Rather than getting pissy, Ava raised a mocking brow at him. He didn't know on whose behalf to be more insulted—his, his former dates' or Ava's.

"This 'arm candy' is armed and dangerous," Dominic said dryly. "So watch yourself."

"I like her already," Martha declared.

He gave the woman a kiss on the cheek and held on tight to Ava's hand. This whole situation was a potential minefield of disasters, but he was here now and needed to make the best of it even if he'd rather be negotiating a hostage release during an armed standoff.

He grabbed a drink off a passing waiter and held it out to Ava.

She refused. "I'm officially on duty."

"Fine." He wasn't going to argue with her. He took it and downed it in one go, then grabbed another. "Where's the whiskey when you need it."

"Dominic!"

He forced himself not to tense up at hearing his father's voice. He put a smile on his face and turned. "Pop. There you are."

Ava squeezed his hand, and he wished he didn't like her quite so much. He had the horrible feeling they'd both invested more emotionally in the other than they'd planned.

He embraced his dad, felt the man's arms squeeze tight around him as if he were trying to anchor him in place. Rather than withdraw and run like Dominic normally did, he allowed the contact for a few seconds longer. Let his dad pull away first.

"Let me introduce you to Agent Ava Kanas. My girlfriend."

He didn't miss the way his father's eyes lit up when he looked at Ava. The guy was a serial womanizer—just like his brother.

Ava tucked her pretty purse under her arm to shake his father's hand. His father smiled intently. "You're the first woman he's brought home in over a decade."

One side of Ava's mouth kicked up. "Maybe I'll start a trend."

"I hope not. I'd like to see you stick around." His father still hadn't released Ava's hand, and Dominic felt himself getting territorial, which was probably why dear old Dad was doing this, to wind him up. Finally, his father let go, and Dominic ungritted his teeth.

"Where is the lovely Tracy?" Dominic asked.

"In the ballroom."

Ava's eyes widened so much Dominic had to hold back a laugh. Didn't everyone have a ballroom?

"Let me introduce you both."

Ava leaned close as they started walking through the crowd. "You haven't met her yet?"

Dominic shrugged. "I've been busy."

"That's terrible," Ava chastised.

"Talk to my boss."

She shoved his arm, but he refused to let go of her hand, and she stumbled into him. She laughed, and he leaned down and kissed her on the lips.

His heart started pounding, and his skin burst into flames when she kissed him back despite being surrounded by strangers. Everything and everybody in the room vanished. Her free hand curled into his lapel to draw him closer.

A loud wolf whistle split the air, and he pulled away. Ava blushed a deep red. She wiped the lipstick off his mouth with an expression that was embarrassed, but her eyes shone with what looked like happiness.

He carried on into the ballroom not caring what anyone thought of him or Ava or the fact they were here together. He looked over the heads of most of the crowd and spotted his dad near the far wall beneath the world's biggest mirror that reflected the world's largest chandelier.

"Wow. You guys sure know how to throw a party. Do you have indoor fireworks too?"

He shook his head. Ava Kanas was an ocean breeze in this stuffy DC atmosphere.

They made their way through the crowd, Dominic nodding to old acquaintances but moving fast enough not to invite conversation. Finally, he reached his father's side.

"Dominic, I'd like you to meet Tracy Fitzgerald. Tracy, this is my youngest son. As I told you, he works for the FBI."

The woman turned, and Dominic was pleasantly surprised. Unlike his father's former wife, Fiona "call me Fe-Fe," Tracy appeared older than he was. Rather than platinum blonde Tracy wore her hair in a short brown bob and had freckles all over her nose. She wore a pretty red gown, and her dark eyes were emphasized with dark shadow.

She looked intelligent and friendly.

Tracy held out her hand—one with an impressive-looking diamond on the third finger. "It's a pleasure to meet you, Dominic. Your father has talked about you so much I feel like I already know you."

Her accent was slightly southern. Not full-on Alabama, but maybe North Carolina.

"Nice to meet you too, Tracy. Sorry it took me so long to show up."

She gave him a warm smile. "I understand you're busy. Your father is incredibly proud of what you do. Well, he's proud of all his children, but I'd say especially you."

Dominic clenched his jaw at the unexpected feelings the words evoked. The Sheridans prided themselves on their stoic demeanors in the face of unimaginable pain, but a little human kindness sent them reeling.

He'd pissed his father off when he'd joined the FBI, but that had been a long time ago. Maybe it was time to get over the old resentments.

"This is Ava." He introduced her to Tracy, as the emotion he was feeling seemed to grow and spread. Contagious. Dangerous. Knotting his throat so that he couldn't speak.

"It's lovely to meet you, Ava." Tracy shook her hand.

"You too, ma'am."

"Tracy runs the Smithsonian—"

"I don't run it," Tracy admonished the governor. "I work there. Stop trying to make me sound more important than I actually am." She pursed her lips then joked, "He's going to get me fired if he's not careful."

The governor pulled her close and gave her a kiss. "You're important to me."

Dominic grinned. Obviously, Tracy was smart, independent and dedicated to her job. He liked her already.

The man responsible for the wolf whistle joined their party and clapped Dominic on the back. Hard.

"Didn't think you'd show up." His brother's pupils widened as he scanned Ava from hair to toe and then let his gaze rest on her breasts. He swayed slightly, obviously drunk.

"Stop leching after my date or she'll shoot you." Dominic wanted to smack Franklin, but Ava was more than capable of defending herself.

"Does that mean she also carries fluffy handcuffs?"

Franklin and his father both sniggered at the innuendo, but Tracy glared at his father.

Ava said sweetly, "How about we find a radiator and you can try them out for a few hours?"

Franklin's eyes narrowed, and his smile didn't reach his eyes. He did not like to be challenged. Dominic's brother was five years older than he was and he'd screwed his way through the female population without thought for years, including the only other girl Dominic had brought home and, he was pretty sure, step-mother number two.

Dominic watched his brother's cynicism twist all the fun out of his face and wondered if that was what he himself usually looked like. If that was the expression he usually showed the world. His stomach churned. He didn't want to be that jaded or condemning or self-isolated.

"Where's Gwen?" Dominic asked when the silence lingered, and Ava started to worry she'd said the wrong thing.

"Over by the punch. She's still dating that asshole Geoffrey. True love." With a sneer, Franklin knocked back his Champagne like it was water.

Dominic blinked.

"I heard the crash you were involved in was pretty bad," his dad said quietly. "Glad you're still with us, son."

"It was just a fender bender."

"You totaled the car," Franklin pointed out.

"The insurance company wrote it off. You know how they are sometimes."

Ava's brows climbed halfway up her forehead.

Franklin reached forward and snatched the dark glasses from Dominic's face. Winced before thrusting them against Dominic's chest. "Looks like a hell of a *fender bender.*"

His father looked aghast at Dominic's fading bruises. Tracy shot a wary look at his brother.

"Airbags," Dominic commented wryly.

"Are you sure the lovely Ava didn't give you a black eye?"

"Why would I do that?" Ava asked in confusion.

"Funzies?" Franklin downed another glass of Champagne. Dominic tried to remember an occasion when his brother hadn't been drunk at a family get-together and couldn't.

"Leave Ava alone," Dominic told him.

"I can handle myself," Ava insisted.

His brother scoffed and wiped his mouth with the back of his hand. Franklin was either an alcoholic or well on his way to becoming one. But it didn't explain why he was so vindictive toward Dominic. Or maybe it was his way of keeping everyone at arm's length. Of not being devastated again should something happen to any of them. Drive everyone you loved away so you never got hurt again.

Dominic's mouth went dry as he recognized the tactic.

"I like this one," Franklin said, as if that mattered. "She's feisty. Not like the last one you brought home. What was her name?"

Dominic glared at his brother. "Ainsley." Whom his brother had seduced and then dumped. The only reason to bring her up now was to drive a wedge between them.

"*She*," Ava said with a spark in her eye and angle to her chin that Dominic knew spelled trouble, "is a federal agent with powers of arrest, so *feisty* is the least of my personality traits."

Dominic put his arm around Ava's shoulders and felt the tension vibrating through her bones.

Franklin grabbed another drink off a passing waiter and Dominic saw the tightening of his father's features. Then he heard a squeal behind him that could only be his sister.

He turned around and she jumped on him, clamping around him like a koala, blissfully unaware of his sore shoulder and ribs.

He wrapped his arms tight around her and squeezed. Maybe his problem in the past was he'd always let himself be pushed away from these gatherings by his older brother's bitterness and his own self-doubt.

"Hi, Gwen," Dominic mumbled when she didn't release him.

"I am so happy to see you." Gwen sniffed into his neck. "I've missed you so much."

His hands formed fists as he met Tracy's soft gaze.

"You could always come visit," he objected.

"You're never there. Whenever I say I'm coming to stay you suddenly have important business out of town."

Dominic grimaced. That was probably true. "That's my job, Gwen. It's hard to plan time off."

She finally let go and stood back.

"Good thing you didn't join the law firm after all, Dom. I can see why you didn't." Franklin raked Ava up and down with a leer. Then he reached out and ran his knuckle over the slope of her breast. "We certainly don't have pussy like this in the office—"

Dominic punched Franklin so hard his brother was out cold before he hit the deck.

Shit.

Dominic squeezed closed his eyes, mad with himself for reacting. His brother had deliberately provoked him, knowing how much their father hated creating a public scene. Goddamn it. Why did Franklin always have to push him?

"Sorry, Pop." He shook the pain out of his hand, then bent to drag his unconscious sibling somewhere private. His father stopped him. He waved over two of his security guards. "Get him out of here and one of you stay with him until he sobers up."

Dominic backed away a step. "I'll leave."

"No," his father exclaimed. "What Franklin did was reprehensible." His dad's hands trembled. "I've ignored his faults for too long. He's always been jealous of you even when you were a baby. Nothing your mother or I ever said changed that. Now his drinking has exacerbated the issue."

Dominic blinked, as much by the mention of his mother as anything else. He didn't remember the last time they'd spoken about her. "Well, I'm sorry for causing a scene."

"I need to get him the help he needs and pray he's smart enough to accept it. I'm sorry, Ava. Sorry, son." His father wrapped him in a fierce hug that Dominic was helpless against. Then Gwen joined in, and he broke out in a cold sweat at the pain radiating from his ribs, but still he didn't break away.

A ball of emotion swelled in his throat, and his eyes burned. All those years of holding back so as to not upset anyone, all the suppressed resentment and grief. Maybe it was the car crash, or being targeted for death by some madman, but suddenly he felt like he could start over. He didn't need to repeat old patterns or failures. He could control his future. His family was flawed, but the relationships weren't irreparable.

Ava watched him, expression uncertain. He could tell she was about to run.

"I warned you my family was crazy," he said as his father and sister finally let him go.

"Hey." She held up her hands dramatically. "My family is Greek. All you need to do is to start tossing crockery, and I'll feel right at home."

He laughed and pulled her towards him, knowing she was self-conscious but wanting her to understand he cared about her, that she was important to him even if he didn't know how to say the words. They'd take the time to figure this out. He didn't want to lose her. They'd do it right.

He kissed her full on the mouth. An open mouth *if-we-were-alone-I'd-be-nailing-you-to-the-wall* kind of kiss. When he pulled back and looked up, his whole world crashed around his feet.

CHAPTER THIRTY

BERNIE WATCHED DOMINIC Sheridan kiss the bitch he was with not once, but twice. And the way he'd stared at her, all smoldering passion and hot lust.

It was so perfect. So fucking perfect. Killing Dominic had been the plan all along but that was too easy. Too…linear. Not enough suffering considering all the harm Sheridan had done. Not enough torture or pain.

Bernie had planned to put something nasty in the punch. Not enough to kill anyone, probably, but enough to have them shitting themselves as they all rushed for the restroom at once.

It would have been so much fun.

Unfortunately, they had servers watching each table, and the opportunity had not presented itself. Someone was always there, making conversation and stuffing their faces.

Bernie did not want to be remembered hanging around the food and drink areas if people started to get sick, so the idea was abandoned.

Security had been too tight to risk bringing in a gun.

Dominic and the bitch and some other guy had gone off to the library but then the president had arrived and there was only so much ass-licking Bernie could watch without vomiting. Leaving seemed like the smart thing to do. Losing Robin had been a blow. Smashing Sheridan's windows had eased the sharpness of the anger but slicing that bitch, inch by perfect inch, would go a lot further to evening out the score.

But now wasn't the time. Instead, it was time to retreat and regroup, leave the area until they dropped their guards again. There was a rush in the thought of that. A sweet, hot rush in the thought of slowly sending Sheridan over the edge into madness to where Bernie lived with only grief as a companion.

CHAPTER THIRTY-ONE

AVA WAS SURPRISED that Dominic kissed her in public, in front of his father even, but as usual when he touched her, her knees dissolved and she sank against him.

This didn't seem like make-believe or temporary. It felt a lot like how she expected love to feel.

Then he stiffened and straightened away from her so fast she almost stumbled. She blinked in confusion and saw the problem. The FBI Director stood with his glare burning a hole right through her.

Shoot.

The director nodded toward Dominic's father. "Governor. Ms. Fitzgerald." Then he stepped closer to Ava and Dominic and lowered his voice. "Let's go somewhere private, shall we?"

Dominic's expression closed down. He nodded. "Come with me."

He let go of her hand for what felt like the first time in hours. Of course, he let go. Their boss had seen them snogging in public, and they were both about to get their asses reamed.

Crap. This could look very bad for Dominic as he was her superior, and she knew how important his reputation was to him.

Dominic led them out of the ballroom through a nearby doorway, down a short corridor and then around into a room that was an actual library. There was a big, open fireplace and wingback chairs. Ava could only imagine how magical this looked at Christmastime.

She waited for Dominic to close the door behind their boss.

"I can explain, sir," she jumped in. "We were pretending to be personally involved so that the UNSUB would not realize we're onto them. Hoping to draw them out."

Dominic's expression flickered as if she'd said the wrong thing. Eyes narrowed. Lips pinched.

"I thought the UNSUB was dead. Killed by you two in a New York State forest yesterday." The director wore an almost bored expression as if killing people didn't bear a personal cost for the agents involved.

"We won't know exactly how many people are mixed up in this plot until we get the DNA back and some other evidentiary data," Ava explained.

"Pity you killed the only living witness then."

Ava straightened in shock.

"The man, Robin Elgin, shot at us repeatedly." Dominic spoke, his voice a low, hard rumble. "He had his weapon aimed at Agent Kanas, and if I hadn't shot him, he'd have murdered Agent Kanas in cold blood."

"And I'm sure she's been *very* grateful."

Fury crashed through Ava and stole her breath. "What the hell does that mean?" Her voice vibrated.

Dominic's eyes widened as if he wanted her to stop talking, but she was done being insulted.

"What does it mean?" The director laughed. "I come to the society event of the year and discover two of my personnel exchanging saliva in a crowded room in front of the Governor of Vermont. The FBI has a reputation to uphold and that doesn't involve agents making spectacles of themselves."

Ava knew she was gaping like a fish, but the director had twisted the situation into something tawdry and ugly. It felt as if he'd slapped her.

"I am the one who kissed Agent Kanas. She simply played along in case there is another UNSUB involved in the multiple murders and serious attempts on my life, and if they happened to have eyes inside this event then she wouldn't give away the fact she's been assigned to watch my back."

"She wasn't guarding your back when I walked in." The director sounded equally furious. "She was goddamned scratching her nails down it."

"That is not true." Dominic defended her.

"Tell me you two haven't been physically involved."

Dominic's eyes were dark with resentment, and his fingers clenched and unclenched, but he didn't deny it.

Was he regretting getting involved with her now? Of course, he was. His career was everything to him, and she was dragging him down into the gutter with her.

Ava dropped her gaze to the carpet.

"At least you aren't stupid enough to lie about it further."

Ava glanced up, anger scalding the back of her eyes.

"You were given another chance after being put on suspension, but you've proven repeatedly you're a hothead who has no place in the Bureau. Worse," the director raked her with a censorious gaze. "You are a bad influence on others. Give me your credentials and service weapon. I will see to it that your belongings are shipped to the address on file. You will not be allowed back onto FBI property." His tone was offhand and derogatory. "SSA Sheridan, report to OPR first thing tomorrow."

"What?" Ava took a step forward. "I get fired and SSA Sheridan gets reported to OPR? In what universe was that fair?" She saw the answer reflected in the director's eyes. The wealth, the power of the Sheridan family, versus the blue-collar impotence of hers.

Ava stared at the director as silence reverberated around the room.

"You can't do this." The words emerged from Ava's lips as a whisper when what she really wanted to do was scream.

"I will do whatever I deem appropriate to protect the reputation of my agency."

Ava kept waiting for Dominic to *do* something, help in some way, but he only stood there, hostility pouring off him in palpable waves.

Bitterness boiled through her veins. She should have known.

His resentment shouldn't feel like a betrayal. But it did. Humiliation flooded her. She would not break down in front of these men. She opened her borrowed clutch and offered her weapon to her boss, along with her creds.

"I'm a good agent," she forced out. Then, without looking at Dominic, she left.

DOMINIC WAITED FOR the fury inside him to subside. He knew how to talk his way out of this. He knew that reactive anger would get them nowhere. He wanted to take Ava in his arms and calm her down, but he needed to calm himself down first.

She wouldn't leave without talking to him. She'd wait for

him somewhere quiet where they could discuss things. He'd fix this.

Dammit. Panic raced through him. No way would Ava stick around after she'd been insulted so thoroughly. She'd leave. ASAP.

Dominic started to go after her, but the director grabbed his arm.

"She isn't worth it, Sheridan."

He pulled away. The desire to put his knuckles through the man's face was almost overwhelming, and he pulled in air to stop himself. He'd already punched his brother tonight. Ava had turned him into someone who would rather use his fists than his words, when it was his words that had gotten him where he was today.

This wasn't who he was. What the hell had happened to him?

Finally, he figured out what he needed to say. "I know she's only a rookie, but she is a damned good agent. She is the first person who figured out we had a killer targeting FBI personnel." His voice sounded like broken glass grinding against itself. "At great risk to herself, she helped resolve a prison siege and prevented the warden from being violently raped while we all sat around and watched. She saved my reputation after the car crash when everyone believed I'd probably had a few too many drinks or maybe snorted a line of coke. She went after the truth and uncovered a drug smuggling ring the DEA had been after for months."

"She's a loose cannon—"

"She's the best goddamn federal agent I've ever met!" Dominic yelled. "And you fired her when *I* kissed her. I'm the one you need to fire." Dominic stuck his finger in the man's chest, sure as shit about to lose his job. But he didn't care.

If the Bureau he worked for treated someone as fiercely loyal as Ava Kanas like trash then he did not care.

He needed to find her.

She'd already have convinced herself that he didn't value her enough to defend her. And his silence while he'd been trying to keep his shit together would reinforce that notion. None of this was her fault. Not getting kissed in public, not him decking his brother, not her getting fired.

This was all on him, and she was the one paying.

He went to hurry after her when the door was pushed open. Rather than Ava returning, his father and his godfather stood there. Secret Service agents hovered in the background.

"Problems, gentlemen?" President Joshua Hague and his dad came in, closing the door behind them.

And normally Dominic would say, *no, sir. Nothing for you to get involved in, sir.* He despised nepotism, but this wasn't about him. This was about a grave injustice being dealt out to an agent he respected and admired.

"A fellow agent of mine, one I happen to care about deeply." The director flinched at that, and Dominic knew he should feel ashamed for using his connections in a way he'd sworn he never would in the past. Except he wasn't looking for favors, he was looking for fairness. And he'd only just appreciated how much Ava meant to him. "Was fired after I kissed her in public."

The director opened his mouth to defend himself, but Dominic spoke over him. "Either the director fires us both, or he gives Ava her job back, and she faces the same disciplinary review process I do. What he does not do is treat us differently because she's a rookie, and I'm the son of a goddamn politician."

The president and his father came toward them.

"Is this true?" his father asked. "You fired Ava?"

"She and Dominic were involved in an intimate relationship—"

"Were?" Dominic snarled. Was he supposed to ditch Ava now?

Deep wrinkles gathered on his father's forehead. "But that's not frowned upon in the Bureau when they are both single."

"Agents have to declare it to their supervisors. They can't work together," the director blustered.

"This *just* started," Dominic said impatiently. He wanted to go to her but needed to fight for her first. "We didn't plan to get involved. We were forced together due to...circumstances." Dominic's gaze flicked to his father and the president. He couldn't discuss an active investigation even with them. "We fell for each other. Hard."

Dominic closed his eyes. Oh shit. He had fallen for her so hard, from so high. His landing zone had been like the cross a parachutist aimed for from ten thousand feet. Tiny and insignificant until you got close. And then when you got closer you knew exactly what to aim for and where to go.

"I need to find her." Dominic looked at the director. "I'll hand in my official resignation tomorrow, but first I need to talk to Ava."

"I saw her out front," his father said. "With a pregnant woman. Senator Tremont's daughter, I think..."

"Mallory Rooney?"

"Yes, that's her."

"Excuse me, gentlemen, but I have a relationship to save."

On the way out, he paused to put a hand on his father's shoulder. "Sorry to ruin your party, Pop. I like Tracy, by the way. I hope you'll both be very happy."

"I like her too. In fact, I love her." His father's hand covered his. "It's all right, son. Go find your girl." His eyes grew watery. "You look at her the way I used to look at your mother when we first met. I want to see you dancing together at my wedding."

So did he, Dominic realized. He wanted to show her off on his arm and go home with her. Which pissed him off all over again that she'd left without him.

Because he hadn't fought for her.

Because, like always, it had been Ava Kanas against the world.

If only she'd been patient, she'd have seen him go to bat for her. Balls to the wall. Mouth set to megaphone. Was he too late? Had he come riding to her defense a few seconds too late? She was pissed but, more importantly, she was hurt. Would she forgive him?

He didn't know. He texted her and waited for her to reply, but the message didn't even show as being delivered.

Dominic stared at the screen impatiently then shook his head as he made his way through the ballroom to the front of the house. He knew how to negotiate a high-stakes game, and this thing with Ava was about as high stakes as anything he'd ever dealt with before.

CHAPTER THIRTY-TWO

MALLORY WASN'T SURE how she'd ended up at Governor Sheridan's engagement party with her mother.

She wore a flowing black dress made of layers upon layers of netting that resembled a tent. It reached her knees—probably—and had a decorative collar covered in shiny costume jewels. The only saving grace was it was loose and cool, and her arms and legs were bare.

Mal was pretty sure she'd attended another engagement party in this house years ago and knew the governor had remarried several times after losing his first wife to suicide. She understood grief better than most. She was lucky to have channeled her anguish into her career on the way to finding Alex. If anything happened to him...she couldn't imagine carrying on.

Except, she ran a hand over her taut belly, she had another reason to keep going now. Another reason to live.

She climbed the steps to the massive front door of the impressive mansion and took one look at the crowd of people milling around inside.

"You go on, Mom. I'm going to sit outside on the bench in the sunshine." She pointed to a garden seat that might hold her weight. "Say hi to the governor and grab me some water, would you?"

Her mother's mouth turned down at the corners. "Are you all right?"

Sweat broke out on Mal's brow, and a wave of lightheadedness rolled over her, but the last thing she wanted was for anyone to make a fuss. Low blood pressure came along with the pregnancy, and she'd learned to move through it. It only lasted a couple of minutes generally. It was the constant back ache like knuckles kneading her kidneys that was driving her to distraction.

"I'm fine."

Her mother squeezed her hand.

Mallory wanted to be alone for a few minutes and instead there were three hundred people ready to make small talk. She'd rather make an arrest. *God.* "I just don't want to go into a stuffy house full of people."

"Okay. If you are sure. I'll say hello to Douglas and Tracy and get you a drink. I'll be back in ten minutes."

Sure, she would.

Mallory smiled reassuringly at her. She loved her mother. What she hated was being treated like she needed a nursemaid.

Alone for the time being, she headed down to the garden bench and sat, sighing as her poor aching feet got some relief.

Out of the corner of her eye she caught a flash of lavender, and her head shot up.

Was that Ava Kanas?

Mal hurried to her feet and walked over to the main gate.

"Ava?" she called.

The woman whirled, and Mal took in her devastated expression. She hurried forward. "What happened?"

Ava blinked suspiciously bright eyes. "Nothing."

"Liar," said Mal. "It has to be Dominic. What did he do?"

The bark of laughter had a bitter edge. "What gave it away?"

"The broken heart you're wearing on your face." Mal put an arm around Ava and held her when the woman started to shake. "Okay, we're going to walk down the street here so that we don't give anyone a free show. I'll call Alex to come pick us up."

Mal one-handedly speed-dialed her husband. "Can you come get me and Ava?"

"The baby?" he asked.

"No, Ava is having a problem with a certain hostage negotiator and needs to get out of here fast." Mal hung up and slipped the phone in her pocket.

Ava straightened and used both hands to wipe at the makeup around her eyes. "Not an agent any longer. The director fired me."

"What? Why?"

"He caught me and Dominic kissing."

"What about Dominic? Did he get fired?" asked Mal.

"No." Ava's lips trembled.

"What did Dominic say?" Heat rose through Mal. A wave of sensation ran over her skin.

"Nothing much. He just stood there looking pissed." Ava shook her head. "I couldn't stay. I had to get out of there."

Mal ran her hand over Ava's back. "I'm so sorry. I am sure Dominic will not let this stand."

Ava didn't look convinced. At all. And then two things happened at once. Mal felt a rush of liquid burst down her legs, and a car pulled up beside them.

"Oh, hell. Here we go."

"What?" Ava frowned and then looked down at the puddle

around Mal's legs. "Uh oh."

Uh oh, indeed. Suddenly the long hours of back ache made a lot more sense. She'd probably been in pre-labor the whole time.

The car window rolled down, and a woman's voice called out, "Can I offer you a ride?"

Mal leaned into the open window. "My waters broke. Can you give me a ride to the hospital, please?" She'd text Alex to meet her there.

"Of course, get in."

Mal turned and gave Ava a squeeze, recognizing the misery in her pinched features.

"Do you love him?" she asked.

Ava blinked like she hadn't known the answer to that question until Mal had voiced it, then nodded despondently.

"Then go back in there and fight for him."

Ava closed her eyes and slowly shook her head. "I can't chase him, Mallory. I can't be another of those women throwing themselves at him. If he wants me, he's going to have to fight for me. Come on, you have a baby to deliver. Let's get you to the hospital."

"Call him? At least give him a chance."

Ava squeezed her hand. "I'll call him." But her sad eyes conveyed she didn't think there was much point.

Mallory nodded. Right now, she had another priority so she slid awkwardly into the passenger seat and held her breath as the pain intensified.

"SUZANNA. WHAT ARE you doing here?" Ava recognized the

woman as soon as she got into the car. "This is Dominic's neighbor," she told Mallory.

Suzanna checked her shoulder, flipped her signal, and pulled smoothly away from the curb.

"I'm one of the governor's donors so I was invited to the party." Her bony fingers clenched and unclenched around the wheel. "To be honest, I'd hoped to talk to Dominic alone, but when he showed up with you, I figured I'd better get out of there before he spotted me. No one wants to look pathetic."

Ava agreed. She took her cell from her borrowed, glittery purse and stared at the screen. She knew she should text the guy so he didn't wonder where she was or waste time looking for her, but emotionally she was still reeling. He'd defended her honor with his brother but hadn't been willing to do the same with the director.

Why was that? Because he believed in her as a woman but not as an agent? Or was too chicken to stand up to the boss? Either way his silence had felt like a betrayal.

She looked at her phone, fingers poised over the text window, but hesitated. She needed time before she contacted the man who'd come to mean so much to her. Time to put up her defenses and shore up her smile, time to figure out what to do with the rest of her life without him or the FBI in it.

She didn't want him to know how much he'd hurt her.

She shouldn't have run out of there, she realized. She was supposed to be watching his back, protecting him, but once again her feelings had guided her actions. Van had tried to get her to slow down, to think rather than react. She was working on it, but obviously not fast enough. Maybe it didn't matter anymore.

Suzanna caught her eye in the rearview mirror. "You look

upset?"

Ava pressed her lips together and hoped she didn't start bawling. She sniffed. "It's nothing."

"I saw him kiss you."

Ava pulled a face. "Yes, well, as you are aware, Dominic is a very good kisser."

"Oh," Suzanna gave a fluttery, little laugh. "We never kissed."

Ava blinked. *What*? "That's not what Dominic thinks."

Suzanna laughed. "Oh, that's adorable. I didn't realize he thought that we... Well, we were both very drunk. I did have the pleasure of seeing his teeny, tiny penis." Her lips spread in a wide smile that didn't reach her eyes. "We didn't have sex though as he couldn't get it up."

Ava raised one brow. This was a weird-ass conversation, not least as Dominic's penis was not tiny. Ava wasn't about to argue the point.

Something felt wrong.

Mallory was sitting very still in the front seat. Eyes closed. Breathing in a measured way.

A car horn honked. The streets whizzed by. Ava leaned forward between the seats. "You missed the turn to the hospital."

Mallory's face was screwed up in pain, and Suzanna was driving too fast.

"Slow down, Suzanna. Turn around. You missed it."

The woman looked over her shoulder but didn't take her foot off the accelerator. Instead, she pulled a P320 Compact Carry Nitron 9mm out of the side pocket of the door and pointed at Mallory's stomach. "Back off, bitch, or your friend and her baby die."

Shit. Ava had made a classic error in judgment. She'd judged the woman with empathy and pity because she remembered what it felt like to wake up with a guy who wanted you gone. Suzanna was not what she'd pretended to be.

Mallory made a keening noise in the back of her throat, a sound torn from her very soul as the reality of what was happening and a labor contraction hit simultaneously.

Ava sat back, pulling the seatbelt across her body.

She texted Dominic the word "help" and then speed-dialed his number, praying he picked up. She hid the cell beneath the material of her skirt.

While their relationship might be in shreds, this threat wasn't over yet. He needed to know that. He needed to help get Mallory the hell out of danger.

Suzanna hadn't noticed the cell phone or maybe didn't realize it was a threat. The woman was off her rocker—insane or a psychopath. Neither was great when she had a gun and the wheel.

"Did you kill Van?" Ava asked.

Suzanna spat out a laugh. "That old fool."

Ava flinched.

"Thought he knew every goddamn thing. He was *easy* to kill. Caroline softened him up with a roofie in his beer, and I helped him home like a drunken bum. Killed him with his own gun."

The constricting band of grief around Ava's heart made it hard to breathe. She'd been right about Van's death, but it didn't make her feel good, especially when she and Mallory were stuck in a speeding vehicle with the person responsible.

"Did you rape him?" Ava asked. The idea horrified her.

Had Van known what was happening? Had he any inkling of the danger he was in amongst the fog of the sedative?

Suzanna sneered. "Don't be ridiculous. I just wanted him to be humiliated in death."

"And you shot Mortimer at the funeral?"

Suzanna's lips pinched. "I should have bought an assault rifle and killed more of you FBI scum. Toss me your weapon," she said sharply. "Quickly before I put a bullet in her."

Ava tried to dislodge the anger and fear that threatened to overwhelm her. "The FBI director fired me because that asshole Sheridan kissed me in front of everyone. He took my weapon and creds. That's why I was upset."

"I don't believe you."

Ava opened her purse and flashed the insides which held a lonely credit card. She pulled her skirts all the way up to flash her panties. "I am not carrying a handgun, lady." She wished she were, although they were traveling so fast Ava wouldn't risk shooting the driver. She was terrified what might happen to Mallory and the baby if they crashed.

"What about you?" Suzanna asked Mallory.

Mallory stared at the driver in disbelief. Sweat stuck strands of hair to her face. "Do I look like a federal agent?"

Even Ava was convinced, but unfortunately, she didn't think Mal was armed.

They were already on the outskirts of town, speeding through the Palisades, skirting the Potomac.

"Let the pregnant woman go. She has nothing to do with this situation. I happened upon her when her waters broke. Pull over and let her have her baby in peace—"

"Why? Why should I? What did the Feds care about my baby?"

"You were pregnant?" Ava finally figured it out. "With Peter Galveston's child?"

Suzanna whizzed through a gap with oncoming traffic honking at her. "That's why I wasn't with him when Sheridan murdered him. I had a scare and had to stay in bed for months at the end. That's why I wasn't with Peter that weekend. That's why he fell for that stupid con."

"You knew what he did to women?" Ava asked, incredulous.

Suzanna snorted. "Of course, I knew. He was a brilliant and fascinating man. Jesus, you are all so stupid."

Better than insane, lady.

Mallory cried out again then seemed to manage to somehow breathe through the pain.

"What happened to your child?" Ava asked.

The wild light was back in Suzanna's eyes, and her throat worked visibly. "He was beautiful and wondrous, but his heart didn't work properly. He died two years ago."

He was the skeleton they'd dug up with Peter Galveston at the cabin. That had to have been the trigger for this woman's appalling actions.

"So, you dug Peter up so they could be together?" Ava asked.

Suzanna nodded. "So, I could keep them both close to me."

"You lived in the cabin?"

Suzanna jerked her chin. "It went up for sale about five years ago, and I moved in with little Pete. I couldn't stop thinking about them all, what they'd done to him. What they'd stolen from us."

"The FBI?"

Another sharp nod. "I collected information on them all and started tracking them down. I've been planning my revenge from the day they killed Peter, but I waited because I didn't want to lose my son. When he died from a heart attack, I didn't have any reason left not to kill them."

Ava shuddered. This woman had hunted those law enforcement officials like dogs for doing their jobs and keeping civilians safe.

"I found out where Sheridan lived in Virginia. I drove by one day about eighteen months ago, trying to figure out the best way to get to him. Then I spotted the house across the road for sale." She cackled. "It seemed like fate."

Where the hell did she get all her money from? Ava wanted to know but figured there were more important questions.

"Why not kill Dominic when you had the chance? He was unconscious in his bed that night, right?" She must have drugged him too. Obviously, it was a technique that had worked for her and her accomplice, Caroline Perry, on more than one occasion.

Suzanna took a turn so fast Ava and Mallory were both pressed against their doors.

"I almost did," Suzanna confessed. "I slipped a knife against his ribs and felt for the space between them, ready to slide it deep into his heart." She came out of the curve, and Ava sat up straight. "It was too easy. I wasn't ready for him to die yet. He needed to understand who was doing this and why he deserved everything that was coming to him."

"You enjoyed torturing him."

"I did." Suzanna's smiling face met hers in the mirror. "I snooped through his house and all his photo albums. I spat in his milk. I stripped him bare and pressed myself against his naked body when he started to rouse. I touched him intimately. I watched his confusion turn to horror, but it was never quite enough. He never had quite enough to lose. Until he met you."

Ava watched Mallory's fingers clench over her abdomen. This was serious. Stalling for time was fine when someone wasn't giving birth. Ava had to get her medical help, but how?

"Let her go. Take me as a hostage, and let her go. She has nothing to do with any of this."

"No." The wild eyes gleamed. "This is perfect. A sign."

A fucking sign?

Mallory was writhing in pain in the front seat, her feet straining against the floor.

"I'm getting a new baby. A gift from Peter." Suzanna smiled like the psycho she was and terror invaded every single cell of Ava's body. There was no way this bitch was getting hold of that baby.

They'd crossed the river and were heading along a quiet road. Ava saw signs to a private airstrip. "You've been planning this for a long time."

"*This* I didn't plan at all. I'd decided to walk away for a little while. To let Sheridan drop his guard. Maybe kill him with another poisoned casserole."

Ava gaped. If Dominic hadn't have tripped over his dog, he and Mallory and her baby might already be dead...and Ava had never suspected a thing. The woman was a hell of an actress.

"When I saw you on the sidewalk it was like all my prayers were answered." Suzanna looked at her with eerily empty eyes. "Peter even gifted me another baby."

Over Ava's dead body.

Mallory was resolutely silent, concentrating on the internal battle she was fighting.

"What about Caroline Perry and Robin Elgin? What was their connection?" Ava needed to distract her. To make a plan. That's what Dominic would do. She slipped the phone into her purse. She hoped he could still hear them talking. That he understood the conversation and what it meant. Record it for criminal proceedings.

Suzanna shrugged. "Caroline was someone I brought home once. She proved useful, especially when she told me that the bar where she worked was run by drug dealers. I kept her around for a while. Then she almost killed Sheridan—without my permission. That would never do."

So, Suzanna had drowned her in the tub. "And Robin Elgin?" Ava pushed.

Suzanna sighed. "Robin was a dear friend. He was involved in our…activities. Peter used to like to watch him with me." Suzanna sobbed and covered her mouth with the back of her gun hand as if overcome with emotion. Ava braced herself. She fought the urge to grab the wheel. If they crashed it might hurt the baby. Ava had to protect Mallory and the baby at all costs.

"*With* you?" Ava said uncertainly. This was what Dominic and other negotiators did to get people talking—mirror key words or phrases. It felt obvious and stupid. And she must be stupid to have gotten in this goddamn car when she'd known the threat wasn't over. But she'd never expected the threat to come at her. Nor at Mallory.

"When we had sex." Suzanna waved the pistol airily like that was a common occurrence. "Peter would have us role playing." The bony fingers that gripped the steering wheel so fiercely had knuckles standing out like a mountain ridge. "It was Robin's idea to take someone that no one cared about to play with for a while. To 'ramp things up.'"

To demean and debase. To torture and kill.

And on the surface Robin had seemed like such a nice guy.

"Although I don't think he realized we'd have to kill her. Not at first anyway."

They were passing through woods now on flat land close to the river. Still following signs to the airport.

"You didn't mind Peter watching?" Ava had no clue how to talk to this woman, and Mallory was busy internalizing her pain.

"Why else would I have sex with Robin?" Suzanna asked as if Ava was the idiot. "You think me having sex with Robin made Peter love me less? *Au contraire.* He knew what he meant to me. He knew I'd die for him. He knew I'd kill for him too."

The vehemence of the words made the hair on Ava's neck stand on end.

She thought about Dominic and what this woman wanted to do to him. She was supposed to be his bodyguard, and here she was luring him into danger. She'd abandoned him when she was supposed to be protecting him, all because of her hurt *feelings.* The FBI director wasn't the reason she'd been watching his back. Investigating Van's death was the initial reason, and then realizing Dominic himself was a target had given her another reason to stick close. He wasn't just a way of keeping her job.

Maybe she really was a terrible FBI agent who deserved to be fired. Unfortunately, she wasn't the only one in jeopardy or else she'd tackle Suzanna for the gun.

Ava prayed Dominic would figure out some way to find them without putting himself in the crosshairs. She felt so helpless hurtling to her doom this way, and the last thing she wanted was for him to be hurt. He might not love her, but he didn't deserve any of this.

"I'm going to be sick." Mallory held her hand over her mouth, and then she let go and vomited all over Suzanna's lap.

"Oh, my god, oh, my god!" Suzanna careened onto the side of the road, brakes squealing, car fishtailing. She held her now sodden sequined gown away from her skin. "That's disgusting. You're disgusting." The smell was rank and bilious.

Ava wished she'd thought of it.

The bush was thick here. They just needed a chance, and they might be able to get away.

"I'm going to be sick again," Mallory warned, grabbing her mouth and heaving. There was no way they could afford to get on a plane with this woman, so this was genius.

Or maybe Mallory was genuinely ill, probably because during what should be the most difficult experience of her life, she was being kidnapped by a mad woman who wanted to steal her child.

Suzanna popped the door locks, and Mallory stumbled out of the car and bent over as if she was going to be sick. But she didn't stop moving. She ran.

Elation filled Ava.

Go, Mallory!

Suzanna aimed the weapon at the pregnant woman and curled her finger around the trigger.

Hell, no!

Ava lunged for the gun. Suzanna jerked it out of reach and fired twice, the noise pounding Ava's eardrums in the enclosed space. The bullets went high, through the roof of the car. Suzanna screamed in frustration.

Ava was fighting for her life, for all their lives. She punched Suzanna three times in the face, stunning her opponent with the unrelenting violence of her attack. The damn woman didn't drop the weapon though. Ava grabbed her clutch and kicked open the door, rolling to the ground as bullets sprayed where she'd been a split-second before.

Ava scrambled to her feet in the high heels, cursing the amount of material in the dress. She slipped on the gravel, finally finding her feet as the driver's door opened. Ava dashed down the short embankment and dove between two large bushes that scratched and stabbed at her arms. She hurtled into the woods after Mallory and prayed they could both escape this nightmare.

CHAPTER THIRTY-THREE

DOMINIC STOOD ON the sidewalk as an Audi sports car screeched to a halt beside him.

Alex Parker stepped out and looked around. "Where's Mal?"

Dominic put his hands on his hips as he searched the empty street. "Apparently she and Ava went off together somewhere."

"But she called me to come pick them up…?" Alex's gaze dropped to a patch of wet concrete on the sidewalk, incongruous with the sun blazing overhead in the sky.

Dominic's phone dinged with an incoming text and then it rang. Dominic answered when he saw it was from Ava but from the echoing silence on the other end it seemed like she'd called by mistake.

Then he heard her say, "Did you kill Van?"

He clenched his jaw as he heard the answer and put the call on speaker, turning the volume up to the max, muting his side of the conversation. He met Parker's gaze. "I think the killer has Ava."

A woman laughed on the line.

He felt lightheaded when he recognized the voice of the person talking to Ava. "Shit. That's my neighbor, Suzanna Bernier."

"Get in." Parker slid into the driver's seat of his car and was half way down the street before Dominic closed his door.

Alex fished his cell from his pocket and used his retina to unlock the screen before tossing it to Dominic. "Open the icon with Mallory's image. Let's see where she is first. If she's at your father's house or the hospital she's safe."

The app connected to a map and a red dot appeared on the screen, heading northwest out of the city at high speed.

GPS. "We have a signal. She's on the move."

Alex said nothing but turned on his car's GPS screen which now mirrored his cell. It seemed likely that both Mallory and Ava were in the clutches of this evil woman and from the conversation he was overhearing on his cell, this was not good.

"Buckle up." Alex accelerated and blew through a red light. A few seconds later a siren started in pursuit. Alex glanced in the mirror. "Get rid of him."

Dominic called his father on his personal cell—thank God the FBI's rules and bureaucracy meant he always carried two—and did something he had never done before. He used his connections for his own purposes. "Pop, don't argue with me but put the president on the line, right now. We have a serious situation."

It took a few seconds and then a few more before the background din of the party receded. Dominic imagined the men standing in the library.

A line up of traffic at another red light had Alex pulling up on the wide sidewalk and bypassing the queue. They bumped down the curb back onto the road with a bone-jarring bounce.

"Hello?"

"Mr. President," Dominic said quickly.

"Dominic." Hague sounded exasperated. "I keep telling you, call me Joshua or Uncle Josh the way you have done your entire life—"

"The thing is, sir, at this exact moment I need to talk to the president, not my godfather."

"Okay," Hague said slowly. "Go on."

"I need you to contact capitol police. There is a woman going by the name of Suzanna Bernier who is a neighbor of mine. I have reason to believe she has been killing FBI agents." He heard a gasp from the older man.

"She currently has Ava Kanas and Agent Mallory Rooney—who is heavily pregnant—in a vehicle heading northwest. I am assuming Bernier is armed. I need traffic units to let a black Audi through as we are in pursuit of a tracking signal, but we have a traffic cop on our tail." Alex reeled off the plate number and Dominic repeated it. Then he told the man the location of the other car and road on which they were traveling.

"I don't know what make or model of car Suzanna Bernier is driving, but the cops can probably figure it out. Order police to put up roadblocks in a twenty-mile radius but don't try to stop our Audi. I have the horrible feeling if we don't catch up with them soon, they're all dead." Dominic couldn't even grasp that idea.

More traffic had Alex cursing and laying on the horn to force his way through.

The president was shouting instructions to his staff. The traffic cop was still in hot pursuit, the siren giving an appropriately urgent soundtrack to Dominic's already hammering heart.

"I have to go, sir."

"Take care, Dominic. Don't go rushing in without back-up."

"Let's hope I don't need to." Dominic hung up and held on as Alex took a shortcut going in the wrong direction down a side street, then taking a corner on two wheels to get them ahead of the traffic. Dominic tried not to remember the wreck that had almost killed him last week. His entire world had been turned upside down since that moment and part of that turmoil had been caused by falling in love with Ava Kanas. Ava was the most important thing in his life, and he had the horrible feeling that because he hadn't held on tight to her hand when she'd needed him most, he was about to lose her forever.

And it was all his fault. He should have defended her faster and more vehemently. He should have tossed in his shield and left when she left. He'd been so damn sure he could talk them out of the situation but had failed. So maybe he wasn't as shit-hot as he liked to think. Maybe he really had got where he had because of who his father was.

The traffic cop abruptly turned off the siren and fell away from the chase.

Thank God.

They were catching up to them. Dominic didn't think he'd ever traveled at this speed before, and he was praying Alex could squeeze even more out of the sports car. He thought he heard Mallory speak, and then he heard the sound of retching and an exclamation. Out of the corner of his eye he saw Alex tense.

The red dot on Alex's screen stopped moving. Suzanna had halted the car. Then the signal that presumably represented Mallory's cell was moving into the forest, and the sound of gunshots came distinctly through Dominic's phone.

AVA CURSED HER heels as she ran into the woods, heading for the dense undergrowth. She heard Suzanna getting out of the car and dared not stop.

Ava instinctively reached for her weapon and silently swore when she remembered she'd handed it in to the fricking director and hadn't worn a backup to the party.

Where was Mallory? Ava scanned the area and saw the other woman pressed against a large oak. Their eyes connected. Ava's lavender gown was a neon freaking sign in the forest. At least Mallory wore black. Ava turned and ran in the opposite direction.

Going to Mallory would get them both killed. She needed to lead Suzanna as far from the other woman as possible.

She remembered the phone in her purse as she sprinted flat out, hiking up her train to stop herself falling and praying the heels didn't twist. She hid behind a big oak and pulled out the cell, tossing the bag. "Dominic?"

A bullet striking the tree above her head had her darting away again. She tripped and sprawled in the dirt, and the phone went flying. She couldn't go after it though. Running was the only way she could hope to escape this nightmare.

Another bullet, feet to the right. Thank god Suzanna was a lousy shot.

Draw her away from Mallory.

Draw the killer into the woods until the cavalry arrived. Ava's pulse pounded, but a strange calm settled over her. As if this was happening to someone else. As if she was in a training exercise and someone would yell "stop" at any moment.

Another bullet hit close enough to make her yelp, and she rolled and scrambled back to her feet, dodging through the trees.

How many shots was that? Seven? Eight? The weapon held fifteen bullets plus one in the chamber, assuming it was fully loaded. Ava paused behind a tree and undid the buckles on the heels, kicking them off. She contemplated stripping out of the dress, but the idea of being found naked didn't sit right. Plus, her skin was equally bright in this environment. No, right now she was a decoy. She needed to keep going.

Sweat drenched her brow, and she wiped it away impatiently. Dammit. So much for training.

She eyed the next biggest tree and ran again, trying not to feel the sharp stones and sticks that bit into the soft soles of her feet. This time the bullet seared her upper arm, and she cried out in pain but did not stop dodging and weaving. Her left arm hung numbly at her side. Blood dripped off the ends of her fingers, soaking into the pretty dress, a dress that was now going to get her killed.

She should have worn a tux. She grimaced at the thought. If she died, Dominic was going to take it so hard. The fact she loved him seemed so obvious now. Like the blinders had been violently torn away. And if she hadn't walked away from him the way she had, neither she nor Mallory would be in this nightmarish situation.

Pride before the fall...

Hell of a fall.

She cut deep into the woods, her injured arm hot and numb and useless. Suzanna had said she'd die for Peter. Ava realized as she dodged bullets in the woods, that she'd die for

Dominic too. And, more importantly, without a doubt, Dominic would die for her.

And if she was strong enough to take a bullet for someone, she was damn sure strong enough to stop hiding from her feelings and pouncing on every excuse not to trust a guy. She was worth loving. She was worthy of Dominic's love. She didn't need to prove anything to anyone.

She just had to stay alive.

Ava darted down a short, sharp escarpment and cut back, pressing herself into the dirt and roots of an undercut rock face. Her heart beat so fast and strong she thought it might explode and flood her insides with blood.

She trembled, fear and despair rushing through her. She wished she could tell Dominic she was sorry for not having his back at the party. Of course, he was pissed at the situation. Of course, he was pissed with the director. And he might even be pissed with her. That was okay. It had been a crappy position to find himself in, and he'd been trying to figure his way out of it by using his strengths when she'd stopped giving him a chance.

If she got out of this alive, she needed to tell him all this. That he loved her. And that she loved him right back. And she wouldn't leave him again no matter how terrifying it got.

They just both needed to survive.

And it wasn't Ava putting him in danger although she should never have left his side, it was this mad woman determined to get her twisted revenge.

Was Mallory safe?

Ava didn't know. She wanted to scream with frustration but held her breath. Danger was close by. She could sense it.

A footstep sounded above her. Dirt trickled down into her

hair and over her bare shoulders. Ava closed her eyes. Didn't move. Didn't make a sound. She didn't want to die.

With luck Mallory was safe and far away. Ava prayed fervently and wished she'd worn her evil eye bracelet.

A laugh rang out, raising gooseflesh in its wake.

The tinkling whisper above her head made her freeze. "Caught you."

CHAPTER THIRTY-FOUR

MALLORY CONCEALED HERSELF behind a large maple, back pressed against the rough bark, and prayed. A contraction hit, and the pain was almost unbearable, a giant slice of sensation that cut her slowly in half. She didn't move and didn't make a sound. She endured.

The best thing about the dress she was wearing was the fact it had pockets. In those pockets was her cell, and she knew Alex would be tracking her. She knew it as well as she knew her own face in the mirror. They just had to stay alive until he got here.

She gritted her teeth and tried to breathe. All her planning. The birthing classes. The private medical professionals she'd lined up. The nightshirt she'd chosen. The comfy pillows. She'd even booked a freaking birthing pool.

Birth *plan*—ha!

The contraction eased, and Mal could inhale again.

She listened intently, not daring to move, knowing this crazy bitch wanted her baby more than anything else. But Mal had no intention of letting her get her hands on their little bean. Even if that meant sacrificing Ava in the short-term. Alex would find them, and he would deal with Suzanna and save them all.

Hold on, Ava.

The other agent was deliberately drawing her away, Mal realized with a rush of love so huge it almost made her sob. As soon as Suzanna headed off after Ava, Mallory went back up to the road. She contemplated getting behind the wheel of Suzanna's car, but Alex would be here soon and if she had a contraction she couldn't drive anyway, and the contractions were coming fast and furious.

Instead Mal shuffled across the highway as quickly as she could and disappeared into the forest on the other side of the road.

Guilt ripped through her, as powerful as any contraction, but she forced herself to keep moving. Away from Ava, away from the danger. She cupped her hands around her distended stomach. No way was that psycho getting hold of her baby. Suzanna would kill Mal as soon as the baby was born. She knew how these lunatics worked.

If only she had a gun, but this stupid dress and lack of a waist meant she hadn't worn one. Plus, she'd been going to an engagement party for a governor for heaven's sake. She should have been safe. She walked through the woods, parallel to the road, each gunshot behind her making desperation crawl along her nerves.

Alex would come. Mal needed to have faith and hold on to that knowledge and pray her baby, and Ava, survived.

Another contraction hit, dropping her to her knees. Agony ripped through her, and she bit down on a scream. Any noise and Suzanna would find her and kill her and steal her baby.

Not happening.

Another gunshot.

She jolted. Damn. But a distraction might save Ava…

Mallory felt as if she were being torn in two both physically and mentally. But this baby was coming, ready or not, and Mallory could only fight one battle at a time.

She spotted an upturned tree, its jagged roots towering into the air. She staggered onwards barely able to move more than a couple of inches per step because of the pressure growing between her legs. Hidden behind the massive roots was a grassy area where she lay down out of sight.

Her improvised birthing plan involved less pillows, more insects and a whole lot less pain medication.

Another contraction pressed down on her, and she lay there panting, forcing herself not to push as it couldn't be time yet. Her fingers closed around a short piece of wood in the grass beside her, and Mal clamped it between her teeth and bit down on the whimpers that wanted to emerge from her throat.

The baby wasn't here yet, but it wouldn't be long. If Suzanna found her before Alex did, she was dead.

CHAPTER THIRTY-FIVE

DOMINIC AND ALEX pulled up beside a black sedan abandoned on the side of the road with three doors thrown wide open. They both had their guns drawn.

A gunshot off to the right told Dominic Suzanna Bernier was nearby. Alex checked his phone. "Mallory is that way." He pointed in the opposite direction, looking torn.

"Go. Make sure Mallory and the baby are okay. I'm going to get Suzanna's attention. Cavalry is on the way." He'd spoken to agents from the WFO. Their SWAT team was fifteen minutes behind them. They'd discovered Suzanna Bernier owned her own private jet at a nearby airstrip and agents were also en route to make sure it stayed grounded.

Dominic didn't think about Ava being hurt or dead. If he fell into that train of thought he'd never survive. Never have a second chance at fully living his life rather than this highly controlled, emotionally stunted effort he'd been deluding himself with.

Alex jogged off in the opposite direction. Dominic prayed Rooney was alive and their baby safe.

"Suzanna!" he cried as he pushed into the woods. A crow took off from a nearby branch, and Dominic's heart screeched in his chest. *Fuck.*

The sound of movement drew him east, keeping close to

the road. He scanned the forest for some sign of them, spotted a trail where the grass had been flattened, possibly by the heavy material of a formal gown. The bright lavender color should be easy to spot in this environment. Too easy.

He moved swiftly, using trees for cover as much as possible. Ava's high heels were tossed behind a tree. Then the glittery evening purse she'd been carrying.

The incongruousness of sequins and tuxedos in a woodland setting was not lost on him. How could a glitzy party turn into his worst nightmare in the space of thirty minutes?

That's what evil people did. Destroy things. Destroy happiness, destroy people. Although he'd done some destroying of his own when he'd let Ava leave, and he'd never forgive himself for getting her into this mess. For letting her down when she'd needed him most.

If only Ava had had her gun...but who knew what Suzanna had done to gain control of the women. If she'd threatened Rooney then Ava would have gotten rid of the gun anyway. The director was still an asshole. The women must have heard him shout when he arrived, surely, so where were they? He saw a flash of movement in his peripheral vision to the left. He headed swiftly in that direction, probing the woods for any sign of Ava in her pale purple dress. He sucked in a harsh breath when he saw blood on the ground. It had to be Ava's. She'd been hit. He took a fraction of a second to reassure himself that if she wasn't lying here dead then she was okay.

"I'm the one you want, Suzanna. Get back here and finish what you started. Revenge for me killing that asshole Peter."

She shrieked, insanity ringing in the echoes. "You shouldn't even say his name!"

Looney-fucking-tune. "Peter Galveston? *That* name?"

A flash of lavender appeared behind all the green, and he held his breath as two people pushed their way through the bushes towards him. Ava—alive, thank god—and behind her, Suzanna Bernier.

The fact Ava was still breathing was a gut punch of relief. The gun pointed at her head was less positive, as was the way her left arm hung limply at her side, crimson blood soaking her pretty dress.

The usual techniques for negotiation might not work here. There wasn't the time needed to build the rapport that might eventually get Suzanna to stop killing the woman he'd stupidly gone and fallen in love with. And if Suzanna found out how much he cared for Ava, she'd kill her all the sooner.

But even as his heart lurched in anger at the realization Suzanna had hurt Ava, his head told him to try. To slow it down. To diffuse the drama. To give time, time. To find out the 'why' behind her actions. Knowledge was power. The SWAT team were on the way and hopefully Alex Parker had taken Mallory to safety.

"You loved him," he said. "You must have been devastated when you lost him."

She made a sound like an animal being snared. "I didn't *lose* him. You murdered him!" She shoved Ava ahead of her. Blood dripped from her hand. Too much blood.

If he'd stood up to the director earlier this wouldn't have happened.

His mouth went dry when he realized that if they survived this and he wanted to win Ava's heart he was going to have to open himself up, to prove himself to her over and over again. Ava's faith was too fragile. She'd been tested too often. He was going to have to use every ounce of the skills he'd learned over the years to gain her trust and after that, her love. He just needed a chance.

"How can I help you, Suzanna?" These were some of the most powerful words to use with someone in distress.

"How about you beg like a dog for her life and then I'll kill her anyway?" Suzanna jeered.

Things didn't always go by the book with psychopaths.

"Her son died," Ava said quietly.

Suzanna jerked Ava's head back with a fistful of hair. Ava grimaced in pain. "Shut up."

"Tell me about your son." Open-ended questions got people talking but if it was a sensitive subject, and obviously the loss of a child was always a sensitive subject, it could backfire.

Where the hell was SWAT?

"What do you care about my son?" The words were choked and bitter.

He tilted his head to one side and threw her an eyebrow flash, telling her to trust him with his body language. "You told me your son was with his father…" And then he realized this child was the skeleton they'd found buried with Galveston.

"What was he like?"

Suzanna's throat moved as she swallowed. "He was smart and loved animals. He had dark hair like his father. My eyes." She trailed off into memories.

Dominic let the silence linger for as long as he dared. He didn't want her remembering Ava. "What happened?"

Suzanna looked downcast, but she kept a tight hold on Ava's hair and the gun did not waver. "He was born with Wolff-Parkinson-White syndrome. He died of a heart attack when he was eight while playing hide-and-seek with his friends."

"Losing a child must be incredibly painful. I am so very sorry for your loss." The child's death had been the trigger for the FBI murders.

"Did Peter know about the baby?" he asked. Ava was watching him with bright eyes. Chin still tipped high in defiance despite the blood seeping from her hand. He wanted to send her a message, but Suzanna would see and react to it.

"Yes. Of course, he knew. He was thrilled with the idea of becoming a father."

Dominic bet he was. Another innocent to assert control over. But in a negotiation, you had to pack away judgment and your own ego and concentrate on the prize. The prize this time was getting Suzanna to release Ava without further harm.

"I'm sure he was a great kid." Dominic stretched the tightness out of his neck. Sweat slid down the side of his face, and he wiped it on the sleeve of his jacket. He was negotiating for Ava's life, and the stakes had never been higher. "So, after your son died you were suffering from so much grief you decided to go after the people you held responsible for killing the man you loved. You feel like you hate us all for shooting Peter. For stealing the father of your child. You blame us for being alone."

The pain in Suzanna's silence was palpable. He let the moment drag out.

"That's right," Suzanna said finally in a small voice.

This was the breakthrough moment he needed, but usually there was a time gap while the psychology of that pronouncement went to work on the abductor's psyche. The woman had murdered an unknown number of FBI agents including his mentor and had maimed an innocent bystander. Now Ava's blood-soaked form stood before him, and he had to push concern for her out of his brain so he could do his job.

If anything happened to Ava, life as he knew it would be over. He forced the newly discovered feelings of love aside. Let a cold and deadly calm settle over him.

"You must have been hurt very badly when your son died, Suzanna. You suffered great pain. You exacted revenge upon the FBI because you felt the FBI was responsible for that pain. It's over now. Time to stop suffering and let the world see what you did."

Suzanna's lips drooped at the edges. "I had hoped to get away with it, but obviously I wasn't quite clever enough."

He'd love to know exactly who she'd killed and how, but psychopaths often lied about their crimes. Plus, he didn't want to remind her that if she gave up, she was going to spend the rest of her days in prison or on death row.

He had only one objective. Getting Ava to safety.

"You have been incredibly effective in your vengeance. We both know you've had several opportunities to kill me but didn't. You made us look like fools. Don't you want the world to know that?"

Was he reaching her? Finding a hold in the madness? "Let Kanas go, and I will make sure you are treated with respect and compassion." Even though it would hurt his soul.

It was the wrong play.

"I'm not in this for the glory, Sheridan. I'm in it to cause as much pain as possible, especially to you." Her words had him bracing.

Her finger tightened on the trigger, and he knew he had to take decisive action. Otherwise, Ava was dead.

He came out from cover. Held his weapon in two hands

pointed at the ground.

"That woman had nothing to do with Peter's death. She doesn't even like me very much." Maybe Ava's technique of shocking the fuck out of people would be effective as a last resort. He hoped Ava didn't believe the lies. "She was an easy fuck but you know how much I hate commitment. I dumped her the moment she got clingy and threatened my career."

"She's in love with you, jackass!"

Dominic froze, his gaze locking on Ava's. Was it true? She sent him a sorry half smile. How the hell had Suzanna figured it out when he hadn't? Then Ava mouthed the word. "Ready."

It took him a moment to read it for what it was. A signal.

He gave her an almost imperceptible nod.

Suzanna pushed Ava forward, and they started walking toward him, Ava stumbling unsteadily on her feet. "So, I'm going to put a bullet in her and you can watch her die…"

Ava used the fingers of her uninjured hand to signal the countdown from "three." She looked undaunted and unafraid.

"And then, even if I don't get to kill you…" Suzanna was going for suicide by cop.

"Two." Ava counted down silently, still moving toward him.

"I'll know that you'll go to your grave knowing all these people died because of you…"

"One." Ava sagged in Suzanna's arms, becoming dead weight that the other woman couldn't hold.

Dominic brought his weapon up and fired three shots straight into center mass of Suzanna Bernier. The woman dropped to her knees and then toppled over. Ava rolled over and snatched the gun out of Suzanna's limp fingers.

"Do you have your cuffs?" Ava shouted. She was on her

knees holding the weapon on Suzanna's inert body. Dominic could see Ava's feet were bleeding and covered in dirt.

He crossed over to her, bent down and checked the pulse in Suzanna's neck. Shook his head. "Doesn't matter. She's dead."

He turned towards Ava. Took the gun from her hands and stuffed it into his jacket pocket. She stayed where she was, staring at the dead woman with wide, haunted eyes.

He pulled off his bow tie and secured it tightly over the wound in Ava's upper arm that was still bleeding.

"We have to find Mallory," she whispered. "She went into labor."

Dominic swept her up into his arms.

"I can walk," she protested.

Ava deserved someone to take care of her for a change. To slay her dragons.

"I've got you." He kissed her forehead, and she sagged against him.

"I know," she said softly.

His throat closed with emotion, and he almost stumbled with relief. She believed in him. She trusted him to be there for her, despite what had happened earlier with the director. She'd had faith in him that he'd come to help her.

"Suzanna killed Van."

"I heard. You did the right thing calling me when you did."

Ava's fingers tightened around his lapel. "She killed him as if a loser like that had the right to judge him."

"She didn't. She was less than scum."

"She was involved in Galveston's crimes. Was on maternity bed rest when you shot the bastard."

Dominic nodded. That made sense. Ava laid her face against his chest, and he felt her go lax.

They reached the car.

"Where's Mallory?" she asked.

Dominic nodded in the direction of the woods. "Parker said somewhere in there."

A rush of dread swept over him at the unholy silence. What if Mallory had been hurt or something had happened to the baby?

MALLORY LAY IN the dirt looking up at the blue sky as a series of gunshots split the air. Sweat stuck her hair to her skin. Her body trembled with exertion. Had Ava been killed? Where was Suzanna? Mal heard a car stop. Thought she heard men's voices but didn't dare call attention to herself in case Suzanna had accomplices they didn't know about.

Had Suzanna left the area? Or was she roaming about like a rabid animal looking for revenge?

Another contraction hit, stealing all her attention, making her bite down on the stick as breath was ripped from her body. Her back arched up off the ground, knees bent, legs wide. It was hard to think, let alone protect herself or her baby.

A tiny whimper escaped, and she clamped down on it, terrified of giving herself away.

Suddenly Alex was crouching beside her.

She spat the stick out of her mouth and grabbed onto his hand.

"You found us." She started panting, pain tearing her apart.

He smoothed her damp hair off her forehead and kissed her there. His eyes scanned the area. His SIG stayed in his hand.

"Is she still loose?" Mallory whispered.

"Those last shots sounded like a Glock. What weapon did she have?"

Mallory laughed and wished desperately for some water. "A semi-automatic. I don't know exactly. I avoided looking at it."

His eyes softened, and a smile played around his mouth. "Sheridan's got this."

"What if Ava's dead? It'll be all my fault—" Another blast of agony bore down on her.

She panted but Alex gained her attention and coaxed her to breathe the way she'd been coached.

"Breathe through the pain, Mal."

Her nails bit into his flesh. He placed the weapon on the ground beside him.

"As soon as this contraction is over, I'll take a look at how dilated you are. Figure out how to get you to the car."

She shook her head. "This baby is coming, Alex. I'm not going to make it to the car."

Alarmed eyes met hers. "You can't hold back a little? Slow it down?"

"That's not how it works! This baby is coming," she hissed. "Now."

She lay back as Alex lifted her skirts and dragged her panties down her legs. "Don't let Suzanna find us," she pleaded in a whisper. "She wants to take our baby as her own."

"No one is taking our baby, Mal. You know that."

She did. But she was still terrified.

Alex nudged her thighs wider apart. Her hand touched the grip of his SIG in reassurance. She didn't pick it up. She wasn't stupid. But it was within reach and if that bitch showed up Mal would put a bullet between her eyes, contraction or no contraction.

"I can see the baby's head."

Mal closed her eyes. Oh crap. All the planning and preparation they'd done and she was having the baby in a grass patch on the side of the road.

"You have to push with the next contraction, Mal." He looked up and met her gaze, his silver eyes filled with concern. "It's time."

Fear overwhelmed her, and panic made her pulse skip. "I can't do this."

He smiled. "You *can* do this."

She wanted to cuss and swear at him, but another contraction hit, and the instinctive urge to push took over.

When it was finished, she gasped out a keening sound, rubbing her finger over the pattern on the SIG's grip.

The pain came again with barely a second of respite in between. She clenched every muscle in her body and pushed with all her strength.

"Head's out," Alex said excitedly. "Next push will get the shoulders clear and it'll be over, Mal. Our baby is nearly here and I've got you both." His eyes met hers and flicked to the gun. "Trust me. Nothing will get past me to hurt either of you."

She withdrew her hand from the weapon as another contraction clenched her body. She squeezed and felt the baby leave her body in a rush. Alex caught him-or-her and placed the warm infant on her chest.

Oh, my goodness. Oh, my goodness.

A perfect, scrunched up little face peered up at her, absolutely unimpressed by the change in accommodation. The baby had a snub nose and a thatch of black hair on its head and huddled against Mallory's chest.

Alex dragged off his t-shirt and wrapped it around the newborn who made a mewling sound. Then Alex cut the gray umbilical cord with a pocketknife. "Sorry. It's the best I can do."

Hopefully it didn't matter. "Help me pull my dress up for some skin on skin bonding."

"My favorite kind," he joked as he maneuvered damp tulle out of the way so the baby could lie on her breast.

She was virtually naked, sitting on the grass in the woods, rough bark poking her shoulders as flies buzzed around. Her baby snuggled into the comfort of her body, and Mallory realized she'd done it. Given birth without the support of modern medicine. And although it had been rough, she'd managed. She was so glad Alex had been here to help.

He kissed both their foreheads and picked up the SIG. "We have a perfect baby girl." His voice cracked. "You are amazing, Mrs. Parker."

Joy shot through Mallory even as she worried about Ava and Dominic. "You're pretty amazing yourself, Mr. Parker."

He shook his head. "Not even close, love. Not even close."

Then the baby started to cry.

CHAPTER THIRTY-SIX

THE SOUND OF a baby squalling cut through the air, and a rush of relief raced up Dominic's spine.

"Thank god Suzanna is dead," Ava spoke against his chest.

"Why?" he asked, tightening his hold.

"She was going to steal Mallory's baby. Claimed the child was a gift from Galveston. Okay. You have to put me down now. We need to go help her."

"I'm not putting you down or letting you go ever again, Ava Kanas." Dominic strode across the road and into the woods still carrying her.

"I—"

"I quit the Bureau by the way. Of course, you ran out so fast I didn't get to impress you with my dramatic exit."

"Don't quit the job you love for me," she said tiredly.

There was blood all over his white shirt. Exactly like the day Calvin Mortimer had died.

"It wasn't for you." He looked into her eyes. "It was for us."

She reached up with her good hand and touched his face. "I'm sorry I was such a terrible bodyguard."

"You thought I was mad with you, but I was trying to control my temper and not lash out."

"You better teach me your technique."

"I've had years of training as a negotiator, Ava, and I still had to work hard not to punch the guy in the face."

"Getting arrested wouldn't have helped anyone." She smiled but then her lips trembled and the smile fell off her face. "Suzanna planned this for a long time. She almost succeeded."

Dominic's stomach churned. "I can't believe I slept with her."

"You didn't."

"What?"

"She said you couldn't get it up."

"Thank god." He narrowed his eyes as realization struck. "The bitch drugged me. No wonder I couldn't remember anything about that night. I felt like shit all year, and it was all part of her plan to make me suffer."

Ava's head started to bob against his chest.

Dominic spotted a bare-chested Parker up ahead holding his SIG.

"Bernier is dead," Dominic shouted.

Dominic walked around a huge fallen tree and saw Mallory Rooney cradling a newborn against her chest, covered by what must have been Parker's shirt.

"Are you okay?"

"Yes," Mallory said firmly. "We're fine. Is Ava?"

Dominic looked down and realized she'd closed her eyes. He gave her a nudge, but she didn't stir.

"She's been shot," Mallory said.

"I put a tourniquet on it." But Mallory wasn't pointing to her arm. He eased Ava away from him and realized there was a bullet wound on her hip, and she was bleeding steadily all over him.

Panic raced through him. He hadn't realized she'd been

shot twice and didn't think she had, either.

"Alex. Call a medivac—"

"It'll be faster if I drive." Alex took the baby gently in one arm and eased Mallory to her feet with the other. Then he handed the baby back. "Can you manage Ava alone?" he asked, putting a supporting arm around Mallory.

Dominic nodded. He couldn't speak. He turned and jogged back to the road. "Don't fucking die on me now, Ava."

He'd barely survived his mother's death. He'd never survive Ava's.

"I can't drive too fast because of the baby, and I don't have a car seat." Alex grabbed a medical kit out of the Audi's trunk. "There's Quikclot in there and bandages. Press down as hard as you can. We're fifteen minutes from a hospital. Twenty from a trauma center. Stop the bleeding, and we can keep her alive."

They maneuvered Ava onto the backseat of what had been Suzanna's car, him on his knees beside her, applying the white powder to the two bullet wounds and checking for more.

Alex got behind the wheel. Mallory climbed into the front passenger seat with her precious cargo.

"I'll call the cops for an escort and to warn the hospital." Mallory buckled up as fast as she was able, kissing the bundle she held to her breast.

Alex executed a quick three-point turn. "We'll probably pass SWAT on the way."

"I'll call them too with an update," Mallory assured them.

Ava was ghostly white, her lips drained of color, chest barely rising up and down.

"Drive as fast as you can safely go," Dominic begged. He didn't want anything to happen to the baby and knew Ava wouldn't either. "But *please* hurry."

CHAPTER THIRTY-SEVEN

AVA WOKE TO a burning pain in her side and an arm that felt as if it had been sawn off at the shoulder.

She stretched her eyelids apart and waited for her vision to settle. Her mother sat on a chair, asleep. That was unexpected. Dominic sat in the opposite corner.

"Hey, what does anyone have to do around here to get a drink of water?" Her voice sounded like a forty-a-day smoker.

Dominic bolted upright, and her mother sprang to her feet.

"You're awake." He grabbed her good hand.

"What happened?"

"You were shot." Her mother said it harshly.

"I didn't think it was that serious." She eyed the bandage on her arm. At least the limb was still attached.

"You were shot twice." Dominic kissed her knuckles. "One bullet hit you in the side of the hip but didn't exit. The surgeon dug it out of your thigh."

Ava grunted. "She shot me in the butt?" Suzanna was a better aim than she'd given the psychopath credit for. "What's the prognosis?"

"Terminal." Her mother hovered over her, clearly upset. "So, you're coming home with me to live out your last days."

If her mom was joking, she must be okay, but it reminded

her about her tanked career.

"Well, I guess you got your wish, Mom. I'm no longer with the FBI." She turned her head away from them both. She wasn't sure what she was going to do now. Dominic had said some pretty nice things in the woods earlier. And quit the FBI, but there was no way they'd allow him to leave. Someone would talk him out of it. He was born to be a negotiator, and she didn't want him to quit a job he loved either.

"What do you mean?" her mother asked.

Dominic squeezed her fingers. "The director rescinded his termination. Said the whole thing had been a huge misunderstanding."

Ava wanted to feel grateful, but she couldn't meet his gaze. "Because of you, not because of me. He wants you to stay even if that means putting up with me."

"Actually, no." Dominic sat on the bed. Her mom threw him a dirty look. "Because Lincoln Frazer, Mallory Rooney, Ray Aldrich and everyone in the Fredericksburg RA, Charlotte Blood, Eban Winters, Mark Gross, Kurt Montana, and a whole swathe of HRT guys threatened to quit if the director went through with your dismissal, which they all considered unfair. Pretty much everyone you've ever worked with." Dominic smiled, and a shot of something that felt a lot like lust, only softer and deeper, went through her. "I haven't had time to formally tender my resignation yet. I decided to wait and ask you what you planned to do before I moved forward with that."

"Ray Aldrich?"

"Ray was pretty repentant after it became clear Van was murdered. He saw the error of his ways." Ava tried to stave off the tears, but one leaked through. So much for willpower.

Dominic's dark blue gaze regarded her seriously. "You aren't alone in the FBI, Ava. You have a lot of people who love you and respect you. Van was one. I'm another." He kissed her fingertips, and her heart gave an unexpected flutter. She'd hoped he loved her but hearing him say it—in front of her mother, no less—felt like a million dreams coming true. She was overwhelmed, unable to speak. Unable to swallow. And that people had stood up for her when she needed it. People she respected. People she didn't…

"Don't leave the Bureau because the director was an ass. The FBI *needs* agents like you." Dominic's eyes flashed to her mother whose expression was pinched but didn't fool Ava for one minute. The woman was pumped Ava had finally found a man.

Dominic misunderstood Ava's silence. "I know I told you I wasn't interested in relationships, but that was before I met you. I can't imagine not seeing you every day. Not finding out how many bad guys you made sorry for crossing paths with you each night after work. I love you, Ava. I've never felt this way about anyone before."

His eyes were intent on her face, and she raised her hand to touch his stubbled jaw. He looked good when he was clean-shaven, but he looked hot as hell with scruff. She wished she had the strength to kiss him until he couldn't breathe but feared she'd end up with the crash cart in here, trying to revive her quivering heart.

"I love you too, Dominic Sheridan. I've loved you from the moment I saw you cutting Van's lawn with your shirt sleeves rolled up."

His grin was pure male satisfaction, and he deserved it. He'd come after her when she'd walked out on him. He'd trusted her to help save them in the woods and carried her out of there bleeding.

She sent her mother a narrow look and teased, "I love you even though you aren't Greek."

Her mother threw up her hands dramatically, knowing when she was being baited. She walked around the bed and kissed Dominic on the top of the head. "You better treat her right, Dominic Sheridan."

"Mom."

"Hey. You almost died because some crazy woman was after him, Ava—"

Ava rolled her eyes. "It's not exactly the first time I nearly died this week, Mom." Her mother looked horrified, but Ava's mouth went dry as she remembered something more important. "Mallory? The baby? Are they okay?"

Dominic grinned. "All amazingly well. Let me call them quick. We might catch them before they leave the hospital."

Ten minutes later, there was a knock on the door. A glowing Mallory and pale Alex holding a baby carrier came in the room.

Ava said, "I am so glad you guys are okay."

Alex brought the baby over for a look. Dark lashes rested on plump, pink cheeks. Tiny, perfect, cupid's bow lips were slightly parted. Gorgeous and in one piece. Ava's heart melted.

"So beautiful." She reached out to touch a tiny finger that wrapped around hers with a grip of steel.

"Makes you want one, huh?" Her mother, subtle as a meteorite.

"One day," Ava said softly.

"One day," Dominic murmured against her ear.

"Georgina Ava Parker, meet your godmother."

"What?" Ava's eyes widened.

"You heard." Mallory grinned widely.

"I didn't do anything," Ava protested.

"Except draw a mad woman away from me so I could escape." Mallory was wearing a pretty dress covered in daisies. No one would ever guess a day ago they'd both been running for their lives in the woods.

"You're the one who saved us," Ava insisted. "I had no idea how to make her stop the car. Throwing up on Suzanna was genius."

The awful memories dimmed the glow in Mallory's eyes. "We got lucky." She smiled over at Alex who watched his wife with careful attention. "We got a lot luckier than you did. I'm so sorry you were hurt."

"I'll survive." Life came at you fast sometimes. Fast. Like a bullet. And wasting a moment of it was foolish. Ava turned to Dominic. "I love you."

His eyes darkened, and one side of his mouth curled up. "You better."

"I want to go home."

"You have two gunshot wounds," her mother said, wringing her hands together.

"You have to stay in for a few days." Dominic laughed at whatever mutinous expression was showing on her face. "As long as you continue to recover, the doctor said you can be discharged in a few days. We can stay at my place in DC until you're completely recovered."

Her mother cleared her throat, and Ava almost choked on a strangled laugh.

"And," Dominic said, clearing his own throat even louder, "there's plenty of room for your mom to stay there too."

"We're leaving," Mallory stepped forward to touch the back of Ava's hand. "We're going to stay in the city for a week or two, while we try to figure out the instruction manual on this little bundle. Call us. We'll come visit." She kissed Ava's cheek, and Ava wanted to hug her hard, but it hurt too much.

Alex hefted the carrier and gave Ava another kiss, then turned to Ava's mother. "We could give you a ride back to Dominic's apartment, Vera, if you want to take a nap."

It was a surprise Alex knew Ava's mom by her first name, but presumably he'd met her when Ava had been unconscious.

"I can call my doorman to let you in, and you can rest for an hour. It was a long flight," Dominic added.

Ava shot her mother a look that begged for privacy at the same time saying she was grateful to see her.

Finally, her mom appeared to receive the message, and her eyes widened as her gaze pinged between Ava and Dominic. "Ah…I *am* tired. I didn't sleep at all last night. I'll come back for the evening visiting hours though and bring you some of your favorite Galaktoboureko so you can have something decent to eat rather than this disgusting mush I see them feeding people." Her mother looked revolted. "You take care of her. Let her rest." She wagged her finger at Dominic and gave him the sort of look usually reserved for customers she thought might dine and dash. Then she ran her hand over Ava's hair, kissed her brow, and whispered, "*S' agapo*."

"What does that mean?" Dominic asked, holding her hand when the others finally left them alone.

"*S' agapo*?"

Dominic nodded, leaning closer.

"I love you."

Those indigo eyes of his smiled. "*S' agapo*," he repeated.

"*S' agapo.*" She gripped his hand tight. "Is this real, Sheridan? Or is it all going to fizzle into nothing in a year's time?"

His grin was as wide as the sky. "Only one way to find out, Kanas."

She smiled back. "I guess there is. You along for the ride?"

He shook his head. "Hell, no. I'm driving the damn car."

She laughed and then opened her mouth as pain sliced through her. "Ouch."

"Don't laugh."

"I'll try not to. I'm just so happy."

"Good."

"I don't remember much of anything after you killed Suzanna." She frowned. "Oh, wait, I remember you carrying me in your arms…" She could swoon from that memory alone.

"We found Mr. and Mrs. Parker having delivered their own baby and then realized you'd been shot twice. Parker drove us all here as we figured it was faster than waiting for a medivac or ambulance."

"I'm lucky you arrived when you did." Ava's stomach twisted at the memory of how close she'd come to death. "If you hadn't called out, she'd have put a bullet in me and then gone hunting for Mallory."

Dominic bowed his head, his throat working. She ran her fingers over the roughness of his jaw, his wide bottom lip.

"I can't believe I didn't figure it out." He captured her hand.

"Everyone missed it."

"Not you."

"She totally fooled me," Ava argued.

He was serious, and it unnerved her. "You saw the truth

about Van's death when nobody else did. That's why Frazer wants you on his team."

"Wait. What?"

Dominic pulled a face. "I wasn't supposed to tell you. I told him I doubted you'd agree."

"Not want to work for the BAU? Are you crazy?"

"They're nothing but glorified computer analysts. Barely ever leave the office."

"Hell, yes, I want to join the BAU. You know how hard it is to get in?"

Dominic opened his eyes wide with fake innocence. "So, you're coming back to the FBI?"

Excitement spread through her entire body. "I am if I can work at the BAU."

"You'll have to start at the bottom."

"I am totally used to the bottom."

"Ah, shit." His brows clamped together.

Ava laughed. That was not what she'd expected him to say. "What is it?"

"Ranger is at the apartment. Charlotte brought him up to DC when my colleagues at CNU discovered the director fired you."

Ava picked at the cotton blanket. "I didn't think Charlotte liked me very much."

"I didn't think she did either."

"What changed?"

"Probably the unjustness of the whole thing—it upset her feminist heart. Tell me your mother likes dogs?"

Ava grimaced. "We never had one so I don't know."

"Okay." He stood. For once he was wearing jeans and a t-shirt rather than one of his well-tailored suits. He looked good in both. "I'm going to call the doorman and ask him to let your mom in and to warn her. Then I'm going to call my sister, Gwen, and ask her to take care of Ranger for a night or two. When they let you out of here and we're both there, he won't be a problem."

Ava watched him make the call. When he was finished, she said, "I'm glad you're getting on better with your family."

"Nothing like nearly dying or losing the woman you love to focus the mind on the important things. I'm tired of being alone, Ava. I never expected to meet you or fall for you, but now, even the thought of being without you for a day or a week, let alone a lifetime is unfathomable."

"I need to let you in on a little secret," she whispered.

He leaned closer. "What?"

"I get really turned on when you use long words."

"Do you now?" His eyes gleamed.

She winced and lifted the covers to check out her wound on the side of her hip. *Ouch.* "So, no long words until I'm able to take full advantage of you."

"I'll do my best." He bent down and kissed her mouth. A curl of want wound its way from her lips through her ribs to her heart.

The feeling was unfathomable. It felt a lot like love.

EPILOGUE

Seven days later.

THE FINE WOOL of Dominic's black jacket was too heavy for the hot, sticky humidity of Virginia in late August. His shirt clung to his back with sweat, making his skin prickle.

Ava reached for his hand even though they had an audience. She wore a plain, black sheath that hung a little loose on her too-thin frame. Flat shoes and bare legs. The glass bead bracelet she favored was wrapped around her wrist.

She'd lost weight in the days since she'd been shot and was struggling to find an appetite despite her mother cooking all her favorite Greek dishes. Dominic, however, was gonna get fat if Vera stayed much longer.

The woman obviously adored her daughter. She was standing on Ava's other side, paying her own tribute to a man who'd helped out her family so many times in the past.

Ava had insisted on attending. He could hardly say no, even though he was worried about her. She was healing well according to her doctors, but she looked pale…

Van's daughters stood beside him. Heads held high even though they must be feeling the terror left over from the last time they'd stood in this same spot. The FBI had stationed sniper teams in all the high locations in the surrounding area. No one was taking any chances this time.

The priest was preaching a lot more fervently than last time. No more hastily arranged words. No speeding to get the man in consecrated ground before anyone discovered he wasn't really allowed to be there.

The crowd of mourners was in the hundreds today. Agents from far and wide had come to honor their fallen colleague with all the reverence and pageantry that Van Stamos deserved. The FBI Director and Assistant Attorney General were both in attendance although doing their level best not to look at him or Ava. Frazer, Rooney, and Parker were here. Fernando Chavez had traveled in from Reno. The Gabanys, Van's neighbors.

All thanks to the woman who now held his hand like he was the pin in her grenade.

He allowed a single tear to fall this time. Van had meant the world to Dominic and he'd been ruthlessly murdered as had so many others. Dominic would always blame himself for not seeing through Suzanna Bernier's facade to her true nature. He'd never be able to make it up to the man, except by taking care of Ava.

Not that that was the reason behind his actions. Loving Ava was a compulsion and one he had no intention of resisting. Free will was an illusion. He was Ava's now. Always.

After the ceremony, Ava and her mother waited for the family to pay their respects before placing flowers on the grave in an old Greek tradition. He watched Ava remove the glass bead bracelet from her wrist and lay it gently amidst the flowers.

Soon, Dominic found himself standing near a familiar, gnarled oak tree trying to keep Ava in the shade while Vera chatted to Van's family.

He looked at her. Taking in her pale skin, bloodless lips. He cupped her face in his hands. “You okay?”

She pushed the dark sunglasses she wore to the top of her head. Shadows underscored her hazel eyes. “Tired,” she admitted.

“Feel up to going to the wake?” he asked.

“I wouldn’t miss it for the world.”

He wanted to put his hand around her shoulder or hug her waist, but the healing gunshot wounds made it impossible. He settled for squeezing her fingers.

“What I really want,” she leaned closer, looking at his mouth. “Is for my mother to go home so we can have some privacy.”

His lips twitched. “Privacy huh? I didn’t think you were up for that yet.”

He was kidding, but her pupils flared.

“We’re clever enough to figure something out.” Her smile was positively sinful.

He pulled her closer and rested his lips against her brow. “I’ll see what I can do.”

Dominic spotted Mallory waving to them, and they headed across the grass to meet her and Parker, who looked ready to head back to their newborn. Ava’s mom steamed ahead like the force of nature she was.

The smell of crushed grass rose up and teased old memories. For once the scent didn’t evoke grief and suffering. It reminded him of the power of love and also of how much love needed to be tended and nurtured.

“I want to spend the rest of my life with you, Ava Kanas.”

She stopped and blinked at him with a shocked expression on her face. “Are you proposing to me in a graveyard,

Dominic Sheridan?"

"I'm not proposing in a graveyard." He turned towards her with a grin. "I'm telling you that I am going to propose to you, and you need to prepare yourself."

"Prepare myself?" she quizzed.

"For being loved by me for the rest of my life."

"Being loved by you is the best thing I've ever experienced." Her hazel eyes grew large. "I don't ever want to lose you."

"You won't, Ava." But he knew what she meant. The way she'd lost her father and he'd lost his mother. The way Van had been taken from them. He gathered her fingers against his chest. "There are no guarantees about how long we get on this earth, but I do know that we carry the people we love in our hearts forever."

He kissed her, and she melted against him with a soft sigh.

"It's funny," she said, pulling away and leading him towards where the Parkers and her mother were waiting for them. "Chasing criminals never really scared me, but being in a relationship, being part of a couple? That terrifies the hell out of me."

"It used to scare me too, but not anymore."

She glanced up at him. "What's the secret?"

He held her gaze. "You are, Ava. You are."

Then he looked up at the sky and knew it was true. Ava Kanas was worth the risk of heartbreak.

USEFUL ACRONYM DEFINITIONS FOR TONI'S BOOKS

ADA: Assistant District Attorney
AG: Attorney General
ASAC: Assistant Special Agent in Charge
ASC: Assistant Section Chief
ATF: Alcohol, Tobacco, and Firearms
BAU: Behavioral Analysis Unit
BOLO: Be on the Lookout
BORTAC: US Border Patrol Tactical Unit
BUCAR: Bureau Car
CBP: US Customs and Border Patrol
CBT: Cognitive Behavioral Therapy
CIRG: Critical Incident Response Group
CMU: Crisis Management Unit
CN: Crisis Negotiator
CNU: Crisis Negotiation Unit
CO: Commanding Officer
CODIS: Combined DNA Index System
CP: Command Post
CQB: Close-Quarters Battle
DA: District Attorney
DEA: Drug Enforcement Administration
DEVGRU: Naval Special Warfare Development Group
DIA: Defense Intelligence Agency

DHS: Department of Homeland Security
DOB: Date of Birth
DOD: Department of Defense
DOJ: Department of Justice
DS: Diplomatic Security
DSS: US Diplomatic Security Service
DVI: Disaster Victim Identification
EMDR: Eye Movement Desensitization & Reprocessing
EMT: Emergency Medical Technician
ERT: Evidence Response Team
FOA: First-Office Assignment
FBI: Federal Bureau of Investigation
FNG: Fucking New Guy
FO: Field Office
FWO: Federal Wildlife Officer
IC: Incident Commander
IC: Intelligence Community
ICE: US Immigration and Customs Enforcement
HAHO: High Altitude High Opening (parachute jump)
HRT: Hostage Rescue Team
HT: Hostage-Taker
JEH: J. Edgar Hoover Building (FBI Headquarters)
K&R: Kidnap and Ransom
LAPD: Los Angeles Police Department
LEO: Law Enforcement Officer
LZ: Landing Zone
ME: Medical Examiner
MO: Modus Operandi
NAT: New Agent Trainee
NCAVC: National Center for Analysis of Violent Crime
NCIC: National Crime Information Center
NFT: Non-Fungible Token
NOTS: New Operator Training School

NPS: National Park Service
NYFO: New York Field Office
OC: Organized Crime
OCU: Organized Crime Unit
OPR: Office of Professional Responsibility
POTUS: President of the United States
PT: Physiology Technician
PTSD: Post-Traumatic Stress Disorder
RA: Resident Agency
RCMP: Royal Canadian Mounted Police
RSO: Senior Regional Security Officer from the US Diplomatic Service
SA: Special Agent
SAC: Special Agent-in-Charge
SANE: Sexual Assault Nurse Examiners
SAS: Special Air Squadron (British Special Forces unit)
SD: Secure Digital
SIOC: Strategic Information & Operations
SF: Special Forces
SSA: Supervisory Special Agent
SWAT: Special Weapons and Tactics
TC: Tactical Commander
TDY: Temporary Duty Yonder
TEDAC: Terrorist Explosive Device Analytical Center
TOD: Time of Death
UAF: University of Alaska, Fairbanks
UBC: Undocumented Border Crosser
UNSUB: Unknown Subject
USSS: United States Secret Service
ViCAP: Violent Criminal Apprehension Program
VIN: Vehicle Identification Number
WFO: Washington Field Office

COLD JUSTICE WORLD OVERVIEW

All books can be read as standalones

COLD JUSTICE® SERIES

A Cold Dark Place (Book #1)

Cold Pursuit (Book #2)

Cold Light of Day (Book #3)

Cold Fear (Book #4)

Cold in The Shadows (Book #5)

Cold Hearted (Book #6)

Cold Secrets (Book #7)

Cold Malice (Book #8)

A Cold Dark Promise (Book #9~A Wedding Novella)

Cold Blooded (Book #10)

COLD JUSTICE® – THE NEGOTIATORS

Cold & Deadly (Book #1)

Colder Than Sin (Book #2)

Cold Wicked Lies (Book #3)

Cold Cruel Kiss (Book #4)

Cold as Ice (Book #5)

COLD JUSTICE® – MOST WANTED

Cold Silence (Book #1)

Cold Deceit (Book #2)

Cold Snap (Book #3) – Coming soon

Cold Fury (Book #4) – Coming soon

The Cold Justice® series books are also available as **audiobooks** narrated by Eric Dove, and in various box set compilations.

Check out all Toni's books on her website (www.tonianderson author.com/books-2)

ACKNOWLEDGMENTS

Despite my best efforts I seem to be getting slower at writing rather than faster. Sorry. Nothing I can do except keep cracking on and focus on producing the best book I'm capable of creating. Thanks for waiting! I have the world's best readers and I appreciate you!

I shook things up a little with this story and took a sideways step within the FBI. Nothing drastic but enough that I wanted to create a spinoff to the original *Cold Justice* books. The reasoning will become more apparent in future books.

Thanks, as always, to Kathy Altman for being my critique partner/savior. We plotted car chases with her intimate knowledge of the area where the book is set. We also discussed donut shops. Now I need to visit because authenticity is *key* and even though no donut shops were used in this book, who knows what the next book will require? Huge thanks also to Carolyn Crane for the beta read—your enthusiasm buoyed me when I needed it most. And you were right, *about everything.* Thanks to Jocelyn Grant for creating the super *Crossfire* logo—you rock!

It takes a team to create and sell a book. Thanks to my cover designer and formatter for their hard work. Also, to Tara at Inkslingers PR for her supportive efforts and getting the word out. Credit to my editors, Deb Nemeth, Joan Turner at JRT Editing, and Alicia Dean, for helping me make the book the best it can be. I appreciate their sharp-eyed and clear-minded observations.

As always, I want to thank my husband for being hero inspiration, and for cooking dinner after a hard day at work when I'm too tired to even think about food. And my kids for being the best people in the world and for putting up with my vague, distracted crazy. Love you guys.

ABOUT THE AUTHOR

Toni Anderson writes gritty, sexy, FBI Romantic Thrillers, and is a *New York Times* and a *USA Today* bestselling author. Her books have won the Daphne du Maurier Award for Excellence in Mystery and Suspense, Readers' Choice, Aspen Gold, Book Buyers' Best, Golden Quill, National Excellence in Story Telling Contest, and National Excellence in Romance Fiction awards. She's been a finalist in both the Vivian Contest and the RITA Award from the Romance Writers of America. Toni's books have been translated into five different languages and over three million copies of her books have been downloaded.

Best known for her Cold Justice® books perhaps it's not surprising to discover Toni lives in one of the most extreme climates on earth—Manitoba, Canada. Formerly a Marine Biologist, Toni still misses the ocean, but is lucky enough to travel for research purposes. In late 2015, she visited FBI Headquarters in Washington DC, including a tour of the Strategic Information and Operations Center. She hopes not to get arrested for her Google searches.

Sign up for Toni Anderson's newsletter:
www.tonianadersonauthor.com/newsletter-signup

Like Toni Anderson on Facebook:
facebook.com/tonianadersonauthor

Follow on Instagram:
instagram.com/toni_anderson_author

Made in the USA
Las Vegas, NV
23 July 2024

92815966R00246